GREG HAAS

The Butcher's Thumb

A Novel

with
Robert Loss

To Walter,
An inspiration,
Greg Haas

iUniverse, Inc.
New York   Bloomington

iUniverse books may be ordered through booksellers or by contacting:

iUniverse
1663 Liberty Drive
Bloomington, IN 47403
www.iuniverse.com
1-800-Authors (1-800-288-4677)

ISBN: 978-1-4502-0607-5 (sc)
ISBN: 978-1-4502-0597-9 (hc)
ISBN: 978-1-4502-0596-2 (ebook)

Printed in the United States of America

iUniverse rev. date: 04/29/2010

ACKNOWLEDGMENTS

I wrote this like I have lived my life: aided by and blessed with more friends than I deserve and as result I can't begin to list them all. The list would include encouragement from friends I grew up with, went to school with, have worked with, and partied with. It would include my family, my teachers and neighbors. Let me simply say to all who've guided me in spite of myself, thank you.

I want to thank my wife Anita and my son Andrew for their patience.

PROLOGUE

Matt's Journal, Day 7

The campaign never stops. At least I used to think that. But now, from me, it's been cut off like a gangrened arm. I woke up today and looked around the vaguely familiar room—the cheap furniture, thick drapes, noisy air conditioner, ice bucket—all the usual chain motel, mass-produced accoutrements. The chairs are begging to be smashed into particle-board bits. I saw my wallet and my White House credentials, tags I used to wear like a proud dog, and I tossed them into the wastebasket like a Frisbee.

I started this journal 1,405 days ago, and I'm all out of bullshit. Bone-dry, not even the residual odor of manure. Through most of my life I seemed to have an endless supply: it got me laid, past difficult interviews with howling reporters, even convinced a few people that I was all right. For someone like me to be out of bullshit is like being out of air or blood, so I fill it with the next best thing: scotch. When a bullshitter is out of bullshit, well, the truth is too horrible to face.

Here's a little recipe I've tried: out of milk, yet still half a box of Lucky Charms to go, I've mixed the cereal into a tumbler with a bit of Bailey's. And when I finally bothered to pick up a Dispatch *today and saw my, shall we say, unflattering visage, I mixed myself a double.*

Seven days until the 2004 election, the polls show "my guy" with a healthy lead, one I helped build. Much of the political world's attention is turned to my home state of Ohio, and I find myself here on the same day as and a few blocks from the president I've defended for too long. It would be funny if it didn't hurt so much. Voltaire was right when he said, "God is a comedian performing to an audience that's afraid to laugh."

The truest form of being lost is when home looks like a foreign world. I used to know this town, Columbus, like I knew the battered streets of Marion, Ohio, where I grew up. (Fitting that I graduated from a high school named for Warren G. Harding, whose administration set the bar for scandal.) But now there's no familiar place to get back to, no familiar face to find.

In the end, what we are is chewing gum. They find us in one piece, neatly formed. They strip us, pop us in their mouths, and chew. Every now and then they squeeze us flat in their mouth, blow hot air into us—and we inflate, all full of ourselves. Then we burst. We're back to being chewed up. They get tired of us and spit us out, and we spend the rest of our days sticking to the bottom of their shoes. No doubt Stephen Shay is calculating every angle, studying the poll results, and, like a butcher, weighing the meat, glancing at his audience to see if he can slip his thumb on the scales and tip things in his direction.

I was his best student, but to challenge him and the rest of Kensington's administration—my administration, for God's sake—would be futile. The media have gone right along with what Shay and Gail have been saying about me, that I'm crazy and vengeful. That headline in the Dispatch? *"Press Secretary's Mental Health Questioned." How about that? It's a true conspiracy, baby, and any explanation I can give is just too easy to dispel: he's a nut job! I should know how the slander works; I helped them do it to Oliver Redgrave. A deflection of fault, of blame. It's like Baudelaire said, "The greatest trick the devil ever pulled was convincing people he didn't exist." Come to think of it, Mickey Rourke said that, too.*

I didn't start out this way, you know. No one starts out thinking they could end up drunk in a motel near the airport throwing their White House creds into the trash can. We begin innocently, even if we're corrupt and just don't know it yet.

PART ONE:
STRAIGHT TO THE TOP, WITH A DETOUR

CHAPTER 1

Near two in the morning, a cheer erupted through the hotel. In a sixteenth-floor bar outfitted with old saddles, framed photos of cowboys, and Broncos pennants, power brokers and contributors and desperate hangers-on raised their glasses, spilling expensive alcohol, and shook hands, hugged, kissed. Those who'd been competitors within the campaign laid down their swords long enough to toast. In the swirl of applause and shouting, Matt Risen watched the big-screen television where an excited political commentator had just finished scribbling on his dry erase board a barely legible 254 under Al Thornton, and a bold 285 underneath Will Kensington.

"And there you have it!" the commentator said emphatically. "We're reversing our earlier prediction and are now declaring Republican William Kensington the winner in Ohio, which puts him over the minimum of 270 electoral votes." The slightly overweight commentator's eyes bulged and twinkled as he tried to speak slowly for the rest of America. He had a slight smile and a regular Joe haircut, not the blow-dry look of the majority of these network goons. "Even if Thornton picks up Iowa and New Mexico, he can't overcome 270. But remember the big picture here, folks. The country—*you*—have voted for a massive shift in ideas."

It sounded like he was calling a baseball game; his excitement about the process certainly covered up any bias … a true pro.

"You tell 'em, buddy," said Matt before he broke away from the television into a crowd of hands and grinning teeth and martini glasses. It was a goddamn nipple-tingle, all right: everyone clapping him on the shoulders, congratulating his work, reminding him that he was going places, straight to the top. And the women! Beautiful young staffers and

1

elegant senators' wives planting kisses on his cheeks. The drug of victory, a super-charged shot of Viagra to the pride, a thrill that emanated from his nipples and washed over his entire body. He'd felt it before, but never at such a high level.

Like some pale midget bull, Stephen Shay parted the crowd, angling for Matt.

"Hot damn!" Matt shouted to him.

"We have work to do," Shay grunted.

"Stop for a second and congratulate yourself, Stephen."

But even as he'd said it, Matt knew it wasn't going to happen. Shay grabbed him at the elbow and bullied them through the rest of the crowd. Despite their celebration, everyone who watched Shay did so with fear. One fool made the mistake of smacking him on the shoulder, and Shay practically growled at him. Yes, he was the architect of the underwhelming president-elect's rise to power, but he preferred the shadows, preferred intimidation over adoration, preferred to control the images of others rather than craft one of himself. Though his face had a hawkish point to it, otherwise it was bland as an egg.

In fact, his looks were unremarkable, except for his preposterously large head, which Matt followed through the packed hallways. The crowds thinned as they reached the suites Matt liked to call the inner sanctum.

"How does the State Capitol look for the acceptance speech?" Shay said, sipping a scotch.

"Great, but the speech sucks."

Shay smirked. "The speech doesn't matter now. Like I always tell you, words don't matter much anymore—"

"It's the visual, I know. But look, I'm the press secretary. Essentially I tell stories, so words sorta kinda gotta matter to me."

Shay shrugged. "Why do you think they call it the big picture?"

An anonymous staffer appeared at Shay's side and nervously whispered that Kensington was about to take a call from Thornton. Shay bolted as fast as his pudgy body could take him into the president-elect's suite, and Matt drifted to a mirror. His shirt was soaked. And was that a stain? He snapped his fingers to the staffer and told the kid to bring him a fresh shirt from his suitcase. The kid didn't look surprised, of course; Matt changed shirts at least twice a day. A necessity of the campaign—and one he enjoyed, coming from a little town in Ohio, having grown up so poor he'd worn shirts with holes in them. Watching himself in the mirror, he loosened his tie and stripped off his tailored suit jacket and the stained shirt. This was the kind of victory that made you think you could talk to the press shirtless, with women hanging onto you, a glass of McCutcheon in hand, a cigar dangling from your mouth. He brushed back his hair, twisting a lock with a dab of forming crème so it looked just a little askew. Didn't want them thinking he'd been lazing around all night. Shit, he'd never been in such a big election.

Twenty minutes later, dressed in the new shirt and pumped up by Thornton's concession—the entire suite had cheered—Matt was once again hustling down the hallway with Shay, this time part of an entourage headed for the elevators to the lobby downstairs. Matt noticed the dandruff on Shay's rumpled jacket and understood again why Shay avoided the cameras.

"Look," Shay said, "when we get to the Capitol, just tell the press that when Thornton conceded, it was very cordial, and leave it at that."

"I thought I'd maybe tell them that Thornton cried."

"That robot? They'd never believe you."

As they rode in the elevators, Matt watched the bodyguards and aides study Shay's enormous head. Though it was covered amply with silver hair, the head looked like a lollipop in danger of falling off its stick. Not that anyone would tell that to Stephen. Oh, maybe someone had, long ago, and now that person was most likely buried in an unmarked grave in the Badlands. Shay didn't even mind that people called him "The S.S." Actually found it flattering. Shay's arm stretched up to Matt's shoulder, his small hand awkwardly giving him a squeeze. Back when they'd met, shortly after Matt had left Ohio to represent a tobacco coalition, Shay had been all bluster and intimidation and had nearly reduced Matt to tears in front of his lobbyist bosses. But he'd stuck, Shay said, and learned. Learned quickly. Well, you tended to do that when a flamethrower was pointed at you.

When the elevator opened, a deafening roar greeted them from the throng filling the ornate lobby. Camera flashes blinded him, and if not for the guards bullying their way through, Matt would have gotten lost. But then an even louder cheer went up. Matt looked over his shoulder and saw, just behind him and to the right, that the secured elevator door had opened to reveal exiting Secret Service agents and the faithful's new commander-in-chief, William Kensington.

He leaned down into Shay's ear and shouted through the din, "I made them cut that God's Will bullshit out of the speech."

"It was in there?"

"Practically screamed divine intervention." He hopped into the backseat of the number one staff car, a tricked-out Escalade he wouldn't mind owning, and extended a hand to Shay, whose stubby legs needed some help. "I figured we'd actually want to take up residence in the White House before we get back to that kind of talk."

"That's campaign rhetoric. Good thinking." Shay looked ahead as Kensington was being escorted into the limo ahead of them. "Should I ride with him?" Before Matt could respond, Shay muttered to himself, "No, I'll just stay here." He snapped his seatbelt and pounded the back of the driver's seat with his tiny fists.

The motorcade lurched into a slow crawl toward the Capitol building. Through the tinted windows, Matt observed the shadowy figures lining the sidewalks, waving their flags, holding up homemade posters. He'd made it. The scrawny, orphaned kid from Marion, Ohio, had totally fucking made it, all right. Riding one car behind the president-elect, learning from one of the greatest political minds of the twentieth century, favored by this man whose preposterously large head suggested the cunning ruthlessness inside it, the total lack of sentimentality. Shay did not take a liking to many. He hated men younger than him. But here Matt was. And why? Because he'd clawed his way into it, because he'd ordered those tailored suits before he could really afford them, and because America rewarded you when you worked your ass off.

Shay's phone rang. "Shit. Thornton's personal number." He flipped it shut. "No good reason for a call like that."

A second later Matt's cell vibrated. That bastard Kelly yakked into his ear, and he hung up. "Lead limo," he said.

"Thornton's calling them, isn't he? Tell me they didn't answer."

"Well, the governor's going over the speech, but I think they're about to."

"I knew I should have ridden with him." Shay lunged toward the driver. "Stop the fucking car!"

The young volunteer, who had been rewarded for six months of her hard work by being allowed to drive Shay's car in the motorcade, instinctively locked on the brakes. Matt clutched the door and then was rocked forward by a collision from behind. "What the hell?" he shouted. The third vehicle, directly behind them, was humping their bumper.

Unfazed, Shay sprinted toward the limo which carried the would-be president and his parents and spouse, along with the staffer Kelly and three Secret Services agents, one of whom was behind the wheel. His lollipop head on his tiny body made it look as if he were about to topple forward.

Matt popped out of the SUV. "Shay, wait!"

The lead limo peeled off. Not good, Matt thought. Protocol required the agent driving the president to hit the gas pedal, dart ahead in case there was some kind of assault on the motorcade, and allow additional security from the local safety forces to surround him. But in the thick mayhem on the streets, the limo could only get so far, and it stopped again as local leos—cops on foot, horseback, and motorcycle—swarmed.

Shay had never stopped his pursuit. In the noise on the street, Matt could hear Shay's tinny voice screaming, and then he spotted a couple of black suits closing in. They would only see a large-headed man with wild hair and a wild look in his eyes charging the car. "Not good," Matt muttered to himself as Shay was tackled to the street.

Matt slammed the door shut and sprinted ahead. "It's Shay!" he screamed. "Get him up off the fucking ground!"

The agent who'd pinned Shay down pulled himself up. Before anyone could help him, Shay rolled over on his back, sat upright, leaned forward, and pushed off the ground with his hands, despite their being chained together with handcuffs. It was fucking acrobatic. He stumbled toward the door of the limo. A wide-eyed Kelly recognized him and threw open the door.

"Somebody uncuff him, for God's sake," Matt shouted as he caught up. "Stephen, what's the big deal about a call—"

"Take his phone," said Shay, pointing with his bound hands to Kelly.

"My phone?" said Kelly.

"Sorry," said Matt as he stripped the cell phone away from the twit; he'd never liked the way Kelly called him Matt Raisin, or the fact that Kelly had cock-blocked him at a party last June.

"Throw it on the ground," said Shay, and once Matt dutifully had, Shay went all *Riverdance* on it, stomping it into pieces. Nothing had been boring since Matt had ducked under the wing of Shay.

Kelly stared at Shay, his eyes syrupy. "Why did you do that to my cell phone?"

"We will speak to Thornton *after* the acceptance speech."

"But the Governor's already on the phone with Thornton."

Shay screeched, "No! Will, get off the phone! Someone get me out of these goddamn cuffs!"

The frustrated agent behind him shouted, "Then stand still!" and Shay froze until he'd been freed.

Matt slumped against the hull of the limo, finally connecting the dots: the robotic Thornton was having a change of heart. Something must have gone wrong, terribly ass-backward wrong. And now he understood what Shay was doing; if Kensington's announcement that Thornton had conceded was televised, by inference it would present a clear image that Kensington was the president-elect. The public wouldn't question that fact.

Sitting in the rear seat on the passenger side, governor Kensington spoke into the phone, wearing his typical look of confusion. "I don't understand," he was mumbling into the cell phone. "You just conceded half an hour ago." Shay forced his way into the limo, leaning over Kensington's classy wife like a drunk on spring break.

Kensington stammered, "Well, Al, don't believe what your people are telling you about Ohio—"

"Will, let me talk to him," said Shay, and when the dumbfounded candidate held it out, Shay barked into the phone, as if he were talking to an obscene caller. "The networks have declared us the winner. Your people don't know shit! The secretary of state is sure, we're sure, everyone's sure: we carried Ohio. You lose, buddy!" He snapped the phone shut and tossed it back to Kensington.

Ohio, Matt thought. Great.

Shay reached inside the limo, grabbed Kelly, and pulled him out of the car. "You're fired. Do not get back in the motorcade." He grabbed the nickel-sized credential pinned to Kelly's lapel and tore it free, with part of the suit cloth still attached.

Looking as if he'd been hit in the stomach, Kelly asked, to no one in particular, "Why?"

Shay was already headed back to their SUV, so Matt leaned into the dumbfuck's face. "I'll tell you why. Because you didn't call Shay or me to clear that phone call. If we had already given the acceptance speech, Thornton would look like an idiot saying he changed his mind and tried to call us back! What did you think he was going to do, offer some helpful hints for the speech?"

Shay had returned, and instead of glowering at Kelly, he was grinning at Matt and nodding.

"Matt, what do you think about the speech?" said Kensington. "Should we go ahead?"

"No!" Shay said, pacing beside the limo.

"I need to get over there now and find out what the press corps knows," said Matt. "That cocksucker, Fagan, was probably letting them know about the call as it was happening. Maybe even bringing the networks into it live."

"Go," Shay hissed. "Fire 'em up. We may need a mob before this is over." Shay held a small finger up to Matt's chin. "Project victory! It's Thornton who's confused. We know we won."

Once Shay had turned back, Matt leaned in toward Kelly. He was dumber than shit, sometimes, but loyal. No one deserved what he'd gotten. "Here," said Matt, handing Kelly his card. "Call me in a week, and we'll find you something new, okay?"

Chapter 2

"Typical lefty backpedaling," Matt said to his flock. He smiled easily and eyed a blonde reporter from Fox. "Thornton looked at the numbers—the facts—and conceded. If he has rescinded his concession, well, I can only assume that his emotions got the better of him. For once."

The flock of reporters tittered. They'd surrounded him, sweat-drenched, their collective breathing emitting a fog. Behind them, on the temporary stage in front of the capitol building, an empty podium beckoned as the world waited.

"What do you know about that second call?" shouted the blonde. Stunning lips on her, like little pillows.

"Nothing detailed. For all I know, Vice President Thornton wanted to talk about global warming. Again."

That got a laugh.

"So is Kensington going to speak?" crowed a humorless old-timer.

Matt felt his face warm and struggled to relax. Always tough to talk to reporters when you had no idea what the fuck was going on. He probably looked like Kensington right now; the would-be president only had two expressions: confused or arrogant.

"Like I said, I don't know the details."

"Is the motorcade heading back to the hotel?"

"I haven't heard, but look, the important thing here is that Thornton *did* concede. And if there is a recount, we'll win again. Thank you."

He twirled around and tried to make it through the flock—they who brought him to the rest of the world, put him on televisions across America, and now wanted their pound of flesh. They nearly trampled him on their way to their next spin-meister.

"Nice work, sir," said his lackey, Broussard. "Should we head back?"

"Give me a minute or two, Chuck."

Matt leaned against the railing, staring out over the human ocean that covered the steps of the capitol building. Its gold seal dome was lit and shining, in stark relief, mystical, like a palace in Saudi Arabia or Iraq. It *was* a palace, the home of three generations of Kensington governors and now, maybe, a president. For the first time since Thornton had un-conceded, the possibility of losing sunk in with a different weight than the one he'd experienced when the networks had originally declared Thornton the winner in Ohio. Then it had seemed early and the networks too eager to flaunt their shiny new exit poll technology; now, though, it was all up for grabs, impossible to predict. He could land in the White House or back on the streets of Marion, Ohio. He'd heard stories of what happened to the losing staff, to promising up-and-comers who'd been crushed by their defeat and branded as losers. As his Uncle Jesse would've said, "It's back to slopping the hogs at your Aunt Marie's farm for you, kid."

Leaning over the rail as, throughout the crowd, flickers of camera flashes sparkled like the sun reflecting off the sea, Matt knew how he must look to anyone watching. That was part of his business. His face was a tool: the bright, confident smile; eyes that made a person feel she was the sole object of Matt's attention; the short, light scar just above his left cheekbone, which showed a little grit and experience. Not for nothing was the president-elect's press secretary a handsome guy in his late thirties, a man whose easy posture and full, wavy hair just screamed "American." He'd take it. Not his fault he'd gotten the best of the family genes. Still, he was surprised to hear the shutter-click of a camera nearby, wondering why the hell this moment, of all moments, was worth capturing.

He turned to see first the giant, black, glassy eye of a camera lens. And then, from behind it, a woman of radiant blue eyes.

"Hell of a shot," she said, grinning.

"Sorry I got in the way."

"Sorry nothin'. It's an historic shot."

He knew her. Or had, at least, seen her. Yes, just a little while ago, pushing her way near the stage, which was not an easy thing to do.

Same milk-white T-shirt and jeans, same cascading and curly hair pulled back in a sharp ponytail. Same figure: five-ten, statuesque, with an ass like a bell.

"I'm just a footnote to history, Ms. …"

"Kris Johansen. And you're no footnote. The young careerist on the edge of history. Clinging to hope. Figuring out how to spin this new dilemma. Very provocative."

"Careerist?"

She pulled a laminated, all-access badge from the tangle of cameras hanging around her neck. "Thanks for the pass," she said, then whirled off down the steps of the platform.

Broussard appeared next to him. "We should get going."

"Did I give that chick top-level press creds?"

"Johansen? Yeah, I think you did."

"Or she used my name." He watched her wedge into a crowd of elephant-hatted, average citizens and start shooting. She changed her angle, made an adjustment, and aimed the camera again. A pro.

"Tricky," he muttered.

⌒ᴧᴧ⌒

She found him again at the elevators in the lobby. It'd taken them half an hour to get back, and he and Broussard were sweating through their suits; but she was leaning against the wall like she'd skipped here.

"Going up?" she said.

"Straight to the top. Where even that pass can't get you in." He eyed Broussard and laughed.

"I'm snapping history here, Mr. Risen. Portraits. I won't embarrass anybody."

The elevator doors opened, and Matt stepped in, sliding a key card into the panel next to the floor buttons. Jamming the button for the sixteenth floor a couple of times, he said, "You photojournalists always end up embarrassing somebody." He waved as the doors closed.

"She's a pest," said Broussard.

"She's hot as hell, Chuck. Who cares if she's a pest?"

"Wait 'til the recount is over."

"Wanna bet she finds her way upstairs?" said Matt, pulling out his wallet. "I'll put fifty on it."

"You're on."

Minutes later, Matt was fifty dollars richer. They'd made the last turn to the inner sanctum, and there she was, arguing with a Secret Service agent. Around them, the hallway was bouncing with aides and staffers in such a hurry they kept colliding. But despite the noise, Kris's voice echoed down the hall, "Matt Risen said specifically that I could take some photos."

"Bullshit," he called.

A momentary look of embarrassment faded quickly, and she winked at him. *Winked.* Damn! A few stray locks were wet, and the rosy undertones of her skin were flushed, but otherwise she looked unperturbed by the stone-faced agent barring her way.

"Come on," he said. "I don't want them to shoot you."

"Matt—"

"Hush, Broussard. Clear the princess's path for her."

She laced her arm into his. "Thank you, my prince."

With a sigh, he gently removed her arm. "Don't get too cutesy, okay? And don't start asking questions."

"Like if you live in Old Town?"

He glanced at her, that familiar urge weakening him; poets called it lust. Attractive as she was, he'd never exactly been a one-woman man.

"Yup."

"I've seen you around. You're always on your phone."

"And you've probably always got a camera in front of your face. Otherwise, I'd remember seeing you."

Her eyebrows arched flirtatiously. Caught! Hell, he'd meant it to be a light jab. Not a good time to be losing control of his tongue, forked though it might be.

They approached a pair of Secret Service agents near the doors to the A-list suites, and he paused a moment and gently led her to the wall. "This has been cute, really, but in there, seriously, best behavior." A pinch of anger sharpened his words—anger that she'd gotten to him so easily? "Piss those guys off and you'll be snapping photos of mall openings and ice cream socials."

"Photojournalists are the most dangerous kind of reporter," she said with a little grin. "The wrong photo at the wrong time can't be explained away."

"So we agree."

"Does your breath always stink this much?" she said.

Damn, this woman could keep him off-balance. Shaking his head, Matt stalked toward the door and told the agents to let her in. He'd learned long ago that you never asked them for anything. They were trained to say no. You just told them what you were doing. As was their custom, the two agents nodded to each other silently and opened the door.

He might have heard Kris compliment one on his tie—they all wore the same ties—but he was immediately drawn to the sight of Shay pacing nervously near the long, dark windows like a duck on speed. The blood-red decor of the room finally seemed apt. Stacks of paper littered coffee tables, chairs, and desks; the tangle of phone and Internet lines made it look like some poor beast had been eviscerated.

Shay grabbed his lapels. "These assholes are throwing it away," he hissed. "Do I have to think of every goddamn thing? Do I have to tell you people to take a shit? Go ahead, take a shit—"

"Easy, Stephen." Never had seen him worked up like this. "I need to tell you to breathe."

Shay wiped his forehead down as Matt heard the snapping of a camera. "We have to go back to every state Thornton won and stir up some shit. Enough to cast doubt. If he wants to make it all about Ohio, we'll turn the tables on him."

"Did you see me with the press?"

"You? Yeah, I saw you, Matt. Good boy, good boy. Go get yourself a treat, and then start working on something fucking brilliant to say! You have to go along with the recount idea—that's what Webb wants. But project victory!"

The next half-hour sped along, Matt spending most of his time crouched with the speechwriting team—two of them Kensington family friends, one a coke addict from Madison Avenue, and the other a former law professor—and watching Kris carefully. That distraction alone was reason enough she shouldn't have been in here. But she stayed true to her word, clicking away silently as dignitaries with credentials packed into the room, filling it past capacity even though there was a tight screen on the guests; family members, stray senators, and Fortune 100 CEOs were getting turned away back to the ballroom downstairs. Women with layers of jewels looked around pensively and whispered to the people next to them. Brooding men studied their Rolex watches and paced in their Gucci loafers, filling the room with a constant din. It was one of those rare moments when everyone had the same amount of information—none. Not that it stopped anyone from talking.

"Yeah, the process of patriotism," Matt said to Broussard. "We can stir that pot." He turned to the young press assistants who worked for him. "I want a one-on-one full court press. Each of you—take a single reporter or producer to babysit." At random he pointed to an aide and tossed him a list of the key credentialed press. "Divide 'em up. Find out who has the best relationships, and make sure none of the big dogs are just standing around.

"Look people … everyone is going to want to talk to me or someone else. I can only talk to so many, so pacify them as best you can." Matt looked at the ceiling. "Okay, I know that's silly. Do what you can. But we won! Thornton is a desperate, sore loser. That is our message. Say it a hundred ways—but say it, say it, and say it.

"Spin under crisis, kid! SUCK! I'm loving it, so are you, now get to work!"

As he strained to stand, a shock of pain flaring in his shoulders, Matt saw Shay impotently whistling to quiet the room. Even he couldn't get the moneybags to shut up.

"Quiet, please!" boomed a familiar, harsh voice.

The entire room was silenced. Dixon Webb, the would-be vice president, had emerged from an adjoining suite into the chaos. Webb's appearance—broad shoulders, a barrel chest, large metal eyeglasses that highlighted his intense blue eyes, and his lips formed in a permanent sneer—caused many to see in him the epitome of arrogance and contempt. However, to his friends and supporters, the gleam in his eyes reassured them that the toughest ballbuster on the planet was in control.

Webb pointed to several people in the room individually and said, "I have to apologize for my roughness, but you need to leave the room.

Please just go next door, downstairs, whichever. Relax and we'll keep you informed."

Some were offended and some were relieved that someone was taking charge, but everyone he pointed to got the hell out of the room.

Matt turned to see that Shay's eyes were locked on Webb; he wasn't mesmerized, he was jealous. In private, Shay had the upper hand, but in public, Webb projected pure self-assurance. Shay usually took command in a small collection of the highest-ranking allies. But all things change after an election, and it was only a matter of time before Webb tried to rein in Shay. That would be fun to watch—if they won.

As the room cleared out, Kris could no longer blend in. Shay spotted her, his little eyes widening. "What are you doing here?" he barked.

Matt intercepted Shay as Kris calmly took several pictures of her charging antagonist. "I let her in, Stephen."

"Are you insane?"

"I thought it would be good to get some dramatic, historic shots."

"Are you *completely* insane?" Shay stared wide-eyed, shaking his sagging jowls. "Here's a history lesson: do you know who she is? She's a big lefty." He turned toward Kris. "Now Ms. Johansen, get the fuck out!"

"Hey, lay off, Steve," Matt said.

"*Lay off?*"

"I'm leaving," Kris said, calmly putting her camera away. "Matt, no need to worry about the quality of the photos. Even Mr. Shay will be flattered."

As she finished packing, Webb started talking, and Shay glared as if he were about to sever Matt's jugular vein. "We have a photographer we control for that shit!" he whispered as she slipped out of the room.

"Yeah and that's what he gives us: shit. You're the it's-all-about-the-visual guy. Don't you want something good for a change?"

"Gentlemen," Webb snarled. "May we continue to decide the fate of our country, or do you need a couple minutes?" The few remaining people in the room snickered, and Shay's pale, nearly translucent skin turned deep crimson. "Shay, give us a rundown."

"We need to be very aggressive. We won: that's our position. Repeat it and repeat it. If they hear us say it once, they won't necessarily buy it, but they will if they hear it a thousand times. They're going to go through with a recount in Ohio; we can't stop that." He glared at Webb. "But we must open the door to a recount in Iowa, Wisconsin, New Hampshire—any state Thornton won by less than 1 percent in the unofficial count. If we don't get the result we like, then we won't let that recount stand. For every recount there can be another recount.

"Ultimately, every election is decided by the House of Representatives, and several legal issues will have to be determined by the Supreme Court. We control both." Shay rose up on his toes, lifting his tiny body and bulbous head as he spoke. "All we need to do is to provide them with the cover they'll need to recognize our victory. We do that by making this a political fight, not a legal fight. Secondly, the media needs to understand that we will not concede. Without saying so, we need to make them understand that they'll see this country torn apart if they stand in our way."

He slowly turned his globular head toward Matt and narrowed his eyes. "That's your job, Casanova. So go downstairs and start spinning the talking heads like Linda-fucking-Blair."

In one part of the hotel, government affairs liaisons were meeting with elected officials; in another, recount experts around the country were being recruited thanks to a list prepared a few days prior by the RNC. Shay wanted the talent on its way to Ohio in the morning, so bags were packed hastily, flights arranged, and breakfasts ordered.

CHAPTER 3

On the streets of the plaza, the crowds waiting for a speech had finally begun to disperse. Exhausted and shivering, their night on the verge of utter anticlimax, the remaining Republican faithful would have been pleased to know, no doubt, that Matt's mind was focused exactly where it should be: on sex.

Specifically, sex with the feline and felonious woman lingering near the balcony of the inner sanctum, her hips cocked to one side as she brushed aside hair that was nearly bronze. She caught his eye, nodded at the balcony, and, in segments of movement, he followed Gail Turner outside.

"I thought you might need to cool down," she said.

"We could steal fifteen minutes."

Girlishly she squeezed together her plump lips and kissed him lightly, quickly, on the mouth. "This is better than sex."

"I beg to differ."

"It's not happening," she said, glancing over his shoulder and through the window at the television set inside.

His shoulders relaxed, knowing she was right, that on a night like this, it was dangerous to miss even the smallest event. Or crisis. Downtime was what had brought them together, beginning in August at a stop in Lincoln, Nebraska—the middle of nowhere, with nothing to do but hole up in a room, order a bottle of wine, and screw each other's brains out. The scandal would have been negligible, really; hookups along the campaign route were about as shocking as birds swarming to bread crumbs.

"It's good that you're upfront, though." She smiled wickedly and yawned, her body like a lioness. "That's what gets rewarded in DC,

Matt. That and success. The Republicans don't give a shit about loyalty, Matt."

She ought to know. With her Harvard Law School diploma and DoD credentials, Gail had practically been raised inside the Beltway; everything about her was as efficient as the campaign she helped to manage, even the way she made love without any tangles or clumsiness, without any interest in him, really. He would keep his eyes open while she closed hers and smiled in a lost, delirious way, and he would study her undulating form, the curves just inside her pelvic bones, the dusting of freckles on her stern cheeks. He'd noticed a week ago that she never really looked at him during the act, never said his name. Just went about her business on top of him.

She said to him now, "I heard about your little girlfriend from the *Times*. Johansen's her name?"

"Shay lost it."

She chuckled. "I'll bet he did. You have a thing for these do-gooders, don't you? Liberal women like Johansen."

"She called me a careerist. We're more than that, aren't we?"

"I'll let you know when I get to the top." Stretching her lithe body again, she turned for a moment to look at the meandering crowds below. "Matt, people who accuse others of being careerists are just lazy, or idealists, or both."

"She was working her ass off tonight."

"So she's an idealist. She's worked for all the major papers. You think she's not a careerist?" Seeing that he was reaching for a cigarette, she put a hand on his, reminding him again how disgusting a habit it was and how none of the serious power brokers in town smoked anymore. "It's cutthroat in there," she said with a crooked grin. "My father taught me how to play, you know. When I was ten years old. You get five balls, and try to knock the other guys' balls off the table before they knock yours."

"I know how to play cutthroat."

"Do you?"

As she spoke, Gail looked again over his shoulder at the monitor inside, and her eyes bulged. Without a word, she broke toward the sliding balcony doors and headed immediately toward the recently woken president-elect's side. He rushed in, having no idea what was wrong until he saw Shay and Webb standing in front of the television, watching Grover Alexander speak live with the cable networks, flapping his old rubbery lips about the resolve of the Republican campaign. With his strict and handsome features and shock of snowy, full white hair, Alexander looked a bit like Matt imagined he would look in his sixties: dripping with wealth and connections.

"Who let this fuck-hat loose?" Shay shouted.

"He's doing all right," Webb muttered out of the side of his mouth. "For a rogue operative."

"I just wanna know if I'm the damn president or not," said Kensington. Gail said something into his ear, and he chortled. Matt still didn't know what connection she had with the Kensingtons, but it went back through her own family.

Alexander looked right into the camera. "Talk of any conspiracy here is absurd. Though a friend of mine once said"—oh God, he was grinning like the Cheshire cat—"that 80 percent of conspiracy talk is BS, which only helps cover up the other 20 percent, which is true."

"Jesus Christ!" Shay screamed. He whirled, and his eyes locked onto Matt's. "Where the fuck have you been? We've lost time on this already."

"Where is he, in the ballroom?"

"I can go," said Gail. "The RNC's up to speed with the recount, my job's done for now."

"No, this is Matt's problem."

"But Stephen, I know Alexander."

If Gail wanted to go face the angry mob for once, then there must have been something in it for her. What had she said? *I'll let you know when I get to the top.* Fuck that, he'd get there first.

And so he bolted out of the room, shouting behind him that he'd clean it up. He shuttled along the hallway, passing through clumps of weary aides sipping their coffee—oops, spilling their coffee—and bitching about having to go to Ohio. Broussard caught up with him near the elevator, ran down their itinerary—airport by seven, with the press—and when Matt explained why he was in a rush, Broussard asked if he should have brought a handful of tranquilizer darts.

If only. Alexander was not a man you could push around. He was *the* elephant of Republican money, an advisor to tobacco companies and defense contractors. He wasn't some pissant K Street lobbyist, he *bought* them—by the dozen. In the press, companies claimed to hire him for his advice, but it was really for his access; in return, he'd raised millions for the party. So Matt could understand why he'd ducked into the spotlight—there he was now, waiting near a camera light and reflecting screen, while a producer from MSNBC was milling around. Alexander relied on visibility—and somebody, somewhere was watching live. Now, thanks to this conspiracy bullshit, his interview would be replayed over and over unless Matt gave them something else to chew on.

Alexander saw him and laughed.

"They send the fox after the hound, eh?"

Matt took him by the crook of his elbow. "You know we appreciate what you do, Grover. Really. We're just hell-bent on this 'Thornton conceded' message."

"I fucked it up, kid. Knew it the second it was coming out of my mouth."

Broussard whipped a memo out of his leather folder and handed it to Alexander. The producer tried to peer in, and Broussard blocked him like a power forward.

"Webb doesn't want you doing anymore interviews."

"Webb? Or Shay?" said Alexander. "I'm not gonna let that little hermaphrodite tell me what to do—"

"We're on the air in two minutes, Risen," barked the producer, "and somebody better be standing in front of this goddamn camera."

They were swimming toward him now, these bloodthirsty reporters, having picked up his scent. We could do an impromptu press conference, they said. What did he know? Was this a conspiracy? Desperate to appease their screaming producers, they began to circle; everyone in the media knew that the entire nation had a clicker in hand and was flipping through the channels. Chunky linebacker-types were hauling over more cameras, more lighting stands. Blood in the water.

"I'm not retracting a fucking thing," said Alexander.

"I'll handle it," Matt said. "They're like children with attention deficit; you just need to redirect them." He patted Alexander's shoulder and looked him in the eye. "Webb needs you on the phones, raising some serious money."

Having surveyed the oncoming wave of reporters, Alexander seemed relieved to be able to slink away. Matt quickly arranged a security aide to lead him upstairs and shake off any reporters who tried following him—that, too, was for Alexander's ego. No one was going to follow him with Matt dangling there like meaty bait in the bloody ocean.

"Appreciate it, Risen," said Alexander. "If you need help getting that press secretary job in the White House, I'll put in a word."

Matt watched him leave as Broussard chattered in his ear about talking points. Why the hell would he need help? It was a done deal.

"Who am I talking to?" he said to the producer.

"Change of plans. We'll field everybody's questions."

"Going live in five ..."

Broussard stepped out of the way. They all do, Matt thought. Especially Gail. When it came to giving a detailed account of Kensington's foreign policy platform, Gail gave the speech, cruising along on her prepared remarks, but when the president-elect butchered the English language, it was Matt's ass on a stick.

The reporters had formed a cylinder more than seven feet high around Matt, holding cameras on their shoulders and above their own heads like basketball players trying to inbound the ball. Microphones were jammed into any opening; one reporter held a mike between the legs of a perturbed reporter in front of him.

"Is there a conspiracy?" someone shouted.

The lights were lit, hot, and he stared into the darkness around their edges.

"The only conspiracy," Matt said, "is that I can't get a Denver omelet here in Denver." The exhausted journalists were an easy crowd; they erupted into laughter. "I guess Brokaw said you got some on your suits, but look, you have Thornton to blame for that. We won. Plain and simple. If he wants to make a mess of this and taint the election process, we'll do what we need to do to ensure that the votes of the American people are counted accurately and fairly. And I'm confident that William Kensington will prove to be the winner. Now let me give you some real news and tell you about our travel plans ..."

CHAPTER 4

The old man, to the surprise of everyone in the café, was quite adept with his cell phone. Though his eyes were beleaguered and his posture a bit hunched, and though he had been stirring his black tea pensively, like a man whom time has passed by, he had been dialing numbers all through the lunch hour, holding the phone out in front of his face and squinting. He would talk for a short time, youthfully, one bear-paw hand quite animated, then hang up, seem to be thinking to himself, and then dial another number. The waitresses giggled about him near the bar, though they had no idea what he was saying. His heavy lips hardly moved.

And so they did not hear him say into his phone, "Finally, someone who knows something useful."

"Useful has its price," said the reedy voice on the other end.

The man's massive hand surrounded his teacup, satisfied at last. "Meet me now, and that price will be worth your trouble."

"Why not the phone?"

"That's no good. Come to the first-floor restaurant in the rebuilt tower of Kitai-gorod. You know it?"

"Sure. Can't get very far, eh, Yuri?"

"One never escapes Lubyanka Square, my friend."

Yuri Nesterenko hung up, eyed the giggling waitresses, and tapped his tea cup. Their girlish attention was harmless; he might have considered it flattering many years ago, but now he was just a doddering old man with bulldog jowls.

"Can I take your coat?" said the pretty waitress as she poured.

"There's a draft," he snapped. "You should have it sealed."

The girl sulked off. A product of new Russia: impertinent, sloppy, carefree. What bothered him more, their ignorance or their carelessness? Or their adoration of this American spectacle on the television above the bar—in fact, he noticed, on *every* television in the café. Over images of the cowboy Kensington waving to his adoring public in the state of Ohio, those puppet journalists were gleefully talking about "possibilities." As if they were covering a real election. It was all part of the grand, fraudulent American imperialist show. Pretending to give people choices.

"Change the channel," he said to the bartender. The whelp quickly pointed a remote and the screen flipped—to yet another image of Kensington. "Again." Another station, another report, this one on the robotic Thornton. "Never mind, never mind," Yuri said, and he angled his chair away from the television and pointed it toward the wide windows so he could see Korovyov approach.

The light today was dim. Growing dimmer across Red Square, across what passed for a government of the people. Still, after his meeting with Korovyov, he would stop by the park and toss the breadcrumbs in his pocket to the pigeons and hope that some children would pass by so that he could regale them with stories of Russia's glorious past. A few pieces of candy, too, of course, to help the lesson go down more smoothly. Had not Russia been a great power? Napoleon had come knocking and been sent away. Hitler, too. Always he would end his stories with the warning that, once in every generation, someone from the West tried to destroy them. And so it would be for their generation. But they had only ever been defeated by themselves.

In time Korovyov appeared in the swirling wind, his short, stuttering steps unmarked by age. So little power in such a hurry all the time; a wonder it hadn't gotten him killed. The former colleague brushed off a ratty fedora and stammered toward Yuri, who decided to feign respect. He stood and greeted Korovyov firmly with one hand. "Nikolai Ivanovich," he said, pointing to the teapot. "Warm yourself?"

"Something stronger, I think."

They had called Korovyov "The Duck" due to a fortunately-timed action during an incident in East Germany, but the nickname might as well have come from his thirst for liquor. Yuri obliged him, ordering a vodka neat for himself. It was necessary, sometimes, to put up with others' foibles, their addictions; patience was not only virtuous, it was effective. Yuri they had called "The Bear."

"I nearly froze to death," said Korovyov in his thin little voice.

"You could have hailed a taxi. You would have been here sooner."

"A man needs his exercise." Korovyov smiled conspiratorially. "Don't you agree? Even at our age. The machine only wears down. Though your jaw is strong as ever, old friend."

Yuri sighed. This would take some time. And it did. Traipsing through the past, as if it were anything to be giddy or sentimental about. Proud, yes, but Korovyov treated everything with a boyish gloss, polishing up his own dismal record. They talked about Russia's new leadership. They talked about their dead wives. Yuri tapped his thick fingers on the table quietly.

"In 1996, Pozharsky took a job with a software firm," Korovyov said abruptly. He'd just sipped the beginning of his second round. "He's the man you're looking for."

"Kostya?"

Korovyov nodded and took another sip. His nails were clacking against the glass. "He took his knowledge with him. Has come full circle. The software is being used by our old family now. Hell, the North Koreans, too, for all I know."

"But he can get it for me?"

Leaning back, the foul little man puffed his chest as he said that no, he didn't think Kostya would be able to do so. "He's still in the game. You're not."

"This is no game."

"All the players have left the board, Yuri."

"Not me. Not yet."

Korovyov grinned and scratched with a nail the corner of his gaunt mouth. "You're like one of those Japanese they found thirty years after the war, still holding their posts. Waiting for the news that the fighting was over."

"Old habits," muttered Yuri, and he frowned when the idiot felt it necessary to complete the phrase. Rarely did anything die softly.

"The software you want is called Orbweaver."

"A spider."

"It catches everything." Korovyov grinned again and drained the vodka from between the ice. "Are you after Americans?"

Yuri stared at him.

"It's just like the old days!" said Korovyov.

Lest Korovyov run up his bill, Yuri thanked him profusely and signaled the waitresses, who had stopped giggling. He enjoyed watching his old colleague's eyes scramble for a stray drink. None was to be found, and, after leaving the least possible tip, Yuri tightened his own gray woolen coat against the cold and proceeded to walk Korovyov across the Square. They stopped at the State Historical Museum where a class of children dragged their feet up the steps.

"Nikolai Ivanovich, you have been a great help. And done a service to your country, even if your country no longer cares." He hugged the frail man, resting a bear paw near the collar of Korovyov's coat, inches from his neck. "Naturally, you mustn't say a word to Kostya. That would be foolish. Yes?"

"Y-yes."

He put a few bills into Korovyov's shaking, waiting hands and told him not to waste it on liquor. Cheap liquor, at any rate. And as he watched his former comrade stutter-step away, Yuri considered that he might have to kill the poor bastard.

He strolled into Alexander Garden, alongside the Manege, and brushed a little snow off a green-painted park bench not far from a scavenging flock of pigeons. One toss of bread crumbs and the flock swarmed, like Americans to money. The pigeons had better manners.

Soon enough, a group of children came by in their shiny, plush ski coats—probably American-made—and Yuri called to them. Four of Russia's only hope, the oldest perhaps ten years old. Did they want to hear a story about the KGB's glory days? Wide-eyed, a bit scared—of course they did!

"Once upon a time, not so long ago, there was a KGB agent feared by many," he said. "A loyal servant of the motherland, a man who traveled all the world because of the love he held for his country. He fought imperialist spies, men who had been allies in World War II and then turned on the Soviet Union out of greed and pride. American generals had considered invasion, but feared the resolve that had defeated Napoleon, turned back Hitler ..."

The thought flashed briefly, as these thoughts do, faster than the mind can register: Kostya, a dedicated man, a brilliant tactician, a man whose full name—Kostantin Dmitrich Pozharsky—was an allusion to one of the greatest Russian heroes, one of only two men honored with a statue on Red Square, just over there. A patriot in the Time of Troubles. Well, they had seen troubles of their own, he and Kostya. And Kostya had always been reliable. And a good friend. But bound by his new employment, he'd be reluctant to give up this software, this Orbweaver. Even for the sake of noble revenge.

Yuri snapped to attention. The children were looking at him expectantly, their noses dripping, their cheeks flush. He concluded as he always did. "You must stand up and defend Russia! Even though we are under the American cowboy boots, we will stand again! You will fight, and you will win! And I, children, will help you, even if it is from the grave."

Awe passed through them. A small boy asked, "How, grandpa?"

Yuri smiled. "Because I am not just a grandpa."

"No?"

Yuri widened his eyes dramatically, slowly leaned in toward the little boy, and pointed to the scar under his right eye which looked like a bloody tear. "*I* am that KGB agent. My nickname amongst comrades was The Bear. But the Americans, do you know, they called me The Butcher!"

He lunged toward the boy, growling like some ancient horror movie monster, his thick fingers frozen in claws. The children squealed with pleasure and laughed, and Yuri grinned, and for their attention, he handed them each a few sweet pieces of *karofka*.

CHAPTER 5

Two weeks had passed since that confusing night in Denver, and the nation still had no winner to praise or loser to ridicule. The months between election and inauguration allow the country to end its relationship with the former president—in this case, a smooth-talking Southerner who attracted scandal the way sweets on a pavement draw ants—and begin its relationship with the incoming president, greeting him like an enthusiastic newlywed, a nervous first date, or a groom on the wrong side of a shotgun. But in late November of 2000, the United States of America had no leader, no husband or wife, only a question mark. As such, it was mayhem.

The history books will show that the Kensington campaign and the Thornton campaign jockeyed for position in the courts, battling fiercely over hanging chads and ballot eligibility. Fairly, squarely. What the historians will not, perhaps, note is that the Thornton campaign ran a lifeless, boring legal war, while Stephen Shay—lurking, as usual, in the shadows—made sure the Kensington effort was nothing less than a crusade for everything good and decent in the American soul, an appeal to the hearts and minds of the country's people. And so it made sense that the showdown was in Ohio, The Heart of It All, and more specifically, Columbus, the test-market capital of the country. Here, there was a bit of everything, as good a match with national demographics as any city in the country: clean, successful, raw, and new—a true break from the rust belt, Columbus was the sixteenth-largest city in the country, but it felt like a small town.

"And it's a place where things come together," said Matt, glancing at the list Shay had prepared for him. In front of him, seated at a long table, his bleary-eyed staff were doing their best to wake up. "The AFL-CIO was formed here, the National Football League, the National Basketball Association, and even—get this—the structure of the baseball minor league system. Even the National Rifle Association was started here. Hold your applause, Broussard. The Temperance Union, the VFW, the first American Legion, and much more. Not far away, Tecumseh nearly united the eastern tribes to fight the Americans. It's where the Appalachians come together with the great Midwestern farm land."

He paused a moment for effect. Broussard was checking his Palm Pilot.

"And it's where our campaign victory comes together," Matt nearly shouted. "That is your message for today: Victory is Coming Together. Right here, right now. Fuck the courts, fuck the Dems; it's inevitable. The recount deadline is almost up, and the nightmare—Thornton's nightmare—no, the nightmare he's *forced* on all of us by being such a pussy—is almost over."

Broussard eyed him, unimpressed.

"Stick to that, and drinks are on me tonight!"

That woke them up. He dispersed them to their tasks—most were headed to prep the morning talk shows—and called after them, "And if I hear one more of you bitch about missing Thanksgiving, *you're* buying!"

He and Broussard collected their papers and crossed High Street to the lobby of the Riffe Center. The day was barely an hour long, and he was already exhausted—by the monotony, more than anything. Each day some new memo came out and would spark him for an hour or so, but reflecting at night, it was the same old shit: we won, Thornton's a sore loser, power to the people. The only thing that had changed? He and Gail had agreed to keep their relationship casual, primarily because she'd flown to Tennessee to stir up some trouble behind the scenes in Thornton's home state—and in the process had run into an old boyfriend of hers from Harvard. And so, two nights ago, he'd bedded one of the local support team, a perky but chunky blonde named Cassandra who talked too much—about Kensington's plans to deal with Iraq, about how poorly her mother had treated her, and about how much she loved God. It was the little details that kept you going in life.

"Why do I need to be at this meeting?" he said to Broussard as they waited for the elevator. "These are state representatives' yes-men."

"Shay said so last night."

"He was drunk last night."

"He's drunk every night."

Matt perused the listings for CATCOs season of plays; he'd never been, but had heard good things. In fact, for a guy who'd gone to Ohio State and worked for the governor, he didn't seem to remember Columbus distinctly at all. Riding down to the city had once been a big deal for the grungy little twerp from Marion, but since he'd left Sonny Allen's staff for the lobbyist job in DC, he'd not been in Columbus for more than one night at a time. Maybe a tour would do him good. Hell, you could never get lost; the city was a perfect square, all the streets parallel and perpendicular, and so long as you could see the sun, you could always find your direction.

—◦◦◦—

Strutting victoriously back into the main office, having demolished his Democratic counterpart Robin Moore—stunningly plush lips, feisty temperament—on national television over some minor memo sent out by Thornton's campaign concerning the recount's use of overseas ballots from the armed forces, Matt was met by applause suitable for Caesar. He looked for only one face in the crowd.

Shay clenched a tiny fist and smiled. "Now they're anti-soldier. Even they must know it's over. Great work, Matt."

"Thanks for the intel," he said with a nod. "That memo wasn't much, but the overseas connection was too sympathetic to pass up."

"Thank Gail," said Shay with a gleam. Gail lingered in the corner of the room in a peach-colored tailored suit, her cell phone to her ear. Still, she nodded at him.

Shay spun him around and walked him away from the staff. Shay's clothes reeked of body odor and cheap cologne, and Matt wondered what he'd been doing all day.

"This is a street fight, and whoever strikes first usually wins," Shay said. "Now let's talk a bit about how you're going to deal with the media in the administration, as opposed to the more gentle method we've all used during the campaign."

"I've been gentle?"

"You know, the kidding around. It's great for our friends, and it puts the more liberal assholes on their heels. But things have to change now."

For Shay, the media fell into three categories; friends, enemies, and eunuchs. Matt had seen him berate a reporter at the top of his lungs, in front of the entire press corps, for what he considered an unfair story—and had witnessed the man go from enemy to eunuch in a matter of seconds.

"We have the chance to turn a corner over the next few days, to frame the image of our presidency." Shay grinned like a shark. "Step it up a notch. Throw the high, hard one, brush 'em off the plate. In the meetings with media enemies, make sure you demonstrate toughness. Don't let down your guard."

"If I start off as weak, I'll never get back the strength."

"You'll crawl up to them like some homeless dog. That's not how we operate. Remember when you were a kid on the playground? Everybody, even the teachers, reacted to the bully and walked on eggshells around him because they knew that his reaction would be unreasonable, irrational, if they pissed him off. That's how we keep our enemies in place."

Matt remembered a showdown between a neighborhood bully and his cousin Cory; as long as nobody dealt with the bullies like Cory had, they'd all be okay.

"So as long as they think I'll come after them," said Matt.

Shay pointed a tiny finger in his face. "No, as long as they *know* it. If there's one thing these people can do, it's smell bullshit. You're going to have to make an example out of someone. Me, I'd pick that snotty bitch photographer you snuck in on election night. I never did rip you a new one for that."

"There's nothing left to rip," Matt said quietly, grinning to pass it off.

"Well, a scotch is calling me. To strengthen my attitude."

Or calm his nerves, loosen himself up, break a mental block. They walked over to the bar that had been set up in the office suite; Shay offered Matt a drink by motioning with the bottle.

"No, thanks, Stephen. Listen, talking about the job ... seems a little early, huh?"

"Oh no, this thing's wrapped up."

"I mean, me. As press secretary. That's a lock?"

Shay's thin eyebrows arched. "You've heard differently?"

"Something Alexander said to me back in Denver."

"That fuckwad. Listen to me. Certainly there are no guarantees. That's the kind of thinking that got Thornton in this mess he's in." He downed a sizable portion of the scotch, cleared his throat, and swung his tiny arms at Matt's shoulders like a penguin, clutching him with fatherly affection. "But I don't know a better person than you for the job. When the time comes, let no one stop you."

After a series of meetings on the Ohio State campus, Matt cut toward the parking garage across the Oval. His old stomping grounds! Beer bongs and darts! When he hadn't been studying. The temptation was to see the infrequent parties and his looser, fifth and final year as the sum of his college experience, and that's how he would have described it to most of the gregarious assholes he worked with, but the truth was that he'd worked his ass off between part-time jobs and classes and the internship that eventually got him in with Sonny Allen. Around him now, college kids draped in OSU sweaters hurried by with their backpacks sagging and their cigarette smoke blowing in the wind—and not a damn one of them voted, he thought; the numbers here were terrible, not surprisingly. The familiar buildings seemed older, rearranged, as if a giant hand had simply picked them up and moved them, but they still had the ring of 1950s-era public works and the hard fist of academia that had slapped him around his freshman year. "Liberal Land," Shay had called it, but like most state universities, the conservative sentiment was stronger than you might expect. Oh fuck: he was starting to think like Shay.

As he walked and gazed across the wide expanse of the Oval's lawn, he saw a woman photographing a small band of protestors. It couldn't be. Jeans and a yellow winter coat, something you'd buy from L. L. Bean. He laughed at the possibility that he'd be the one to sneak up on Kris Johansen this time. He darted across the lawn toward that beautiful bell-shaped bottom. She had only two cameras this time, and she kept moving, probably trying to capture what was left of the light.

"Hey, no press allowed," he said, out of breath.

She turned—thank God it was her. Sizing him up, she said flatly, "Don't bother me when I'm working," and turned back to the five or six kids marching in a tiny, rather ineffective little circle. Their posters were calling for an end to Kensington's illegal campaign to steal *blah blah blah.*

"You go from photographing the best election night ever to this?"

"It's all important," she said. "It's all history."

Jesus. Was this the same woman who'd flirted with him in Denver? Who called him "my prince"? No, of course not: she'd only needed something from him then. A woman using her looks to get what she needed—go figure. Maybe Gail was right, maybe he was naive.

"Well, hey, it was nice seeing you, Kris."

He turned back to the garage and angrily clapped his gloved hands together. No woman had ever achieved what she, without even trying, had achieved. Maybe Erica Schultz, back in the third grade.

"Matt Risen's a quitter!" she shouted behind him.

"Quitter! Quitter!" chanted the students.

He turned, and she snapped a photo.

"It won't come out anyway," he said as he stormed back, the protestors not relenting in their chant. She snapped another photo and laughed. "Did you pay them?"

"I told them you were a Republican."

"Quitter! Quitter!"

"Look, you little punks," he said, "it's your guy who quit—"

"Okay, okay," Kris said, still laughing, pushing him back. "Leave them to their freedom of speech. I've lost the light here anyway."

They strolled away. The silence was beautiful.

"So, you don't call, you don't write," she said.

"You didn't give me your number."

"Would you have used it?"

"On the party's dime." His hands in his coat pockets, he swiveled around. "Where's your car?"

"I took the bus. Public transportation all the way."

Now the silence turned uneasy. It never turned uneasy; he always filled it, gracefully, bombastically, whatever the situation called for. Something about this woman tied up his best asset: his tongue.

"Your team's winning this thing," she said, affecting a motherly pout. "You should be glowing. Why aren't you glowing?"

He answered, too quickly, "Anxious. Weirdly anxious, don't know why."

"It's that winter sun. Sets too soon." She nodded like she had all the answers, like she'd been here before. "Or it's Shay. How is Egghead?"

"Still pissed at me for letting a hippie-dippie liberal photojournalist into the inner sanctum on election night."

"Really? With all that's been going on?"

"He knows how to hold a grudge." Matt sighed and studied the white reflective panels of the Wexner Center. "He needs control; I'm used to not having any."

"Maybe you should try having a little more."

"Oh, hell, I do try, but then Kensington calls Africa a country—"

He stopped himself, and she burst into laughter again—rich, free laughter from the gut.

"Don't worry, I can keep a secret," she said.

"Do I look worried?"

"Like a Chihuahua." Kris grinned, which made her seem younger, mischievous. "Look, I've dealt with Shay before. He's made it clear he doesn't like some of the views I've expressed in my artwork, but unlike your friends at Fox, who try to pretend they're not right-wingers, I admit that I'm a godless lefty." She brushed a thick partition of hair over her ear and pulled a knit cap from her pocket. "But I'm a journalist first. I separate what I do in news and what I do in my art."

"So which is this?"

"You and me?"

His heart shook a bit. Just hearing the words "you and me," joined by a lovely conjunction was all it took to reduce him to a jibber-jabbering idiot? *Smooth.*

"No, the photos, there, with the—"

"What are you doing here anyway?"

"Recount … thing," he said. "I went to school here."

"You're from Ohio?"

"Marion, about forty-five minutes—"

"Northwest, yeah. I've been there. Huh." She explained that she'd done an extensive tour in 1992 with the Democratic candidate—"the winner," she noted—and then had come back a few years ago to do a feature on the Ohio River's long string of cancerous coal-burning plants. "So you know this town pretty well, huh?" she said.

"Like the back of my hand."

"Give a girl a tour?"

"Sure. Absolutely."

Once they reached the garage, and, bowing a little as he held the door open for her, he flipped through a quick mental list of restaurants, night spots. Buckeye Donuts wasn't going to cut it, although there were times late at night it had looked like a blurry oasis. He hopped into the driver's seat and, as he leaned over to buckle his seat belt, got a good whiff of a lilac perfume mixed with the surprisingly appealing scent of cold-weather sweat. The smell of reality.

"Does your boss really believe that God elected him? God's Will Kensington."

"That comment was out of context." Matt hunched forward and wiped the fog off the windows as he drove. "Can we not talk politics?"

"Right now? No. We have to."

"I believe in most of my party's values, okay? A strong America means a safer world for everyone. Look how much better off we've been since Reagan broke up the Soviet Union."

Kris looked shocked. "I thought that was Yoko!" She laughed and then shook her head. "Wait, I'm starting to sound like you guys. Blame the woman instead of the four guys with more money and drugs than they knew what to do with. It's the same way you conservatives look for scapegoats in your foreign policy."

"There's your conspiracy," he said, turning right onto a street clogged with students. He screeched the brakes at a crosswalk. These guys just didn't care if you hit them, did they? The Focus crawled along the winding road, and he eventually turned them onto what he was sure was Neil Avenue. As they proceeded more smoothly to the south, he pointed out a rancid hole-in-the-wall he'd lived in his junior year. "My neighbors reeked of pot."

"Liberals!" she said.

"Hey, I have liberal friends."

"Please. You wouldn't know a liberal in this town if he came up and bit you on the ass."

His ears perked up. Was that a drawl? "Are you from the South?"

"Shit, is my accent showing?" She covered her mouth and grinned, exposing those rosy cheeks he could kiss all night. "Texas born and raised. Surprised I'm not a right-winger?" she said, letting her accent stretch absurdly. "Not all Texans are. I am a socialist, communist, Marxist journalist of Swedish and Irish descent from the great state of Texas. And I've got a great ass."

"Well, I'll take you to a Democrat bar, how about that?"

As he took a right, he couldn't keep his eyes off of her and nearly rimmed the curb. The brick streets jiggled the chassis of the car, and she joked about Shay's turkey neck wobbling when he walked. Matt was reminded by the bricks of his apartment in German Village, and though he could no longer recall its street name or what the front of it looked like, he did remember the way the morning light poured through the front windows, as if the sun were reaching down into his bedroom. He saw himself there, and suddenly Kris was with him, nestled, living with him.

Oh shit.

They rolled to a red light. "Where are we?" she said, craning her neck to see past him.

"On our way downtown. I know this great restaurant."

"Downtown's that way."

She pointed out his window, to the cluster of buildings nearly blocked from their sight by the 315 overpass. Lost. Well, not entirely. The sun was low over the horizon, burning the treetops, so he still had some sense of direction. But yeah, it had been awhile since he'd been home.

—◦◦—

"But if you know a place well, the history of it, I mean—it looks different," Matt said, leaning over his basil soup. With a cut of Due Amici's flatiron steak in her mouth, Kris nodded, watching and listening so intently that he had to remind himself what in the hell he was talking about. "Okay, an anecdote: this one winter I was sledding with a girl.

We were about twelve, I guess, and we were talking about where we were going to live when we grew up. She said Boston, and I asked her why, and she said because she could feel the history of it when she was there. She asked where I wanted to live, and I said, 'Here.' This girl—her name was Angela Snyder—she said, 'Why? There's so little history here.' And I pointed out that the top of the hill we were sledding down was a two thousand-year-old Indian mound. If you know a place, you can see its secrets and it's always exciting."

Kris sipped her merlot and cleared her throat. "But you don't live here."

"Huh?"

"You moved."

He wiped his mouth. "Okay, but you're missing the point." He scanned high brick walls and black exposed ceiling for another way to put it. What, he wondered, had once stood here? "All right. One time I was driving myself and Sonny Allen, the governor—"

"Yeah, yeah, taught you everything you know," she said.

"This, too. We're driving in the Hocking Hills, I think, and we come up on this curve in the road that appeared out of nowhere for no apparent reason, and he said, 'You know why this curve is here?'"

"Because he let his cronies carve it out?"

"Nice," Matt said. "I see what you did there. No, Allen said that these roads are built on the land the settlers made *their* roads on, and they made 'em on trails the Indians used, and the Indians were following the trails the deer made, and *they* were following a path some charging woolly mammoth made thousands of years ago. So we just went around that curve 'cause a woolly mammoth got a whiff of mammoth pussy."

With a twinge of horror he'd skidded right into the governor's punch line, trying to stop himself at the last second to no avail, cringing until Kris broke out into that carefree laugh again, so loudly the rest of Due Amici's patrons—a few of them journalists and politicos—lifted their heads liked spooked gazelle.

"Mammoth pussy," she gasped through hooting she was trying to stop. "Something about the words ... oh, God."

"So you see my point?"

She only cut up more.

By the time they emerged through the frosted doors and handed their ticket to the valet, Matt was pretty sure he could marry this woman. If the timing was ever right.

"You hardly ate," she said as they turned from Gay Street onto High.

"What'd you eat, that soup, and the calamari, right?" She leaned in and sniffed him. "You, sir, smell of fennel."

"At least it's not my breath."

"Now who's holding grudges?"

Up the street, the Hyatt Regency loomed to the left. Nearly seven o'clock, enough time yet, he supposed. She wasn't even bothering to ask where they were going anymore, only teased him by pointing to random buildings and asking him what they were. And then Broussard called. It'd taken him longer than Matt expected. Winking at Kris, he said he was getting a feel of the mood of the electorate, and that he'd be back, yes, yes, cheerio. He hung up as they approached a parking lot in the Short North.

"Do you ever get tired of lying?" Kris said.

A familiar cold pit opened in his stomach.

"I don't lie."

"Oh, I didn't mean *lie* lie. I meant, to that guy, Broussard." Her voice softened as she said, "Just a joke."

"Not a good one," he said, but he turned to smile a little—no harm done—and saw that she'd leaned her head against the window.

"There's a spot."

It took a little while for the mood to lighten, courtesy of Mr. Jack Daniels. He introduced her to the Short North Tavern—"a Dems hidey-hole," he said—and ordered a round. For her part, she seemed to drag herself out of whatever thoughts she'd gotten stuck in back there in the car. A few Democrats strolled over: one he knew from his time with Sonny Allen; three of them were law consultants for Thornton's campaign, and their jokes were as forced as their candidate's smile. Ever magnanimous, he bought them a round, too, expensive enough to rub his impending victory in their faces. All of them leered at Kris, and she seemed to take a genuine but minor interest in them; she seemed curious about everything, asked questions, but never forced it, as if she knew quite well when her limits were reached. And she drank like a woman who knew how to drink. There was no easy way to pin her down, no category to lump her into, which was troubling for a man used to looking for two-word catchphrases that could turn an argument.

Also leering at Kris, from the darker end of the bar, was Robin Moore. The woman he'd destroyed on national television today. When Matt caught her eye, she toasted him silently.

"It's like a neighborhood bar," Kris said, straining over Springsteen's "Dancing in the Dark" blaring from a CD player behind the bar. "You know, for a city bar."

"This is probably the most liberal neighborhood in the city. Didn't use to be much to it, really, until a few people had the balls to invest, and then a city council staffer and a couple of creative types got involved, and bam, they turned it around."

"You?"

He laughed. "No, for once I'm not talking about myself."

An absolutely feline grin parted her lips. Besides the rather innocent daydream he'd had about German Village, he'd barely thought about having sex with her; it was like some part of his brain had been closed off for most of the night. Probably for the better.

"Look, forget what I said in the car. I try not to make assumptions."

"I spin things. I guess it's deserved."

"No, no." Her eyes were studying him, and after a suspenseful silence, she said, "So what happens when this is over? For you?"

"I'm not sure."

"Something in the White House? Press secretary?"

The urge to say "Yes," to brag and give her a Tom Cruise smile, dissipated quickly. She drew the honesty out of him like a needle.

"Shay said not to worry, but I'm worried. A lot of names are going to jockey for that job."

"Shay's got your back?"

"So he says."

"Then what's to worry about." She patted his knee—oh, Christ!— and said, "I'll be rooting for you, tiger. Like Mary Jane and Spiderman, but the Mary Jane who finally got out of the house, you know."

"You're buzzed," he said.

"A little."

Sometime later, his phone rang again. Then again. Second time in what, ten minutes? Broussard. Fuck, that stupid promise he'd made in the morning. Eight forty-five. Taking the call, Matt hardly let his assistant speak. "I'm on my way, but I'm not rushing, all right? Fuckin' grow a pair!"

But the return couldn't be avoided. Nothing important had come across his BlackBerry, just some shit from the current president trying to stir some sympathy for Thornton. Still, there was a limit, and he knew that the calls would be picking up and give him no peace.

He let his hand grace the back of Kris's coat as they stepped outside. Opened her door.

"Radio?" said Kris.

"Sure, anything. I like it all. The Boss. That jazz they had going in Due Amici's. Southern rock, classical. Hell, I'm all over the map."

She smirked. "Don't know what you want to be when you grow up?"

"A big shot," he said. He could feel the liquor in his words. "I'm a careerist, remember?"

"God, you do hold a grudge."

"Teasing, teasing."

But a silence he couldn't control descended on them, and they rode silently down the High Street drag strip. Despite the angst, it was nice to be able to be silent with her, to have a moment to think; in Washington, if you didn't have something to say immediately, you looked like Robin Moore had this morning in their face-off: a bug-eyed fish caught on a hook.

"Don't tell me you have a husband," he said.

Her chuckle seemed directed at herself. "Nope." She wet her lips, lost in some thought, and said suddenly, "I'm not just some piece of ass."

"Did I say you were?"

"We girls in the secretary pool, we talk."

His guts bottomed out. Maybe she'd done some digging in the weeks since he'd seen her. Maybe, given his ways, there wasn't much need to.

"You're different," he said quietly.

"I know. Too different."

When they'd pulled up to the Renaissance, he unhitched his seatbelt and turned to her. Her eyes—like his, he imagined—searched and danced away, and finally she leaned in an inch, more, and their lips met in a manner he could only think of, later, as frustrated.

"At least let me call you when I get back," he whispered.

Tucking her upper lip, wincing, she pulled a piece of paper out of her coat pocket, held it for a moment, and then put it in his hand.

"Old-fashioned," she said, unearthing her cameras from underneath the coat he'd left in the backseat before she opened the door. "I'll be the one with the camera in front of my face."

———∿∿———

The hotel barstools were stiff. The in-house system was playing Mariah Carey. The staff members he'd sent off in the morning to spread their message were frolicking—the only word he could think of for their weird, paganish gyrations—and drinking his wallet dry. Fuck it, he'd charge the campaign. They were all going to be rich. Victory was coming together. He sat on the barstool and stared at the row of liquor bottles, the cheesy Ohio postcard lodged between the register and the mirror, and a disposable camera someone had placed by the beer taps.

Too different.

Well.

Worse, Shay had been waiting. Said he'd sent two texts, where the fuck had Matt gone, where was the outlook plan for tomorrow, who was doing CNN, who was doing Fox?

"Are you shit-faced?" Matt said to him.

Shay's eyes flared; he wheeled around, stumbled, regained his balance, cursed at one of the staffers and otherwise left wordlessly. Even his silences were bludgeoning. If effective.

Matt wondered if he still had a job in Washington.

CHAPTER 6

The Sunday deadline passed, the recount was over, and the Thornton campaign was a free-floating barge in the middle of the ocean. "They're going to the Supreme Court," said Shay, "but we'll kill that off." And so Matt was free, again, to escape the campaign for a day, renting his own car and heading for Marion to see his Uncle Jess and his cousin Cory.

Driving up Route 23, he was amazed at the growth and prosperity he saw at the start of his route: new shopping plazas where there'd once been cornfields, high-end box stores just north of Worthington and 200k housing developments. Forty minutes later, he was a witness to the depression that had stricken Marion. Though most streets were lined with towering, proud trees, many of the houses showed signs of distress. The factories were empty. How long had this been going on? As he pulled into the Oakland Heights neighborhood, he smiled at the names of former neighbors on mailboxes and the old, inviolate tavern with the juicy, cube steak sandwiches; but on the other corner, the second-hand furniture store, pharmacy, and ice cream store had been torn down and replaced by a drive-through beer dock and a bar. Marion was a rusty, welded together city, half manufacturing, half agriculture, and all transportation, like the state itself.

"Glad you could make it," Jess said gruffly from the porch.

"Things have just been so crazy—"

"Well come on in. You can have some leftovers."

No manly hug, no crude jokes. Just a grunt and a nod of the head. Jess had supposedly long ago made his peace with Matt's politics.

"Where's Cory?"

"Down at some bar with that Carrie girl. He didn't know if you'd actually show up."

Matt paced around the living room, touching furniture that had been in the house since the late 1960s, as Jesse stood in the kitchen doorway, arms crossed over his massive gut. Six-five, built, it seemed, from an oak tree. In a photograph on the mantle, Uncle Jess dwarfed his first wife, Cory's mom, Angeline. They were standing by that bright yellow '66 Chevy Nova Wagon—the same school bus color as Kris's winter coat—with Cory and Matt and Matt's parents, a handsome couple, his father's charm shining like a new dime, his mother's stern beliefs tightening her Irish mouth. That old Chevy. Matt peered at the photo, remembering the way the Nova's carriage shook on bumpy roads, remembering the night Angeline and his parents had left the boys with Jesse and driven out to Bucyrus for an auction. He and Cory had danced all over the Naugahyde furniture, rooting on the Buckeyes in that grueling 1970 game at the 'Shoe against the boys from up north and celebrating with secret sips of Uncle Jesse's beer when the call came from the county police.

"Your folks loved that car," said Jesse.

"Thirty years," Matt said distantly. "Angie was a real looker, Jess."

"Ain't all about looks, you know."

Matt turned but Jesse had slipped into the kitchen, where he was talking with his third wife, Paula. He looked back at the photo. Almost thirty years to the day, and he'd nearly forgotten.

A squat, cheerless woman, Paula emerged with a cold plate of turkey cutlets and stuffing. Matt thanked her, sat nervously, and began to eat while Jess loomed in the corner of the room, pretending to watch CNN.

"Nothing good on there," Matt said.

"Suppose I've gotten my fill. Don't know how you do it."

Thank God for Cory, who bounded in minutes later, bringing back the sun of the day and descriptions of Carrie O'Malley. He bear-hugged Matt and said, "You're looking pale on that TV set, brother."

"Like you seen a ghost," said Jesse, settling with a huff into the red Naugahyde chair.

"Jesus, Dad, a little couth, please." He eyed Matt with that mischievous, optimist's glint. "So are you guys done torturing the rest of us with this recount?"

"I bet it was tearing up folks at the Ag Department, huh?"

"My money was on Kensington all the way," said Cory. "Though he doesn't know a damn thing about corn. You think he'll disband the Agricultural Department?"

Matt chuckled. That was Cory, always preparing for the worst, full of schemes and stories about the inner dealings of one of the federal government's most boring departments. If you didn't know him, he'd come across a little hard—too jovial, almost cocky—but the truth was, he'd been as scarred as Matt by the car accident in '70, and he'd turned that pain into integrity. That might've been his best-kept secret.

As Matt finished his meal, Cory described his beer with Carrie, how her ginger-colored hair lit up in the afternoon light, how she sang along to Johnny Cash with that crystalline voice of hers.

"Always figured she'd make it big," Matt said.

"Ah, she's happy," Cory replied, gazing out the window. Apparently Carrie had talked about visiting DC sometime soon. It was about time his cousin manned up when it came to his third-grade crush. For ten years he'd pined for a woman he'd known from work, Tess-something-or-other, who'd died suddenly. Sometimes he acted like a widower.

But today he and Cory were kids again, cruising the back alleys and sidewalks of Oakland Heights. The air was crisp, refreshing; there was only so much a man could take of air-conditioned hotel rooms.

"So Jess hates me now," Matt said.

"Aw, he's just pissed you didn't come to Thanksgiving at Aunt Marie's."

"I couldn't get away. Especially not all the way out to Fredericktown."

"He'll get over it."

Jess had been his northern star; it'd been his suggestion for Matt to go to Staunton Military Academy in the seventh grade, even though it meant being without Cory for a couple of years, and when the school closed, bankrupt, in 1976, Jess had brought him home even though Aunt Marie said she had work for him on the farm. "You got a gifted brain, kid," he'd told Matt, "and I ain't gonna let you waste it on horse shit and chicken eggs."

"I'm gonna need him," Matt said to Cory. "I'm gonna need you."

Cory tried to brush his curly blond hair down into his eyes. "Well, gee, Matt, I'm just a corn-shucker at the Ag Department."

They crossed a glass-covered alleyway by Edison Middle School. Had the streets always been this littered, this dirty? He remembered them cleaner, wider—but then, he figured, that's how everyone remembered their hometown.

"I was thinking about you a couple days ago," Matt said. "Shay gave me this lecture—"

"There's a shock."

"He was prepping me. I might not even get the press secretary job, you know."

Cory stopped. "You're shitting me. After all that work?"

"Success, not loyalty," Matt said. "I guess dedication's not even a factor."

"I'd call your campaign successful. Even if Kensington's a dope."

"He has his good points."

Raising his arms like he was being mugged, Cory iterated the phrase Matt so often heard here: leave politics at the front door. The posture reminded him of that autumn day.

"Warren what's-his-name," said Matt. "Remember that fight?"

"God, man, I haven't thought about that in years." Cory peered down the alley. "Must have been right over there on Woodrow, huh? Warren Welch. Big motherfucker."

"That didn't stop you."

The instant he'd spotted the frail Derrick McGahern in Warren's grip, Cory had sprinted the two blocks; Matt had followed out of instinct but froze once he saw his cousin leap on Warren and pull him loose from the scrawny victim of life. Without pausing, Warren jabbed Cory in the face.

"And you wanted a fair fight," Cory said now, laughing. "Against that guy. He was like the Juggernaut."

"I was stroking his ego. First time I learned to do that, I guess." As if drawn by the memory, they'd wandered toward Woodrow Avenue. "Besides," Matt said, "it was supposed to give you a chance to run."

"I thought I was dead."

"I did, too. You always seemed so much bigger than me, Cor, but that day, well, not so much."

Until, Matt thought. Until Cory, looking like a red fox circling a grizzly bear, asked Warren if he could take off his coat. The big jackass grunted, "Sure," and Cory ripped off his coat, tossed it over Warren's head, and kicked him squarely in the balls. The Juggernaut bent in half, fell to the pavement, the coat draped over his face—no protection from Cory's punches. Finally, with Warren's moans muffled, Cory had stood over him and said, "If you ever pick on any of these other kids, you'll get some more." And by God, he'd said it like he meant it.

"It was a miracle," Matt said with a grin. He sat on a fire hydrant painted green. Back then, he was sure, it'd been painted red. "This be hallowed ground."

"Of course, a few days later, he pounded the shit out of me."

"Yeah, but the resolve on your face, man! 'Even if you kick my ass every day, nothing changes. You'll be sorry one way or another.' Classic stuff."

"I got to him," Cory said faintly. "It was my face that was bloody, but his voice, it was shaking when he laughed." He looked down the street, suddenly despondent, his shoulder slumped. That was the flip side of Cory, you had to understand. It'd just started the past ten years or so. You got him going, all carefree, and then something burst. Into sadness or anger, the latter voiced not like some bombastic sergeant but the steady, terrifying voice of a lieutenant: cold, commanding.

Matt tried to leaven things by asking, "Why that day? I mean, he'd been torturing us for years and then—bam!"

"It was the right time and place," said Cory. "But you gotta be willing to lose if you take on a bully." The optimist's smile returned. "But, hey, what's so bad about losing if it makes you feel good about yourself?"

"You think Thornton feels good about himself?"

"No fucking politics! Not until we get back to DC, okay?"

—⌁⌁—

That night he slept in his own bed. Cory was just down the hall. Awake, staring at the Indians pennant he'd bought with paper route money, he'd been thinking again about what Kris had said about them being too different and how she might change her mind if she met Cory, when he heard a clanking in the kitchen.

He found Uncle Jess at the table eating a cherry pie out of a plastic container. A slime of filling in his white beard, Jess grunted, "Paula got it from this great little market, and I hate to see it go bad. Two days old already."

Matt pulled out one of the ancient chairs from the table and sat. It'd been a serious blow to his pride when Cory'd revealed the reasons for his uncle's anger. Pride in his job, in who he was. How he was known. But that flare-up had passed once he'd begun thinking of Kris. How she made him feel the way Cory and Jess made him feel: solid.

"I wish I'd been here for Thanksgiving," he said.

Jess shoveled up another bite. "Wish so, too."

"I don't always know how much I give up for my job until it's too late. I end up looking over my shoulder."

"You got to ask yourself: am I willing to ride to heaven on the devil's back?" He reached for a mug of cold coffee and slurped. "But shit, Matt, you're in a world I don't get. You and Cory both. Don't listen to a pig farmer like me."

"You teach math."

"Basic math. For kids."

"You should come out to DC soon. I know Cory'd like you to visit. You can bring the beautiful Carrie O'Malley with you."

"And leave Paula here?" said Jesse. A crazed, lusty fire lit his eyes, and he wiped the filling from his mouth. "I may just do that," he said with a cackle.

Cory was the strong, abiding oak's branches, Jess the trunk and the taproot. You could go anywhere, Matt thought, you could weather anything, so long as you knew where to find that tree, so long as you came back to it now and then.

"I won't let 'em change me, Jess. In DC If I get the job."

Jess wrapped his humongous arm around Matt and about near choked the life out of him.

"You still got your pop's naïveté in you, boy. Everything changes." He pushed a gnarled fingertip into Matt's face. "Question is, into what?"

Chapter 7

Maybe it was the flight into DC, watching that white slate of government buildings come into view; or maybe it was the number of calls he'd gotten from Broussard and Shay and Gail; or maybe it was the effect of getting too much advice from too many people—a cyclone of well-intentioned words that blurred together—but for whatever reason, by the time Matt Risen returned to his apartment in Alexandria, his mind was wholly focused on securing his position as the press secretary to the forty-third president of the United States.

He'd not been home for nearly two months, had not collected his mail, fed his cat, or picked up the paper, but it was a given that Shelly Ray, his thirteen year-old neighbor, was watching out for him and Larry Bird, his enormous and deceptively slow tabby. The cat's blond and yellow fur reminded him of Bird's curly mane, and, like the great one, the feline Larry Bird was confident, always in control, but not much of a coach. Matt made no apologies for the name; it reminded him of his childhood, the lamentably bad Cavaliers, and the more preferable, either good or great Boston Celtics, whose every game he'd followed from Ohio.

As he backed into his parking spot, he noticed that the Ray family's Volvo had a major dent and a broken headlight. They must have had another drunk driving mishap, he thought and shook his head in disgust.

Shelly's home projected the image of loving parents: remnants of Shelly's youth, the almost symbolic swing set, tree house, and an elaborate sand box. Shelley hadn't used them in years, but they served their function for anyone who didn't look too closely. To Matt, the signs were obvious: strange people coming in and out of the house at all hours, the muffled sounds of impromptu parties, cars parked with wheels up on the curb. One morning, Matt had found one of the Rays' Volvos with its doors left open all night and the snow that had fallen a few hours earlier dusting the interior of the car.

Larry Bird greeted him with a pissed-off meow, not unlike Uncle Jesse's greeting back in Marion. With a whoosh, he swept the purring cat off the ground, holding his pudgy body in front of him. "You, sir, have gotten fat," he muttered.

Maybe if he didn't get the job, he'd turn into one of those people who walked their cat on a leash.

He'd not been home more than twenty minutes when Shelly's familiar voice was chanting his name as she sprang up the steps of his brownstone. She dropped a clutch of business shirts, a UPS package, and a stack of mail and rocketed into his chest, her eyes crudely circled with what looked like crayon.

"You're home!"

"Is that mascara?"

"Eyeliner. *Such* a difference. No wonder you're terrible with women."

His eyes crinkled. He kept his lascivious activities hidden from her best he could, but surely she'd seen a woman or two coming and going.

"So are you back for good?" she asked, digging her hands into her back pockets.

"Should be."

"You look pale on TV. They don't feed you enough."

He descended on the couch, sloughing off Larry Bird. "Exhaustion, kiddo. Stress. Grown-up things." He slipped a piece of paper from his jeans and handed it to her. "Could you pick this stuff up for me?"

"Are they going to the Supreme Court?" she blurted.

"With my grocery list? No."

"They've got a point, you know. That secretary of state in Ohio is a bitch."

"Easy, Shell. And watch your mouth, huh? You're a bad example for Larry Bird. Who, by the way, looks like he's gained a few pounds."

"Answer my question."

The beauty of youth: that she'd literally stomped her sneaker onto his hardwood flooring but was demanding to be treated like an adult. Precocious little brat. Like he'd been.

"They did go to the Supreme Court, and they got struck down. Two days ago. And no, they can't go back. Not without losing what's left of their dignity, Shell." He sat up. "It's like when you keep asking someone to go out with you, over and over, and they keep shooting you down."

"I wouldn't know about that," she said sweetly.

"Ri-ight. There comes a point where you just say forget it and move on."

Appeased, she plopped down next to him and looked at the list. How she'd love to go get his groceries, "like a servant," she said. If only a certain matter of contractual obligations could be fulfilled.

"You need money?"

"You *owe* me money. Without me, your house would fall apart."

"I doubt that."

"Besides, isn't that what the government does, hand out money?"

Sighing, he dug out his wallet. A hundred? She stared at him coldly. Two months, she reminded him. He'd been gone two months. He gave her three hundred and told her to scram before he changed his mind.

She stared at him again, one eye squinting.

"What?"

"Did you meet someone?" she squawked with more than a little jealousy.

"How about you hang up my shirts, Karnak."

Took him awhile, but he finally got her to trudge upstairs and give him a moment's peace. She'd take on more responsibilities if he let her. Her feelings for him were mixed: she loved him, at times, like a parent or the big brother she never had; at other times there was a hint that she had a crush on him. She was clearly careful about the latter; she knew that if she ever made Matt nervous or uncomfortable he might feel forced to pull away.

Given her lush chestnut hair, big blue eyes, and already-developed figure, it was a good thing she was so perceptive. He would have pulled away from her if things got strange. He wasn't stupid: she was, without a doubt, the little sister he'd never had, and his protectiveness of and brotherly antagonism toward her were simple. But being in the public eye in a time of great sexual cynicism, problems could arise. The evil thoughts of others could chill a great friendship.

Shay had once visited his apartment and met Shelly; Matt could read Shay's mind, and it made him ill. "I'm only talking about the appearance," Shay had said, to which Matt responded that he'd tell other people what to think, and otherwise, they could go fuck themselves.

As Shelly hung up his shirts in the hall closet, Matt walked into the laundry room and started sorting through his suitcase. His clothes reeked of something he couldn't name, a placeless-ness, a weird lack of smell more than anything. Larry Bird strolled in and tried to insert himself into the suitcase; the laundry room was his domain as much as the Boston Garden or French Lick, Indiana, was the realm of his somewhat more insecure namesake.

Shelly walked in. "Laundry?" she said efficiently. Christ, maybe they were like some old married couple. "Do you want to go to Tyson's Corner this week?" she said. "Soon as you get a break, anyway? I need new clothes."

"You're starting to look like a hippie."

"That's kinda the objective. I'm a hippie, dude." She held two fingers up to her mouth as if she was smoking a joint. "It's not like I've gone Goth or anything."

"I thought that was the point of the mascara."

She shook her head with not-so-subtle disgust. "For a guy who spends all his time thinking about appearances, you sure don't know much about them."

"I have people for that."

"Ugh. So how about Tyson's Corner?"

He thought of the million things that needed to happen, the party tonight, the hands he'd have to shake just so the job was locked up. Even now, he could hear his BlackBerry buzzing where he'd left it on the coffee table. The fucking campaign never stopped, all right.

"We'll see," he said too briskly. "It's just a busy time, Shell."

Her eyes fell. "Okay."

"I just don't want to promise and not deliver."

"Sure. Oh, I almost forgot why I came over. Cory stopped by."

"Did he leave a message?"

"I didn't talk to him. I just saw him knocking on the door, and he left that package for you." She pointed to the box she'd left on his credenza.

Inside the box he found a basketball with a note: *Any time you feel your head getting too big, call me. We'll take this to the court, and I'll bring you back to earth.* Matt chuckled. Just what a couple of guys approaching middle age should be doing on their day off.

After Shelly left he fired off an e-mail to thank Cory. *Any time you feel man enough*, he wrote, signing it, *Your friend, Warren*.

———∿———

The bar was set off from the avenue, a shadow in a shadowed alley, and, while a few young people in three-hundred-dollar suits milled around the oak bar top in the front room, the real money was petting itself in the back room beyond the staffer who looked like a wrestler, through the oak double-doors affixed with dull, brass handles thick as a ship's tie-lines, and lit by faux gas lamps, a chilly chandelier, and an honest-to-God hearth. The heat and the vodka: lethal combination, thought Matt.

Grover Alexander's cottony white hair was slicked back by some kind of miracle cream, and, with a self-satisfied slur, he said, "You're a regular Clark Kent, Risen. They call you, and you duck into a phone booth and fly off like Superman." He turned to the woman sitting next to him. "He saved my ass in Denver, tell you that." With keen eyes, sparkling from either the booze or some scheme, he grinned at Matt. "Wanna make some *real* money in the private sector?"

"He's White House-bound," said the woman, a think-tank hot shot with SecNav connections. "Aren't you, Matt?"

"Nothing's guaranteed, Sue." He tightened his lips around an unlit cigarette and played with it for a moment. "Everyone's got their man."

"Not me," she cooed.

"More money in the private sector," Grover said before he knocked back his tumbler.

Shay emerged between the thick bodies and the cloud of cigar smoke, holding two cigars of his own, each wrapped. Even in this low light, his skin was pale.

"A word," he said, tossing a cigar into Matt's lap. "You weren't going to smoke that piece of shit, were you?"

"Not now."

Shay looked down at the think-tanker, whose blouse, Matt had noticed, seemed to open another inch every hour. Not surprisingly, she smiled at Shay the same way she'd smiled at him—that was the game, the meaningless flirtation everyone played, even if she'd decided to bed Matt, and he her—and even less surprisingly, Shay stared at her as though she were a lump of anthracite coal.

"You're in Middle East economic prediction," he said flatly.

"I'm flattered, Mr. Shay." Sue rose a bit from her leather chair, extending a hand.

"We'll need you down the road," Shay said without taking her hand, waddling toward an empty corner of the room. The former, philandering president he was not. Matt grinned at the stricken thinker, who'd snapped her hand back to her drink, hoping no one would see the dis. In Shay's eyes, intellectuals would always be recondite outcasts, good for their information but naively sequestered, untested by the pressure of having to make a decision and see it succeed or fail.

It took Matt a few minutes to reach the dark corner where Shay waited; at every turn, there was a hand to shake, a name to learn in the din of the room and its vaulted ceiling. No one bothered Stephen Shay; he bothered you, and you feared his approach; thrilled, too, at your contact with the underside demon of DC conservatism. The effect had nearly worn off for Matt over the years, and when he finally reached Shay, he said, "She's got a thing for you, boss."

"I'd like to get paid to sit on my ass all day."

Shay lit his cigar and held the flame toward Matt. Over the tip of the cigar and the small fire, his eyes narrowed. With one hand, Shay balanced his half-full scotch, and with the other, he motioned to a floating waiter. "Fill mine, fill his," he growled. "He's going to need it."

"Celebration?"

"Not yet," said Shay, his smile crooked. He shouldered into the corner of the wall and gazed over Matt's shoulder. "Webb has someone else in mind for the press secretary position."

"But I—"

"Easy, easy. Lots of allies here. On your side, all of them. You need to rally." He smirked and sipped on the scotch. "Unless you'd rather bow out gracefully, like Thornton."

This wasn't supposed to be a dogfight. Win the election, win the job: that's what Shay had said back in June. Matt swirled his scotch—Shay's scotch; same brand, same glass. He thought he'd passed all the tests there were to pass.

"Who is it?" he said.

"Gail."

Backing away, Matt shook his head and scratched at his ear, chuckling through closed lips. Epithets hissed through his clenched lips. "She's got Kensington's ear, too. She's tight with him. Goddamn it, Stephen, why isn't she going into a policy position?"

"Where she belongs? There's your first argument."

"She doesn't know how to work a question."

Shay's thin smirk remained fixed. "Do you think she'll be a problem?"

"Damn right she will. Webb's backing, Kensington's—he'll want to show he's equal opportunity."

"And Alexander. Grover's got her in his pocket."

Matt's head snapped back toward the cluster of chairs he'd just been sitting in. Son of a bitch.

"He make you an offer?" Shay said.

"It'd be quieter work. Less spotlight."

"Sure. And another Republican candidate could come along in the next, oh, I don't know, twelve years," said Shay. "Of course, it'll be Kensington's brother. And then, shit, his cousin, I don't know. They'll always look at you as a campaign man, a guy on the ground."

It was one thing to know you were being manipulated. Another to think you were above it, that you'd done your time in the trenches, and now you deserved your medal—and *still* they were manipulating you.

"Just fucking level with me," he whispered to Shay. "I have your vote?"

Shay nodded absently.

"You want me to do this?"

"Ah, want. That's a strong word, Matt. Ask it of yourself. Because if *you* don't want it, with every ounce of fluid in that soft little spine of yours,"—he reached around to tap the back of Matt's suit—"then Gail *should* get the job. This is not passion on the football field in that cornhusk state of yours. This is not breaking down doors. This is surgery. A scalpel, correctly inserted. A vertebra snapped."

His breath medicinally sour, Shay withdrew. Impossible not to feel the cunning and power he possessed. If they'd been standing any closer to the fire, he'd have looked like the devil and not some harmless, pudgy leprechaun.

Matt gritted his teeth against his own drink. He'd never liked scotch.

"I'll make some calls."

"No," said Shay. "Work the room. It's just another campaign."

There was no point in digging up dirt on Gail. He *was* the dirt. A clump of it, anyway, a bit of country sod stuck to her heels, some Ohio farm boy she'd fucked on a lark and now could wipe off her shoe and toss in the trash. Webb and Alexander and Kensington: it was tough to imagine more potent backers. And Gail had spent her whole life in the Beltway scene, gaining credentials in the DoD and across the Congress, always appearing at the right cocktail party, the right evening at the Kennedy Center, the right bar at the right time. He'd been in DC for six years and never knew the Round Robin Bar existed until he met Shay. In some ways, moving to Washington was like moving to a small town: it was easy to get to know people on a superficial level, but there'd always be some who viewed you, forever, as a newcomer.

When Staunton had closed in '76, he was received in Marion like he'd never grown up there. He'd fought his way back in, scratching and clawing for every ounce of respect he got.

The day after Shay's ominous news, Matt worked the phones to raise some backing of his own. No one had the clout of Shay, though, and when Matt told them he was up against Gail Turner, he could practically see them turn pale. One influential DC newspaper editor said he ought to consider calling in a team of SEALs. Matt found Kris's number on his phone and nearly called her. For sympathy more than anything. But, no, this was the kind of back-biting, dirty politics that she couldn't stand, apparently.

Near midnight, his doorbell chimed. In the fish-eye lens of the peephole, Gail was primping her wavy hair. He flung open the door and asked her just what in the hell she thought she was doing.

"Canvassing the neighborhood," she said. "Are you going to let me in?"

He backed away. A limo pulled off as she came in, letting her coat fall to the floor. She wore a black negligee, panties, hose, and heels.

"There's a meeting tomorrow night," she said softly. "We'll meet in the Round Bar, then go up into a room in the Willard. An election wrap-up, strategy meeting." She played with the unbuttoned flaps of his shirt, running her nails gently across his chest. "I imagine that's when we'll find out who got the job."

"Are you insane?"

"Matt, Matt, Matt. Nothing has to change."

"But it could. For me."

She sat on the black couch he'd bought a few months ago from overseas—real Italian leather—and crossed her slippery legs.

"You underestimate yourself," she said. "Never thought I'd have to tell you that. You're like a … sheep in wolf's clothing."

"So we just put this whole thing aside, knock back some cabernet, and go upstairs?"

"We could do it right here," she said, patting the taut leather.

Whore, thought Matt. And then what was he, exactly? Like he'd never thought there'd be an advantage to sleeping with an up-and-coming consultant.

Larry Bird waddled up, and when Gail cooed at him, he stopped in his tracks, bunched his paws, and glared at her.

"The meeting's a big deal," said Gail. "McCowan will be there, probably Alexander."

"I'm sure you saw to that."

"I don't tell a guy like that what to do." She rose, slithered over to him.

The scent emanating from her skin—skin as smooth as the petals of a tulip—God, the scent was inhuman. Celestial.

As he led her upstairs, he wondered about his father, his grandfathers: had they been as weak as him? Had Jesse? Or was he the only Risen in the world who couldn't resist a little high-class tail on the night before his loyalty was deemed worthless?

CHAPTER 8

The Nesterenko family line, such that Yuri knew it, extended back to the Bloody Sunday riots of 1905 and to his great-grandfather. A blacksmith, Mishka had joined the march to the Winter Palace, the home of Tsar Nikolas II and his family. "An idealist," Yuri's grandmother called her papa, "a peaceful man, our Mishka." Presenting to the Tsar a petition that demanded nominal civil rights for workers and a representational government, more than one hundred thousand peaceful but misguided men, women, and children waited, shivering in the snow, their feet wet, their noses running. Mishka, lost in the crowd, was killed when the palace guards opened fire—killed not by a bullet, but by chaos, by the hoof of a horse. Great-grandpapa, little bear; Georgiy Gapon and the rest of the devout Orthodox gathered at the Winter Palace: misguided. Why? Because they underestimated the necessity of force and the willingness of the aristocracy to use it. Lenin, whose older brother had been executed for plotting an assassination, never made the same mistake.

Yuri pulled onto a narrow access road weighted under looming, overhanging trees and proceeded down the dark tunnel until he came to its end. A car idled with its lights turned off. Sliding next to it, Yuri rolled down his passenger window. The other car's driver did the same, and the turbid voice of Kostya Pozharsky sang along with the American singer Bruce Springsteen's "Dancing in the Dark."

"A reminder, yes?" said Kostya. "Of more exciting days."

"When we collected files on American pop singer trash? I suppose."

Both shut off their cars, and Yuri met Kostya where the road ended at a sandy path, which they followed to the wide pier of the North River

Terminal overlooking the Khimkinskoye Reservoir. To their right, near the terminal itself, a single, four-deck passenger liner was unloading under the yellow light of the gaudy star affixed to the spire of the terminus. Few meandered close to where Yuri and Kostya stood under a lamp, until they turned to the left, down the long pier, where they would not be seen.

"My wife and I enjoyed river cruises," Kostya said, "before she passed. Look how the water's become black as oil. It's a shame."

"Yes, it stinks."

"Less care is taken, these days." He rubbed the bridge of his nose where his glasses rested. "But then, things are different."

Yuri chuckled and lay an arm across his squat friend's shoulders. "Don't be so morose," he said brightly. "We had a good past, thrilling adventures. And I hear you're doing well for yourself. What is the name of the company? Molniya-something or other?"

"ACO Molniya. Where did you hear that?"

"I bumped into The Duck a week or so back."

Kostya's dim eyes widened. "Nikolai? How does he slake his thirst these days? Whiskey or gin?"

"Vodka. So predictable."

They strolled on, Kostya railing as he always did against the evils of alcohol and tobacco, noting the faint scent of a cigar on Yuri's thick wool coat and chiding him for it. Bits of icy debris knocked against one another in the reservoir. Near the point where the pier turned at a sharp angle—in a better season, and during the day, passenger liners would be docked this far, full of music and children screaming—Yuri gestured toward an empty bench with his gloved hands, allowed Kostya to sit, then spread his heavy coattails and sat himself.

"If you'd wanted a job, you could have just come to my place," said Kostya.

"Thank you, but I get by. My retirement package is enough."

"I left too young." Kostya blew his breath into his cupped hands. "But when I'm done with Molniya, I'll retire with grace. I'm in the Pokrovsky Hills, you know. Americans, French, British, Indians. Very interesting people. That's what I regret the most about those days; we never took the time to know other cultures. We were so afraid."

Yuri muttered something like an agreement. Though it pained him to think of Kostya all alone in what must be a luxurious townhouse, it was more painful to hear him talking of fear.

"All of our business is not finished," said Yuri. "My business, perhaps."

"What happened in Florence?"

"Yes. That is my only job now."

Like a frustrated teacher, Kostya grunted and leaned his back into the bench. "*Extinguished gaiety of years, which sunk in madness.* Is that it? Yes, I believe so. *Presses on me like a hangover, restless.* Yes, *restless.*" He looked up at Yuri. "Pushkin. I used to know the entire poem by heart."

"I am not mad."

Kostya's thinning brown hair caught in the wind. "You want something of me."

"I believe it is called Orbweaver."

Kostya exhaled dramatically, eyed Yuri as if to check that he knew what he had just said. Since he'd met with Korovyov, Yuri had done some poking around and verified that, indeed, Orbweaver would suit his purposes. A massive search engine designed by ACO Molniya in 1998, the program could hack databases of considerable security and automatically sift through gigabytes of information at a lightning speed, renewing its search each day, a task Yuri was having more and more difficulty with.

A bilious laugh erupted from Kostya. "You wouldn't even know how to use it, Yuri."

"Then you could help me."

"I would have to make a duplicate; I'd be fired if I removed it from the office and fired if I was discovered. Even then, you'd need a powerful computer. Does your pension provide—"

"Damn it, Kostya, have you forgotten?" Both of his thick hands he wrapped around his compatriot's forearm. "Florence. The Americans, the slaughter. That bloody elevator. Has a desk job made you fat in the head, too?"

Kostya giggled. Childishly.

"Ah, Yuri. If you knew what I worked on, how my projects help the FSB. The technology is replacing us. You were wise to get out in 1995; things have changed."

"I see that."

"I cannot help you."

Yuri faced the black water of the Khimkinskoye. Lights from across the basin reflected like vicious embers that refused to be put out. He pursed his thick lips and stood. "Come, let's get a coffee somewhere."

"At this hour? No thanks." Kostya stood with a slight wheeze and gazed across the reservoir. "A little more time here, eh? I'm not that cold." He wandered a few steps toward the water. "I'm glad you picked this place to meet, Yuri. When I'd take the river with Margarita, I'd always stare over here at our old haunt. Many secrets exchanged in these shadows." He turned to Yuri, who'd come up beside him. "You needn't worry. I won't say anything. The days of reporting every little thing are over."

"Even with new leadership?"

"Well. I hear they're going after Pavel Zaitsev for that Three Whales affair. Our man will seize the reins, I'm telling you. Once KGB, always KGB."

"Indeed."

"And now the Americans have their cowboy president again. It's a cycle."

"He's a fool like the rest," Yuri said.

"Thornton gave up too soon. He would've been a good president."

"You sound smitten."

"Well, the Americans fascinate me," said Kostya with a quick smile. "You're like the man who's fallen in love with the twin sisters, revenge and justice. You're loyal to both. Forced to choose, you can't tell them apart until it's too—"

Yuri reached out his gloved, paw-like hands and, with a savage groan, snapped Kostya's neck.

He eased his friend's body down to the ground in front of him, laying him on his back, and stared at the small eyes frozen in a dull reverie. Always a bit slow, and now grown soft. He'd allowed Yuri to slide behind him too easily; in the old days, he'd have broken at least one of Yuri's wrists. Maybe all that about revenge and justice …maybe he sensed his end was near. Years ago he'd not have kept a wall between his subconscious and conscious, and he would have acted on his instincts.

Down the pier, all was still, and a thicket of trees protected him well from the highway. He knelt and opened Kostya's jacket, patting down the pockets in the lining and then those in his colleague's pants until he found the wallet, the keys, and the keycard that would get him into Molniya. Credit cards and money, too, and then his license—the former to create the illusion of a mugging, the latter to buy himself some time.

Without looking at Kostya's face, he dragged the body to the pier's lip and slumped it into the black, nauseating water. It was only as he held the chapped leather wallet in his hands that he let loose a sharp sob. The wallet seemed so small, its brown leather worn at the edges where day in and day out Kostya had put it into his pocket. Among men, an untouchable object. To handle it was an affront to a man's dignity.

"Kostantin Dmitrich Pozharsky," he moaned. "Was it worth it?"

Then he spun the wallet out into the water and stalked back to the sandy path. His breath was ragged. The muscles of his arms, gone weak and stringy, burned.

CHAPTER 9

When Gail Turner walked into the Round Bar, all heads snapped to attention. Matt leaned over his club soda and tried to keep from throwing the fucking thing across the bar.

Shay was, of course, oblivious. "You can never be too sure," he continued. "Four years goes by quick. The way it happened, we're going to be in a hole. We'll need some breaks—and need to make our own breaks."

"I couldn't agree more," said Gail.

Shay grinned, produced three Cuban cigars, and put his arm around each of them.

In the polished brass doors of the Willard elevator, Matt imagined Shay's face reflecting a golden glow. He felt his heart pounding and Gail's knowing stares, like a lioness about to make a kill. The woman had supernatural senses.

They walked into the private suite with one large table in the middle of the room, and Shay immediately bitched about the coffee pots and ice water and lack of alcohol. "What is this, the PTA?"

Gradually, the others emerged from the elevator, first Grover Alexander, then General Marshall McCowan. The general was a tall, good-looking sixty-two-year-old. He had a warm smile and inviting eyes that were the kind of physical features that the public would find reassuring. Soldier first, politician second ... or even third. Gail recognized early in her Defense Department days that he was perfect for television and used him repeatedly for public appearances after she joined up with Kensington. Score another one for Gail.

Finally, Webb tottered in, somehow purposeful and driven despite his limp and hunched posture. To Gail he gave a wink; to Matt, an icy stare.

"Well, General, since you're the chief of staff, do you want to start the meeting?" Shay asked sappily. Anyone could see through the false deference.

"I think you've got a prepared agenda, Stephen, so this is really your meeting," the general said, carefully studying the room.

Matt was relieved that Shay had agreed to work inside the White House as special assistant to the president and deputy chief of staff; it would make Matt's job as communications director that much easier. If he got the damn thing.

"We have just 1,414 days until election day, so today we begin the reelection campaign. The greatest advantage we've always had over the other side is that we know the campaign never stops. It's how we won Ohio, and it's how we'll get support for our agenda, and it's how we get reelected."

Shay's voice maintained an energy that seemed endless, which meant he was warming up to one of his mini-speeches. It often sounded like he'd been preparing his comments for days.

In a voice at least two decibels too loud for the room, Shay said, "All elections are won or lost based on the two great messages: hope or fear. And all strategies are ultimately either motivate and unite, or divide and conquer. Hope and fear are symbiotically connected if you're waving the Soviet red threat in the public's face. That's how you justify a defense buildup: in the hope it keeps us safe."

Matt nervously scratched the tablecloth with manicured nails, wondering how or when he could cut in.

Shay propped up his balloon head on his arms. "The last administration ran on hope. They succeeded because of the economy, and we left them that gift."

Shay held up an erect index finger. "First, our reelection will not be won by running on some notion of hope. Secondly, we'll stay focused on the people who matter. They're the people who are, tonight, not talking about this election, or at least not much. They're talking about stocks, sports, and SUVs. Those are the ones we need to reach. We have to make sure they understand that the world we live in is a scary place and that we're the ones who'll keep them safe and happy."

"Some of these people, Stephen," said Alexander, "these people in the middle? They think we stole the election."

"What about Kennedy?" said McCowan. "He stole the election in 1960 and it didn't matter."

"I don't give a shit about Kennedy," Shay said. "And this isn't 1960. We have twenty-four-hour-a-day headline news, and we can ram this fear message down their throats so hard they'll forget about the election. Because, I'm telling you, we cannot dismiss our horrible starting point."

"When do we get the polling information?" Alexander said.

"Tomorrow, but the numbers aren't going to tell me anything I don't know." Shay brushed his hair back and stared down Alexander before he continued. "Thirdly, we have to keep the oil flowing in and the cash growing. Before this administration is finished, we are going to do something about Iran and maybe even Iraq. If the last administration had any balls, they would have secured the region, but they blew it."

"Blow jobs were a specialty of theirs," Alexander quipped.

No one laughed.

Matt leaned forward, seizing the gaping hole left by the old perv. "We have control of both Houses, we have the agenda. We've got to seize our opportunity to create a strong presidential image—and I've got a few ideas how."

"We can't know how quite yet," Gail snapped.

"We can start sketching it," said Matt.

"We begin now," Shay roared, "and seize the opportunity when it appears. Even I won't pretend to know when or what that will be."

Gail, Webb, and Alexander glanced at each other subtly.

"An opportunity will present itself," Gail said coolly, looking right at Matt.

"Most importantly, when our numbers go up, we can pursue our international interests," Shay said.

"Which is going to be difficult," Gail said, showing off, "because this country's always had a significant isolationist reflex." When she spoke like this—with the same arrogance she used when speaking to reporters—her lips curled into a very Webb-like sneer.

"We need a strong wholesale message," said Matt. "Something people need to fear, so I can deliver the retail message." McCowan raised his furry eyebrows at that. It was like a gift. "Wholesale is basically what I've been doing these past six months," Matt said in a rush. "It's a broadcast message, the one everyone hears; retail is a message that is delivered in or to a small group."

"Or individual to individual," Shay said. "And the messages needn't be the same."

"The key is to be aware of where and when you use each message," Gail said. "When it comes to networking, the NRA provides the greatest retail political support in the country."

"But that's a volatile group," said Matt with a nasty little grin. "The evangelicals are good, and they're growing by the day." He turned to McCowan. "With these groups, you can tell a joke in the morning, and, by the next day, it's in every coffee shop, break room, and barroom. That's powerful retail impact, particularly in dealing with Congress."

Shay said, "The mistress stuff on the last president—"

"But all those stories broke in the tabloids," said McCowan.

Alexander gave a sympathetic nod to the bewildered general as he said, "The grassroots pounding a message and the tabloids blaring headlines allows our friends at Fox to start up. Then the rest of the media are forced to pick up on it because it's so widespread."

"If it's popular enough, it becomes news," Matt said. "We don't have to tell them what to say. They know what to say when they see the opportunity."

Shay said, "The key ingredients are the influencers that other people listen to. They shape politics more than most people realize, they're the real warriors in this battle. You have the large influencers, like the networks and newspapers, that shape the wholesale message. But underneath them are the micro-influencers, the people willing to talk about politics person-to-person and who have the credibility to change the course of history. *If* we keep them on board. The campaign never ends."

"Which is a must," Matt blurted.

"Very astute," said Gail.

By the end of the meeting, his shirt was soaked through. His hair probably looked like a bird's nest. It seemed any time he'd made a gain,

Gail would zing him or follow up with more specific ideas—especially when they rolled back around to Iran—and fear.

As Shay huddled with Webb and Gail got on her phone, Matt shook the general's hand. McCowan was a fucking hero, frankly, and they'd treated him like a fifth-grade student-council president.

"Didn't Roman generals ride through the streets on a chariot after victories for the empire," said Matt rather sourly, "with a slave whispering that all fame is fleeting?"

"That's true," McCowan said sternly. "Don't forget it."

The general excused himself and passed through the double doors with Alexander trailing him like a Feist dog, which left only Matt, Shay, Webb, and … no Gail. She was gone.

"Matt, a word?" said Webb.

Where the fuck had she gone? And how? A secret panel?

"Give us a couple minutes, Matt, then come back in, if you would. We'd like to do an interview."

He stared at Webb dumbly for a moment. An interview. Was he fucking kidding? But he managed to keep his mouth shut and slinked out into the hallway. There, Gail was checking her teeth in a full-length mirror.

"Get a drink?" she said.

"I can't. I'm meeting with Webb and Shay."

"Oh, your interview. Had mine." She rubbed his damp shoulders and eked out something like a wink. "Give me a call later if you like."

She stalked down the hallway without a word. He could think of none, either. That confident air, the swagger. He only felt it when he was spinning to the frantic press. He couldn't spin for himself worth a damn. Maybe it was best if he didn't get the job. A fishing lure salesman: now that he could see. Or a sportswriter for a small-town newspaper. Or a homeless drunk with a fat tabby.

"Matt," said Shay.

He sat across from Webb at the tip of the wide oval table. Shay paced a moment and finally broke down and poured a cup of coffee.

"So this is your pitch," said Webb. "Pitch."

"My record during the election and recount speaks for itself," said Matt. "You saw it. Twenty years' experience in this business, and I know how to spin the hell out of things, especially in SUCK." Webb chuckled.

He'd always gotten a kick out of the acronym. "Gail has a great mind. But she doesn't know how to talk to regular people—or to the press."

"Argue *your* credentials," sneered Webb.

"All due respect, but you know my credentials." He inhaled sharply. "I feel that you should know this about Gail: back in Denver, she told me one night that the Republican party doesn't reward loyalty."

Webb and Shay glanced at each other. Maybe he'd hooked them.

"She went on and on about success. I think she'll turn on this party the instant it becomes more profitable—"

"This *party?*" said Webb, cackling at the word.

"The Republican Party."

Webb leaned forward, so close Matt could see the grayness of his lips. "Do you know who we are?" he asked quietly. Nearly in a whisper. "Loyalty is cheap. Success is expensive, Matt."

"Gail was right," said Shay. And just as his dinner was about to surface, Matt heard through a dizzying whine, "And what time of night did she tell you this in Denver?"

His face burned, baby, burned.

"We've … she's been coming to me, Stephen. Mr. Vice President. Given the nature of this job, I should have told you before, but that night we were just—"

Both men broke out into cacophonous laughter.

Through tears, Shay said, "Matt, we know. We know."

"It's good to get a little dirt under your nails, Risen."

A duck-billed platypus would've had more grace: Matt blinked too often, smacked his dry lips too often, and generally, he figured, looked like the country hick he'd been exposed for.

"Welcome aboard," said Webb.

"I've got the job?"

"Of course you do," Shay said, practically leering.

More blinking, more lip-smacking. At a moment when he should have been clicking his heels together like Fred Astaire, all Matt could do was gaze in shock at the two white-hairs before him. A sizable rage was working its way out, and burst, "Then why the hell did you make me sweat?"

Webb leaned in again. "Because we could. And don't ever forget it."

Matt's Journal, Day 1,412

Going with Shay's advice and encoding this. Never know who might see it, or when.

It's taken me the two days since the meeting to come down from this high, or low, depending on how you look at it. The panicky turbulence in my gut in the days leading up to their decision—if you could even call it that—I replaced that night with too much Jameson. Hard liquor for the first time in years. Because we could. That's what Webb said. I see his point now. Power, the flexing of it. Like Shay said I'd need to do with the media, go on the offensive. Have I forgiven Shay and Webb, and even Gail, who was in on it the whole time? Fuck it, do I need to?

The announcement of the team began to trickle out yesterday. Gail first. She'll be Webb's chief of staff, which makes sense. His right hand, cloaked in shadows. Swore I saw Kensington give her a little wink as Webb made it public to the media. Note to self: keep an eye on those two.

Grover on the outside is a natural. Those who are long on belongings are there, and they'll pay him well to protect and expand those belongings. McCowan on the inside is a coup. Sure he's politically naive, but both parties respect the hell out of him. The general reminds me so much of my commandant at Staunton Military Academy: stony features, not afraid to look the fool in order to get the job done. Total, absolute dedication.

(So many memories are linked to my years at Staunton. It connected me to the rest of the world, gave me discipline and order, and I learned to respect the military, respect my elders. By the time I went back to Marion, I was a man. No more Oakland Heights mafia, a group of guys who weren't nearly as tough as we thought; the night we got arrested for joyriding in our neighbors' new Mercury, the leader of our group cried like a baby and confessed to everything we'd ever done—and even some things we'd only thought of doing.)

Unlike Grover, Shay doesn't care about money. I'd be lying if I didn't say that I'm relieved Shay's coming inside; his experience is one benefit, but maybe even more significantly, Shay won't be as likely to second-guess me if he's part of the team. I prefer to have him inside the tent pissing out, not outside the tent pissing in.

It's a great fucking team, I have to admit. Even with Broussard as my deputy. But hell, I need someone around who I can beat in poker.

Jess said he'll e-mail the article from the Marion Star *when it comes out. They were already out to talk to him. I'm being treated like a success story in the paper, but the hometown of Warren G. Harding is treating me with a bit of caution. The psychic make-up of the city is a strange fusion of Republican Harding's philosophies and those more sympathetic to early twentieth-century socialist Eugene V. Debs, Harding's one-time presidential opponent who spent more than a little time in Ohio. If I'd never gone to Staunton, I'm sure I would've ended up falling under the spell of the liberal propaganda. It's not easy to be on the side that is fighting in so many ways to keep us safe. Not all of us carry guns, but all of us know that safety is not an accident.*

I haven't called Kris yet. She's so certain we're a mistake for each other.

Oh. Gail's at the door. Gotta go.

Chapter 10

Matt climbed into the back of the limo, stretched his legs, and called Gail to see if she was ready, while the limo driver drove toward her Georgetown apartment. He quickly checked his tie, having perfected the art of tying the knot in a moving car. A person could get used to the limo. Hell, the tux was becoming a nightly occurrence. Gail was waiting on the front step, stone-faced and rigid. A beautiful Rodin that came alive only when the clothes started coming off. She climbed in the backseat, returned his cold peck on her cheek, and absently placed her hand in his lap. His lack of a response did not seem to affect her; a few seconds later she pulled her hand away and opened her purse to check her makeup.

Their first stop of the Inaugural Ball tour was a cocktail party at the home of Grover Alexander. The reception in his stylish home was the most sought-after event that wasn't part of the official inaugural festivities. As Matt and Gail entered, a large crowd closed in around them; to most of the outside world, they were the campaign. Matt made the rounds, circulating among wealthy contributors, think-tank policy whizzes, and many of the talking heads that had been invited, including a particularly strong delegation from Fox News. Glancing around the room, Matt spotted Stephen in the shadows quietly drinking with a few friends. He didn't recognize them, but they didn't seem to be any more interested in receiving attention than Stephen typically did.

"Scotch neat?" Matt said smiling.

"Of course. Another one of your celebrated entrances. You must be the most popular guy in town."

Whether or not that was true, Shay's colleagues stepped away, melting into the shadows and the crowd.

"Gail and you seeing a lot of each other?" Shay said with a smirk.

"Thought you knew my every move."

The idea of Shay being interested in Gail, or in picturing Matt and Gail together in the sack—well, it was more than a little sickening. Or as Shelly would have succinctly put it, "Nasty." Besides, it'd long ago struck him that Shay was probably asexual.

A day that had begun with a prayer meeting in St. John's Church across from the White House became a blur of champagne, dancing, and introduction upon introduction. The Inaugural Ball was so large that, even in a city designed for big receptions, the event had to be spread out into several regional ballrooms. States and departments were assigned one of seven inaugural locations, and the new president and his entourage would visit each. For Matt and Gail, it ended at the National Building Museum. In the speech Matt had helped to craft, Kensington had talked confidently of men created equally in God's image; looking around the museum's high balustrades and the long lines at the bar, Matt wondered if God indeed looked like a silver-haired crow with false teeth and Gucci loafers.

"Am I supposed to remember all these names?" he shouted to her over the din. "I'll fail pathetically if I am."

"You're hopeless," she said with a thin smile. "I remember their names, the names of their sons and daughters, where they went to school."

He challenged her to a test, and with savant-like detail, Gail spit out details like a human computer, even for the scads of out-of-towners that they'd bumped into. "Couple of minutes for goodbyes, huh, and then we should get out of here." She fluttered her long eyelashes at him.

And maybe because he'd been thinking forward, he felt a wave of boredom at the redundant, uninformed conversations surrounding him. He drifted away from the crowd onto a portico off the side of the ballroom. While the night air was frigid, he had his own space here. And lost in his reverie, he didn't hear Kris the first time.

"I said, 'Stealing a smoke?'"

He blinked once or twice. Or three times. Beautiful was not the word. Transcendent. Two black straps falling lightly off her creamy shoulders, just enough fabric tucked near the waist to expose her strong hips. All made up with hardly any makeup that he could see.

"Still trying to quit," he said. "Have you been making the rounds?"

"Sticking to one place, mainly. Getting bored."

"It's more exhausting than the campaign."

"A party, exhausting? Well, my friend, you've never been to Bosnia."

Her words held a moment—the insult was there—but she smiled away the distance between them. Almost. Where, he wondered, did politics stop? Where could you just love someone?

"I know a café," she said. "Big honkin' omelets."

"Denver omelets?"

"Sure."

"Matt?"

Gail stood in the shadow of a column with her hips cocked, her purse tight to her chest, her breath steaming out of the darkness into the cold light of the moon.

"I ..." he stammered.

"It's okay," said Kris, her eyes judicious and even. "Go. We'll catch up."

"Absolutely."

He went to hug her and found that he could only give both of her shoulders a friendly squeeze.

He followed Gail to the limo, and to his surprise, she didn't say a word about Kris. As the vehicle started to move, Gail stripped her gown away from her back and climbed on top of Matt before he'd even settled in. Had she taken off her underwear in the bathroom, or not worn any? He glanced to make sure the shield between them and the driver was up.

"I hope that glass is one-way," he muttered under her neck.

"Who cares? Might make it more interesting."

She unbuckled his belt as something heavy struck the side of the car. Through the tinted windows, strange shadows formed a wall along the sidewalk; square shapes bobbed against the dark blue horizon. Protestors. There'd been thousands of them.

"What are they throwing?" he said.

"Eggs," Gail said breathlessly. "Dear, they've been throwing them all night."

PART TWO: MARS

CHAPTER 1

Who could have predicted that the groundwork for so much sacrifice and controversy would be laid down during a summertime presidential power walk in the mountains of Colorado? Certainly not Matt, who'd chugged along in Kensington's pack dutifully, a thin bead of sweat along his barbered hairline. The pace along the ranch trail was slow by normal standards, but not Webb's; the vice president gasped for air as Kensington grinned back at him. "Let me know if your chest starts hurting too bad, Dixie!" He gestured toward the team of onlookers in suits and sunglasses. "But don't worry, the docs here ain't horse doctors. They're pretty darn good."

Webb groaned as the Secret Service men, with their smooth, long strides, kept their watchful eyes on him. No one seemed too concerned about Shay, who was kicking his tiny legs in double time, his big head wobbling like it was about to break off.

They'd been at it for a good twenty minutes before Webb brought up Iran. "Mr. President, we'll have … an opportunity, soon we believe, to justify an invasion." He inhaled like a drowning victim come to the surface. "They're moving ahead with their nuclear program. We have to think of the necessities."

The word "invasion" perked up Matt's ears, all right, and he surged ahead to hear the president's response.

"I don't know, Dixie," Kensington said effortlessly. "I told the American people we wouldn't get involved in no nation building."

"But Mr. President—"

"Guys, when we're working out, call me Will. Guess when I'm workin' out, I like to think I'm not president."

Shay, now at a full jog in order to keep up, said, "Okay, Will. Believe me, I was all with you on that during the campaign, but it wasn't a promise so much as a statement of intention."

"Will, hold up," Webb labored to say, and with a more-direct-than-usual suggestion from a Secret Service man, the entourage lurched to a halt, reminding Matt of the motorcade on election night in Denver. Webb bent over, resting his hands on his knees. "Iran will use its capability and direct it at Israel before long. We'll have little—or no—warning."

The president said, "Maybe, but something tells me war with Iraq isn't a good idea."

"Iran, Mr. President," Webb said quizzically. "We're talking about Iran."

"What did I say?"

"Iraq," Matt said gently. "We were talking about Iran, sir."

"Oh, yeah. Guess it was wishful thinking. You know I don't like that fat fuck in Iraq, and he's crazy enough to lash out like a rattlesnake, too."

Webb smiled slightly as he said, "In time sir, no doubt they're a concern; we can't confirm what Iraq has in terms of weapons, but we know Iran is working toward the bomb." He squinted at Matt, like he expected him to be taking notes. "Besides, Iran is a much easier target. There's still an organized middleclass in Iran. Much more homogenous demographics."

"Homo-what?" The president smirked.

"Homogeneous, that is they are—"

"Just joshin' ya, Dixie. You know I like to play as dumb as people think I am. Hell, even my family thinks I'm a dumb shit." He squinted at the mountain peaks. "Sure would like to take it to that fat motherfucker, though."

As they made their way back to the Kensington family ranch compound, the president beaming at Shay and singing, "You say Iran, I say Iraq, let's call the whole thing off," Matt couldn't tell if he admired Kensington's acting or was terrified by it. Had it been Johnny Carson or Phil Hartman on SNL who'd played Ronald Reagan acting dumb with the press, doddering as he had his picture taken with a Girl Scout—and then, behind closed doors, was calling all the shots?

—⁓⁓—

The first seven months of the new administration had been, the president was fond of saying, "like herdin' cattle." More thoughtfully considered—and perhaps it was by Kensington, but he kept whatever depth of intellect he may have possessed buried under a mountain of aphorisms and folksy charm—February through August had been much like the campaign, especially for Matt Risen: a series of crises to respond to, most of them the result of the president's meager proposals and their frosty reception in the Senate and the barely Republican House. It felt like a battle of inches: limits on abortion counseling; federal funding for faith-based initiatives; protection of human embryos in stem-cell research; and even rumors of a bill to enforce mandatory school prayer—all of it much to the delight of that minority of the country that truly considered Kensington to be God's Will.

And so it had continued through the first half of 2001. Matt's days were longer than they'd been during the campaign—he'd yawn awake at five o'clock, spend the day shuttling between the press briefing room, his staff offices, and the various offices on the first floor until his feet were burning; he'd fetch lunch from the mess, eat at his curved mahogany desk, stare out the three windows at the sunlight, watch it disappear, and then, if he was lucky, return home around eight in the evening. Peace and quiet? None. The press secretary's expansive office was the operational hub of the floor, a checkpoint for nosy journalists—many of whom he delighted in turning away—and his phone might as well have been continually ringing. Sometimes, when he deigned to have a gaggle with the press, so many packed into his office that the tubular light fixtures shook with their footsteps and voices. Private life? There wasn't one, except for a few cobbled-together hours with Gail or the occasional chat on the steps of his brownstone with Shelly, who was already calling herself his maid and demanding an appropriate raise.

And Kris? He'd caught her a few times by phone, but their intricate and unpredictable schedules never quite matched up, and she was on assignment for nearly two months in Afghanistan with some hot-shit reporter from the *New York Times*. And maybe that was for the best. A campaign could inebriate you with possibilities, all that forward-looking, all that imagining; emerging one damp night from a sleek limousine at some benefit at Lincoln Center, flashbulbs strobe-lighting the reflective hull of the limo, it struck him that all his life he'd done nothing but pursue possibilities, and that he had finally reached them—and he ought now to focus on keeping them secure.

Besides, he and Gail were the quiet celebrities of the Inner Belt. The national media couldn't care less, really, but the DC papers included the couple on their social pages religiously: dancing at a benefit ball at the National Gallery of Art; slumming it with Broussard and a friend of Gail's from Harvard in a back corner at Zaytinya; applauding the American premiere of a new Russian opera. Their romance was never more than implied, but the message was sold and they benefited greatly; distant acquaintances and even far-left Dems opened up to Risen-Turner in public, if only to establish contacts inside what had quickly become an inscrutable White House. In DC, everyone rooted for a love story until it failed, and then, when the blood hit the water, they converged like sharks.

Still, despite himself, on many nights, even the nights he and Gail disturbed and dampened his bed sheets, Matt found himself thinking of Kris and that night in Columbus when they'd been as free to explore the city as its namesake. And then, as if steering himself toward a sturdier, more familiar shore, he would push away the memories and the possibilities and lull himself back into a restless sleep.

~⋀~

Then came Kansas City—and an innocuous early August visit by the president to an elementary school. As Kensington stumbled through a children's book, one reporter took Matt into the hallway and whispered, "Is it true the CIA and the White House are digging their heels in against the Hassan bin Chalabi intel?"

Matt asked him to repeat the question.

The reporter's source claimed a CIA operative was preparing to go public, claiming that the White House was ignoring considerable chatter which proved that Hassan bin Chalabi was planning a major strike this fall on American soil. "Using commercial airliners," the reporter added with a hush. "He says you guys are hoping for some reason to use the Star Wars system or go into Afghanistan, maybe Iran. What do you think?"

Matt's eyes tangoed back and forth between the classroom and the reporter, whose intense glare had dimmed a bit. "Off the record?" The reporter nodded. "Off the record I'd ask you why you're buying that shit."

"I'm just telling you what he said. I'm not going with anything now, it's obviously way out there. But it's too important, Matt. You know, if there is any truth to it, maybe you can dig around and see what's fallen through the cracks."

Within fifteen minutes, pacing on the school's blacktopped and broken playground, Matt had called Shay and relayed the story. Shay responded gruffly, "It's probably bullshit. Who's this agent?"

"He wouldn't say. I know it's probably nothing."

"I'll check it out."

Two days later, in Webb's office, Matt was being praised like a holy saint. At that very minute, fifty-seven arrests were taking place around the country, mainly along the Eastern Seaboard and down in Florida; would-be hijackers were being rooted out of their homes, detained, and cuffed in airports and even a few flight schools. General McCowan pumped Matt's hand and said, "This country owes a great debt to you and your reporter. We nearly had a tragedy of epic proportions on our hands. Who knows, maybe several floors of a major skyscraper could've been wiped out. It's hard to fathom."

Gail, Shay, and Webb nodded in near unison. "To put it mildly," said Webb, prowling behind his desk like an agitated tiger. "We also owe this CIA agent. See if your friend can get a name for us?"

"I doubt he'll want to give—"

"The man is a hero," Webb snapped. A vicious cloud passed through his eyes, it seemed, and he settled into his chair.

"I'll find out," said Shay.

Hassan bin Chalabi admitted in a video that, while this attempt had indeed failed, he wouldn't stop. Protests broke out across the Middle East, many claiming that this so-called terrorist threat had been manufactured by the CIA to justify a war. And in the United States, the public was just as furious at being inconvenienced by strengthened airport security. If the terrorists had been captured and the system had worked, why were their trips to Disney World being delayed? What could justify that kind of intrusion?

The answer came soon, in the first week of September: within minutes of each other, terrorists attacked two college football games, first in Boise, Idaho when a small plane loaded with a deadly nerve gas and pulling a U.S. flag and a banner with the name of a car dealer was shot down just two miles from the blue turf of Bronco Stadium by the air force. Ironically Boise State was playing Air Force. Given the hardware that often accompanied Air Force football games, it was a foolish target, and the terrorists' plot wasn't helped by the sloppy and brazen manner in which they'd stuffed the body of the plane's pilot into a tool cabinet at an airport hangar.

In Madison, Wisconsin, on Interstate 90, a semi jackknifed in the road, shutting down all four lanes while a small plane was briskly rolled out of its trailer, its wings quickly unfolded as four men pushed it past the semi, beyond the reach of the terrified motorists who could only watch and reach for their cell phones as the single-prop taxied down the empty highway.

Just two miles away at Camp Randall stadium, a lone sniper standing high and alone in a heavy rain carefully took aim as the small plane made its way toward a capacity crowd. He waited for the radio to crackle and give him the authority to move ahead, watching as the plane dropped low across Lake Mendota and arced southwest toward the stadium. He could make out the form of a man's face. "Take your shot," said a voice through the static. Time seemed to slow into a series of framed photographs, the sniper would say later to the press. His shot was perfect. The plane dove and smacked across the lake surface before exploding, spraying water and debris several hundred yards ashore, the concussive blast knocking a few bicyclists off their path. In the stadium, panicked fans poured out onto the field, screaming, while others bolted for the nearest exit. The opposing coach, in a thick scarlet sweater vest, snatched the mike from the head referee and begged the crowd to stay put until they knew what was going on; meanwhile, the coaching staffs and players of both teams locked arms to help slow the crowd, and the home team's band leader cajoled his students into playing, and together they managed to keep half of the stadium filled and avoided a deadly stampede.

Matt watched the country plunge into chaos, recriminations, and a need for vengeance; the obligatory gratitude that no one had been killed, except for the lone pilot near Boise, vanished within a day of the attacks, and, as he stood first in the airborne Air Force One and then safely at the podium in the White House, he was amazed that so many of the questions concerned what they, the administration, would do next. He stalled, throwing out active but meaningless words: "evaluating," "assessing," "investigating," and so on. But there was nothing much to investigate by the end of that day; the major players were known, and another video message from bin Chalabi admitted to defeat once more.

The president stood before the cameras and urged America to unite against "the threat of evil"—Matt didn't care for the religious implications, to say the least—and then suggested, oddly and completely off-script, that Americans should "go shopping" to bolster the economy.

Meanwhile, America was turning on itself: mosques were ransacked in eleven major cities including DC, New York, Cleveland, and Detroit; police forces were tied up with thefts, beatings, harassment, and murders committed against legal citizens who had the misfortune to look vaguely Middle Eastern; countless calls rose from the far right to keep all borders closed through the end of the year and to halt immigration; and, though Matt steadfastly praised the work of the air force and the marines, whose sniper had taken down what was being called "The Mendota Plane," cries erupted from both parties for someone's head on a platter—how, they wanted to know, had the terrorists gotten so close? The violence usually took place overseas, they all but admitted. It *belonged* there. *Do something.*

Four days after the attacks, Matt's stomach churned as Air Force One banked hard over Idaho, where Kensington had just delivered a speech at the Boise pilot's funeral. In the mist and grayness, one of the two F-18s assigned to protection detail climbed higher into the clouds. The military politics of Air Force One were as balanced as its wingspan. The plane was flown by the air force, and the army was on board to work with the Secret Service on all communications. In addition to providing for all the president's outside-the-White-House food needs, the navy was also responsible for all of his personal needs; his clothes were packed and laid out by a navy seaman. Marines were everywhere, both ceremonial and official—marines flew the president's helicopters—and it was a marine whom Broussard ducked past in order to motion to Matt that he should pick up an in-flight phone.

Kensington greeted him cheerily. "I got something to say to a couple of key media folks. You know, the ones we can count on." He snickered and told Matt to bring them back to his private office in ten minutes.

"Gentleman and ladies," the president said once they'd settled in. "I want you to know that I'm on a new course, and we need take powerful steps to protect our country. We need to take all of this at Iraq. That country is the key to *stabilitizing* the region."

Had he heard that wrong? Iran, he screamed to himself. Iran, not Iraq. But the president was already talking about God and duty and bin Chalabi's ties to the Iraqi government, and, judging by the faces of the reporters—a mix of horror, confusion, and a perverse kind of hunger—there was no way to undo what Kensington had just said. As he ducked into the plane's massive hallway and called Shay, he remembered that jog in Colorado. Please God, Matt muttered, staring out a window at the other F-18.

"Stephen, I thought you and Webb said Iran?"

"It's Iraq now."

"But remember what he said in Colorado—"

"Yeah," Shay said, chewing something gristly. "You're not a policy-maker, kid. You don't get to be in all the meetings."

That evening, in the president's private office on the second floor of the West Wing, Matt waited with Shay, Gail, and Webb for Kensington to finish dinner. Webb was chewing on the pale flesh of his upper lip. "Iran's off the board, for now," he said bitterly. "I don't like it, but we can make this work."

"The public isn't going to be with us yet," said Shay. "The system worked, and when it works, it's hard to say we need a strategy change."

"We have our *raison d'être*, Stephen: that they made it as far as the—"

"That only works for the hardliners, Dixon." He whirled around the room, undulating the knuckles of one tiny fist. "Crazies trying to kill Americans isn't enough. If the Japs had run out of gas and crashed on their way to Pearl Harbor, the day wouldn't have lived in infamy."

Webb peered above his glasses at Matt. "We have the bully pulpit, the most powerful tool a president commands. Baby steps, Risen. It starts with you."

The president strode into the room accompanied by a fleet of assistants and one other conspicuous guest: Grover Alexander.

"I know you're disappointed, Dixie, but heck, maybe this really is God's will, you know?" He smiled with an idiotic kind of self-satisfaction. This was the version of Kensington that Matt couldn't stand; maybe it was the Ohio in him, but the whole religion-on-the-sleeve thing just seemed spurious. "In any case, fellas, we're committed to Iraq. No second guessing."

"I don't disagree," Webb said, returning the president's gaze.

Matt watched Shay's eyes dart between Webb and Alexander, who was towering silently in the corner of the room, his arms folded across his chest like some dead Egyptian pharaoh. Shay had explained to Matt just an hour ago, in the privacy of his office, that "an asshole like Grover Alexander" preferred Iraq; the arms dealers Alexander represented—and who didn't he represent?—lusted after the possibility of a longer, more hardware-intensive conflict that would certainly transpire in Iran's divisive neighbor. Was that what swayed Kensington? And was the vice president going to rip out Alexander's throat with his teeth?

Alexander crossed to a chair close to the mahogany desk as he said, "War's a great opportunity for visuals, Stephen."

"Yeah, I don't doubt it: rubble and smoke, the president walking alone across the lawn or visiting the troops." For a moment he seemed to lose himself.

"I can rouse some folks to beat the right war drums," said Alexander.

For the first time, Gail spoke. "I've got Defense Department friends who'll stand behind us on Iraq. Harvard professors, if we need to slum it a bit."

They all looked to Matt.

"Just tell me what to say."

"All the right things," Kensington said with a snicker.

Later, over generous amounts of scotch at the Willard, Shay confided that he'd have preferred Iran. "Not that I'd ever have admitted that to

Webb. Iran is a towering threat, easier to use. Kicking around Iraq, that's a harder sell."

"They were helping bin Chalabi."

Shay smirked, one eye squinting. He nearly broke into a laugh. Rubbing the bottom of his tumbler across the wooden bar, he said, "You've got some serious work ahead of you, kid. Drumming up support falls onto your shoulders. I'm going to suggest that Kensington let you work more with his speechwriters—we can't have this hyperactive Christian missionary talk creeping into the speeches. If he wants to see a crucifixion, well, he can just wait and see what the press does if he keeps that shit up." He grinned just widely enough that a single tooth showed under his gums. "We need the language of war. That's on you. So get out your thesaurus, your dictionary, and brush up on your goddamn history. It's everywhere you look. This was a hangout for President Grant, and it became so well-known that people would crowd into that tiny little lobby over there and wait to see him, wait for hours. They were called favor-seekers, but they came to be called lobbyists. The history and words you're looking for are everywhere."

Driving home, Matt left the windows down so the breeze would cool his hot face. He couldn't rid himself of a moment from Webb's office after the reporter's CIA contact had helped to avert the first series of attacks: Webb, prowling, had said, "History will record it as just another August. The intelligence community did their job, and in one year the name Hassan bin Chalabi will be forgotten by 90 percent of Americans." Then he'd stopped and gazed at the hard reflection of his face in the desk. "You know, it's horrible to even think," he'd said softly, almost to himself, "but we may have lost something here. This could have … well, you know they say we've lost our *raison d'être* after our success in tearing down the Iron Curtain. But with the terrorists, we've got a new *raison*. And America needs to know."

How disappointed Webb had seemed that night—he'd never have admitted to it—and how begrudgingly pleased he seemed tonight, how invigorated despite his wrinkled brows and the fact that he and the rest of the neo-cons had been overruled. "I don't want to wait on the next camel jockey with a nuclear backpack riding into Des Moines," he said crudely once Alexander had finally left. "We're on the offensive now. We move fast, boys, and we'll soon get Iran back in our sights." Aggressive action. Hard to disagree with that. No more sitting back and waiting for them to do something. You only had to be wrong once. Driving, Matt liked the phrase, repeated it once, and then recorded it on a pocket-size Sony he always kept nearby.

CHAPTER 2

Less than a week later, Matt had to get out on the town. Just for a night. Coaxing the press to back off the Iraq question had proven impossible, and he wasn't getting much help from Webb and Shay, and certainly not the president. Was there going to be an invasion? More UN sanctions? What had the president meant by "take all of this at Iraq"? Dangling like a piece of fresh laundry on the line, he concentrated on the mantra he'd come up with after a weekend of reading: *over there* had invaded the safety of *in here*. It was a motif that reached back into antiquity and played to the most primal of fears and human needs. A threat from overseas. The relative safety within our borders has been tested. They invade you? You invade them. Proof that Iraq had anything to do with Hassan bin Chalabi and his army of terrorists would have helped, of course. Would, in fact, have made him seem like less of an idiot to the press. They had the taste for blood now. Back in January, before the inauguration, he'd taken Shay's advice about getting rough with the press: he'd crafted a memo demanding fairness from all the reporters who were still sore over the election, and then, during a series of low-profile lunches and dinners, he'd shown it to the nation's most powerful publishers and media moguls and the men who controlled them—their lawyers. It'd worked like a charm. No one wanted to invite a lawsuit. But the resistance by the press corps was palpable, and they knew he'd been behind it, and now, unleashed, they didn't mind barking at him that he was spinning bullshit. If the marines didn't invade somebody soon, he told Broussard one day, he'd need a rabies shot.

The finest distraction came in the form of the Kennedy Center's opening night of *Camelot*. He'd always been a sucker for musicals, ever since Aunt Angeline had sat at her upright and pounded out "Singing in the Rain" and "Everything's Coming Up Roses" like Ethel Merman's long-lost twin sister. And so he'd collected six tickets, fifth row center, and convinced Gail that it would be only a momentary distraction and another opportunity to get her picture in the papers. With Cory tagging along to assess Gail—it was long overdue—and Shelly bouncing off the walls with two of her friends, each of them dressed like they were going to the prom, he sighed with some satisfaction as the limo crossed the Memorial Bridge. In the spring, this would be the best way to come into the city and capture a breathtaking view of the cherry blossoms, their baby-pink hue softening up a city filled with granite statues of the dead. Of course, the view would be lost on Gail.

"Ladies, please," Gail said to Shelly and her friends. "A little less noise, huh?"

"They've never been in a limo," Matt said.

"And they never will again," she muttered, smiling coldly at Matt, "if they act like Britney Spears wannabes." She turned to them like some sorority big. "Seriously, girls, this is a chance to show some very important people that you're made of high-class material."

So severe was her tone, despite the encouragement, that the girls lapsed into a demure silence ... for about a second.

"Methinks I hear the echo of someone's parenting," Cory said.

"Never too young to start," she said, checking her lipstick.

They passed the Saudi Arabian embassy and cruised to a halt in front of the towering Center, its rather cold exterior bedecked in Camelot posters, flashbulbs popping under the high overhang like bursts of contained heat lightning. When they'd reached the entrance, Cory stepped out first with the girls, who couldn't help but wave at the photographers, and then Gail and Matt emerged, taking a few strides toward the massive glass doorway before the photographers picked up on them. Leave it to a *New York Times* reporter to spoil the mood. "Ms. Turner, what's your role in the response to Iraq?" She only smiled, her cheeks bunched tightly, and led Matt inside while Shelly asked a photographer if she could get a copy of whatever pictures he'd taken of her and her friends.

"So it's a done deal," Cory said to Gail and Matt as they waited in the Grand Foyer. "We're going into Iraq."

"Not exactly," Gail whispered.

They'd been seated in the Eisenhower Theatre for only a few minutes—the girls craning their necks at the vaulted ceiling, chirping to each other about their school's "lame-ass" auditorium—when Gail, reading from her BlackBerry, whispered to Matt that it had begun.

"What's begun?"

"The coup. In Iraq."

The noise in the hall seemed to drain away, and momentarily he realized that the lights had dimmed and the hush was only the prelude to the applause. Still, his gut churned. A coup? How? What bothered him more: that again he'd been left out of the loop, or that somewhere in a darkness as deep as the one into which they'd been pitched now, Webb and his buddies were capable of engineering the overthrow of a country?

As Merlyn talked the young Arthur down from a tree and instructed him to take care of his responsibilities and to think for himself, Matt asked Gail if maybe they shouldn't leave.

"The coup's not waiting for us." She patted his wrist and planted a kiss like a pinprick on his cheek. "Try to enjoy yourself."

This was easily the tenth different production Matt had seen of *Camelot*. Of all Broadway musicals it was his favorite and, feeling invisible in the darkness of the theater, he mouthed the words to his favorite parts. "Let it never be forgot ... that once there was a spot ... for one brief shining moment that was known as Camelot." The anonymity could continue a little while longer, thank you. How had Kennedy dealt with the constant pressure? The worst was to be seen as a hero; it made you greater than human, and no person could live up to that lie for very long. Some, like Gail, seemed to think that day of reckoning would never come; even now, she couldn't stay away from the updates she was receiving on her BlackBerry, and her face, in the pale blue glow of the device, looked too pleased, too assured.

Despite her, Matt allowed himself to sink away into the story and the lush music, nearly foreign in its innocence and beauty, and he recalled Aunt Marie's rants about the days when a soundtrack for a musical like *Camelot* could top the charts. That quiet traditionalism that Shay always talked about—Marie had it, Jess had it, Cory had it ... he had it. For all his sleeping around, Matt had never given up on the idea of finding a true love, of recreating some romance that could live up to the past. It wasn't Gail. Not at all. There was nothing in Gail to share, nothing in Gail but Gail. As Lancelot eased into "If Ever I Would Leave You," Matt slipped further into his chair, mouthing along with the words as if repeating some long-forgotten prayer.

After the curtain fell, he and Cory waited on the River Terrace while the girls and Gail used the bathroom. Staring across the black and glassy Potomac, he explained to Cory the connections that had been made between the musical, the myth, and the Kennedy administration.

"Glory ends in ruins," said Cory.

"But the dream never dies," Matt responded. "Tom of Warwick."

A profound look of sorrow passed over Cory, and Matt blamed himself for the aura of melancholy that had settled on them both. "So Kensington is, who, Tom of Warwick?" said Cory. "The next hope, the revival of idealism?"

"Let's hope he's not Arthur."

"He already is," said Cory.

A crowd was moving down the terrace under the row of trees, and, as they neared the ebullient blue fountain, he saw Kris and she saw him. The dancing light from the fountain only added to the regal beauty of her tall figure in a black cocktail dress, adorned with a simple strand of pearls. She winked at him and began singing "If Ever I Would Leave You" in a voice that could've peeled paint.

"You seem to know the words to a lot of the songs," she teased.

Matt blushed. "And you should stick to photography."

"Hey, I sound great in the shower. So are you auditioning for a part in the company? I thought you were going to stand up in the middle of the audience and give them your best Robert Goulet."

Cory rolled his eyes and looked at the ground as he whispered to Matt, "I told you this would happen someday."

"I thought it was adorable," she said.

Matt only heard "adorable" and almost nothing of what Cory had said. In fact he nearly forgot to introduce Cory, his "smart-ass cousin."

"I've heard a lot about you, smart-ass," said Kris as her friends drifted over, one a woman who looked like some trendy trash from New York and the other a well-dressed man whose five o'clock shadow and seemingly electrocuted hair just screamed journalist. Maybe the hotshot from the *Times*. Cory, too, was sizing the man up, and as the small talk circled through them, Cory shot Matt a tiny smile and subtly shook his head.

With a fluency they'd mastered since their adolescence, Cory distracted Kris's friends, giving Matt some room to work. "You look … alive," he said.

"I should hope so."

"You know what I mean. Afghanistan? How was it?"

"Dry," she said. "And foreboding," she added, her eyes falling. With some effort she smiled again and took his hands. "Feel like a tour around DC? You probably know it better than Columbus."

"I know my way from my apartment to the White House and back."

"Then how about dinner? I mean it. No excuses."

As if on cue, Shelly emerged onto the terrace with her friends, followed by Gail, who was staring at her BlackBerry. Seeing Kris, Shelly bounded up to her; the girl had a sixth sense about the women he was interested in.

When Gail finally looked up, you could have chilled a keg with her demeanor. Thinly she smiled and shook Kris's hand, and Matt felt an urge to jump into the Potomac.

"*Every*one's out tonight," Gail said. "What did you think?"

"Of the play?" said Kris. "Oh, I thought it took on a new light."

"Really?" Gail batted her eyelashes; she may have been truly confused, but with her, like Kensington, it was hard to tell. "In what way?"

"The context," Kris said. Damn it, she was enjoying this! "The idealism."

"We can't forget the way things ended," said Cory.

"And … cut," Matt said, clapping his hands horizontally in front of him. "This is veering into politics." He put his hands over Shelly's ears. "I wouldn't want to scar the young."

"I can still hear you," said Shelly.

With some awkward goodbyes, the two groups parted. He ushered Gail back into the Hall of States, and looking over his shoulder, he saw Kris smiling at him. Maybe it was the impending war, gathering like the dense night on the other side of the Potomac. Or maybe it was the memory of their parting at the inauguration—another opportunity missed. Or maybe it was something simpler than all of that. In any case, he held his hand to his ear, his pinkie and thumb extended, and nodded to her; she smiled again, and the world seemed even more dangerous. Pleasantly so.

—⁓—

The floodlights outside the White House cast a warm, butterscotch-colored hue on the front portico, an almost Rockwellian image if not for the shadow of a sniper patrolling the rooftop. As they'd neared the North Portico, Gail told Matt, over the excited talk of the girls, that Iraqi dictator Abu-Omar Pachachi's eldest son, Omar, had managed to pull off the coup without a hitch, which was rather remarkable considering he was the more dimwitted of the two sons. She smiled in satisfaction and said to Cory, "He was afraid his father, and brother, Othman, would kill him. Paranoia makes for wonderful opportunities."

"He killed his own father?" Cory said in a terse hush.

"I'm assuming you'll keep that to yourself," Gail said, "your being Matt's cousin and all. Because the story will be different in the papers. And maybe in the history books."

"Don't worry," Cory said as the limo came to a halt, "I'm a regular spy."

"Maybe you're our mystery CIA leak," said Matt.

Gail glanced at him, her eyes firm.

"You mean about the August attacks? Hey, it could be me," Cory said kind of pathetically.

Matt smiled and patted his cousin on the shoulder. "The only spying you've ever done was trying to peek up Carrie O'Malley's skirt. And you got caught."

He thanked Shelly and her friends for the lovely evening, promised he'd fill Cory in as soon as he could, and stepped out into the warm fall night. He could already feel Kris slipping away.

"Shay's got a lead on the CIA leak," Gail hissed. "Some nutcase."

"So that doesn't rule out Cory." But the vehemence in her voice soured him, taking him back again to Webb's near-tirade about the guy the day of the arrests. "Who is it?"

"Ask Shay."

Again out of the loop, and again tossed to the wolf pack: inside, Broussard informed him that the press was snarling, that the news about the coup had already leaked. "Shay and Webb called a press conference; they're waiting on you in the Oval Office."

"Please tell me we're taking a wait-and-see stance."

Broussard stopped and combed a hand through hair so frizzy and thick it seemed pubic. "Not exactly."

In the situation room, or what they called "the woodshed," not a single person was without a telephone, including Kensington, whose feet were propped on the massive oak table as he chatted, his western twang cutting above the noise. "And we got *The Godfather: Part II* to thank, Andre. Yeah. Young Omar got the kiss of death from his younger brother. Yeah, he was just doing what he saw some Russian diplomat do, but one of our boys showed Omar the movie and—oh yeah, I know, that did it."

Matt lingered for a little while, wondering what in the hell he'd be expected to say at this press conference, which was, according to Broussard, supposed to start in half an hour. Finally he pulled Shay from his phone.

"We only have slim details, and that's all you need to tell them."

"What details, for Christ's sake?"

Shay couldn't suppress his glee: the eldest of the Pachachi boys had attended a football match with his family. In a private booth, the Iraqi president was waiting for the national anthem to end, after which the curtain in front of him would be opened and he'd emerge to his adoring-or-else public. Just as the song began, Omar reached under a catering table for a Beretta, and, as a few shadowy figures dropped the guards in the hall, the eldest son executed his father and his brother. With a little help, and within seconds, he'd slain two top deputies and a waiter. As the song neared its finish, Omar was carefully shot in the shoulder by one of the foreign accomplices, and when the curtain opened, the people of Iraq saw the brave son, the last of the Pachachi clan, his face streaked in blood as he held up the traitorous waiter by his hair, a Beretta in his limp, bloodless hand.

"Of course, there *were* no foreign accomplices," Shay said with a twinkle.

"There weren't."

"No. It was all Omar's idea. Somehow this numb-nut also managed to pull off consecutive bombings in three palaces, a kidnapping of the foreign secretary, and the sudden capitulation of the information secretary—but no one's going to ask how. At least, not yet."

"So he foiled a plot to overthrow his father?"

"One perhaps undertaken with the thought that Pachachi couldn't withstand a coming American invasion. That *they* could, these—usurpers. No, don't use that word."

"So now he's in charge."

"Yes. We're pleased. Emit optimism."

With a giggle not unlike that of the Pillsbury Doughboy, Shay tottered off.

Soon Matt's fingers were wrapped tightly around the edge of the podium in the blinding lights of a room full of hungry reporters. There was a reason the deep end of the pool below was directly below the podium and not the press, a fact he would normally joke about. No dice tonight. Yes, the president would speak, but probably not until the morning, when more facts were known. Yes, the basic reports seemed correct, but he hesitated to go into details until they'd been confirmed. No, the United States and its allies had not been aware of the attempted coup. Yes, the United States and its allies would provide air support to maintain stability in the region. As the questions flew, he tried to slacken his posture, tried to seem almost disinterested. Just another day at the office. Even the busty Fox News reporter couldn't bait him into hypothesizing on the way this had conveniently occurred so soon after Vice President Webb had noted again the connection between Iraq and bin Chalabi's forces. "Things are different over there," he said dryly, "but I can promise you that the president will be looking into ways to build from this, uh, that is, to find a way to strengthen our security here at home."

Broussard waited near the salvation of the blue door out of the room and handed him a bottle of water. "Rough crowd. Shay wants to see you."

"Christ. Where?"

"The bowling alley."

Matt just shook his head. It was a perfectly absurd location, and as he and Broussard navigated their way through a number of unfamiliar halls, he wondered if the ghost of Richard Nixon would be waiting for them.

Instead, there was an enormous bald man whose head was as rounded and shiny as one of the pins. He had the slanting eyes and long nose of a wolf, and the scant blond hairs on his eyebrows made it look like he had no eyebrows at all.

"Broussard, get lost," Shay said.

One steely glance from the stranger and Broussard was very lost.

"Matt, I want you to meet my friend Carl." Matt nodded to Carl, who gripped his hand with all the gentleness of a grizzly bear. "Looks like a WWF wrestler, don't you think?"

"Only on the weekends, Stephen," said Carl, his voice like a bass drum.

"Now that you've met Carl, remember one important thing: you have never met Carl. Understand, Matt?"

The Middle East was coming unglued and all Stephen could think about was some amateur cloak and dagger bullshit?

"Yeah, never heard of the guy."

"Carl is retired CIA. He did a little of everything, including PSYOP."

"The psychological operations used to induce behavior conducive to a predetermined outcome," Matt recited from the last LeCarre novel he'd read.

"You've read some spy novels," Carl grunted.

Matt hesitated. "That's … right."

"Carl has developed a few techniques, Matt, that could be useful to you." Shay adjusted his glasses and leaned against the ball rack. "Fact is, I watched that piss-poor conference of yours; you need some of these techniques. There was no optimism. And you're hung up on words. Words are fine, Matt, they can be manipulated, they can be shaped, carved, shaved, whatever. But you're forgetting the visual. Carl, explain your priority words messaging."

"As we all know, people often don't hear every word, but they do hear power words," Carl said professorially, despite his leather jacket and jeans. "Years back, I thought if we could select the right words at the right time, we could convey a hidden message. We did studies, measured words on a one-to-ten scale. Simple words like *the* and *it* get no value. A word like *time* ranked between a one and a three. Words like *murder* or *execute* ranked a ten."

The more he talked, the more his Jersey accent leaked out. Thinking of the chaos upstairs, Matt crossed his arms and cocked his head. It all made sense, but seemed, again, a bit amateurish.

Carl said, "The word terrorism, before the last couple of incidents, was probably a seven or eight, but today it's an eight or nine. When, or if, something happens with a massive death toll, it'll be a ten. Now here's the important part: the response to these word-value associations will vary depending on their bias. People tend to link eight-nine-ten words together."

Matt felt Shay's eyes scanning him as Carl continued, "So, Matt, your comments and speeches should link terrorism with Iraq and Iran."

"Which you did a piss-poor job of tonight," Shay muttered.

"I didn't know what the fuck was going on tonight, Stephen. I still don't—"

"It doesn't matter," Carl said, one of his bare-seeming eyebrows fully arched. "Any subtle phraseology could tie Iraq directly to the attacks here, if done correctly. And as soon as you start linking Iraq to freedom, you'll get a spike in the polling numbers. Spread democracy abroad—we love that shit."

"Our God-given mission," Shay scoffed, producing a red apple from his coat pocket.

"For instance, all you have to do is say a sentence like, 'We're keeping our eye on Iran and doing what we can about the terrorist problem.' You haven't said that Iran is full of terrorists"—Carl beamed—"but you *have*. See?"

Shay was now staring Matt down unashamedly as he took tiny bites from the top of the apple. He always ate apples that way, nibbling in systematic rows around it until it was gone. All of it: core, seeds, and stem.

"From time to time, you'll be too direct," Shay said through a full mouth, "but the people are so eager for a fight, they won't scrutinize what you say."

Carl said, "Or the way you say it. Body language techniques: you, or one of your team, turn a certain way when Iran is mentioned, and then do the same thing with other hot button words. So you're always speaking the same way when you say the words Iraq and Hassan bin Chalabi. Use your hands, if you want—that's another subtle clue. Wave a hand to the right when saying Iraq, then wave it again when saying Hassan."

The gravity and manipulation of what Carl was suggesting—and Shay, by proxy, demanding—couldn't prevent Matt from picturing the *Camelot* actors waving their hands, their precise marks, their measured genuflections.

"Matt, this is not some bullshit Carl just made up. It's been tested, and it's worked. The president could never manage all of this choreography. You can."

"I'll work with my staff."

"Work on yourself first," Shay snapped. "You look dazed. Do you not understand that what's happening right now—the success of it—will either get us reelected in '04 or sink us to the bottom of the mother-fucking Atlantic?"

So abruptly had his anger surged that Shay seemed to catch even himself by surprise. His thin voice echoed down the single lane and the cramped walls.

"I understand, Stephen."

"Carl will keep an eye on you," said Shay. "For support."

"I'll do my job," Matt said, his voice monotone. Then to demonstrate, he faced the pins at the end of the lane. "This country is under attack, and the terrorists"—he pointed an index finger at the ceiling, then lowered it—"are at our door." He raised his index finger again and added, "Meanwhile, Iran remains a danger to this country and our people."

Carl nodded, though he seemed unimpressed. Shay, too.

Matt's Journal, Day 925

Shay jokingly calls the coup in Iraq the Caine Mutiny. But Kensington won't stop calling Omar Pachachi The Godfather. Thank God he hasn't let that slip in a speech. Anyway, finally have a handle on the whole story, and it's an example of paranoia and power—Richard III, *maybe. The youngest of Pachachi's two sons, and always his father's favorite, tried to assert himself too much with his older brother. Our intelligence sources convinced Omar that his younger brother and ailing father were conspiring to kill him, to head off any problem that might arise if the president's health declined further.*

The family's psychological makeup is bizarre at best. No psychological study can prove which has greater impact on the sanity of a child as he grows, nature or nurture. With this family, only both could have such a powerful impact. Some boys might be allowed to light firecrackers; the Pachachi boys were given a box of hand grenades. A teacher who had once insulted the rather dull older child was forced to play Russian roulette at the boy's request. But the boy had a change of heart just before the teacher pulled the trigger. The father was furious that the boy had shown remorse and forced the teacher to pull the trigger. The gun clicked. The father glared at the boy and ordered the teacher to pull the trigger again, adding, "The first was for the insult to me. Now, for the insult to my son, pull the trigger." Urine dripped into a puddle at the feet of the teacher. The boy remained silent, and the teacher died that day.

But Pachachi knew, and we knew, the son had a softness that his father could never accept, and the second child became his father's likely successor that day.

By carefully identifying the right agents, and after years of painstakingly detailed study of the "sit-reps," we made our way inside the president's small circle of confidants. Didn't hurt, of course, that Pachachi had once been an ally of ours—we'd backed him in 1981 against Iran, naturally—and his delicate mental state was always both a concern and an opportunity. Our guy was Iraqi; he'd studied in England, and he made a fine militant Sunni; he got as close as anyone ever had to Pachachi, but he warned that we'd never control the father. The eldest son, however ...

For an intelligence community steeped in psychological research, understanding and manipulating lunatic leaders has always been a little easier than sane leaders. (With anyone who has the ego required to lead a nation, the definition of sanity is relative, of course.)

Anyway, Iraq has a new leader: insane, unsophisticated, dim-witted and completely under the thumb of a man who is now the richest CIA agent in a long time. Using The Godfather *movie, I have to admit, was a stroke of brilliance built on luck built on planning; was it Branch Rickey who said that "luck is the residue of design"? Anyway, Kensington's calling Omar The Godfather, which means our guy is now Consigliore. And I thought John LeCarre really made all that shit up, you know, the nicknames, the codes. The Godfather of Iraq's first request of the United States? "Send me Diane Keaton." At least the wacky bastard has a sense of humor. A dark one. When a picture of his dead brother popped up on a television screen, he said, "With a few more bullet holes in him, my brother could be called Sunni Sonny."*

Don't worry, Shay says. The impress of the Pachachi name will keep Iraq under control. (That's not what we're hearing from the State Department, but since when did we listen to them?) Of course, not all in Iraq support the new Godfather, and battle lines are being drawn: Iran is waiting to pounce in the east, Syria in the west, and Turkey in the north. "We'll soon get Iran back in our sights," Webb said a few weeks ago. I wonder if he can see them now.

CHAPTER 3

Matt jammed the gears into park, locked up his Escalade, and hustled down the pier, adjusting his tie as he neared the glowing white yacht. As he reached the gangplank, he tried to put the misery of the afternoon behind him—the vacant stares of his rookie staff members, the stiffness of his goddamn fingers from all the pointing—and he nodded at the steward and guided himself up the shaky ramp. On the deck stood a wall of men in thousand-dollar suits and women in beaded gowns, their gold and silver hues catching the late sun descending over the banks of the Potomac and the Alexandria skyline. Their chatter was bubbly, carefree, as if they weren't an exclusive confederation of the most powerful people in America meeting just a few days after The Godfather's coup.

Gail flagged him down on the cramped dinner deck and led him, after a cold peck on the cheek, to the post Shay had set up for himself near the bar. That journey, crossing the thirty-foot-wide deck, took them a good fifteen minutes as Gail stopped to chat with everyone she knew—which was everyone, it seemed. Each face introduced to Matt lit up as if in the presence of a celebrity. Shay had made sure Matt knew how reluctant Webb had been to invite him, just as Shay made sure to point out that he'd been the one to insist that Matt come along. "These people want to meet you," Shay sneered. "The big celebrity. Besides, it's time for the face to meet the brains."

He huddled with Shay as the yacht drifted from its mooring and arced out into the muddy green waters of the river. Holding his scotch over the rail, Shay looked at the mansions across the Potomac and asked how the training had gone.

"Oh, fantastic," Matt lied.

"I doubt that."

"You would be correct."

In the relatively confined space of his office at the White House, Matt had gathered his troops and tried to teach them Carl's techniques—never once mentioning Carl, or Stephen, for that matter. Broussard picked the techniques up quickly enough, but rolled his eyes and sighed throughout the meeting, which had probably inspired one of the rookies—a red-haired geek named Joe—to openly question the point of the techniques. Five publicists and spokespersons aiming their fingers at the wall, fumbling to coordinate their words and their bodies, unenthused and eager to go home. Joe nearly poked out Matt's eye.

"Well we might have another message for you to throw in the mix. I got a lead on that CIA leak awhile ago."

"In Kansas City?"

Shay glanced around the sunlight-drenched bar and nodded. "Guy named Redgrave. Yale professor. A real nut job. Probably working on his memoirs. Always chatting to the press. And other people."

"I don't know him."

"You will," Shay said with a taut grin.

Webb led his dog, Charlie Brown, up onto the deck. As the basset hound poked around, he seemed a little more light-footed than usual, giving him a princely quality that contradicted his sad eyes. Everyone knew to at least acknowledge the dog with a polite grin, a cootchie-coo. Webb had six true loves: his wife and four daughters, and the nine-year-old Charlie Brown. Webb's glacier-blue eyes melted into warm pools at the mere presence of his family or his dog; often, during an intense conversation, Matt tried to shift Webb's eyes away from the humans in the room and toward Charlie Brown.

"That dog pissed on my shoes once," Shay muttered.

With the skies clear, the yacht's overhang was retracted for the dinner, which was signaled by the ringing of a triangle by the yacht's owner, Grover Alexander. While there were a few bigger boats around, Shay had noted, letting Grover host was all about his liaisons with the key coalitions that supported the president. In a somewhat campy white-and-black tuxedo, he shouted, "Dinner's served," and the guests laughed. The rich seemed to enjoy lowering themselves, as it was never more than a corny facade. And these were the super-rich—Gail had pointed out the billionaires—a collection of individuals both powerful and heartless who owned media networks, defense companies, tobacco companies, oil companies, and pharmaceutical companies. Real power, real wealth. They could afford throwing anyone overboard, even each other. Even Dixon Webb.

He dined with Shay and Gail, picking at a rack of lamb. His appetite had been scrawny the past week. What with an impending war and all. But here a string quartet was playing and the chatter continued as it had before; how comfortable these people were, how safe they felt. The only expressed fear he'd overheard was about their money, their companies. Otherwise, they stood behind the scrim which separated them from the rest of America, from the poor players strutting and fretting and never to be heard from. These men—and they *were* mainly men, white and white-haired men and their trophy wives—would never become the focus of media attention or legal attention; their lawyers could tie up any case for years and threaten countersuits to scare off corporate bean counters. The interest groups they financed never showed up in anyone's campaign reports; they had minions for that, mere millionaires for those roles. Matt guessed that a man like Redgrave ought to fear their attention just as much as Shay's.

The river met the sky's orange and pink colors, which swirled like a Van Gogh painting, and subtly the yacht's deck lights came to life. Matt was on his third or fourth glass of some impossibly expensive chardonnay when Shay suggested he cut back. This was business, not a party. Even Shay kept close tabs on his alcohol consumption with this crowd.

Webb straightened his crooked back, clinking the glass before him. "Thank you all for taking the time to join us this evening, and thank you, Grover, for the use of this lovely vessel." In the polite applause, Webb gathered himself. There was a reason he'd never been a serious candidate for the presidency: he spoke stiffly, like a condescending school principal having a bad day.

"This nation is starting to wake up to the dangers it faces. Hassan bin Chalabi has indeed roused a sleeping giant, and that giant is pissed." Cheers scored the deck, and a few knives were pounded against the tables. "This is our time, our opportunity, our responsibility to make this country safe," Webb continued in his stilted way. "Many in our nation have always had a false sense of security. Too many Americans believed that the oceans between the new world and the old world would keep us safe. Many of our own ancestors believed when they left Europe, it was all behind them. This isolationist reflex has slowed our growth at times and left us vulnerable. Many historians and academics have been so concerned with the minutia of historical facts, they ignore the reality of our global manifest destiny. They can't see the mighty river for the streams, for even the drops of water."

Webb sipped from a glass of water as the last red beams of sunlight settled behind him. Matt wondered if "ol' Dixie" figured he was gonna be the only vice president on Mount Rushmore.

"But there have been a few of us, with an understanding that we are not safe, who have always been committed to staying strong, staying alert. Now, after the events of August and this month, the heroics and actions of many have spared us bloodshed in the short run—but left too many still sound asleep. We must get the nation behind us so that we may take our place in history and see America's role in the world fulfilled. As Shakespeare said, 'Once more into the breach, dear friends, once more.'"

More ravenous applause. If Matt had ever doubted the reality of a coming storm, here were the winds pushing it along.

Still, concern and questions tightened the men's faces. Webb was peppered with questions from unusually eager billionaires, and a loose dialogue careened across the dinner tables as young waiters cleared the plates. When the conversation shifted to Iraq, one man in the crowd said in a sandpaper voice, "Of the three major targets, Iran, Iraq, and North Korea, why Iraq? Iran has nukes, North Korea is breathing down Japan's neck. We can go after one, but not three at the same time."

A voice in the red night called out, "If we spin 'em right, we can do it."

Faces aglow in just-lit candle centerpieces turned to Matt. Shay nodded almost imperceptibly.

"We're taking steps to join together the, uh, the big picture," Matt said. "So the American people see the connections—"

"And how exactly are going to do that?"

"And that still doesn't answer my question, Webb," said the man with the rasping voice. "Take out Iran, and Iraq's a domino."

Near the vice president, a man rose and cleared his throat. He was so tall he could have been a retired basketball player, and the silver hair on his head seemed shellacked into place. "The reasons we started with Iraq are several," he said almost impatiently. "It was a coup, not all-out war, and now that The Godfather is in charge, or," he chuckled, "now that Fredo is The Godfather and we're in charge of him, perhaps the Iranians will do something stupid. Any offensive action they take will unbalance the guts of their society. I'm convinced, and Webb here is convinced, that if we put the heat on them, convince *them* that war is inevitable, they will indeed make such a mistake. The Fort Sumter effect: the South struck first because they thought war was inevitable, which gave Lincoln all the cover he needed. All wars start with a provocation, sometimes real, sometimes … enhanced."

"The Boston Massacre gave us the Revolution," said Webb. "The Alamo was the call to arms that brought the full force of the United States into the war with Mexico."

"I'm all for a call to arms," said a man Gail had introduced earlier as a defense contractor. The crowd broke into a heinous laughter.

The elder continued, "The sinking of the *Maine*, the *Lusitania*, Pearl Harbor, the Gulf of Tonkin—all provoked by the bad guys. The attacks of the past month were thwarted, yes, but they *were* attacks. On our soil. Right now the country's anger can easily be directed to Iraq. After that, a simple blunder by the Iranians—if, for example, Muslim extremists with Iranian ties were to bomb some friendly event in Europe, say the Cannes Film Festival, and a lot of people, even a few movie stars, get killed—"

"Good riddance!" one guy in the back yelled.

Another stood up, smoothing down a thick beard and mustache; he seemed half the age of the rest of the cabal. "Where's Shay and Risen?" he barked, following the heads parting like a sea toward Matt's table. "I read today that only 33 percent of Americans think Iraq had anything to do with the attacks. Now, Lord knows I'm just a humble computer technician"—the crowd tittered at his feigned modesty—"but for Christ's sake, you've got a tall hill to climb, and I'm not sure you can make it."

Shay launched up, and with his stubby arms planted on the table, he snarled, "Then maybe you should stick to *Law and Order*, Mack—"

"That's one of the few shows I *don't* own, but I do own about a hundred others—"

"Because if you believe one poll is worth a damn on its own, then you've got no business watching the media."

Matt couldn't help but catch the same fuck-you attitude and stood next to Shay. "Every time something like this happens, the media get up on their high horse," he said in the voice he used with the press. "It's a process. The other side is having its push, and then we'll rope them back in."

"Like cattle on the president's ranch," said Grover Alexander from a few tables over. He shot Matt a wink.

"They have to report what we tell them," Matt said. "That's the news."

"Well, you'd better get busy, or all this talk is for nothing," said the computer magnate. "You better make your spin stick." He let his pointed finger hover in the air, then sat down as a chorus of voices took the place of his and carried on the inquisition.

Some two hours later, the yacht had turned around and headed north, and the discussion was finally over. The suits and the gowns were mingling to the strains of the quartet, and Matt was leaning on the port rail, tipping his glass delicately between his thumb and index finger. War, not only in Iraq, but also with Iran, was inevitable. These people would see to it. Maybe McCowan could head it off. He was a military hero and the chief of staff. Why the hell wasn't he here tonight?

Webb sidled up with Charlie Brown glumly trailing behind. The leash, Matt noticed, was studded with an American flag lapel pin. Webb grinned tightly and put an arm around Matt's shoulders. "Who's worse?" he asked. "The press corps or these guys?"

"I'd like to sic them on each other," said Matt. "Please tell me that one guy was just daydreaming with that Cannes bullshit."

"No one's talking about framing the Iranians," Webb said pensively. He slipped his arm away and balanced himself against the rail. "But things happen, and when they do, you capitalize."

They were silent awhile, staring at the green-black water cascading past.

"For what it's worth, Matt, I think you're doing a hell of a job."

"Thank you, Mr. Vice President."

"This business is all about adjusting, improvising, suiting the chaos of everyday events to your long-term goals. That's tough on a press secretary."

"But it's my ass if we tank."

Webb tapped his fingers on the railing and said, distantly, "You know how things work."

"I appreciate that you don't bullshit me, sir."

Webb cackled. "Eh, I'm too old for that."

"So is this the big conspiracy meeting everyone talks about?" Matt said with a shaky smile.

"We don't hold regular meetings, if that's what you think. Hell, half the people on this boat have never met, and they won't ever see each other again. But are we working for the same goal? Yes." Webb studied the black water, his chin dancing the rest of his stiff skull along to the violins, the viola, the cello. "That word, conspiracy—such a wonderful word. Planning sessions in dark mysterious rooms, meetings at a hidden lodge in the mountains, old WASPs sipping brandy."

He nodded at Matt's glass. "Or scotch. Conspiracy is just the gravity an idea holds. The idea is a real thing. The idea *is* the meeting place; it holds those that come to it in its orbit. It's nearly … celestial. Mars. High in the sky."

Matt imagined the look on the president's face if he heard his veep talking this way, dreaming of a necessary war.

"Look at one of the greatest American conspiracies, freeing the slaves. Did John Brown, Harriet Beecher Stowe, Salmon Chase, Frederick Douglas, and Abraham Lincoln meet and plan? None of them saw the issue exactly the same way. Frankly, they hardly agreed on much of anything. Yet their various actions led to the war." He shook his head and sipped from the glass of merlot he'd been balancing on the railing. "It's a strange dance the players make in a conspiracy, guided not by other people but by an idea."

"But the people make the ideas."

"I don't know, Matt." Webb raised his nose into the air, as if scenting something. "I'm not sure of that. Look, I know what you're thinking. 'Old Webb, he doesn't care about regular people.' The greatest dilemma of leadership is how many lives you will lose in the interest of the many. A leader must ask himself, is knowingly losing one life worth avoiding the loss of a thousand?"

"Hiroshima."

"Yes, then how about killing thousands to save hundreds of thousands? Where do you draw the line?"

Whether it was the alcohol or frustration, Matt felt a unusual desire to challenge Webb. Hell, the old guy seemed to be begging for it.

"Sometimes I think that the Nazis told themselves the same thing." Webb bristled and glared. "Not that I'm comparing us."

After a pause Webb regained his composure. "It's not just our side that takes advantage of events," he said. "The opposition does the same thing. Kent State lit the fuse that ended Vietnam early. Galvanized the opposition. The bad news for us, in the long term, was how it strengthened a belief in isolationism. The good news was that it defined the liberals as anti-soldier."

Matt thought of Kris, whom he had yet to call since that night at the Kennedy Center. He couldn't imagine her being anti-soldier, but of course, only the label counted. You couldn't run a campaign for hearts and minds on complex realities.

Still, he said to Webb, "Is it really that pared down? Just two sides?"

"It is." He peered at Matt and tugged Charlie Brown's leash. "Come with me. I want to introduce you to somebody."

They ambled along the port side, from the stern toward the bow. With no idea who they were meeting, Matt decided to ride the moment. As they passed a clump of egregiously dressed passengers, Gail poked her head out from the crowd and glared at him. He winked. It was good to be seen walking close to Webb. And his dog.

Tom Langdon had indeed played basketball—in college, 1956–58. After which he'd gone into the navy and emerged not only a fighter pilot but a scientist; then, with the easy success Gail always moaned about, he had fallen in love with the darling of one of the world's wealthiest families and worked his way to the pinnacle of the family business, which just happened to be science and technology. Divine intervention or careful calculation? The darling was somewhere else on the boat, and Tom Langdon was now holding forth to Matt and Webb on the efficiency of the military machine and how quickly any insurgency in Iraq would be crushed. At least he hadn't mentioned the Cannes Film Festival again.

They sat at the bow of the yacht, beyond a seemingly invisible line which no one was willing to cross. Langdon paused, and, studying Matt's face with his dark eyes, he said, "Do you know what that place is over there?" He pointed to lights atop a steep hill on the western shore.

"Mount Vernon."

"Home of General and President Washington. I'm a reader, Matt, I like to read. Hell, old-timers like Webb and me, we got plenty of time on our hands." He leaned in and whispered to Matt, "Don't let him fool ya, I know he just takes naps in that office of his all day."

Webb chuckled and petted Charlie Brown's head.

Langdon sat upright and explained that we, the people, had forgotten that during the Revolution, Washington conducted a war on the natives in the West to break the Iroquois and the Ohio Union of tribes. "The natives fought him off good until he starved them into submission," said Langdon. "Thousands died. But today there is no more revered and honored a man than Washington. Why? Because he knew, and history proved, that a strong western front and an expansionist nation was a safer nation.

"Someday what we do will be equally revered," he continued, "but it won't be easy, will it, Webb? It's going to get messy. There'll be collateral damage. But by God, we will make this a safe country."

"The liberals don't like collateral damage, Matt, because it's messy," said Webb. "For the price, they don't think Iraq's worth it down the road."

"And one our greatest weaknesses, Matt, including some Republicans, is an inability to look ahead," Langdon said. "I won't name names."

Webb smiled gently. The string quartet played a melancholy waltz in a minor key.

"Look ahead, Matt," said Langdon. "What do you see?"

Matt closed his eyes and tried to conjure a world map. "Iran jumping in. Maybe Syria."

"Good," Langdon whispered.

"Afghanistan, of course. Pakistan."

"More," Langdon said. "Bear down, Matt, like a bitch on a bone."

Matt inhaled, widened his view. He saw Africa, totally disparate, in chaos. That's not where the Tom Langdons were looking. Then it became obvious.

"China," he said.

"Told you he's a quick learner," Webb said as Matt opened his eyes. Both men smiled at him paternally. "Global positioning: China is aligned with some of the extremists, especially in Pakistan, and that won't help them with oil, which they desperately need, but what if those extremist factions align? What if they regroup and succeed in oil-rich countries? Who will those fundamentalists favor, us or China?" Webb's voice shook. "We must seize control of the Middle East because our economic position with China will be progressively more delicate."

"No one talks about that," Matt said.

"No one needs to," Langdon said flatly. "Not in public."

Webb hesitated a moment. "We've worked on this for years, thoroughly. Something may postpone our vision, and it may not happen in this administration, and yes, it will have to be led by a confederation of heroes and hoodlums, including some people we'd rather not tolerate. Yes, we've befriended the enemies of our enemies. That's what it takes. My daughters will not grow up terrified by extremists and communists."

His voice had regained its quivering edge, and to relax, Webb again scratched the basset hound behind the ears.

"You don't maintain safety and the highest standard of living," said Langdon, "without a squadron or ten of F-18s." He looked at Webb, a gleam in his black eyes. "Granted, some of those weapons manufacturers over there, they're just a bunch of pimps."

Webb chuckled. "They want what we want, for different reasons."

"Matt, that guy right there, the one in the pinstripes and tossed blond hair? He votes Democrat. But he sells missiles. He follows the money."

"We follow the path of country," added Webb. "Money dies. Not a man or woman here is older than this country, Matt. No one should outlive it. I'm damn sure not going to."

The Woodrow Wilson Bridge was coming into view, just the faintest streak of light on the horizon to the north. The quartet had continued its somber set list; the violin was swooping from low to high under a nervous sustain by the cello. Probably Democrats themselves.

"Would you look at this?" Langdon said, staring at his empty glass. "All out of Johnnie Walker Blue."

"I'll get you a refresher," Matt said.

That's what the waiters were for, Langdon told him, but Matt was already feeling guilty enough watching those poor bastards zipping around the yacht. He threaded himself through the crowd and at the bar ordered Langdon's scotch, one for himself, and Webb's Beringer.

"Told you to slow down," Shay said behind him.

"I'm okay, Dad," said Matt. He turned back to the bar, away from that unbearable, monopolizing stare.

"What shit's flying out of Webb's mouth tonight?"

"I think you heard the best of it."

Shay touched his sleeve, tightened his grip just a tad. There was no choice but to look at him.

"Just remember, kid: you dance with the one who brung ya."

His furious eyes were practically shaking, and he didn't wait for Matt to respond; he just slunk off into the throng. Possessive little bastard.

As Matt returned, Langdon smacked Webb on the thigh. "Why are you making this poor kid listen to us old farts?"

"Because," Webb replied, looking at Matt, "he needs to believe the things he's going to say."

"Amen," said Langdon. "The press can smell insincerity."

"Because they invented it," Webb muttered.

Langdon clutched Matt's knee with a wrestler's grip. "Matt, I want you to do something for me. Okay? I want you to make this modest and worthy cause of ours the fight of your life. Nothing is more important."

"Those numbers that one guy mentioned," Matt said. "They're correct. Across the board. We've checked a few different polls."

"Shay got his panties in a bunch, didn't he?" cracked Langdon.

"Thirty-three, maybe 38 percent, max," Matt said. The pessimism felt obvious on his face, like a rash.

"The scale of public opinion is almost always in balance," Webb said. "All political leadership is strapped to it. FDR wanted to wade into the war in Europe for a long time. But the scales were too closely balanced until Pearl Harbor. When two ideas find balance, then it takes people who have talent to tip the level. The way a butcher puts his thumb on a scale to drive up the price of a cut of meat."

"They do that?" Langdon cried in mock distress. "Shit, no wonder I'm not as rich as I could be."

"My wife caught our butcher doing it once, back when we had to do that sort of thing for ourselves," Webb said. "When the ideas on the scale are peace-and-love versus safety-through-strength, we win every time. We must avoid the union of the isolationists and the peaceniks. If that happens, we've got some problems. Overwhelming support keeps the agenda moving forward at the right time. And this is the right time."

Langdon said, "You gotta keep the hippies from the hicks."

"And how do I do that?" said Matt.

"You tell us," said Webb.

Matt's thoughts fell quickly, as if by instinct, to the people back in Marion, the farmers near his aunt in Fredericktown. They just wanted to stay out of it.

"But they can't afford to," he murmured. "The isolationists. We turn them."

"I think so," Langdon said.

"That gets us the 20, maybe 25 percent we need," Matt continued. Phrases began to form in his mind. *A call to arms. The call of duty. There comes a time a man has to lay down his shovel and defend his home.* "I arrange a push in the middle of the country. We can get the president out there once or twice before the end of the year. It's just another campaign."

"Yes," Webb said brightly, "and a different kind of election."

CHAPTER 4

"You have a sense of the architecture coming together," said Ryukhin rather dreamily, his nose tilted high above his neck. "Pieces stacking, one by one. The accordion, the female vocalist, that gypsy violin, yes. But the words! Ah! That slow tease, each element in its time, until the story is known in its entirety."

His porcine and feminine lips planted a wet kiss in the air as the song ended.

Yuri sipped from a mug of weak coffee. "And this song," he said, "you teach it in your courses?"

"I teach all of Leonard Cohen's songs, Mr. Likhodeyev. 'Dance Me to the End of Love' is the pinnacle, though." He parted his squat legs and attempted to pull one foot onto a knee. "The crime of Communism was to keep this man's music out of Moscow."

"I can think of other crimes," Yuri said with a chuckle, gazing out the window of the professor's home study.

Ryukhin had once been a thinner man, no doubt, whose corpulence had now overwhelmed his skinny, ineffectual arms. He breathed laboriously and fidgeted with the single pen he kept in breast pocket. Supposedly he had a wife who was out shopping for the day, but Yuri couldn't imagine that any woman, let alone a devoted wife, could allow her husband to maintain such a ridiculous cut of hair, flatly cropped against a greasy brow, or those awful sideburns.

"From these little architectures rise the greater architecture of history, Mr. Likhodeyev. And an understanding of Western Christianity. Cohen is a prophet, speaks to the future. Less Jesus than John the Baptist, perhaps."

"Let's hope he doesn't meet the same fate."

Ryukhin grinned and asked if Yuri—Mr. Likhodeyev—minded the window open. The season was still warm, and the poor man was sweating through his shirt. With the window propped, birdcalls danced into the room, and Yuri thought of Alexander Garden and those poor children to whom he often spoke. He had maintained his habit of feeding the pigeons their bread and the children their lectures, even as he'd begun tracking down a few slim leads provided by the Orbweaver software. Leads mainly to do with some petty and unfinished internal business. None of that, unfortunately, paid very well. And to carry out his most important vendetta, he'd need cash.

"So you've just signed on for the year?" said Ryukhin. "From St. Petersburg?"

A breeze blew in optimistically, ruffling Yuri's thick silvery hair. "Yes, a three-two schedule. Nineteenth century and the Russian press. Beginning with Tsar Nicholas, of course."

"Strange that I haven't heard of your appointment."

"It's just come through. And I'll be hosted by history, not journalism."

"Ah, I see."

"I wanted to see you to get a … leg-up, I think the term is? Your work, Ivan Nikolayevich, is well-known."

Ryukhin harrumphed. "Too well-known in some corridors."

Yuri feigned a bit of confusion, though he knew Ryukhin, until only two years ago, had indeed been one of the most Western-friendly journalists in Moscow, eager to expose any "malevolence" of the KGB, its contemporary, the FSB, or the Russian mafia. His friends overseas were legion.

"So you are not a fan of our new president?" Yuri said.

"Bagh," Ryukhin spit. "That grave-dancer? He'll drag us back, kicking and screaming, into the Dark Ages." The fat man looked at him queerly. "You know as well as I do how the press can be controlled, manipulated. Coerced. It's a dangerous time for journalists."

"God will see us through," Yuri said briskly, forcing the words out. Leaning forward as Ryukhin reset the CD, and as Cohen's music began again, Yuri felt along the bottom of the end table which separated his chair from Ryukhin's. With a tug, he removed the tiny device, and when Ryukhin turned around, he held it up to him.

"If we are but a little observant," Yuri continued.

"My God, where did you find that?"

Yuri crushed it in his massive hand, imagining the squeal that would be recorded back in Lubyanka Square on some computer. He pointed to under the table and whispered, "There may be others. You should have your house fumigated."

"I'll call some cleaners," said Ryukhin. He fell heavily into his chair and picked the mechanical carcass from Yuri's outstretched hand. "I thought I'd left that behind once I entered academe."

"Our pasts follow us."

"The past isn't dead, it's not even the past. Faulkner said something to that effect."

There were, Yuri knew, exactly two other devices remaining in the room: one in the phone, naturally, and another on the back of the highest shelf of Ryukhin's bookcase. Judging from the dust on the footstool near the case, Ryukhin did not like to exert himself.

"I hope I can speak frankly," Yuri said in a careful whisper. "You spent a little time in Florence, didn't you?"

"Lovely city," Ryukhin said just as cautiously.

Yuri leaned close. "Were you there when two KGB agents were killed?"

With his glassy orbs, Ryukhin scanned the room as intensely as he seemed to be scanning his memory. "No, that was after my time." He wiggled a bit in his chair. "You're not—"

"No," Yuri said. "Though, Ivan, you've been forthcoming, and so I will be forthcoming with you." He continued in a whisper out of necessity, though the hushed tone would also convince this simpleton of the lie he about to tell. "I was an agent, many, many years ago. One of those dissidents who find their way into the service. Troublemakers. A bit *off* in the head. But you have no need to fear me. I hate the KGB as much as you."

Ryukhin nodded with a childish grin. "I did know an American," he said. "Enormous man, bald head, no eyebrows. I suspected he was CIA."

The description didn't latch, set off no bells or whistles, but then so much was foggy in Florence. He let Ryukhin ramble on for awhile, mainly about the architecture of the city, its beautiful bridges.

The gypsy violin swayed from the speakers of the professor's little stereo, and finally Yuri stood and said he'd taken enough of Ryukhin's time.

In full voice now, with no worries of his inquiries being caught on tape, Yuri said, "This is a wicked world, my friend. It infects us all."

Yuri reached for his overcoat, which he'd carefully hung on the back of the study door, and Ryukhin stood, nodding academically. "Is that why you study the past, to escape the terror of the present day?"

"Not at all. As you said, the past isn't even the past. I'm infected like anyone else."

"Like these radiation poisonings we've been hearing of."

"Oh, yes." Yuri nodded, thinking immediately of Zaryana, pushing her memory just as quickly from his mind. "A dishonorable way to kill."

"There is no honor in death."

Yuri grinned sadly. "No, I suppose not. But murder, perhaps. Killing Hitler, for example."

Having put on his heavy overcoat, he pretended to pat himself down for his wallet, his keys, apologizing for his forgetfulness. He looked at Ryukhin squarely. "Ivan Nikolayevich, no man escapes the architecture of history, as you call it. We are all scaffolding."

"Very true."

"A man may engage in business deals," Yuri said slowly, "to further a greater cause. Deals which he finds pedestrian, even, beneath him."

"Oh, don't I know it. Even here, at university—"

"Infected," Yuri said as he drew out of his coat the Luger fitted with a silencer, "we nonetheless press on toward our greater cause, no matter the cost."

Standing transfixed, Ryukhin's bulbous lips quaked. A dark stain spread from his crotch down his pant legs. Just as his heavy body was about to will itself into motion, Yuri shot him once in the chest. Ryukhin stumbled and crashed onto the end table and slid and fell with a thump onto his back. Yuri stood over him—the man's breathing was not so shallow now, was it?—and kicked him over as one would roll a log, then shot him once in the back of his skull.

From a pay phone Yuri dialed the number, waited for the tone, and punched in a three-digit code. Hanging up, he padded toward the Metro, his nostrils thick with the odor of diesel and cordite, and he wondered if he had the energy to go to the park and feed the pigeons.

He had departed the Metro at Okhotyi Ryad and was walking the remaining block to his apartment when his cell phone buzzed; a voice, masked and deepened, confirmed that his payment had been transferred. Six million rubles. Had he known he'd be forced to listen to that insipid idiot talk and to the idiot's fetish for American music, Yuri would have asked for more.

He hung up his coat and surveyed his bleak one-room apartment for signs of mischief; you could never trust the man who hired you, even when your reputation was rather foreboding. There was little to survey: an unmade bed, a single drafty window, two worn-out cloth chairs he'd bought at a thrift store, a narrow kitchenette, a black-and-white television, and of course, the rickety desk he'd stolen from Lubyanka Square. No one missed it, apparently. On that chipped and malformed hulk sat the reason he lived in such a dingy apartment: the gleaming, state-of-the-art computer that had set him back a few kopecks, as did the cable Internet and the external hard drive he'd needed for the Orbweaver, which was running smoothly even now. On the floor beside the desk were piled stacks of thick file folders, floppy disks, CDs, and crinkled reel-to-reel tapes, evidence he'd kept from the old days.

Zaryana would never have allowed such a mess. Even in the advanced stages of her thyroid cancer, she'd picked up after him incessantly in their old apartment.

He brewed a cup of tea and sat at the computer, first accessing his bank account—yes, there it was, all of it, enough to finance his operation for at least two years—and then beginning the long and tedious work of sifting through the numerous photos of American agents he possessed, some confirmed, some not. An enormous bald man, Ryukhin had said, without eyebrows. The words sparked no memory, but nearly an hour later, the image did: a man with heavy, militaristic features, his head nearly shaven, the stubble a nearly translucent blond. The same with the eyebrows. The surge of excitement coursing through Yuri faded quickly: the agent, nicknamed The Wrestler, had supposedly left Florence a year before that fateful night at the Hotel Bernini Palace. Yuri paged through his memory of that night, the confusion in the hallway, shots erupting from all angles. Two Americans, a man and a woman. An ambush between the polished brass walls of the Bernini. The American bitch tumbling, bleeding, into the elevator, and then an explosion. From the floor he saw a third assassin, a mere bumbling rookie trying to reload, his young face pale and wet. But the percussion of the explosion was still ringing in his ears, and his muscles did not seem to even want to respond—a blunt shock sent him back to the ground. Then Nikolai had gone silent. Then Mikhail. Too slow. You only needed to be too slow once.

He'd sat up once more and reached for his gun—the third assassin was right there, crying over the dead woman—but a voice called out from around the corner, "I've got something you want! Don't shoot!"

The young American in front of him looked just as surprised as he.

"Let the two of them go—the woman and the man—and I'll slide you a briefcase," the voice said. "Full of goodies. Useful goodies."

Yuri's heart beat frenetically. He doubted he could even shoot straight. "And then we all walk away?" he said in broken English. Yes, the man promised, and Yuri had set his gun on the floor. "I do this for my country. But this, between us, is not over."

The young man was beginning to drag the woman away when an arm extended around the hallway corner and tossed a briefcase toward Yuri. He opened it and found a stack of maps of Afghanistan, floppy disks, and a psychological profile of Hassan bin Chalabi. By the time he looked up, the Americans were gone.

Now he stared at the photo on the computer. This bald man was not one of the assassins that day, no, but he may have been involved. He may even have been there, despite what their intelligence said: The Wrestler had left the country to meet with Hassan bin Chalabi, whom the Americans were supporting back then, calling him a patriot defending his homeland against communist invaders. How little they believed this was proven by the ease with which the voice in the hallway had given up state secrets about him in exchange for the life of one of their agents.

Yuri grinned bitterly. What had the professor said? The "architecture of history"? If there was such a thing, it was stained with the blood of coincidence. Zaryana visiting her sister near Pripyat, Ukraine, late April of 1986. And the blood of pride. The Americans presuming they could tame Hassan and his Islamic extremists and use them against those nasty Reds. And his own slow, doddering hands, covered in his own blood and the blood of his friends.

CHAPTER 5

Women were not supposed to make him nervous. He was Matt Risen, gigolo and verbal con artist. (So one feminist had called him on a CNN roundtable. He'd hit on her once, though, during the campaign. In Nebraska. Which shouldn't have counted, really; after all, nothing ever happens in Nebraska.) Behind the wheel of his Escalade, Matt checked his BlackBerry. He'd been afraid it'd be a typical Saturday night, complete with a last-minute call summoning him back to the White House. But there were no messages, and a part of him panicked for the lack of a diversion. As he neared her part of Old Town, he smoothed back his hair and repeated to himself what he and Kris had promised each other on the phone: no sudden moves, no pressure to spend the night or to start something serious. As a joke, he'd considered showing up with a U-Haul trailer and a wedding dress.

She answered the door hurriedly, peeking around the edge in a white silk robe. "Running late. Sorry, sorry." Her long hair was surprisingly straight and wet. "I just have to run upstairs and throw my clothes on. Just a few minutes. Promise." She smiled that elegant smile of hers. Brighter than the moon.

"No problem. It'll give me a few minutes to inspect your apartment."

As she scrambled up the steps, she said, "Don't look too closely, there's no telling what you'll find."

Her apartment was tasteful. Elegant, naturally. On exposed woodwork had been mounted giant paintings warmed by track lighting from the high ceiling. Yet a set of golf clubs and a softball bat were propped near the door, next to a pair of silver and blue tennis shoes.

He was leafing through a coffee table book titled *The Villages of Tuscany* when she came down the steps wearing a maroon, knee-length dress, sleeveless, with an open back. She whirled a bit, her calf muscles flexing athletically.

"You work out?" he said, trying to sound innocent.

"Carrying fifty pounds of gear is all the workout I need. Have a drink?"

He tapped his watch. "It's my fault."

"No worries, then."

"Maybe I'll take a rain check."

She arched her eyebrows. "Oh, will you now?"

The restaurant was small, their table intimately tucked into the corner of the only room. Over the candlelight, she seemed to be talking; but it seemed he was floating above, watching Kris and himself from a slight distance.

"Pretty boy," she said, snapping her fingers. "My eyes are up here."

"Oh, I …"

She let him squirm for awhile, then admitted he'd been eye-level. "For such a big shot, you're so gullible." Neatly she wound angel hair around her fork and pushed it into a pool of marinara. "So I heard you had a little shouting match with Buddy Porter."

"You know him?"

"We've worked together." She sipped her wine, peering at him. "He said you're really laying down the law on the press corps."

"I'm just taking fewer questions."

"Dangle the bait and take it away."

His gaze drifted. The past few weeks, well, he had been firmer. Partly to stick to the message, partly to limit his chances of giving someone the finger as he tried to use Carl's techniques.

Her silky hand slid across his, and she peeked down to meet his eyes. "Buddy's not pissed at you or anything. They know you're just doing your job. We all have to compromise a little in our work."

"Even you?"

"Even me." Spearing a wedge of zucchini, she held it in the air a moment. "When I was in Afghanistan—"

"You slept with that guy, didn't you?"

"Keep up, Risen, keep up. We were in this village near Peshawar, and I was taking photos of some refugees." Her voice was softening, descending into memory, quizzically, as if it was a memory she didn't quite understand. "And out of this hut burst this ugly man, and he had this little girl by her wrist. She couldn't have been more than ten years old. And he slapped her across her butt, and then her face." She held the forked zucchini out—a tiny javelin. "And I thought what I've thought a thousand times before: do I take this picture? Or do I stop what he's doing?"

"You stopped him."

"In Afghanistan? Hell, no. Jesus, Matt, do you know these countries you guys want to invade? I took the photo. It's what I would've done anyway. Most of the time." She smiled bitterly. "So you're not the only one."

"We're not invading Afghanistan."

"You should."

"We haven't invaded Iraq, either."

"Oh, Risen." She patted his hand. "You don't have to lie to me."

⌣~⋎⋏~⌣

They'd finished two bottles of wine, pouring the last drop into her glass, when she brought up the rain check. The night cap. He nearly fell off his chair.

But the look in her eyes remained cool, balanced, as she opened her apartment door. Rarely had he met a woman so laid back. Compared to Kris, Gail came on like a bulldozer.

"What do you want to drink?" she asked.

"Whatever you're having." He leafed through the book about Tuscany and held it up. "Have you been here?"

"Yes. Hope to live there someday."

"I've been to Italy a couple times, but I can't seem to get out of Rome or Venice. Cory seems to be in Europe or the Middle East all the time; he travels a lot for somebody working in the Ag Department. In fact, he lived in Florence for a little while. So he says, anyway."

"Ah, Florence," she said, "my favorite."

He carefully selected his position on the couch three-quarters of the way from the end, which gave Kris the option of either sitting in the cozy, smaller section to Matt's left, or at the other extreme, the far right, meaning she wanted to keep her distance. Or the in-between choice, to Matt's immediate right. Jesus, it was like choosing your spot at a big meeting.

She placed the glasses of wine in the middle of the coffee table and sat to his immediate right, looking over his arm at the pictures of Tuscany. Promising enough, he thought.

"It's very romantic," he said.

"Tuscany is unbelievable."

"No, I meant in here."

Her indigo eyes flashed with skepticism, maybe a little desire.

"You," she said.

"Me?"

Leaning back, she sighed, thought a moment of something—lovely, pensive Kris—then burst up from the couch and growled. "What am I doing with you? You work for Stephen Shay, for God's sake."

He wasn't sure if he should laugh or not. Finally, when she just kept staring at him, he said, "Steve's not as bad as you think."

"You do not call him Steve."

"No, I don't. Look, his mother was a librarian and his father was a high school principal. A very strict man. His parents hated each other, and because his dad was such an asshole, his mother doted on him. He was friendless–"

"I'm shocked—"

"—and spent all his time reading in the library. What happened to compromises? And what does this have to do with me?"

"There's a line, and I know: you're not Shay." With a huff she sat on the couch. "Hey, I've got my hang-ups like everyone else. I look at that guy, I look at all the neo-cons, and my skin crawls."

"They just want to protect the country."

"How, exactly? By way of that memo you guys sent out last winter? Or, I'm sorry, I mean, the memo you strong-armed the publishers into sending."

"What's wrong with asking for a little fairness?"

"Nothing, except that it was a threat. And reporters already realize they need to be fair. To be trusted. Because if they're not, they're fired."

Slowly she turned away. Dejected, pessimistic. This was going splendidly, wasn't it? They sat in silence, and his eyes drifted to one of her paintings, a sort of abstract landscape, olive-green and muted reds, and birds painted in clay and earth tones and black.

"I feed birds," he blurted.

She squinted at him and burst into that ridiculous, free laugh of hers. For the first time all night, he noted.

"Down at the Starbucks near the Potomac. Not the one on Union Street. Outside, you know? I sit out there and toss 'em crumbs."

Astonishment seemed to have entranced her. "You're a weirdo."

"You sound like Shelly."

"Okay: you're a mass of contradictions."

"Do you ever look them in the eye? The sparrows, when you feed them? They look back at you, like they're saying thank you. Then they fly off with a morsel of scone in their beak."

She giggled and took a long swig of her wine.

"I've got some property out near the Shenandoah park," she said, then stopped herself. "Tell me how you guys are looking at this. How you're approaching this Iraq thing."

"Tell me about Shenandoah instead."

"If I'm going to be with you—" This time she caught herself abruptly. "As friends, or maybe more," she crooned, "we'll see, so keep it in your pants, pretty boy, and tell me how you sell a war."

"Let me tell you about my favorite bird: the mockingbird." She growled again; he could listen to her growl all night. "They're always the loudest at the top," he continued, "like at the apex of a roof."

"They're just imitators. The war, please."

"It's a finer thing than that," he said. "They choose three other bird calls at a time."

She wrapped her hand around his mouth, flared those intelligent eyes of hers, and said, "Tell me. Because I care about these things. Please."

He nodded and she released him. For the briefest of seconds, a familiar wariness kicked in, as if Shay were hovering over his shoulder and saying he couldn't trust this liberal commie. An imaginary finger flicked Shay off into the nearby wall.

He explained that it was a lot like the campaign, that the argument was defined around general messages of safety, patriotism, and revenge. Religion, too, but that was a much more targeted message.

"Aimed at the fundamentalists," she said. "Saving souls overseas."

"Yes. And they get all worked up. Look, it's just tactics."

She raised a hand. "I'm not judging. Go on."

"Well, the real opposition is two groups: the isolationists, and the liberal Christians and Jews. Shay calls them the John and Yoko clans."

"I'm a liberal Christian," she said. "Faith put to work. Call me crazy, but I'm not hung up on a death trip, you know? The whole 'the end is nigh' thing."

Well that was new. Matt wished he'd known it when he was on the yacht with Webb. He'd have been blown away.

"Anyway, Shay's been saying that prosperity is never spoken, only implied. Nobody likes to think they'll support a war for cheaper gas, but a lot of us will."

"And you get this across how?"

"I just keep it on the agenda. Mention how gas prices keep climbing, and how concerned we are."

"And you keep calling everything 'collateral damage.'"

"Lately it's been 'outcomes.'"

"That's even more bland."

"That, my dear, is the point. Sometimes, plain language is safest." He reached desperately for his wine, certain he'd rambled on just long enough for her to notice just how much he sounded like Shay. "So," he said, "now that you're repulsed …"

She was staring at him with the slightest of smiles—elegant! classical!—and then she leaned in and kissed him. His breath stuttered as their mouths opened, as their tongues found each other, and just as she finally pulled away from him, she planted a short, sweet kiss.

"I'm very confused," he said breathlessly.

"Me, too."

A kiss had usually been a pleasurable means to an end—the key step to getting what he wanted and an opportunity to analyze his next move. This was different. He would be happy to sit on this couch all night and look at pictures of Tuscany and argue like lovers, real lovers, argued. Or how he'd always imagined they would.

She graced her hand along his cheek, her eyes concerned. "You're a good guy, Risen. And I … I guess I've always admired people who are good at what they do. It's a turn-on. Intellectually. And otherwise."

She stood, picked up her wine glass and handed him his.

"What about our deal?" he said.

"What deal? I don't remember a deal." She'd walked to the stairway and now laid her head on the banister.

"And Shenandoah. I want to hear about Shenandoah."

She started up the stairs.

"Follow me and I'll tell you all about it."

———∿∿∿———

In the aurora of the next morning, she lay on top of the covers, and he followed the strong lines of her broad shoulders, her narrow waist and wide hips—an intoxicating blend of femininity and athleticism. She'd brought out something of an athleticism in him, too, last night. He reached down to pull the comforter over her hips, and just as he covered her, she spun and grabbed his arms, pulling herself on top of him with a laugh.

"Shouldn't you be on some talk show this morning?" she whispered.

"Not every Sunday. I don't work that hard."

She kissed his neck, bit at his ear. "Could've fooled me."

An hour later they retrieved their clothes from the heap on the floor. He suggested they shower, but she said that was a line she wasn't willing yet to cross. "Men are grubby," she grinned, "and my shower is pristine."

By the time they'd made it downstairs, drunk their coffee, and begun to share the *Post*, it was closing in on noon. With a jolt he remembered to call Shelly, a call that went about as he should've expected: the girl was absolutely giddy he hadn't come home.

"You always scan the photo credits?" she said.

"It's how I start my day. Credits and bylines."

At some point, he'd need to roll into work for a few hours. If he'd been inclined to forget his duty, three messages waited for him, one from Shay and two from Gail. Their names seemed ugly here in Kris's apartment.

She slid to him a story on the attempts of the administration to gain support for the war from evangelicals in the Midwest. "You'd think you were the press secretary or something," she muttered over his shoulder. One preacher from a little town in Illinois had been quoted as saying, unabashedly, that "Jesus is on our side."

"That's what Plato called the Noble Lie," Kris said. "A myth told by the elite to ensure order. These people talk democracy, but they're terrified of it."

She had a point. May have even been right. And without a doubt, she was the right one. He knew it. Here, in her kitchen, in her apartment, he felt at home. And it wasn't about the kitchen, and it wasn't about the apartment.

He finished his coffee and got up. "I don't want to leave. But I have to go in. Tell me you're free for dinner?"

"Not tonight, I have to work. And I'm going to Toronto on Wednesday."

"We'll be in the Dakotas by then. We get back Saturday."

"Next Sunday for me," she said.

A worried, nervous look must have crossed his face. She bunched his cheeks. "At least part of our promise has to hold up, okay? No demands, no expectations. I won't ask about Gail. Just disinfect yourself afterwards."

"I'm not going to see her anymore."

"Or maybe you should just spray her down first."

"I mean it."

Gently she kissed him on the lobe of his ear. She whispered, "I know you do, but … just take it a day at a time, okay? You and me, we're a long shot. But we're adults. So let's just play the odds."

CHAPTER 6

Kris was right. Kris was right about a lot of things. Not everything. But Kris, she could go toe-to-toe with Gail. Maybe even Shay. Kris. Such a crisp name, fresh. Kris, Kris, Kris.

"Mr. Risen?" said the cute old lady, a venerable reporter from Bloomberg.

"Ellen, I'll tell you," he said, gripping the podium, "I've been thinking about my answer since you became the first woman in the Gridiron Club." The packed-in crowd, cramped and sweating, tittered.

He continued, "The president's aware of the delicate balance in Iraq between the Shiites and the Sunnis right now, no doubt. The problem we face is that Iraq's been a breeding ground for terrorism." Casually he let his right hand drift and pointed an index finger at the wall. "By supporting Omar Pachachi's new regime, we're helping to eradicate that threat. It's simple, really. But on the other hand, we've got Iran to deal with." Again his index finger drifted and pointed; by now, it'd become second nature. "Iran is troublesome, all right, and we're keeping an eye on them."

Having in no way answered her question, he watched the reporter's eyes narrow. Quickly he took a question from the back.

"What is the timetable for the insertion of American troops into Iraq?"

"You want me to give away state secrets—who is that back there, Chuck? Is that what you want me to do, Chuck?"

Barely a van Gogh-esque mirage of colors and a shaky voice, the reporter replied that the American people just wanted to know what to expect.

"I think the American people understand the need for security," Matt shot back. "It's you folks that are pressuring us. To support this new regime, we need to employ some tact," he landed on the word and paused, like they'd never heard it before, "and in all senses of the word, use some diplomacy." As he'd been working on, Matt frowned on the last word. That limp, boring word! Diplomacy would never work, would it? And he didn't even need to say with whom!

If she had been watching, Matt thought as he stepped away from the podium, Kris would've at least begrudgingly commended him. Since his first real date with her in October, the press had been amping up its intensity, its vitriol, and two dates later—which, it seemed, was how he marked the days—the lefties in the media weren't letting up. Shay's tutorial had come just in time. And his staff was kicking ass, too, even the greenies. A real fighting unit. Thumbs, power words, and waving hands everywhere.

If anything, the past two months had been a revelation. He'd never doubted he could do this job—in fact, in the earliest months of this year, he'd been too sure—but after the rollercoaster and body blows of August and September, he'd found a new ease in his work. Replies to the press came quicker, and the razor-sharp razing of a few media had come honestly and cleanly. Barely any meat left on the bone. It was just the way things had to be done. Yes, he had misgivings—grave misgivings—about the path Webb and Co. were leading the country down, but he could needle his opinions into the tapestry and that was about it. It's not like there weren't terrorists (index finger) or Iran (repeat) on the loose.

Who deserved the credit for this balancing act? Kris. Kris Johansen. Hi there, Broussard, have I told you about Kris Johansen? (Well, no, he hadn't. Better to keep it hushed-up for a while.) With Kris you could talk for hours. With Kris—she was right—there were shades of gray. Jobs with any power required a reconciliation of extremes: morals, ethics, beliefs. She'd taught him that. Taught him to breathe a little. And yet he was still *shtupping* Gail. Less frequently, less ardently, but still taking her into his bed. Kris was right about that, too. And even knowing that, he was still *shtupping* Gail. Why? The thought came again—a fallback plan while he tested the waters; because he'd believed you could only act one way, pick one side, and that his professional allegiances demanded he choose Gail—but if he'd allowed himself to, you know, actually dwell on it, he already would've broken things off with Gail.

The truth was that now was a complex time, and that he worked a complex job, and thus, things were … simple.

Matt was strutting into the Oval Office—these guys owed him a fucking medal for that conference—when the general's shearing voice struck him like jet exhaust: "You guys are baiting the Iranians! Why in God's name are we going down this path?"

McCowan sat at the lonely end of one couch, Webb at the other end of the opposite ivory couch, and the president in one of the blue-and-white-striped chairs. Shay stood behind Webb (a first?) and was glaring a hole in the general's forehead while Gail lingered malevolently behind the soldier. Custer could not have been more thoroughly surrounded, and the odds were nearly as bad.

Matt plopped down on the general's couch. "Mission accomplished," he said. "I think I made some real headway with the press."

He trailed off, everyone staring at him now, except for McCowan. The Christmas tree lights blinked obscenely.

"We have steps that we can take to stay out of the crosshairs," said McCowan.

"The crosshairs were aimed at us, General," Webb said coldly.

"Really? Because my intel—all of it—says that Pachachi and his sons were party boys living in chicken-shit imitations of the Playboy mansion. All the crazy old bastard needed was a red felt smoking jacket, a skinny pipe, and a couple of bunnies drooling over him." Kensington stifled a laugh, apparently pleased with the image. "The way to keep this guy happy and under control was easy; all we had to do was go to Hugh Hefner and ask him to empty out his garage, basement, and attic, and send the junk to them."

"Well, now, we just need a party for one," said the president. "For The Godfather. Hell, McCowan, it's a budget cut."

"Not in three years," McCowan shot back. He turned to Webb and rose as he said, "Do you know what you've unleashed on our military? Babysitting a civil war?"

"It'll never get to that," Webb said, struggling to stand. His eyes were narrow, on fire. The veep wasn't bored anymore. "We're in charge as long as he's in charge."

"You've got Sunnis claiming the Shia are out to obliterate them—"

"Let 'em," Webb shouted.

"Let's settle down, fellas," the president said with a desperate chuckle. "You're both hotter than two hookers in Tijuana." Slowly Webb sat, but the general turned to the president, his eyes searching. "General, I respect your opinion, but I'm thinking Dixie and these neo-cons are right: we can't wait around. I learned a long time ago that in a street fight, the guy who gets to throw the first punch usually throws the last. In football, everyone always says the best offense is a good defense; well, I think, sometimes a good defense is a good offense. And we got helicopters and what-not to protect The Godfather, right? And that oil. Gonna need that oil for the rebuilding. So we blow 'em away, these ... uh, what're you calling 'em, Gail?"

"Insurgents, sir."

"Insurgents, then. And with little risk to our boys."

McCowan sat down heavily, all but raising his hands in defeat. The rich dark brown hue of his face was slowly turning green. Measuredly he said, "Spark a civil war, and it'll be more than a risk. Provoke Iran, and ..."

Webb bounced his leg against the rug, his glowing face beaming at the general. "The rebuilding process will be quite expensive," he said. "Even if we limit the violence."

The general glared at Webb, his eyes on fire but his mouth sealed, and Matt watched his eyes shift to the president and then to the flag, like he was falling into it. McCowan understood what the opportunities were: Webb and the president had a lot of friends in the rebuilding business. McCowan sagged, stared at his knees. He'd tried to bring the gravity of all the options to the table, and Matt had thought he'd actually had a chance at getting Kensington away from the simplistic bullshit. But now, well, it was like watching two massive iron doors slowly shut; the exits were barred, the options narrowed to one, and now—*now*—they'd start to make sense of the situation over there.

"We must get the country behind this, which won't be easy," Webb said. "I just don't want to lose our message. We have to maintain a focus on the war on terror."

Shay looked at Kensington. "I agree."

The president pointed with an index finger at both Webb and Shay and said, "I sure as fuck know that whenever I hear you two agreeing with the other, it's time to listen. But now we got some kind of speech-planning meeting, don't we?"

An aide had been patiently standing at the door of the office. The rest were already waiting in the Roosevelt Room, she said, and the slaughter was over. McCowan rose lethargically, his dark skin sagging under his eyes, and when they had some space from the others, Matt said, "I just wanted you to know how much I support your position—"

"There's only one position," the general said. "The president's position. And as of this minute, we all must support him. Put your ego in check, Risen."

Matt felt the sunburned sting of shame across his face.

"You're right, I understand."

As they all crossed the hallway into the Fish Room, Gail collared Matt. What was that about, she wanted to know. Nothing, he told her, adding that he probably still had a lot to learn.

Matt had yet to spend much time in the Roosevelt Room—sometimes called the Fish Room after FDR's aquarium and JFK's famous sailfish—but it reeked of history. Power and permanence. Above the mantel hung a portrait of Teddy Roosevelt from his Rough Rider days, different days indeed. Seated already in the hard brown leather chairs, Broussard and the two top speechwriters, Gregory Maurer and Dan Farrell, were joking about something while Candice Byrd, the head of the NSA, listened to them, apparently bored out of her skull. A few aides floated around, waiting for the major players to take their seats. McCowan sat at the far end of the long table, next to Secretary of State Knotts and directly across from Secretary Byrd. Once Kensington had seated himself in the middle of the table next to Greg, Shay pounced on the chair across from him. Gail whispered something into the president's ear as she took the chair to his left, and Webb placed himself near McCowan, separated by a nervous aide who probably had heard all the shouting. Seating, of course, was everything. To keep the president's attention, it was best to be on the opposite side of the table from him so he didn't have to try and look around obstructive heads. With a playful jab at Broussard's shoulder, Matt seated himself next to Shay.

"State of the Union, boys and ladies," Kensington said. "What do we got?"

All exhausted eyes fell on Maurer, a man in his fifties whose cheekbones were pointed and whose voice carried considerable gravity. He'd been an editor for the *National Review*, and prying him away had been possible only after the 2000 victory. Eloquently, he laid out the agenda for the speech, paraphrasing and directly quoting when he needed to, and Matt ticked off each of the points on a legal pad, imagining how each media outlet would respond. Gail, he noticed, was frowning, and, with a subtle glance behind Shay's bulbous head, he saw that Webb was practically giving Maurer the evil eye. Shay was wetting his lips, a nervous habit he possessed when he wanted—*needed*—to jump in, and yet he was letting Maurer finish. That's how much clout Maurer had.

Still, they clobbered him. Economic policies should be minimized and tail-ended, Shay said, adding, "Guess you didn't get the memo, Greg: we're at war. Merry Christmas."

"Under no circumstances mention war," Webb snapped.

And with this, the dog pile began; Shay and Webb leapt on the folksy rhetoric, which Matt actually preferred, but it wasn't a fight worth fighting. Hell, even the distressed McCowan had a few words of advice, suggesting the address to the troops be lengthier and more substantial. "They're the ones doing our dirty work," he said, looking at his reflection in the mirror of the polished table.

"And it makes you look sympathetic," Shay said across the table.

"I am sympathetic," the president whined.

Dan Farrell was taking down notes at a court reporter's clip; Matt knew he'd done the bulk of the work on the foreign policy language, and it was mainly his work getting hammered. With a broad, generous face and an arching, receding hairline, Farrell was a young guy who looked old school, and he was not good at hiding each blow to his pride.

"Dan, in my research," Matt said evenly, "I've found that the 'in here-out there' message hits a nerve. Check out Hannah Arendt on violence and language."

"Jesus Christ," Shay muttered.

Matt didn't bother to look at him. "You could even get an anaphora going."

"What's that?" Gail said, as if she were hard of hearing.

"You don't need to worry about it," Matt said in her direction. "String together a bunch of antitheses."

Shay wiped his left arm across Matt's legal pad. "If you're done showing off, Matt, we can get to what I think is the knockout punch. You mention a tripartite alliance. That's from Bodansky, right?"

Maurer nodded. "You don't like the term?"

"The American people won't know what the fuck you're talking about."

They both glanced at the president, who was staring at his coffee mug and most likely dreaming of his Colorado ranch, fluffy snow, and eggnog. It wasn't just the American people Shay was concerned with; that phrase, tripartite alliance, was a landmine buried in the text, waiting to go off on national television as it exploded out of Kensington's mouth. A mumble-mouth bomb.

"Simpler language," Shay said. "I've been telling you guys—"

"Syria doesn't belong in there," said Gail. "It pales in comparison to the other two."

"North Korea," Webb muttered. "Has to be."

The president nodded and ran his finger around the lip of his mug.

"Simpler language. Triangle of …" Shay drifted off, tapping an apple he'd pulled from his jacket pocket on the table. "Triangle of Hatred."

But he grunted, displeased, and Matt thought of the also terrifying notion of two tr sounds spitting out of Kensington's mouth like chewing tobacco. Shay ought to have known better. Doodling on his notepad, a bit in awe of the silence that had descended on the room, he searched through his mental filing cabinet of history; scarcely did he have a good use for it at press conferences, or on television—choosing the wrong allusion could be a disaster.

"Axis," Matt cried. "Call up all those old memories."

"Iran and Iraq hardly form an Axis, Matt," grumbled Webb, rolling into another one of his professorial explanations.

"It's brilliant," Shay interrupted. "People aren't going to care, Webb. Not the ones who matter, anyway."

The president blurted, "Axis of Sin." He held his hands out, his face caught in that perplexed-chimp mask.

"Axis of Terror," Shay said. "You get all of the allusion, plus the contemporary situation."

"I can live with that," said Kensington. "Why don't we take five?"

But there was too much to work out. They combed through what was now the "Axis of Terror" portion of the speech, swapping Syria for North Korea, nudging Maurer's list of possibilities into the extreme: chemical weapons, blackmail, even kidnappings.

When they finally did take a break, Shay all but pinned Matt against the mantle. "Came on pretty strong, kid," he said, peering up and over his illusory eyeglasses. "But you fucking nailed it. Just keep your ego in check, huh?"

"McCowan told me the same thing."

"Well, he isn't half-bad."

They soon reconvened, and Shay launched into an invective about Farrell's description of Omar Pachachi. He was not "a bright ray of hope," or some such nonsense. "He's a stabilizing force," Shay said. "Repeat it over and over." He smacked Matt's shoulder—the touch like a wet rag, though to Shay it probably felt manly—and reminded Matt to do the same. Dutifully he made the note.

Stabilizing force. Like that George Carlin routine about lifeless, contemporary American words. Suck the verve right out. And of course, when it was so bland, it was harder to tell what was true, and what wasn't, and so the rest of the country could go on believing that Webb and his cronies wanted Omar to keep things stable. Of course, they wanted the opposite. A shake-up. An invitation. It was better that way, he was convinced; on the yacht in the Potomac, Webb had made that pretty clear. Still, it was a lie, and this they were stuffing down American throats: sudden change was almost never a good thing, and not the way the United States did business, but when it happened (over there) we would step in to benevolently steady the hands of history.

"So are you going to tell me?" Gail shrieked on the top step of his brownstone. Even with her standing behind him, her perfume was oppressive.

"Tell you what?"

Larry Bird barely looked up at them from his perch on the coffee table. As Matt passed, he scratched the fatso's ears before loosening his tie.

"'You don't need to worry about it.' In the meeting. What the fuck was that?" She ripped his tie away from him. "You don't talk to me like that. Ever."

It was, he had to admit, the way Shay casually and yet, somehow, with all the brute force of a Mack truck dismissed a person. Not Matt's style, or, not the style he wanted to maintain.

"I don't know," he said limply. "I'm tired, okay?"

"You think you're the only one who puts in eighteen-hour days?"

"I only know one person who whispers in Kensington's ear like that."

"Oh, Jesus," Gail said, and she laughed. Brayed, perhaps. "So, what, you think I'm fucking the president? And that would give me Teflon skin?"

"I was talking shop with Farrell and Maurer." Matt pounded his fist against the recently-painted wall. "Just let it go, okay?"

"You're jealous of my connections."

"All you *have* are connections."

Oh, to get that one back. Like a fishing line you could reel in and cast again. It wasn't nearly the entirety of the truth—her point about cutting Syria was dead-on—and she glared at him now in full confidence that he knew how petty he was being. Holding his eyes a moment longer, she slipped off her heels and carried them upstairs.

With a grunt he tugged off his own shoes and collapsed on the couch. Not a bad bed for the night, though LB was liable to walk all over his face. Fuckin'-a, though, it was *his* house. He hadn't even invited her over. She took him for granted—at least as much as he took her for granted. You slip into a thing, you get lazy, and next thing you know, you're sleeping every other night with a person you can hardly stand. Would he have stopped the car and gone running over to Gail if he'd spied her on the Oval at Ohio State? Had they ever just toured around DC, looking for whatever came next?

He trod upstairs, expecting to speak his peace, but she lay on her side in a pink negligee she'd been leaving in his bedroom. Tomorrow morning, he thought. First light of day. She'd already be on her way out.

Sometime later, he woke violently. A dream lingered just beyond the curtain of sleep, but he could only see shadows of it: a white tower, thin like a church spire; he'd been running; someone was shooting at him. He rolled over and saw that Gail was gone.

Creeping out of the bed, he let his eyes adjust to the darkness before edging toward the bedroom door. You never knew when some lunatic would strike; that was the world now: always primed to explode. From his study down the hall washed an eerie blue light. It blinked once: the shadow of a head and shoulders. Along the carpeting he moved with a hush. Should've bought that goddamn gun. But, no, Cory had said. Guns only cause trouble. Instead, a Depression glass candy dish, which he plucked carefully from the table in the hallway. He glanced a moment at the Picasso sketch he'd bragged to Kris about. The last thing he'd ever see. Well, damn.

Barely an arm's length from the study door, he stepped on a loose board. It creaked like some old battleship. The light blackened as he whirled around the door jamb, scrambling for the lights with the dish raised—but even in the shadows, he could see Gail, one of her slim hands planted on his desk near his laptop.

Which was blinking. Still on. He never left it on.

She giggled. "What is that, a vase?"

"What the fuck are you doing?"

"Checking my e-mail. Couldn't sleep."

"Bullshit." Finally he flipped on the lights. "Bullshit, Gail!" He pushed past her, opened the laptop screen and saw, at the bottom, that his journal document was still open, a dialogue box still asking for the password.

And she was still giggling. "What if I'd been a thief?" she said.

"If?"

"Matt. You know me." Her eyes softened. "I'm a little … thorough."

"What were you hoping to see?" he shouted.

"It's Shay, Matt. He asked me to see if you and Kris were—"

"Oh, bullshit, Gail. Shay would never ask you to do anything. He'd get his CIA lackeys to do it." He set the candy dish on his desk, afraid of what he'd do with it, and scraped his bottom lip with his teeth. "You are a fucking gossip. You snoop around. You use people. That's what you do."

She had nothing to say. Straightening her posture, she headed for the hall with an affronted sashay.

"It's over," he said before she'd made it through the doorway.

"What's over?"

"The fucking."

"The literal, or the figurative?" Gail said.

"The literal!"

She blew air through her lips as if exhaling cigarette smoke and this time stomped out of the room. Momentarily his bedroom light came on. He powered down the laptop. The thought of her reading his innermost thoughts, Christ, it sickened him; even at work, they didn't share ideas or talk about their pasts. She did her job and informed him of it. Most of it. Some of it. And he did the same. Information. Not opinions, not vulnerable beliefs that could be hacked away at, or even nudged in different directions.

He found her at the foot of the bed, collecting a silk blouse. Throwing it into the workout bag she always brought with her, she spit out, "One mistake and you're through with me."

"Oh, come on, Gail. This was about your career and my career."

"Mine doesn't need yours," she said emphatically. She sank onto the bed and started to button up the red blouse she'd been wearing earlier. "I'm not going to make an enemy out of you, Matt. You couldn't take it, and I'm above that. No matter what you think." Her eyes fluttered closed, and he could see the damp impress of moisture. Actual tears, rimming her eyelids, too afraid to fall. "Your stupidity, your gullibility, your pride; the fact that this Johansen bitch is going to walk all over you; even that I suffered through that horrible musical and your tighty-whitey cousin and those insufferable, dim-witted little girls—all of that, I am not going to hold against you."

Picking up her bag, she stalked out. So much rage had balled up—tighty-whitey? insufferable?—that he couldn't speak, could only follow her downstairs, and even when she insulted Larry Bird, calling him as fat and washed-up as his namesake, Matt could only stare at her. At the door she reached into her purse, pulled out a photo of them at the inauguration—she held it up to his face, her eyes inflamed, the tears dried as if they'd never been there—and then she neatly ripped it in two.

"Do you think everyone gets what they want, Matt? That everyone's dream comes true?" Flecks of spit leapt from her lips, and she stuffed her half of the photo into her purse. The torn half of him floated to the hardwood. "Let me tell you something, motherfucker: save yourself. Otherwise, you're going to be incredibly disappointed. We ask for a dream, but we get a block of wood. So we carve out what we can. Kris? She'll break your fucking heart. This job? It's going to kill you. Or maybe not. Maybe you'll get all your dreams to come true like some fairy tale. Me, I'll still be fighting for everything *I* get, and I'll be goddamn happy to get it."

A yanking of the door, a slamming, and she was gone.

His shoulders relaxed. He breathed.

After a moment, he picked up the torn photo. Pieced back together, it would have formed an ideal picture of an ideal couple: the image she had in her mind. That was the thing. Her mind, her ideals. Out of that block of wood she'd carve herself a living doll, one of these days. But it wouldn't be him.

CHAPTER 7

He'd been afraid that Kris would work through the holidays, but she flew in by the twenty-second, giving him enough time to see her, to woo her, and to bestow upon her the fitting gifts for a queen before he left with Cory for Ohio. While at her apartment the night she'd returned, he'd made a list of every Van Morrison CD she owned, and the next day he bought the ones she didn't own.

The next night, by the fire-lit hearth, you might have heard angels, cooing trumpets, and the Harlem Boys Choir. Shelly had helped him to hastily string up decorations—nearly three hundred bucks' worth—since her own family had made their effort, a dry midget tree and a waving Frosty the Snowman that used to light up. For her part, Shelly demanded some face time with Kris; they ate Italian take-out, watched *Christmas Vacation,* and dragged the poor girl through some Christmas carols. And then gifts: for Shelly, four tickets to the Green Day concert in February (her hippie phase long gone); for Matt, from Shelly, a ridiculous red-and-white knit cap, since he refused to wear hats because they'd mess up his hair; for Kris, from Shelly, a photo of her and Larry Bird, in color, LB uncomfortably propped up like a grumpy elder; for Kris, from Matt, the Van Morrison CDs, a subscription to *Orion,* and a gift-to-be-revealed. When they'd finally shooed their young friend out around ten o'clock, he and Kris retired to the bedroom, and some two hours later, about to step into the shower together, Matt produced from his jeans pocket a red velvet box. A pearl earring.

"Not to sound ungrateful," she said, "but, just one?"

"That's one for your left ear." He grinned like a damn fool and reached into his other jeans pocket. "And this one—"

"You are a cheesy son of a gun."

"I don't get much of a chance at the White House."

"Tell that to the press corps."

Tauntingly, he arched his eyebrows. "Hey, I can take them back."

"I love them. I do."

The words echoed, and apparently she saw them bouncing around in his lovesick head. "Don't say it," she said. "Too early."

They stayed up late that night, making love again, showering again, drinking cold coffee until four in the morning. Delirious despite their sleeplessness, Kris's hair frizzy in the moisture and barely tamed by a hair band, they traipsed through the slush on Oronoco Street and turned onto Royal to meet Cory at Gadsby's. Over a few Bloody Marys, they recounted *Camelot,* that night on the terrace, and the way Kris had managed to stump Gail. Just a little, Kris claimed, but Cory insisted it had been a thing of beauty. A regular *coup d'état.*

⌒〰⌒

Returning to DC just after New Year's, Matt felt like a new man. He and Cory had spent considerable time together, "man time," drinking beer and talking about women, and, lo and behold, definitive plans had been made for Carrie O'Malley to finally grace Washington DC with her presence. For such a frigid time of year, love was in the air, a sentiment that not all shared. Gail, for instance, who spoke to him only when it was absolutely necessary. Shay loved only his work. It was grim enough to bring a lovebird to earth.

That process began the night they convened once again in the Roosevelt Room to discuss "the big speech," as Kensington had taken to calling the State of the Union. Conspicuously absent were McCowan and Ed Knotts from the State Department. Their vacancies had been filled by Tom Schillings, the CIA director, and Rick Dimmesdale from the Pentagon, and the room possessed a heavier air than it had in December.

Once again, Maurer ran through the speech, a revised version Shay had been tinkering with over the holidays. Terrorists had been rounded up in Iraq with our help. Allies were flocking to our cause. Though tested, our resolve was strong and would remain strong. Though we'd thwarted attempts on American soil, we could ill afford to take our eyes off the threats still posed. And so on, until Maurer read the "Axis of Terror" portion.

Kensington raised his hand like a schoolboy. "Not strong enough," he said.

"What's not strong enough?" said Shay.

"That term, buddy. Axis of Terror." He glanced down the table at Dimmesdale none too subtly.

"If anything," Gail said, "'axis' is too complicated for young people." She stared Matt down. "They don't remember it."

"Bullshit," Matt blurted. "Every textbook—"

"For me, it's the word terror," said Schillings. "Too blunt. Doesn't create a visual."

"The hell it doesn't," Shay said.

"I'm with Tommy," the president said. "Plus we're saying the goddamned word in every other sentence already."

"But you don't have a suggestion?" said Shay, tapping his fingers.

"Nope."

A pall of silence descended on the room. Unbidden, the word came to him. The word the president was looking for. And it seemed to want to push itself out of his mouth. His chest tightened and he scanned the long, tired faces; it was a table full of heavy drinkers just a few days out from the heaviest drinking holiday of the year, and nobody was thinking straight.

Why shouldn't he say it? The president would be pleased. Then again, the president would be pleased.

Once, he'd told Kris, when he'd been in military school, he'd been taught to obey. He'd been taught that the men above him were there because they belonged there. They had proven themselves; if they hadn't, they wouldn't be there. And it wasn't just military school. That's how life was. That's how work was. No matter how much you bitched and moaned about the men and women above you—yes, he'd caught himself that time, and Kris looked pleased—and even if you coveted their jobs, you had to admit: they'd made it, and you had not. Not yet, maybe not ever.

The room was still silent. Webb seemed poised to say something, then winced. It wasn't as if they'd immediately take Matt's suggestion. He didn't have that kind of clout.

"Evil," Matt said.

The president lifted his eyes from the table, and with those eyes alight, he grinned from one enormous ear to the other.

———∿∿∿———

"Our first goal," the president said, his head stiff as he gazed across the House chamber, "is to confront and prevent any attacks on our country or on our friends and allies. We have begun such work by supporting the stabilizing force offered by the new Iraq regime. Still, Iraq is beset by insurgents who would do us harm, insurgents who are attempting to carry on the failed mission of their fellow terrorists. North Korea has and will continue to expand its nuclear capabilities. And Iran, with its long history of threats against the United States and her allies, and with its proximity to our project of hope in Iraq, once again proves itself dangerous."

He paused, glanced down, and returned his squinting stare to the assembled. When he spoke, his voice had never sounded firmer.

"These states, and the terrorists they support, constitute an Axis of Evil. We have seen such forces gather before in our history, and we will ensure that they meet the same end."

The chamber shook with applause and calls and hurrahs. Near the end of a row, claustrophobically pushed against the wall, Matt had been mouthing just about every word the president said, checking against the copy of the speech he held. But when that phrase came up—that phrase, the one he already regretted, the one that had pushed itself out of his mouth like the vomit it was—Matt had pursed his lips tightly together.

"Fuck it," Shay said to him beneath the applause. "I can admit when I'm wrong."

"It'll play in Peoria," Matt responded.

"It'll play in New York City. We're going to release some of the details of the plans by the August plotters to give us a boost. You know what their target was?"

"You can tell me later," Matt said.

"Surprised you didn't hear it from that asshole Redgrave. Fucking loony. Even a blind pig finds an acorn sometimes." Shay sat down as the hall quieted and the president continued. "He's simmered down a bit, but I'm telling you, the guy's going to be a problem," Shay whispered. "At least the people on the interior of the country think *they* should be afraid. And that's good."

"So we should give him a medal."

"The fuck we should."

As soon as he could, Matt slinked away from the House chamber and made his way home. Kris had texted. *What the hell was that? Axis of Evil?*

He promised to explain. He didn't know how yet, but it sure as hell would involve a story about his properly outraged dissent, how he'd been overruled, and how, as they'd often discussed, life was simply full of compromises. And then he might ask her about this Oliver Redgrave guy and if he was as cozy with the press as Shay said he was.

———～∧∧～———

The Christian Right preened its white feathers; God's Will had given them a gift. The neo-cons gravely nodded their heads, their fleshy jowls wiggling; Kensington finally had the guts to tell it like it is, they said on talk shows across the country. By the end of the week, gun sales were skyrocketing, though it'd take awhile for that to show, and in lonely corners of cities and suburbs, Muslims kept their eyes on the sidewalks in front of them. "A holy war is what they want," one preacher called to his congregation in the vast and Technicolor-splashed cavern of an evangelical church in Iowa, "and a holy war is what we'll give them."

When the numbers came in, Matt was alone at his desk in the White House. He still hadn't had the courage to put a photo of himself and Kris on his desk, and now he wondered if it was because she'd always be looking at him while he worked. Broussard knocked, beaming, and handed him a memo:

Percent surveyed who believe Iraq is responsible for thwarted terrorist attacks: 77 percent

Percent surveyed who believe Iran is a greater threat than Iraq: 65 percent

Broussard hugged him.

Downstairs, in the situation room, he entered to applause, and Kensington reached forward for his hand. "Helluva job, Matt. Helluva job." Shay, with his bland face, bland and colorless as a fried egg, grinned. Even Gail was clapping.

On the screen, a live feed from an army base showed C-130s being loaded.

That night, he ate alone and watched reruns. Kris was in the Congo for a week, and with a fresh horror, he realized that now, in all likelihood, she'd be dispatched to cover the war in Iraq. And it would become a war. Already the Shiites were challenging their supposed Godfather, the Sunnis were arming, and the Kurds were watching—they feared the unknown, just like Americans, just like anyone. And into that fray were headed, Webb had said, ten thousand troops. And Kris, armed with her camera.

He pulled Larry Bird onto his chest as he lay on the couch and stared at the ceiling. The press corps was in shock over the polling numbers. The Democrats, too, with a spicing of outrage. Already, on the nightly cable news shows, they were saying the White House had conned the American public. Astutely they pointed to the term Matt couldn't now bear repeating in his head—it repeated, though, over and again—but how conveniently the press forgot that while Matt and his crew, and Shay, and Webb, and Gail, and the president were all spinning, they had remained silent. Knowing they were culpable, Matt thought sadly, the press and the Dems would let it pass. Preach to their most agreeable choirs, and then sing along with that big choir smack dab in the middle. Those 77 percent. If they wanted to keep their jobs.

Cory had already called. Three times. "Monstrous ignorance," he'd said in one message. But really, Matt would tell him, once he had the stomach for it, really, wasn't it plausible deniability? Keep us safe, the American people shouted, and spare us the details. You did *what*? Well, we didn't know *that*.

Maybe all you could say was that you'd done your job. You listened to those men above you. The ones with years of experience. The ones who lived and breathed the details, who could name remote towns in Iran the way they recalled their first kisses. Maybe all you could say was, "This is my job, Kris. I don't make policy. I make the policies popular."

If you wanted to cast blame, go to the source. He was just the stream. The wind. You couldn't ask the river to stop flowing, could you?

He rolled over into the back of the couch, its leather warm, the scent somehow relaxing, and he let Larry Bird free to roam. The justifications continued. Sleep couldn't come fast enough—or Kris's arms too soon.

PART THREE: BLOOD IN THE WATER

CHAPTER 1

In the year and a half since President Kensington's Axis of Evil speech, Iraq had broken apart; its wounds had festered and been administered to by an increasing number of American troops, the bones reset, the fractures fused, the skin sewn—and still the wounds had reopened, and each time they were worse. In January of 2002, Allied troops totaled hardly over one thousand. By early June 2003, the number had reached one hundred thousand. Most of them were American, since the majority of the Allies had withdrawn their forces.

There was no clear battle plan, claimed the critics; what had begun as the stabilization of a region and a pursuit of reported terrorist cells had quickly devolved into nation-building in the midst of a civil war, that is, in the midst of a nation that didn't know how to rebuild and wasn't even sure it wanted to. Kidnappings, roadside IEDs, young men barely sixteen years old strapping bombs to their chests with duct tape and skulking into crowded markets: these had only increased, and, by the spring, had reached a fever pitch. Nearly eighty thousand Iraqi civilians had died, reported various bureaus—estimates disputed by the White House.

Meanwhile, Iran had kept silent across the border, like a patient in the waiting room—nervously observing the activity, listening to the screams, offering encouraging words to its brothers, mainly the Shia, and otherwise biding its time, content to begin construction on a uranium-enrichment facility near Qom which would not be discovered for many years to come.

In the United States, a civil war raged on in the thoughts, minds, and hearts of either side, though to say only two sides existed was a simplistic device, used only by face politicians and the harpy-like members of the media. The 77 percent of the public who believed Iraq was involved in the terror plots of 2001 begged for answers and results; as they were denied, month by month, their numbers had dipped closer to the median, the dreaded deadlock. Those on the middle ground were less anxious than they'd been—despite a bombing in Madrid, a bombing in London, and the thousands of bombings tearing Iraq to shreds— and kept to their daily lives, working and playing in the habits they knew, even as the far Right and the far Left grew louder by the day. For those extremists, the war changed their lives—and it was now a war, they believed, which the middle resisted—and they spent weekends and vacations picketing each other, claiming the war was a mission of God or crying that the entire war had been fabricated by Kensington and his cohorts. The isolationists clung to the middle, fearing expansion, yet unable to deny that threats against their homeland still existed. The churches remained split according to their denominations. There were no easy answers, few simple positions, in a country so vast. And yet, in the fever of that early summer, you had to claim a spot; even if you tried to avoid it, even if you believed you had been able to avoid it, you were forced to stake your claim, somehow, by someone. Because no one could escape. Whether it was the price of gasoline; a sister or lover being shipped overseas; mid-term elections for Congress or for small-town mayors; the traffic downtown during a protest or the lonely picketer at the end of a suburban road; the relived pain of a veteran; the mysterious past of a cousin; the songs being sung in the high school choirs and the churches; a get-rich scheme selling flag lapels; the ceaseless questions of a young next-door neighbor; arguments at work or arguments on the bus, at the bank, in the bars; or the draping of that heavy red, white and blue cloth over a casket—there was no escape.

⌣⌣⌣

At the top of a verdant hill at the edge of Shenandoah National Park, Matt waited in the cool of twilight for two headlights to appear on the dirt road. Kris's plane ought to have landed three hours ago, but then, flying the Baghdad Special, as she called it, wasn't exactly like hopping on Southwest from Cleveland to Phoenix. Still, he checked his watch and shouted to Shelly, inside the cabin, to see if there'd been any disasters on the news. She came to the door, holding Larry Bird on her shoulder like a sack of flour. "You're a worry-wart," she said.

When Kris had proposed the idea of a weekend retreat—complete with Shelly, Larry Bird, Kris's sister, Margaret, and his cousin, Cory, neither of whom could make it until Saturday—Matt had been skeptical. The past few months had been rough; she was gone a lot, he was busier with plans for the reelection campaign, and the national strain was taking its toll on them; the sparks created by their friction, their passionate yet tolerated differences of opinion, were either fading like embers or threatening to burst into out-and-out flames. Week to week, it was hard to tell, and so he'd wondered if she wanted this getaway to re-evaluate him, to see how far he'd sunk working for Shay and Webb and Kensington. But that was before she left for Baghdad. And before thirty-seven people had been killed near her newspaper's bureau. Before the e-mail from her that said she'd been part of an interview with a now-legless insurgent. Before she'd ridden along to Falluja, for Christ's sake.

You did this, he told himself. You gave her a new place to go die.

Finally, her headlights broke over a hill, and her rickety pickup was bouncing up the road. He called for Shelly again, and, amid the darkness lit by errant fireflies, they watched Kris approach. When her truck lurched to a stop, they practically attacked the door.

She looked exhausted. The creamy texture of her face had been burned and dried, her lips chapped as if cut a hundred times by a paring knife.

"Hey, beautiful," he said, kissing her. She seemed to fall into him. But when they pulled apart, she didn't look him in the eye, and merely reached for Shelly and Larry Bird.

"The creek," she said distantly, pronouncing it "crik." "I want to take a bath in the creek."

"Right now?"

"Yes."

"Okay," he said slowly. "Let's get your bags inside."

"Did you bring us pictures?" Shelly said.

"Later, you," Kris said, smiling sweetly, but a tincture of pain in her pale blue eyes.

They unloaded what luggage she'd not bothered to unpack at her apartment in Old Town, and, taking a Maglite from the cabin, treaded down the backside of the hill, Kris bundling the fresh set of clothes Matt had brought for her. She had been in Baghdad a little over a month—"It's a crucial time over there," she'd said—and already it was plain to see that something had changed in her. Maybe it was just the exhaustion, Matt told himself. But when they reached the creek, Kris stripped off her T-shirt and her bra without any warning.

"Whoa," said Shelly, backing away.

In the gloomy shadows of the overhanging trees, Kris lowered herself into the creek wearing only her underwear, until she was up to her waist. As Matt sat on the bank to kick off his shoes, he swept the Maglite across her accidentally, and it lit an enormous bruise along the right side of her abdomen, a continent-shaped mass of purple and yellow.

"Water," she groaned happily before she dunked herself.

"Isn't it cold?" Shelly said like a true city girl.

"Not nearly cold enough," said Kris, splashing.

An hour later they were getting drunk on chilled wine, Shelly was falling asleep, and in her fresh athletic shorts and Texas Tech T-shirt, Kris was—out of nowhere—talking about her ex-husband. "The main thing that destroyed us was his loss of passion," she said. "When I met him, he was full of life, interested in everything. But he was in corporate law, always worried about moving up the ladder. It took him over."

"Is this a warning or a marriage proposal?"

They were lying in the crook of a seventy-foot oak tree's gnarled roots, and she leaned against his left shoulder, wincing, then looking down the hill into the dark. "Neither," she said. "Well, maybe a warning. It's why I was reluctant when we met. It's easy to get consumed, to get caught up in the neo-con grasp. Sometimes, for your own sake, you need to step back."

"Are these the lessons of Baghdad?"

"You could say that."

He kissed her neck firmly, put his fingers to her cheek, and kissed her lips. When he opened his eyes, she was staring at him. He smiled gently.

"How'd you get the bruise on your side?"

"A car accident." She patted his hand, squeezed it. "Just a regular old car accident. Our driver last week was not a defensive driver. Over there, no one is. Or everyone is, depending on you look at it."

"Was it serious?"

"Serious enough for a bruise," she said.

"Did your ex mind you puddle-jumping all the time?"

She sneered. "Gave him a chance to 'get to know' a few women." Shifting her weight away from her right side, she looked at him again with those distressed eyes. "He hated my photography. At first I thought he was just like my dad, that he just didn't get it, you know?"

"I thought your dad bought you your first camera."

"He did. He came around; Paul didn't. He eventually admitted that he'd never believed—never—that I had talent."

"Clearly he was an idiot."

"Shh. What are those birds?"

He listened to the worried warbling from the tree above them. "Not sure. Tell you what, though, today I've counted about ten different types of birds by their songs in this tree alone," he said. "A veritable orchestra. Two types of orioles, the Baltimore and the orchard; a couple of song sparrows; finches; wrens; even a blue jay. And of course, way up at the top, a mockingbird. That's the real difference from the city: there you get a lot of noise, but not the mixture of sound you get out here."

"A mass of contradictions," she said, smiling weakly, and he wasn't sure if she meant him or the birds—or maybe the war. "I'm glad you like it out here," she added, her face drooping, "because I think I'm moving out here. I think I'm giving up photography."

—⁓⩗⁓—

She wasn't kidding. Her voice clenched and heavy, she explained the horrors she'd seen in Baghdad. If you stayed in the Green Zone, life didn't seem so bad, but the instant you drove away from it, you had a sense that your life was tenuous, even meaningless—and if she thought that, then what did the orphans and widows living in filth think? Or the army kid from Ohio who'd just been standing there in Fallujah, just standing there, when a blade of gunfire disintegrated his legs?

And she'd captured it. The sun-beaten stares, the boys bleeding in the sand. That's when the idea had started speaking to her. This was horrible. Impossible.

"But it's all I know how to do," she shouted, her breath sour from the wine.

They fell asleep in the hold of the tree, nothing resolved, nothing except, for Matt, the sureness that he'd driven her to this place.

In the chill and mist of morning, Cory's car rambled up the road, followed an hour later by Kris's sister, Margaret; even then, Kris remained subdued, fixing home fries and bacon on a heavy cast-iron skillet with a sad smile while Margaret and Cory traded stories about the two lovebirds. The cabin was cramped, and Matt watched in frustration as Kris stewed and he was unable to talk with her. After breakfast, he wandered outside, hoping she'd trail him, but he sat on the hillside alone for a good twenty minutes, the air still cool enough for the steam to rise out of his coffee mug like dragon's breath, before Cory ambled down to him.

"Kris's sister's the spitting image," he said. "Shorter, though. Cute ass—"

"She's a train wreck, Cory," he said, unwillingly thinking of Kris. "Stick to Ms. O'Malley. You talk to her recently?"

"She might come out in July, unless I have to go overseas."

"Yeah, I've heard that before."

Cory sat heavily on the grass beside him. His cousin's cheeks were a little plumper, his thighs a little thicker; too much time behind his desk at the Ag Department, Matt thought. Overseas, my ass.

"I've been thinking about Tess lately," Cory said. "A lot."

After a moment, Matt said, "That'll get you nowhere."

"She was a wonderful woman, but in death, I've made her perfect. Nobody could live up to that. Wouldn't be fair. And I never want to get hurt like that again." He inhaled deeply, squeezed his cheeks tightly. "Ah, it's just the season. And these politics. She had some strong opinions—"

"Doesn't everyone."

Now why in the hell was he picking on Cory, especially about his dead lover? Sure, Tess had been Cory's excuse for years of avoiding anything real with Carrie, but why pick that scab now?

Cory leaned into his line of vision. A challenge to the territorial man.

"What crawled up your ass and died?" Cory said. "Planning another third-world takeover?"

Matt slid his eyes toward his cousin, then away, fighting the urge to throw an elbow, like he'd have done when they were twelve. If only the problems of the world could be solved with an elbow to the head; if only that meant a hundred thousand people wouldn't die.

"That job'll kill you," Cory said quietly. "Look, Matt, you know I've met a lot of people over the years, people up to their elbows in foreign affairs. And I know you see me as just some guy who travels around the world studying crops."

"No, Cory, you don't know how much respect I have for you and your job," Matt sneered. "I know for a fact the only agriculture experience you had before you got that job was growing a few marijuana plants in your college dorm. Now you influence the world's food supply. That's impressive."

"Don't get pissed, Short Fuse."

Matt laughed. "I remember, back in your drinking days, the time you pissed on a stack of BP oil cans because they didn't have a bathroom … right in front of everyone."

"Quit the bullshit, Matt, come on. We need to talk."

"No one's stopping you."

"Okay. Over the years I've made these contacts, and I can tell you it's the consensus of everybody outside a few military hacks—and even a few of them would agree—that the president, the way he's talking about Iran, to Iran—well, it's a terrible mistake. It's almost like he's taunting them. And we're getting deeper in Iraq every day—"

"My job isn't policy."

"But you have the ear of Shay. You convince him, and he convinces Webb in political terms." Cory grinned optimistically, the trainer urging his champ to get back out there and fight.

"Shay listens to me on small things. Nothing like this. He'd think I've lost my mind if I—"

"But maybe you could get him to talk to more people. My friends can talk to people in the State Department, other voices at the Defense

Department, even the CIA—they'd love to get the chance to speak up. You know they have other strategies they've been working on?"

"Who the hell do you know at the CIA?"

"Just a guy or two. There's so much to this that hasn't been thought through. The consequences, Matt." His voice pitched up as he leaned in, rambling on about the same things Shay and Webb talked about daily, and with glee: destabilizing the Middle East, empowering Muslim extremists, taunting Iran, taunting Pakistan and their bomb program. He clutched Matt's forearm. "Get some goddamn outside sources, call in old favors. Do it for yourself, even if it's futile, even if Shay fires you."

Matt glared at Cory. He thought of the kid from Ohio with his legs blown away. Thought of Kris snapping his picture, her head in crosshairs.

"It's bigger than me now," he said distantly.

Cory shook his head. "No, it's these guys, these men driven by greed and power. That and the people's monstrous ignorance of the world."

"Do you really think that Webb, Shay, and I are responsible for 77 percent of the public believing Iraq was behind the terrorist attacks?"

"It's down to 53 percent," Cory said quietly.

"I know. But that's what got the ball rolling. People want to stay ignorant." He bent forward, craning his neck in a grotesque posture. He'd been given the way out, hadn't he? "'Oh, politics are in such a hurry,' they say. 'It's too complicated,' they say. 'Leave us out of it.' These people don't have a fucking clue, and they don't care. You know who did care? Those 23 percent who knew the Iraq connection to the attacks was bullshit."

The word rang down the hill. After a silence, he stood, awkwardly planting his foot on the downward slope, righting himself and pouring out his coffee. So what if Cory knew? It's not like his cousin was about to stand up on a soapbox. At least not to anyone but Matt.

"I haven't given up on this country, Matt."

"Neither have I. But maybe some of these people are smart enough to understand: let those in the know decide what's best. That's what I do. I do my job and otherwise keep my fucking head down."

He started up the hill, torn between dashing the mug against the chair-tree and throwing himself down the rocky slope and hoping for a concussion. And they had another whole night to get through.

"You can't be proud of those numbers, can you?" Cory said below him.

His face turned bright red, but he managed to bite his tongue until the anger faded. He remembered the gleam in Shay's eyes when he'd seen those numbers. At least Cory knew him well enough to know he was bothered by it. At least he was still somewhat recognizable.

He continued up the hill without answering.

The rest of the weekend had gone about as smoothly as the C-130 nosedive into Baghdad that Kris had described. Margaret, who was indeed a train wreck, spent most her time flipping her hair over her shoulder, cursing her ex-husband, flirting with Cory, and attempting to teach Shelly a lesson or two about the evils of men. Kris took to pacing, trying to block out her sister, and sometime in the afternoon began snapping at everything Matt said. And when the conversation over Monopoly turned to the war, turned to the White House, they all looked at Matt, this liberal coalition—even Shelly, who hated Kensington for the way he talked and "laughed like a chimp"—and Matt was forced to sit there and take it. Did he tell them how to do their jobs? Did he suggest Kris boycott black-and-white photography? Did he insist to Cory that the fields of Belarus were prime for corn, not soy?

When they'd arrived back in Old Town at Kris's apartment, she didn't invite them in. He protested until she sighed impatiently. "I need a little time to decompress," she said at his car door.

"Maybe we should have put off the trip until next weekend."

"Well, we all make mistakes," Kris said. The effect was chilling. Was he the mistake? Had she realized that he was the mouth of the enormous war machine which hadn't just sent her to Iraq but had put into place, like a movie set, every horror she'd witnessed?

As he drove Shelly and LB through the dusk-settled streets, the last thing he needed was his fifteen-year-old neighbor's advice. But she gave it, in her blunt fashion, "Man is she pissed at you. I'd back off awhile."

"What did she say to you?"

"She said you're going blind."

"Cory talked to her."

Shelly nodded and turned up the radio. He turned it back down, though he said nothing and had nothing to say.

"Guess you're gonna have to wait to pop the question, huh?"

"I guess."

"Yeah," said Shelly. "I'd wait, too."

CHAPTER 2

The sour turn of the weekend still weighed on him the next morning when Shay burst into his office and tossed a newspaper across his curved desk, scattering memos and a rundown for the noon press conference.

"Where the fuck have you been?" said Shay.

"Off the grid. Why?"

Shay stared at him as if it should be obvious. With a blustery sigh, he pointed to Sunday's *Washington Post* and told Matt to read the editorial page. There Matt found a lengthy diatribe about the administration's manipulation of the situation in Iraq, written by a terrorism expert named Oliver Redgrave.

"This guy again," Matt muttered.

"Yeah, this guy. Again." Shay simmered a moment, then calmly shut Matt's office door. He plopped into the red cloth-backed chair opposite Matt, glanced away, then said coolly, "Something needs to be done about this."

No attribution, Matt noticed. Not good. Whenever some dirty shit needed doing, nobody's name was used as a subject. Except for his own.

"We've headed off every plot, Stephen. He's just pissing in the wind."

"And it's coming back on us." He folded his hands across his lap. "We need to get information out there. To the media."

"What kind of information?"

"Without our fingerprints on it, you understand?"

One of Shay's thin eyebrows arched. As Matt swept back his thick hair, Broussard called to ask where the eight o'clock meeting was being

157

held. The Roosevelt Room, Matt told him, adding that Broussard should start the meeting without him.

"This won't take a minute," Shay said. "Redgrave was definitely your reporter friend's source back in August of 2001." Shay grinned, licking his lips. He pulled an apple from his jacket and took a nibble, as if he was waiting for Matt to piece something together. "He's CIA, Matt. Redgrave has been a CIA agent since the early 1980s."

"How are you sure?"

"Avenues and back alleys. Doesn't matter. He's been demoted, I've heard, and in fact"—Shay leaned forward greedily—"he's under investigation for treason. He sold secrets to our enemies."

"Is that empirically true or speculatively?"

"Totally true. It's confirmed," Shay said slowly. "You will choose a few trustworthy reporters, and you will spread the word: Redgrave is a CIA traitor." He leaned back and cut into the apple with his tiny, rat-like teeth.

Matt stared at him, remembering what Cory had said. *You convince Shay, and Shay convinces Webb.* Sure, Cory. Have you forgotten that shit rolls downhill? When Stephen Shay walks into your office with a command—stiff and focused, almost certainly taking an order from Webb—then you, naive country boy, do as you're told.

Still, for Cory, Matt took a chance. "I don't know. This is pretty coarse."

"Don't forget what he did," Shay said. "It was years ago, and now the guy drives in and out of Langley in a top-down convertible, his wife looks like a supermodel—anyone who wanted to know he's an agent, well, they could find out pretty goddamn easily." Glancing at the apple, he held it up to Matt and pointed at its green skin. "A perfect apple is a beautiful thing. But one worm, burrowing its way inside, can ruin the whole fucking thing. And this isn't about one worm, Matt. It's about a thousand others, waiting to fuck us. The message to them would be, 'Hey, CIA loudmouths, are you ready for the world to know your identity? No? Then don't fuck with us.'"

"The man saved thousands of American lives—"

"But he's going to cost thousands if he keeps on like this." Shay placed the apple on a memo, the juice leaking onto the paper, and peered over his eyeglasses. "Matt, I'm proud of you. The past two years, you've really kicked ass. You've been the bully with the over-the-top reaction, but you've done it your way. A little charm, some careful choices. Those faggots in the press corps eat out of your hand." Shay beamed.

Matt couldn't help but smile, even though he knew Shay was greasing him. Shay didn't grease up just anyone, and it was comforting to know that his relentless work over the past two and half years in this godforsaken office had at least earned him a little clout.

"We need this, kid. This doesn't have to be a big story. If it's just mentioned in a couple of columns, we'll have what we need. Pick the reporters you know will go to jail to protect their source. Then you have nothing to worry about."

Matt lowered his head, staring absently at the letters on the keyboard of his laptop, staring so long that he began to pick out the letters in Redgrave's name.

"How soon?" he finally muttered.

"Right away."

Shay stood, collected his apple, and took a final incisive nibble.

———٨٨——

Knowing the drinks would be on the company dime, Buddy Porter had suggested they meet at the bar in the Hay-Adams, two blocks north of the White House. And so, after calling Shelly and asking her to stay at the house a little later, and after calling Kris to see how she was doing—her voice was distant, shaky, but she insisted she was fine—Matt found himself crouching over a Tanqueray and tonic and watching the clock behind the venerable bar tick closer and closer to eleven. Still time to back out, his instincts murmured. To take a different approach. To lay this at the feet of a different journalist. To pass the whole fucking thing off to Broussard. But what was the worst that could happen to a guy like Redgrave? He was writing articles and teaching courses at Yale, for God's sake, so he was hardly an active agent. Shit, he'd probably get a book deal out of the whole thing.

It was the ongoing love-hate affair between Matt and Buddy Porter that made the diminutive and overweight journalist such an appealing first choice. Flattered, Buddy would go to Gitmo to protect Matt's identity. And he knew Kris. When they'd first begun dating, she'd told him not to worry about that blow-up the two men had had in the Press Corps office; months later, Buddy had winked at him and said, with those salacious eyes of his, "You got a winner there, Risen."

At quarter past eleven, Buddy tumbled into the bar, aptly named Off the Record, and squeezed himself into the booth across from Matt. Sweating like he'd been walking in the midday July sun, Buddy ordered a highball and launched into one of his frantic monologues of inquiry. What was that bullshit today from McCowan about going into Afghanistan? Were that guy's days numbered, or what? Where'd Kris flown into? "How did she like the 'Dad?" Buddy said with a sneer that revealed a newly-capped tooth.

Two drinks in and fifteen minutes before close, Matt said, "Buddy, you've been good to us. Fair enough, you know? I owe you one."

"The wheel's already lubed, Risen. Gimme something substantial."

"You're not talking to me."

"I'm talking to a ghost. Come on."

Matt flattened the cocktail napkin around the edges of his drink. "This Oliver Redgrave shit storm," he said. "We've got data that contradicts his. And he's the supposed expert."

"The guy's a crackerjack."

"Yeah, well, he sees what he wants to. And we think he has an axe to grind." Buddy's furry eyebrows perked. "We just want a fair shake."

"What's the grind?"

Matt's stomach tightened. "You probably already know this, but he's CIA."

Somewhat unimpressed, Buddy told Matt to continue.

"There's an investigation going on—"

"About Redgrave?"

"Into treason charges. Yeah, Redgrave. He sold off some information."

Buddy slumped back, the same grotesque hooked-fish sneer on his lips. "This come from Webb?"

"No," Matt said quickly. "Far as I know, he doesn't have a clue."

"And, what, you think Redgrave's trying to get in a few digs before he gets taken down?"

"I can't speak to the man's motivations."

"You said he has an axe to grind."

"He's CIA, Buddy. They all do."

Buddy grinned. "Half those guys are nuts."

"Look, he's a pencil-pusher, far as we know."

"Who sold secrets. Why's this just coming out now?"

"I don't know, Buddy. Christ, I'm just the messenger."

The bartender rang an old-fashioned bell and called, "Last call!" Matt ordered them another round, though the periphery of his vision was getting starlit and fuzzy.

"You want me to write about this?" Buddy said slowly.

Matt eyed him. Now that he'd forced out the lie, the familiar methods of manipulation were a relief. "Do what you want with it," he said off-handedly. "But you were talking to a ghost tonight, understand?"

Buddy nodded. "A midnight creeper."

While Buddy chewed on the info, Matt stared out the hotel bar window. Through the trees of Lafayette Square, the pale glow of the White House was eerie and potent.

Once Buddy had tottered off, Matt interred himself in a men's room stall. Too much liquor in too short a time. An old nervous habit, one he fell into whenever he was scared shitless. He retched a second, desperate time. "Making offerings to the porcelain god," Cory liked to say, when they were younger and could afford to be stupid.

He got off the phone with Nesbit from *Newsweek* as Judy Hill from *The New York Times* strolled into his office, a Cheshire grin stretching her already wide face. She nearly hopped into a chair. Damn it; Buddy had already gotten to her.

"I just want to know if this is legit," she said, bouncing one knee over the other. "Or if it's payback."

He clicked off the television on the bookshelf, itching for a cigarette like he hadn't all year. "Maybe that's your story, Judy."

"Maybe it is."

"Haven't I been good to you?" Matt said, letting his eyes droop just a tad. "Privileges on Air Force One, private time with the president. Why would you jeopardize that relationship?"

"Why would you lean on it?"

"He's biased. Redgrave. That's all."

She squinted and jotted down a note. "You realize the ramifications of—"

"I told Buddy: Redgrave is low-level, doesn't leave the country anymore."

"How do you think he evaluated the terror threat in Iraq?"

Matt laughed, even as his stomach spiraled. He'd only scanned Redgrave's latest editorial. Shay had never mentioned a recent overseas trip.

"Very carefully," he struggled to say.

"Is Shay talking?"

"Come on, Judy."

"Webb?"

"He's not in the loop on this." He laced his fingers. "You don't have to publish it, you know."

She stiffened. Damn right, thought Matt. Even if she wanted to go with the White House cover-up angle, their message would get out, the message he knew Shay really wanted broadcast: *don't fuck with us.* And how could any journalist—especially one working for a print newspaper with a declining readership and that had accustomed itself to the Internet age about as well as his Uncle Jess—pass up a story like this?

As it turned out, Hill was the only one who did pass it up. By the following week, the other four journalists he'd turned to weren't exactly singing the administration's song, but they had all revealed Redgrave's association with the CIA. And once they did, calls flooded Matt's office. Had the White House known about this? What was the president's stance? Don't bullshit us, they all hissed, practically in unison, jealous, really, that he hadn't picked them. Most had obviously put together what was going down, but proving it was a different matter. The best way to try to loosen up the facts on something like this was to hit Matt as hard as they could. He took his seventh call before 8:00 AM, batted away the questions, again heard the word traitor—applied to Redgrave as a question but subtly aimed at him, he felt—and once the conversation had ended, Matt tapped the receiver against the edge of his mahogany desk a couple of times, then stretched his arm back and with full force slammed the receiver down, which sent a piece of it flying against one of the three windows overlooking the North Lawn. Chunks of plastic littered his desk.

Shay poked his head into the office. "I heard," he said, beaming.

"Me killing my phone?" Matt shouted. "Everyone knows what we did."

"That's not what's in the papers."

"Between the lines, then."

"Just keep your shorts clean. You did what needed to be done. It's over."

You did. Not *we.* Shay was still beaming.

"I need to get backed up here," Matt said. "The Sunday shows are gonna be all over my ass. Why don't we get Gail on this?"

"No need to push the panic button yet. They can guess all they want."

"But Stephen, you didn't make the phone calls."

"Neither did you," Shay said with a wormy smile. "They can't prove shit. Stop acting like a pussy. Get your head right and start focusing on Ohio."

"What the hell does Ohio have to do with this?"

"The election."

Shay's laser-like stare fixed him. He pinched his eyes shut and massaged a throbbing blood vessel over his ear, struggling to redirect his thoughts.

"This Massachusetts gay marriage amendment has the Midwest all fired up. We can play it somehow—"

"I'm disappointed, Matt. You think I'd be slow on a thing like that?"

"But how does that help us in Ohio?"

"We get an amendment on the ballot *banning* gay marriage," Shay said with a wink. "The Christian Right comes out in droves. We've lost some mojo with them over the war. Shit, we'll even go into states that already prohibit it."

"Including Ohio."

"Gail's already on it. Ohio or bust."

"What makes you so sure?"

Shay backed out of the doorway, saying, "It's like your birds, kid: instinct."

CHAPTER 3

Three deadbolts clicked and the door of Yuri Nesterenko's apartment gracefully creaked inward, followed by the massive Butcher himself, dancing to a tune stuck in his head, a swaying gypsy-like tune, the source of which remained deep in his memory. With a playful but lumbering kick, he shut the door and set his groceries on the counter. He began to brew some Woland-brand dark roast coffee, and while it bubbled, he danced over to his computer, entered his password, and rubbed the white soul patch under his lips as he studied again the name that had given him so much pleasure: Oliver Redgrave.

In his photo, the American's peppered hair was swept back and parted in the middle, as if his skull were being primed for a hatchet. With the stern, baggy eyes of a man accustomed to long days and nights of reading, Redgrave stared at him. A stranger, this man. He had not been in the hotel bloodbath that night in Florence. But he might have been connected to those who were.

Meanwhile, the Orbweaver software sifted through terabytes of information, much of it painstakingly digitalized by Yuri over the past year: surveillance photographs, operation debriefings, hurried sketches, journals kept by Nikolai and Mikhail, and personnel logs.

Yuri poured himself a cup of coffee and swayed back to the computer.

He worked for hours as rain beat against the rattling, half-open window, the hot air gusting in despite the fans oscillating in two corners of the room. Redgrave's photograph was saved, affixed to his file, and run through a image-recognition program in the Orb against photos of known and suspected CIA agents. Likewise, an interview he'd given on American television, available on YouTube, was processed by a vocal-recognition program—if only Yuri had known! How much time would have been saved! The gleaming new casing of the external hard drive vibrated and a rich cyan light blinked patiently. Alternately hunched over the computer and pacing, Yuri watched the meager results. For more than a year, nothing had checked out.

In fact, when he'd seen the search result this afternoon—a number of articles from American newspapers—he'd thought it too good to be true. And yet all of the stories said the same thing, implying that the man's biases had gotten the better of him, and that he'd sold information to America's enemies years ago.

Innocently the computer beeped. His heart drumming martially, Yuri clicked on an entry in the Saboteur data file, a compendium of businesses suspected of being CIA fronts. In 1986 Redgrave had worked for Wisconsin Food Laboratories, supposedly a grain researcher, primarily, but also, the Kremlin had suspected, a provider of food to dissident Soviets and Afghan infiltrators in the motherland. They had operated out of Moscow from 1985 to 1986 and in Florence in 1987. And, once he'd narrowed down the search parameters, Yuri discovered that three suspects in the hotel execution had also worked for Wisconsin Food Labs.

So few photographs, really, compared to the mountains of names and aliases, and yet here were three passport photos, like gifts from Lenin himself: the man with black-as-shoe-polish hair and a pale face; the other man whose blond and curly hair made him seem very young, very idealistic; and the blonde bitch who'd died in the elevator. He quickly compared them to surveillance photos from the Hotel Bernini Palace; you could just make out the shellac shine of the pale man's hair and the woman's undignified strut. Undoubtedly the same. And the rookie with the curly hair—well, he'd never forget that face.

"I have you," he whispered.

It was early morning, the rain had subsided, and the pavement hissed with the sound of bleary traffic. Eagerly he filled a paper bag with thick *karofka* pieces and stuffed some loose change into his pants pockets. This was a day for splurging on the children. Just one day of giddy, youthful relief. And then it was back to a butcher's work.

CHAPTER 4

TRAITOR IN THE WHITE HOUSE?

So read the headline on *The O'Toole Factor*'s special Sunday night edition. The goddamn *O'Toole Factor*! Fucking allies!

Kris sat with her knees hunched to her chest, and Matt tapped his foot nervously at the other end of the leather couch. Some idiot from the RNC was not helping matters by downplaying Redgrave's CIA status; it was too obvious a move, and even if he hadn't been covert, he'd worked with covert agents. That much was clear now.

"Tell me this is bullshit," Kris said.

He glanced at her: pale-rose cheeks, worn-out eyes.

"Matt?"

"I can't talk about it," he said at a clip.

Standing, he cracked his knuckles. Apparently Kris hadn't seen the morning roundtable shows. He'd done about as well on *Meet the Press* as this RNC goon. Glancing again at Kris, he saw behind her eyes a landscape of worry, of disappointment. Wheels grinding, exit strategies formulating. She'd sacrificed, gone to Iraq, put her feet on the soil there, and so had Redgrave—again, helpful information Shay might have shared with him, not that it would have made a difference. Redgrave and Kris moved in the light, he and Shay in the cool summery shadows.

"I've got to call Shay."

"Do what you need to," she said quietly.

"We didn't do this."

"Then why are you calling Shay?"

Twenty minutes of obfuscation later, he was speeding to the White House. Shay had called a meeting for a little later in the night, and as Matt climbed the stairwell to his mentor's office on the second floor, he kept tugging on his staff creds. They could throw him under the bus. Shit, maybe this was Gail's revenge—she was Webb's chief of staff, his ex-lover, and a woman with connections like a 1950s switchboard.

He pushed open Shay's door. "I want protection," he blurted.

Shay peered up at him with that wormy smile.

"Hell, we'd all like protection, Matt. Getting it's the problem." He swiveled a bit on his chair and put his hands behind his globular head. "You're a praying man, right?"

Shay's laxness insulted his own quaking.

"Why me?"

"Because I want to ruin your life, Matt, drag you down into the pits of hell!" Shay laughed like a drunk and homeless old man. "Come on, kid. What the fuck do you think? You're the best. The press loves you. Shit, you're the only one in this administration they're happy to protect. Just play your part: deny everything. Think of what we did during the primaries in Carolina."

"This isn't digging up some dirt on an opponent."

"You didn't just dig it up, you fucking slathered it, Matt."

Again with the *you*, not *we*. He put his hands on the back of the only other chair in Shay's office, which was Spartan to the point of nothingness.

"I didn't even realize I'd broken the law until the third time a reporter brought it up."

Shay's face bloomed violently. "Broken the *law*?" he said, his hands slowly descending from behind his head to clutch the arm rests of his red leather chair. "Human behavior. Needs and desires. *Those* are laws." Shay lurched forward, his glasses askew on his nose. "Everything else is politics, and the laws written down, you want to tell me those are absolutes? Yeah, go find me a fucking judge who thinks *that*. We make the laws: we, the people in power." His face shook, his cheeks as red as a sunburn. "Did you break some pissant law? Who the fuck cares? *How* it gets done is for the sewers. *What* gets done, that's important. That's history."

He'd worked himself into such a furor, he was standing. He snapped open a desk drawer and whipped out a bottle of McCutcheon, and as he wiped a tumbler with his handkerchief and splashed out a double, he said, "You're worrying me, kid. I thought we'd been through this. When the shit sprays, the person on the podium can't duck and cover. He has to take it—all of it—the scandal, the screaming, the outright disloyalty. It'll just slide right off you."

"It's too late for me to duck and cover anyway."

"I told you that Amazon woman would be a problem—"

"Leave her out of it."

"That she'd get in your head. Listen to yourself. She already has."

Matt jumped back and shoved the backside of the chair. "I'm not going to tell you ever again: stay the fuck out of my personal life."

Silently they stared each other down. Then, slowly, Shay's lips pursed into something like a smile.

"Take a little time off," he said.

Which was usually code for "leave so we can tear you apart behind your back."

"Yeah, that won't look suspicious."

Shay waved his hand, lowered himself into his chair, and said they could discuss it at the meeting. "Gail's going to do a little damage control. A few journalists, a Cabinet member or two—throw them in the mix. Just to muddy the waters."

"Her own name's coming up," Matt said, not that he gave a shit.

"Everyone thinks this was Webb's plan."

"It wasn't?"

Shay downed the rest of the scotch, gulped, and said, "You just keep your mouth clamped shut, kid. All storms pass."

⌒〜ᴧ〜⌒

But this one took its sweet time. Judy Hill, who'd passed on the story at first, penned a column in the *Times* that Friday which did more than just imply the White House's knowledge. Her op-ed piece ran down all the good Redgrave had done over the years—including his most recent trip to Iraq, where he'd found no evidence of the terrorist training camps Kensington had mentioned or any evidence of a terrorist infrastructure before the attacks in 2001. In short, she said, all Redgrave proved was that American meddling in Iraqi politics had created a civil war and a new market for martyrs. *Would the dissent of a thirty-year veteran of international politics be enough to provoke this administration?* she wrote. *Would they stoop so low as to ruin an American citizen's professional and private life over a difference of perception? The Cold War is over. Hasn't he done enough to atone for his treasonous acts—if they even occurred?*

Matt was on the phone with her before breakfast. "You're killing us, Judy."

"You're killing yourselves," she responded, then hung up.

It got worse when Cory came home from one of his Ag Department trips the next day. He'd been bombarding Matt with calls and texts, all of which Matt had carefully ignored; so maybe Matt shouldn't have been surprised to drive up to his brownstone and see Cory on his stoop, hunched over in a red polo shirt, chatting with Shelly and stroking Larry Bird's rippled fur.

Without even giving Shelly a chance to extricate herself back into Matt's apartment, Cory said, "Tell me who did this."

"Cory, please." He tried to take a step past, but Cory leaned in front of his knee. "I'm exhausted." He studied his cousin's face: Cory's eyes were pink and weighed down by grayish bags, his curly hair uncombed. "You come straight from the airport?"

"I've been home since Thursday. We got finished early."

Matt shrugged and wedged his knee past Cory's face, not too delicately, nearly losing his balance on the stoop. "I've got some beers."

"Goddamn it, Matt."

Shelly's watery eyes were on him; she was used to his own self-loathing, and she'd even gotten used to his tiffs with Kris, but never had she seen him confronted like this by Cory. What *was* she seeing? A failing? Cracks in the armor? Or maybe she'd already seen those—Christ, what did a kid know anyway?

Pushing into the cool, stale air of his apartment, Matt loosened his tie as Cory followed, ranting about the way lower-level employees got shit on by the administration, by every administration, and how he was tired of taking it. "Tired of seeing people die," he blurted.

"Seeing who die?"

Cory slid his eyes toward the bookcase, where Larry Bird had climbed. "Suicides, I mean. The stress. It's taken down a few of us."

Shelly had passed them and gone into the cluttered kitchen, and she emerged with three beers in hand and passed one to him and one to Cory.

"Put that one back," Matt said.

"Dude," Shelly said, traipsing back to the fridge, defeated. "You guys are stressing me out."

"Oh, what's a little law-breaking, Matt?"

"Like you've broken a goddamn law in your life."

"You're both cussing a hell of a lot," Shelly muttered.

"I've broken some doozies," Cory said, "but I've never given up a CIA agent."

"Neither have I."

Cory took a slow swig, eyeing him over the lip and long brown bottle, then set it firmly on the banister. This was the Cory that you feared, the fire-eyed idealist who'd never been wrong. No, be honest: the idealist who'd been proved wrong many times, who'd learned, been battered by love, by the death of a lover, of *the one*, and still hadn't given up. Frazier in the fourteenth round. The lieutenant with his cold, killer voice.

"Was it Gail?" Cory said.

"We're going in circles."

"I guess we are."

He nodded at Shelly, told her to keep an eye on Matt, and stalked out the front door.

Matt had turned back to the day's mail that Shelly had piled on the credenza when she said, still standing in the kitchen doorway, "That's why I don't get politics. It's so urgent."

For a moment he was disappointed by her. In the past two years, she'd pulled her grades out of the sewer and revealed herself to be an intelligent young woman. But still, she was fifteen. Her personal war with her parents was just that: personal.

"Thirty-something people died near the building Kris worked at in Iraq," he said quietly. "It was urgent to them, whether they knew it or not."

After another brief silence, she asked if Redgrave was going to die.

"No," Matt said, too quickly to believe it himself. He couldn't be sure. It was all slipping out of his hands.

Chapter 5

One man can only know so much, Gail Turner thought as she jogged along the Tidal Basin path, holding her back straight and her head high, looking for the next body to get through, past, or ahead of. The whole story was bigger than any single person. The key was to spread little morsels around—a name to this journalist, a date to this one. It only made them hungrier to find out. Everyone wanted to get to the source of the story, its white-hot center. Maybe that's what was so goddamn exciting about this job; she was as near to the center as she could be, where the heat boiled the sweat out of your skin, baptized you day after day.

Gail slithered through the crowd, sticking out her elbows to make a cut between other joggers and pedestrians, carefully judging her angles. As she sped along the path, she scanned through the crowd and nearly stopped dead in her tracks. Tightening her eyes, she focused on the woman on the bench, doubted for a second, brushed past some old fart on his Sunday run, and saw with certainty that Kris Johansen was massaging a sore calf.

Not even glancing over her shoulder to judge if she'd cut anybody off, Gail gracefully curled around to the park bench.

Pick a couple people you want to get dirty, Shay had told her last week. Patsies, he'd called them; the man needed to leave the 1950s behind. Well, it hadn't taken her long to come up with a list—twenty-three names in all—and guess who'd been in the top five?

"Kris!" she said.

"Hey, Gail. Beautiful day, huh?"

Gail glanced up, still running in place, kicking up her knees like a drum major. "It is. Bad thing about nice days, though: too many people. I prefer running in the rain."

"I hadn't noticed the crowd."

Of course she hadn't. Open space, open skies—yes, that was why she hated Kris; it wasn't Matt or her politics, it was how she strode through life so effortlessly, a lone runner on the beach. Gail had to run through a jammed Times Square. It wasn't right.

"Long trail. You pull something?"

"Old war injury," said Kris with a modest smile.

However, the sun shone on every dog's ass once in awhile: Kris's hand was next to a chunk of still-wet, gray pigeon shit. Oh God, thought Gail. Just an inch. She could try to sit down next to her. Lean over, stretch, hope the motion would guide Kris somehow.

"You must be busy," Kris said.

"Always."

"Me, too. I'm only getting two laps in today."

Fucking bitch. Lying fucking bitch.

"I'm surprised you're not clicking a few pictures of sweaty senators."

"Sweat's not my thing."

Gail winked. "That's not what Matt says."

An embarrassing mistake. Jesus, she was talking like some middle-school hussy. That was the thing: you had to be careful. Gail didn't waste her time on hate; disdain, yes, because disdain required no energy or thought, just immediate dismissal. Hate, on the other hand, required effort. Valuable thinking time. Thinking that could be devoted to other pursuits. Which was why she hadn't pinned anything on Kris yet. Those two Sunday talk show hosts, sure. The columnist from *Newsweek* who'd called her "The Queen of Lies"? You're damn right. But Kris? Well, she'd told herself, maybe I just need to get over it.

"Good pieces in the *Times*. Though I could do with a little less editorializing."

"My photographs editorialize?"

"It shows, honey, it shows. How's Matt?"

"Good," Kris snapped, leaning just a bit to her left and toward the bird shit. Come on, Lord. Do your faithful servant a favor, huh? But, no, Kris stretched without moving her hand, then glanced down and saw the droppings. "Whoa," she said, "that was close."

"Oh, yeah," Gail said. "You have to look out for yourself."

Kris popped up from the bench, towering over her with that WNBA frame. Those meaty thighs of hers could feed a village in the Sudan. "Gotta keep moving," she said.

"Yes, indeed," said Gail, waving as Kris jogged off lightly down the path.

I hate you, she thought. And you should feel special.

Gail continued west in the cleansing heat of the sun. It wasn't too late to stir Kris into the mix. The blood was in the water, the sharks circling. But, no. Kris was the type who never got dirty. Never put her hand in the bird shit. Flew to Iraq and came back with only a strained calf muscle. Load up her shoulders with rumor and it'd just slide right off. And the bitch would never know how close she'd come to being tied up in it all. Goddamn, it wasn't fair.

———∿∿———

While Gail was sprinting in the opposite direction as Kris, a few hundred miles to the north, Stephen Shay finished picking his way through the brunch buffet. Roman Mercer always had the best food: fresh shrimp imported from God knew where, and those little pâté sandwiches on rye bread. Wiping his fingertips on the bulges of his hips, Shay strode across the lawn toward the media mogul. Children danced by in broad-rimmed hats, like some odd re-creation of the 1920s. Mercer's youth, Shay thought with a chuckle. Christ, we didn't want to go back to those times, did we? Better we return to the 1950s, the height of American power. In the summer breeze, he remembered a similar day many years ago—his youth—when he lay on his chenille bedspread, his door closed, all alone, chewing an entire pack of Beemans, gawking as he opened the magazine, his heart filled with lust, and unfolded the slick, glossy, full-color pictures of the 1956 Republican Convention. The power brokers. Those sharp suits. He could still recall that chenille bedspread and its little circles of raised fibers knit carefully—precise, just how he liked it.

The Australian mogul's gaunt face dampened when he saw Shay. His hair, gelled back and flat, was a serious achievement; Reagan would've been proud. "I need a word," Shay said bluntly.

The kiss-asses surrounding Mercer eyed Shay like he was some squat imp. Sycophants. Guys like Mercer loved to surround themselves with minions who knew their place. A role usually reserved for an asshole like Grover Alexander. And like Alexander, they could be easily dismissed by the man calling the shots: with a nod from Mercer, the yes-men dispersed toward the wedding bough erected near the lake's edge.

"Make it quick," Mercer said to Shay. "Shannon's only my granddaughter for another twenty minutes."

"Yeah, congratulations on that. I need you to scale back your coverage."

"Of the Redgrave shit? You boys are taking a beating, that's for goddamn sure." Mercer sighed. "You could've called any number of my people, Stephen."

Shay glared at the old fuck's disjointed eyes, so askew it looked like they'd been drawn by Picasso. Would he have shown up to a fucking wedding if he could've just made some calls?

"I can tell the RNC to stop beating down your door for alms."

"If I bury this," Mercer said.

"Deep and dead."

Mercer gazed over the wide lawn, decorated like an Easter egg.

"You have a way of bringing the shadows with you, don't you, Stephen?"

Shay shrugged. "What can I do to—"

"Get that bumbling idiot reelected," Mercer snapped. "That's what you're supposed to do."

"Working on it." Shay grinned. He had him. Easily he slid his hands into his pockets. "You help bury this, and we have a better shot. The Dems are leaning toward Raymond Kirk. I can sense it. He'll be easy pickings, but not if he can play this against us."

"The dutiful CIA agent and his wife," Mercer said.

"It'd make a helluva movie, I'm sure," said Shay. "In about twenty years."

Roman Mercer laughed—a hoarse, deathless croak—and began to amble toward the wedding scene. "I assume you don't just want me to piss down my chain of command. You want me to reach out to my peers." He nodded without an answer. "Well, the ones who hate me still listen to me. Should be easy enough."

Having gotten what he'd come for, Shay resisted the urge to sprint away. There were only a handful of men on the planet you strolled with until they let you go, and Roman Mercer was one of them.

Together they gazed at the back portico of the mansion; a plump girl in a fluffy white dress was hopping anxiously. "There she is," said Mercer. Shay bit back his tongue. The girl looked like a dumpling. "You never can tell how the whole thing will turn out," Mercer waxed. "It's all part of a grander scheme, isn't it? Bigger than Shannon, there, bigger than dirty politics." He grinned. "Even bigger than me."

Chapter 6

A month later, the well was dry. Or so it seemed. The calls to Matt's office had evaporated, the columnists had found other scabs to pick. Redgrave was still alive and not under arrest. And though there was talk of a committee—a committee to investigate the need for a formal committee, which would then recommend how to proceed, if they ever found anything out—and though the CIA was calling for a criminal investigation of the leak, the truth was this: both investigations would die in the water. And for this, Matt was grateful.

No more so than on the night he fell onto a plush bed in the Plaza Hotel. He'd flown up to New York from DC on an early commute, enjoying the combination of businessmen and vacationers from all over the world before he fell asleep, and now he felt as though he could sleep again. The nightmare past and the familiar ground of an election ahead, it was as if the world around him was firming back into shape. He opened a bottle of Pinot Noir and poured himself a thin glass, pacing the empty hotel room, imagining Kris's long body stretched naked on the sheets, her rosy skin flawless except for the barest yellowish remnants of the continent-shaped bruise on her side.

She was due at LaGuardia in a few hours. She'd gone on assignment, tough soldier that she was, dipping her toes into the healing waters of her work, which was more effective than any Shenandoah creek. Though she said it was only because she was bored and didn't know what else to do, maybe, he hoped, working would bring her out of her gloom and signal an end to this rough summer. Maybe by the end of the weekend, he could think seriously about buying her a ring.

Tired as he was, the thought of her put him into a mood, all right. Kris, three shows in two days, and dinners at some of the world's finest restaurants: he danced across the bed, channeling his inner Fred Astaire, and, as he leapt off the bed, he grabbed his phone. Staring it down, he turned it off. A daring gesture. For a daring man! Oh sure, he would check in from time to time, but it was not going to disturb him, not this weekend. Kris would like flowers, he reasoned, so he dashed to the lobby flower shop, grabbed a bouquet of lilies, brought them to the room, and mixed them across the bed. A long shower, plenty of primping in the mirror—manly primping, of course—and the slow, self-seduction of dressing-to-impress. If you believed you looked good, you did.

As he was tying his tie, the door handle unlatched and he peeked around the corner of the bathroom. Her eyes were weary and serious, but she threw her bag to the floor and draped her arms over his shoulders, burying her lips against his neck. She held him away with both hands on his cheeks, her smile formed with the optimism of a nurse.

"You look good," she said softly.

"It's New York," he said. "I'd better. How was the summit?"

"Boring, thankfully."

"You needed it."

She nodded, and he sashayed toward her, offering his hand for a pirouette. Taking it momentarily, she said she was starving, and that he should wait for her at the bar while she showered and changed. "You'll only distract me," she said.

"And that would be a bad thing?"

The flicker in her eyes was half-hearted. A tired line she'd heard from him before. He puttered around while she unpacked, making small talk about London, asking who she had seen and where she had gone. Her answers were prompt but distracted.

"You okay?" he said, rubbing her tight shoulders.

A shadow passed through her eyes. "Sure," she said.

Ordering an Absolut on the rocks at the bar, he figured some anxiety on her part was normal. She could be an anxious woman—the curse of thoughtfulness, he'd told her once. The assignment had been a fluff piece on a UN summit in London, mainly snapshots of world leaders shaking hands and sternly eyeing each other across long oak tables, and it ought to have brought her back to some semblance of her normal self. That carefree laugh and those quick verbal jabs, the anxiousness rising only on occasion.

Having made a point to drink his cocktail very slowly, he was just finishing it when Kris, wearing a short black dress, strutted into the bar. How could any man not ogle her? How could any man want to drink so badly, he wouldn't notice her? Well, he got his wish: tongues were being rolled back up off the tablecloths. Sorry, gentlemen, he wanted to say. She's mine.

———∿∿———

Bald Mountain had been running for a year, though Matt wasn't sure how. Even with two Hollywood actors in the lead roles, it was nothing but a humorless comparison of life at the time of Christ's Crucifixion and the American 1960s, with heavy doses of contemporary political jibber-jabber; Shelly had more intelligent things to say about U.S. politics. In the modern sections of the play, set after the Kennedy assassination, a family endlessly accused each other of betrayal, of alcoholism, and even of incest, and then the patriarch of the family said something about democracy in America being reborn. Kris was agog.

"You have to see the flaws in that play," he said over their second bottle of wine. "It glorifies this populist notion that's just … well, it's more complicated than 'we can all get together and save the world.'"

"At least they bother with that message," she said.

With a slur, he informed her that he, himself, had an idea for a play. "A musical, actually."

"Naturally," she said softly.

He felt a pleasing warmth kick in, a wonderful confidence. "It's about how parents live their lives through their children, these talented kids in music, sports, um, politics, even, all for their own egos. It's called *Stage Fright*. This one scene, a pop singer's mom sings, 'There's no telling what I might be, if I only had a mom like me.'"

Had he actually just sung that out loud?

"Picture a child just receiving some kind of award, and the mother is crowding her way into the spotlight."

"Okay," she said. "You're cut off."

"A second song would be kind of like that puppet scene in *Chicago*, with parents pulling the strings and their children dancing to the song, 'Let Me Pull a String (or Two),' and there's Thornton's dad, right, this bass singing '1600 Pennsylvania Avenue, that's the place for you.'" Now he really was letting it fly, sounding so top-notch that everyone in the restaurant was watching. "'All the good you can do, the wrongs you can right ...' And then Thornton, he's still a kid, okay, but he sings, 'I came within a hanging chad, Dad—'"

"Maybe you could just whisper it to me," she said, firmly taking his hand. His chin nodded heavily, seemingly of its own accord. "So there's no political bias."

"None. I hit my boss. A young Kensington sings, 'If you don't keep me outta Vietnam, you're gonna have to deal with Mom.' Kensington's dad sings, 'What do you do with a brat like this? Just make sure they never test his piss.' All in all, I got about a dozen tunes. The storyline flows awesomely."

Kris looked at him, a little dumbfounded. "I think that's enough wine for you. Don't worry, I won't tell a soul ... for a couple of reasons."

"I could see Shay's face if he heard the last song ... and his hairy ears, man he has hairy ears inside and out—"

"Matt."

"Like a hobbit—"

"Matt. Please."

For a moment, despite the sparkling wash of her face, he sensed she might be upset. He hiccupped and ate slowly for awhile.

"There's a club down the street."

"Not a good idea," Kris said. "You're getting a little too rowdy."

"It'll be great."

He threw money on the table, grabbed Kris's arm, and led her to the door. What all those people must be thinking! That dashing man with that beautiful woman on his arm! Wait, isn't that? I think it is. He could hear Kris talking to people he left in his wake.

"You're a little wobbly," she said to him on the sidewalk. "Take my arm."

He snatched his arm away like a toddler. "No!" Then he let loose a cackle and ran ahead down the street. The night was muggy, infused with the smell of trash and a sharp wind—and the rushing faces of the city's denizens—Hello! And hello to you! How sharp and alive everything was!

Kris caught up again, steering him away from a steakhouse, and she'd nearly convinced him to give up when he spotted the club's busy doorway. "There!" he erupted, as if he had just discovered gold.

"Everyone's staring at you, and you're listing like a ship."

"They know me!" he giggled, and he very seriously announced himself to the bouncer. "What good's any of it if I can't cut a line, you know?" he whispered to her as they entered. Strangely, she winced as he spoke.

The club was nothing more than an opened-up warehouse, it seemed, a long, wide corridor dressed up with neon blue lights; the walls were painted black matte, and they seemed to go on forever. Before she could stop him, he ordered himself a scotch. "Anything incredibly expensive," he shouted to the bartender, and he told Kris to get what she wanted. He pulled his designer sunglasses from his coat, removed his tie and tied it around his head, and paraded into the sweaty, hedonistic tribe with his glass raised. "Who says Republicans don't know how to party?" he shouted behind him to Kris, assuming she was still there. A honey in a lavender, strapless dress rubbed against him, and he swirled ...

His eyes opened. A black velvet painting, curb's eye-view. A Japanese man had been singing with broken English into a karaoke machine.

"He'll be fine," Kris said. From somewhere.

Another man spoke in a low, professional tone. Craning his neck away from the velvet landscape of the sky, he saw the bottom of Kris's long legs, the gray pavement, and a man's brown loafers—then the face: a well-groomed beard. Handsome.

He rolled to one side, and a yelping pain took over momentarily. Kris fussed over him, but he got to all fours and stared at the man. "Who the fuck are you?"

"A friend," the man said with a suspicious grin.

"This nice man had a camcorder, Matt. He works for the *Daily News*."

"You owe me a ride on Air Force One, Risen."

"I see."

He came to his bearings a bit more, leaning back onto painfully cramped ankles, his stomach a hot mess. He'd stumbled, apparently, out of the cab in front of the hotel. The glowing fountain looked so goddamn good, he could've jumped in. In fact ...

Kris caught his sport jacket, holding him firmly by the shoulders. "You're more tired than you know, big guy."

"Me?" Matt said, looking around for the man, who'd disappeared.

"Jon Stewart would've had a week's worth of material," she said, holding up a small tape. "You got lucky."

The brass doors parted; doors and elevators vanished and appeared, and slowly his neck muscles seemed to be turning to stone. And he swore he heard Kris say something about the sign she'd been waiting for.

～ΛΛ～

He woke the next morning to himself: there he was on the television, hair smoothed and carefully combed to the right, defending the honor of Oliver Redgrave and promising full White House cooperation. For a moment he wasn't sure which version of himself was awake.

Kris stepped out of the bathroom fully dressed: T-shirt, jeans, cowboy boots. Her valise was packed and waiting on the credenza.

"What are you doing?" he said sleepily.

For a long time she looked at him, sometimes studiously, her eyes blinking, her hands working in and out of each other. She took a deep breath and said, "I'm flying back to Washington."

His stomach bottomed out with a force he used to experience at the top of the roller coaster hills at Cedar Point.

"Why?"

Shards of the previous night reminded him. But still.

She sat carefully on the far edge of the bed, her hands locked as if in prayer. "Matt, you scared me last night."

"I was just blowing off some steam—"

"That's not it, though," she shouted through him. "That's not the real problem." Clutching a fold of her thick, wet, curly hair, she pushed it back hard over her skull. "At first I thought you'd just forgotten. Let this whole Redgrave thing slip away like a bad dream. And I thought,

'How can he be doing that? How can he just forget?' But then I realized you haven't forgotten, and you were just getting drunk to … to fucking ignore it, Matt." She finally looked up at him, her eyes hard and glassy and wet. Just a little moisture, the Kris Johansen equivalent of sobbing. "Isn't that what you were doing last night?"

His face felt like plastic, his lips heavy rubber.

"It's been really stressful—"

"Don't whine. I don't have time for it. You've got to take some responsibility."

Two large bright blotches had spread across her cheeks, a terrifying shade of crimson, anger and embarrassment that her emotions were visible to him. Her eyes darted from one corner of the room to the other as she rose and launched into a speech, speaking at a pace and with an intensity he'd never witnessed. At what point did "just doing my job" stop, she asked. She knew he didn't believe in everything the administration was doing, but the worst part was that he never bothered to look at the consequences of its actions.

"But you have," he said.

"Yeah, I have." Her voice hardened. "Is there something wrong with that?"

He couldn't stop himself. "We'll get you a medal."

"Oh, fuck this," she muttered, and she sprang from the bed.

"What do you want me to do, Kris? Tell me and I'll do it."

"You could start by having a little compassion."

"Compassion?" He swung his legs out of the bed, surprised to see that they still worked; sobriety, painful as pinpricks, was coming to him, though. "Why should I? For them? For us? For who?"

"Everyone," she seethed, her eyes narrowed. She pounded the bed with a fist. "Because you people don't think about the consequences—"

"Us people?"

"You just roll right through anything you want. And try to look good doing it." She cocked her head and said mockingly, "I was right about you the first time around: all you care about is your fucking career."

She muttered that she was stupid, stupid, stupid as she packed her toiletries into her suitcase and zipped it up.

"You're more naive than I thought," he said, "if you think no one considers the consequences. Years of planning, Kris. *Years.* For Christ's sake, Iran has the bomb!"

"And you want to go to war with them."

"And you want peace, love, and understanding—"

"Diplomacy would be a start," she shouted, her valise swinging as she pulled it over her shoulder.

"Why start something that won't work?"

"That's a good goddamn question, Matt." With a shake and a growl, she grabbed her suitcase and valise and turned for the door. "It's a question I've been asking myself all night."

He leapt from the bed and grabbed her by the shoulders. "The information's there, Kris. It all points to what we're doing now. And there's a mountain of evidence; I don't care what Redgrave said, I've seen it myself. We just can't make it public—"

"And yet you guys expose him. Make *him* public. As far as I'm concerned, that's not just political vindictiveness, Matt. It's treason."

His face slackened. Unbidden images of McCowan and his old commandant at Staunton appeared before him.

"What are you talking about, treason?"

"Maybe not legally," she said, "not by the strictest definition, but morally? Yeah. Everyone knows it was Shay. He's the only person besides Webb who's sleazy enough to do a thing like that."

But he was still dwelling on the word and its martial sting. Hangings and firing squads. Why had the word traitor not been the same? Because it wasn't legal? Or because treason was an act, an act he had committed with his mouth, with the touch of his fingertips to the phone ...

"Oh God," she whispered. "Matt. Matt, tell me."

"It wasn't me," he said limply, staring at the ground.

"Oh, fuck."

She shoved him back, pinning his hip into the sharp corner of the credenza.

"Don't lie to me!" she screamed. "I thought they were insane, those people saying your name. 'No fucking way,' I thought, 'must be some of Gail's bullshit.' But look at you. No wonder you got so goddamn wasted." She erupted into a bubbling stream of whispering. "I thought I meant more ... that something good ... that it'd be you."

Like some impotent schoolboy he stood there, watching her whimper and try to blink her way back to calmness.

"Be honest with me, Matt," she muttered.

If he explained, he'd only seem worse. And he couldn't lie to her, not anymore. She had a gift for sniffing out his bullshit, and it'd been by the grace of luck, he supposed, that she'd believed in him long enough not to suspect.

All he could say?

"No one's gotten hurt."

Her eyes shut, almost dreamily, and she exhaled deeply, wrapped her fingers around the doorknob and looked at him with faltering eyes of expansive pale blue.

"That's not true," she said.

She shut the door quietly behind her.

CHAPTER 7

Blood dripped from the marred eyes of Thomas Kaplan into the bucket of ice water in which his feet were submerged. The poor fellow must be writhing in pain, Yuri thought, a little surprised by the man's lack of resolve. Kaplan and his partner had run like rabbits.

Yuri sat backward in a chair opposite the American, his square head resting on his hands, in the middle of a blackened, once-burned warehouse outside of Moscow. The electricity only worked here, at the north end of the massive hangar, and he'd affixed a hot work lamp to a wire hanging from the ceiling. He batted it like a cat, which, ironically, was Kaplan's nickname among the KGB and, now, the FSB. Besides the man with the tar-black hair, Kaplan and his partner were the only active, covert agents connected to the events in Florence who were still alive. Perhaps it was Kaplan who'd slid him the briefcase.

"How is your friend Hassan bin Chalabi, Mr. Kaplan?" Yuri said slowly in turbid yet punctuated English. "Still a freedom fighter?"

"Fuck you," the man muttered.

"If only we had won," Yuri said, trailing off. Then, "Do you remember Florence in 1987, Mr. Kaplan? A beautiful city. A beautiful hotel called the Bernini Palace."

Kaplan struggled to open his eyes, and with that enormous effort finally glared at Yuri. Drool spilled over his lips and into the ice water, mixing with the pinkish blood.

"You were ... selling shoes," Kaplan said.

"Yes! You recall!" Yuri smacked his heavy lips and ran his paws over the edge of the metal chair. "All that leather—ugh, disgusting." He peered at Kaplan. "So we are not going to play any games, then, are we?"

187

Kaplan stared at him.

"Fifteen years on," said Yuri, "you've aged. You look ready to close up shop."

The man's jaw quivered, and then his whole head jerked. He was a thin man, and his entire body shook with the pain. And they hadn't even gotten to the drugs yet.

With a screech, the metal grate door lifted, and Korovyov's gaunt frame appeared, a silhouette in the moonlight until he took his tiny steps into the warehouse and the dim lighting.

"It's done," he said breathlessly.

Yuri smiled sympathetically at his captive. "Kevin Mendelsohn is swimming in a barrel of acid," he whispered. "You could say that your partnership is disintegrating."

Korovyov laughed with a kind of hiccupping.

Grunting, Yuri rose above the chair and kicked one massive leg over it. He nodded at Korovyov, and the little man opened his case of old syringes. Kaplan moaned, perhaps because he knew what cocktail Korovyov was preparing, or perhaps because he'd been taken so easily. Yuri had overheard the last bit of his conversation with Mendelsohn in Tver, before he and Korovyov had jumped them.

"I came as soon as you called."

"You called me."

And then that beautiful silence of recognition. Ah, the oldest trick in the book, really, and now Mendelsohn—seemingly the feistier, more anxious of the two—was dead and Kaplan would confirm everything Yuri suspected.

He turned as Korovyov was removing the needle from Kaplan's forearm vein. A specialty of his old colleague's, particularly the use of SP-17. The American's face hardened, and in a few moments the stubbly top of his right lip twitched.

"You almost escaped my notice, Mr. Kaplan," said Yuri. "I was so pleased to discover Mr. Redgrave and the others."

"One has to account for all of the players on the board," Korovyov said with a boyish glee.

From a manila file folder, Yuri removed a few photos. "You will tell the truth now. You have no choice."

"I'm going to kill you," Kaplan sneered.

"Good," Yuri said, though Korovyov had gasped. It seemed like a truthful statement, after all, and was followed by Thomas Kaplan's admittance that he was a covert agent for the CIA, known in Ukraine as Hutchins, known in Afghanistan as Ferrier, known everywhere as The Cat, and that he indeed had worked Florence in 1987 under the strategic guidance of Oliver Redgrave.

"He was in charge?"

"He thought he was," muttered Kaplan with another sneer.

One by one Yuri demanded the names of the individuals in the photographs, and his heart tightened as each was confirmed: two field agents—the man with the dense, glossy hair, and the woman who'd been shot in the elevator; and two "pencil-pushers," one of them Redgrave, the other the sandy-blond agent who looked little more than a teenager at the time, but who had managed to kill Nikolai and put two bullets into Yuri himself.

"How did you find out about us?" Yuri growled.

"You," Kaplan stuttered. "Ball made you. In surveillance."

"Is he still alive? Where?"

The American fought, the veins in his neck swelling as he twisted his skull from one side to the other, but finally the drugs forced him to admit that Ball was working out of Serbia these days, when he wasn't in DC or Moscow.

"A new front? Tell me its name."

"Ag Department, th-that's all I know."

Yuri glanced at Korovyov, who shrugged, then stood and circled back to the rusty work table, from which he retrieved his gloves. He put them on and scratched the bloody tear-shaped scar under his right eye as the American rocked back and forth, attempting to gain some momentum. But Yuri had tied the man's hands to the chair himself; at best, he'd simply topple.

"And the younger agent? The man?"

"I don't know," Kaplan seethed. "He works on the orbit of things."

Yuri nodded, his bottom, heavy lip pushed up toward his nose. He circled again toward Kaplan. Out of respect, or fear, Korovyov backed away, and the American rocked furiously, less catlike now, more like a primate.

"Was it you who slid me that briefcase?" said Yuri. "Mendelsohn perhaps?"

"No way. Neither of us."

"Then who?"

"Ball said he did it."

"Mr. Kaplan, you have served your country well until tonight. Perhaps we'll meet again in hell."

With a satisfying pop, Kaplan's neck broke in his hands.

Releasing the sweat-slicked skin, Yuri checked his own breathing, closing his eyes. Lately his heart had been racing, and it wouldn't do to collapse when he'd only begun his vendetta.

In the expanse of the room, a safety clicked.

Korovyov pointed the small metal thing at him, his hands vibrating. With an odd twitch, the little man said, "The old family will take it from here, Yuri."

How unreal. Little Duck, still in the game.

"You went to them after you helped me get to Kostya."

"Yes," said Korovyov. "Naturally they wish to speak with you."

"Naturally."

"Y-you have to come with me."

Yuri studied his old colleague a moment, and judged the distance between them at six, maybe seven meters. Although there were three ways to kill Korovyov in this situation, none involved the avoidance of taking a bullet. He sighed monstrously. Just when his work was beginning to pay off.

"All right," Yuri said, gripping the chair behind the slumped American.

Korovyov relaxed for a second, and, with a roar, Yuri hurled the slender American, the chair, and the bucket of ice water toward him. Chest burning—something cold in there, too—he sprinted at Korovyov as the wiry traitor sprang aside with a yelp. The first shot came on like a Kamaz at full speed, and his left shoulder seemed to drag behind as the rest of him surged toward the panicked eyes of Korovyov. The Duck had banged into the work table, spilling onto the floor—there came a second shot, and a third—before Yuri's hands clutched the haggard old neck. "Please," Korovyov managed to squeak before the eternal silence.

Yuri rolled over. A primordial howl escaped from his bloody mouth, and breathing shallowly, he patted down along his chest, feeling the second entry wound under the left side of his ribs. The idiot. Turncoat alcoholic *idiot*. And what had the FSB thought, that Korovyov would succeed? Or get himself killed in the process? Fumbling for his cell phone, Yuri spat a wad of blood onto the cement. A chill seeped through him. He was in the park. The chiming voices of children, the day dimming to night. To black. *No,* he thought. *Not yet.*

CHAPTER 8

In late August 2003, as a torrential downpour that was shouldering away a week-long heat wave in central Ohio beat against the roof, Matt stared through the one-way mirror at the people seated on the other side in a room barren and cozy like an interrogation room was cozy. Standing next to him, Shay nearly had his hooked nose pressed against the glass and was stroking the loose flab of his neck, not unlike a turkey vulture about to tear a slab of sun-baked meat off of some road-kill rabbit.

Despite the coffee, juice, and doughnuts each had been provided, the members of the focus group looked about as relaxed as rabbits: the northwestern Ohio fundamentalist was fidgeting with her purse, glaring at the pastor who'd brought her; the two men—one a small-business owner from central Ohio, the other a blue-collar guy from Dayton—spoke awkwardly about NASCAR and the Buckeyes, never looking at each other; the inner-ring suburban soccer mom was scrolling through her phone and being watched carefully by a petite, elderly black woman from Cleveland. Shay had been looking for what he kept calling his "key five," and here they were, their every word, spoken and unspoken, about to be videotaped, transcribed, analyzed, and used in the campaign.

"The gay marriage ban," Shay muttered. "That's our main focus."

"The facilitator's going to warm them up first," said Matt, nodding at the man in the white button-down and one-hundred-dollar tie. He was running through the ground rules: let each person speak, and speak for as long as you need to, and so on. Meanwhile the technicians were fixing them with lapel microphones and adjusting the ambient mikes in the room's corners.

Shay pointed a vein-streaked finger at the fundamentalist, who'd been sitting, silent and reserved. "Somebody forced her to come to this."

Behind Matt, Carl cleared his throat. "Yeah … her influencer."

"But that's good. I want to see the interaction. Start with her. She's the most important, her and her preacher."

"We're getting too much noise from that rain," a technician said from the other room.

"Why all this attention to influencers?" Matt said.

"I've always paid attention to the informed voter and his influencer." His lips smacked, and he sneered as he usually did when a point was to be made. "Think of it this way. There are a thousand people like the pastor there in the state of Ohio, but each of our 'key five' represents hundreds of thousands of voters. We have to know how to play the influencers so they spread our message to the informed voters, who spread it to the rest. From the bottom. Grassroots. We do that, we squeeze out another hundred thousand votes, and we can't lose."

"The vice president's coming up," said a technician who'd just come back into the observation room as he nodded toward a video screen.

Shay sighed theatrically.

The magnified sneer of Dixon Webb appeared first, and someone in DC panned the webcam back a bit until Webb's icy eyes and furrowed brow were a bit more proportional, if still imposing.

"Did this charade get started yet?" he growled.

"We're about to," said Shay, turning his back to the screen.

In his snidest voice, Webb rolled through all the reasons this was a terrible idea: the money, the time, the money. The same speech he'd given a week ago in the White House. All the pollsters agreed with him, and, Matt had to admit, the case was decent. "Hell, Carl has had his people researching these losers for months," Webb was saying now. "This whole idea of identifying influencers, then targeting people in their sphere of influence—well, no polling expert has ever done anything like this. It's not scientific, Shay, how are you going to measure—"

Looking at Matt, but loud enough for Webb to hear, Shay said, "Conventional wisdom is never wise, and wisdom is never conventional. Fuck the experts. These so-called losers will decide this whole fucking election. They trust no one in the media; they don't trust us, or our opponents. But they do trust a handful of people they know personally. They accept much of what they say, but not everything. That's the key: I'm trying to segment the two." Then he said bitterly to the screen, "And I didn't ask you to watch this."

Webb looked as if he would spit on Shay if modern technology had developed the ability to teleport mucus.

Just as his focus on Ohio was unquestionable, and inevitable once he'd decided on it, Shay's focus groups were going to happen no matter what Webb or anyone else thought. Matt looked at Shay with a familiar, but nearly extinct, admiration—in two-plus years, Webb had yet to overpower Shay, and you had to admit that when Stephen Shay believed in something, he fought for it. Rabidly.

The facilitator asked all the participants to do a quick mike check, and after a minute or two of chaos, he looked at Lynn Curtin, the fundamentalist. "Tell us what you think about the war, Lynn."

With no small amount of terror, she slowly unraveled an answer. "Well, I don't like how much we talk about it in church, you know. It's God's house and I think politics, especially war talk, is too dirty to talk about in his home." She slid her eyes toward her pastor, who smiled bitterly.

"I think the pastor gave us the right person," said Shay, "but he's the wrong person to be selling to her."

"Here's something interesting," Carl said, staring at the notes he'd compiled—God knew when, or how. With a raise of his bare-seeming, fleshy eyebrow, he said, "Her sister's a dyke, and this prude went to the wedding. The sister lives in Toledo where she teaches school."

"And Lynn is from one of these evangelistic non-denominational churches, right?"

"Yes."

"Matt, before our guy goes into the gay marriage ban, have him ask something about gays in the workforce. Not teaching, per se, but something like, 'Should an employer be able to fire an otherwise good employee if he finds out that person is gay?'"

Matt typed the question into a computer that relayed the message to the facilitator.

They went on for a while about the war, and Lynn consistently drew the conversation back to her Harvest Life Church and pastor:

the reasoning for the war, her support of the troops, her belief in Kensington's "mission," a word she landed on hard. When asked about gays in the workplace, Lynn muttered that she didn't think they should be fired, so long as they kept it to themselves.

Finally their middleman said, "How do you feel about banning gay marriage?"

"Well, I'm not for it, if that's what you mean."

The facilitator raised an eyebrow and leaned back in his chair. "You're *not* in favor of banning gay marriage?"

The pastor smiled at her knowingly as Lynn began to speak. "Oh I'm against gay marriage … I thought you meant that."

"No, the question is: do you favor a ban on gay marriage?"

"Well, I'm for that," she said tentatively.

"That's very interesting," Shay said, his breath fogging the glass.

"She's just embarrassed that she misunderstood," Matt said.

"That's not my take. How about you, Carl?"

"She tensed up in her shoulders, not her face; she wasn't feeling embarrassed, but an impulse to argue."

Shay jotted down a note. "The issue isn't homosexuality, per se. She doesn't hate gays, or lesbians, obviously; it's too complicated for her to apply the rhetoric of the church to the people she sees and knows. So the answer is to *not* think about it. Like the war: keep it out of discussion. But we're *making* her think about it, and she's pissed. She isn't where we want her on this."

As if to prove his point, the pastor was railing away, glancing at the facilitator and Lynn. "The gays have taken over the Democrats; they own Hollywood and the whole East Coast. We have to put our foot down." Bluish veins stuck out on the side of his shaved head as he ranted, and Lynn's body only tightened into a surrendering ball. But in her eyes you could still spot the defiance.

The pastor seemed to sense that he was losing Lynn, and his voice dropped to a quiet pleading, almost whining that it was their duty as Christians to stop the perversion of marriage. "Look, Lynn, I know you agree with me, and I pray every night for Robin, but this is the work of the devil, and I can't let it go. I'll never let it go."

"Talking about it is just so unseemly," she blurted.

"But we have to," the pastor said, leaning into her face.

Behind them, Webb said with a crackling of static, "Fill me in later, boys. I'm on the edge of my fucking seat, really, but I'm going to make some phone calls." The screen went to a test signal.

"Thank you," Shay muttered.

Matt checked down on Carl's notes and peered at Lynn Curtin again. Her reticence and shyness reminded him of some of the women who lived in Marion or out near Marie's farm in Fredericktown. She had an appropriate name: she lived in a house on a country road which, most of the year, was surrounded by corn with a row of trees in front. A fort. Afraid of everything. Schnell was her maiden name—German; her grandfather was probably one of the isolationists in 1940 who wanted to nominate Charles Lindbergh for president. Until Pearl Harbor. Attack us, and you got attacked. Otherwise, she just wanted to build a wall around everything and trust God to protect the United States like he protected her and her husband.

"Let me try a little Shay analysis," Matt said. Shay chuckled, and Carl, ever the obedient lapdog, did not. "She was appalled by the last president's philandering. It was attack on decency."

"Brilliant," Carl said with an exaggerated roll of his eyes.

"Button it, Carl," said Shay. "He's onto something."

"Being gay is 'don't ask, don't tell,' but don't ask her to defend gay rights, either," Matt said. "On *any* level. Anymore than you'd ask her to defend my straight but, well, active sex life. Hell, sex in general is 'don't ask, don't tell,' and yet the Christian Right was obsessed by it during the last administration. 'Unseemly' was the word she used. Imagine her watching Pat Robertson talking about oral sex. That had to drive her nuts. She's favored banning books in libraries and here are her own people yakking about the intimate details of a blow job. I'll bet we almost lost her."

Checking his records, Carl nodded slightly. "She didn't vote in '96 or '98."

"So we can't be crude," Matt said.

"But we still have to get her to vote," said Shay. "She's not motivated yet."

"Because we haven't been attacked again." Matt stepped back from the glass, listening as Lynn explained why she still loved her sister; the others in the room seemed to be nodding their heads. Just a bit. "For her, the gay marriage ban has to be about the fear of public legitimacy and condemning promiscuous sex. Because if gays can get married, next you thing you know, we'll be blabbing about their sex lives on the radio the same we would a straight person's."

Shay grinned, his cheeks doughy and flushed. "You still surprise me, kid."

"Me, too," Carl huffed.

Inside, the facilitator was moving on to Esther Johnson, the frail-looking black woman from Cleveland. Matt filled his coffee cup, patting the backs of the two technicians who'd been working all morning without a break. To have Shay's admiration back was a good thing. His panic over the Redgrave leak was damaging, maybe even damning, and Carl had made no attempt to cover up his suspicion of Matt's loyalty and guts. And balls. Even now he could sense The Wrestler burning a hole through the back of his head. Shay would keep him in check, though.

"She's our hardest sell," Shay said as he pointed toward Esther. "Black Democrat in Cleveland, you'd think it'd be impossible to get her on our side."

"What she has in common with Lynn is the church," Matt said. "And distrust of big organizations. Government, unions, businesses, from the IRS to the RTA. Even church organizations. So she follows a preacher, not a church."

Esther's pastor was her influencer, too, a large man with a cheerful, rotund face who sat next to her with his hands calmly folded.

"I see my neighbors' boys and girls going off," Esther was saying. "Seems like they always take the poor ones, you know, and ship 'em to war."

"But do you think the war is worthwhile," the facilitator said.

She shrugged. "Ought to be spending that money here. Wasn't supposed to be no war, anyway." She cocked her head and smiled wisely at the facilitator. "You all pulled the wool over our eyes with that one."

Count her as one Matt hadn't been able to reach last year. And, hell, he couldn't blame her.

"Let's shift to the gay marriage ban," said the facilitator.

"Let's," Esther said.

"Would you be in favor of it?"

Esther and her preacher exchanged a glance, then, tellingly, shared a firm nod. "America," she said, her voice rising a notch, "has lost its moral focus. I see it every day. Not that nobody asks me. But you have, and so I'm telling you."

"We run programs for the homeless in our church," the preacher said.

"And half of them are drug addicts, right back out there the next morning."

Shay was pacing, and for a moment Matt wondered why he wasn't watching her. But as he looked away, he heard the melodiousness in her voice; it was so expressive, it told you everything you needed to know.

"She's different from Lynn," said Matt. "We can be more aggressive with her. She doesn't mind talking about this stuff in church. It's Christian liberalism, God's tasks become our tasks. Faith through works. She sees prostitutes and drug addicts on her street; this is Sodom and Gomorrah stuff to her."

"But she's against us on everything else," said Shay. "We've got to count on her minister to bring her home for us."

"I can see her voting for the gay marriage ban, then voting against us."

"Maybe not if it's a guy like Kirk."

Matt gazed back through the one-way mirror. Esther had taken off her Sunday hat and was saying the same things as Lynn about not disliking gays, but she was shaking her finger at the facilitator as she did it.

"Let's break pretty soon," said Shay, "and see if we can't get some interaction between her and Lynn during the break."

Thank God, thought Matt; he needed a cigarette in the worst fucking way.

⌒〜⌒

By the time Matt could escape, another hour had passed, and all of the "key five" had weighed in on the gay marriage amendment: the suburban soccer mom was as fervently against the ban as she was the war; but the two men seemed hesitantly in favor of it, particularly the barbershop owner from Newark. Standing under a metal overhang as the rain continued to drum down, Matt thought about the suburban mom, Marge Scarborough, as he lit a cigarette, inhaled, and eased into bliss. That woman had been a Republican in 2000, but she'd slipped away from them, and it was hard not to think it was his fault. Although it would've helped to have a president who spoke English.

He tossed the nub of the cigarette into a small lake forming in the parking lot, then lit another one. For little more than a month now he'd been smoking, drinking nearly every night—scotch, rum, gin; his old aversion to hard liquor so 2000, you know?—and perfecting the art of leaving esoteric voicemails for Kris. Sometimes he'd just say where he was. Some nights he recited a line of poetry he found in his old college anthology. More than once he'd declared himself a prophet whose sole vision was that they were meant to be together. She never answered his calls and now he was pretty sure she never would. The wreckage was piled on the shore, so to speak, and rather than sift through it, he figured a little more of it couldn't hurt.

A sleek golden Escalade pulled into the lot, and in a moment Gail emerged from the backseat, ducking under the umbrella provided by her driver. Around the hood of the massive tank appeared the Ohio Republican Party Chair, Eddie Burgess. Only a few years older than Matt, Burgess walked like he was being led by his cock, and Matt noticed how low on Gail's hip the chairman's hand fell.

"How's it going in there?" Gail said.

Matt nodded, stoking the fire on his cigarette. "Shay's pretty convinced we need to go with this gay marriage ban."

Shrugging, Gail said she'd figured it was already a foregone conclusion. She scanned him up and down. "Smoking, huh?"

"Old habits."

"Die hard," she said with a slight arch in her eyebrow.

Like it needed to be said. He sighed eloquently, he hoped, and held the retrofitted warehouse door open for her. The eloquence would signal that he was not the old Matt Risen who'd sleep with a hot piece of ass just because she was there. This, of course, wasn't exactly the truth.

Inside, the interrogation had continued, and Gail was hardly in the observation room before she relayed that Webb wanted to know what they'd learned.

"Fuck him, and shut up," said Shay. "Let me listen to this."

Gail's neck stiffened; behind her, Burgess's eyes were aflame, like he was some white knight who would come to her rescue. Even Gail was starting to take shots, a sign that the campaign was closing in. It'd be fun, all right, like watching two snakes striking at each other at the bottom of a musky abandoned well.

The man named Tree Morgan was talking about the economy and how it'd "gone to shit" around Dayton. His influencer was some guy in a Cincinnati Reds hat, but Tree, an enormous man as imposing as his nickname, kept mentioning a friend of his in the UAW. The Reds fan twisted in his chair and rolled his eyes every time the UAW guy came up.

"We'll lose this guy on the economy," Shay muttered.

"We'll lose all of them on the economy," said Matt. "Except Lynn, it's not a big issue for her at all."

"Then we make it an issue," said Gail.

"No," Matt said. "Do the math, Gail. It's four to one. We bury it."

"Forgive me, but I thought we exploit strengths."

He slid his eyes toward her. "When the fuck did you become a domestic strategist?"

"When did you?"

"Shut up, both of you," said Shay. He hadn't moved from the glass, and the look on his face was dour, anxious. "Or go get a room." Chewing on his lip, Shay seemed transfixed. "The other guy tensed up. Matt, what's his deal?"

"Uh, Jim Tucker. Vietnam vet. Wounded in action. But he's run his own barbershop for years and done just fine. So he's got a lot of pride— he *should*, you know?—and he probably doesn't trust government. Not just over the war, but his medical experiences with the VA. His buddy there all but said so."

"Which is why he tensed," said Shay. "He doesn't want the government too involved in the economy."

"Which means we've got him with the wholesale 'keep the government out of your life' message.'"

"Even though a gay marriage amendment is doing exactly the opposite," said Gail.

"Only if you're gay," Carl said.

Matt continued, "The best the other side can do is back him off a little, and maybe he doesn't vote."

Shay glanced at Matt. "Very good."

Even as Matt's stomach sank, even as he thought of Kris and Cory trying to steer him left at the cabin in Shenandoah, he could feel the jealous heat of Carl and Gail staring him down. If only they knew how empty Shay's approval felt now, even if it was necessary. When all the grips eluded you, desperately you grabbed for the ones still offered. What was he these days but his job? Cut him up, and you'd find nothing but a shell.

The facilitator thanked each of the participants, handed them checks for a hundred bucks, and led them out into the lobby. Shay called another break, after which they'd convene in a meeting room down the hall, and Gail bolted like a greyhound. She wouldn't be coming back, Matt knew. She hated this kind of work, considered it plebian, a waste of her precious time. On the campaign trail in 2000, it seemed like she believed that anybody who didn't make at least $200k a year carried a rogue virus.

He'd collapsed into one of the vacant technician chairs, checked his messages, and was about to make a routine return call to a media wonk, when he saw Carl drifting into the vacant interview-cum-interrogation room. Shay followed. "… body knows this state's going to be a bitch," Shay was saying quietly, "and after listening to these people, I'm convinced we need to get creative."

Matt glanced over his shoulder at the rest of the empty observation room, and nudged up the volume dial. They must have figured the techs turned the mikes off.

"How creative?" Carl said with a grin.

"What'd you find out yesterday?"

Carl cracked his neck, sighed lazily. "The security in nearly all of the boards of elections are a joke. We can get in and out at will. I swear, my twelve-year-old granddaughter has tighter security on her diary."

"But we'd have to get in twice: before and after the election to reset the machines. And there has to be zero fucking chance we get caught."

"Some boards have closets with those push-button handle locks, like a bathroom." Carl sat on the table edge, his hands animate; sans volume, you'd think he was talking about the Indians. "Steve, keep in mind, too, the day before the election, things are nuts. Offices are filled with temporary staff. Piece of cake. And the day after, everyone's a damn zombie."

"We'd have to change pre-punched cards in some boards, and reseal the electronics in the boards that use electronics. That's a lot of gear to haul."

Carl scoffed. "No problem. Most ballots are stored in easy-to-get-into containers. Hell, in Mahoning County they use fish boxes."

"You sound more confident today," Shay muttered.

"I'm more confident we can."

"But maybe we don't need to."

"What alternatives do you have?" Carl said.

Shay crossed his arms and glanced at the mirror, and Matt jolted before Shay looked away undisturbed. Still, Shay, ever paranoid, whispered, "The Ohio secretary of state, for one. We can get a good deal of help from her. Changes to voter registration rules, ballot issues. All of it last minute, so the Dems don't have much chance to react." He beamed, adding that the simplest way would be the most effective: fewer machines in the urban areas. "They're already way off from where they need to be, and if she denies them machines, *and* if we get the turnout we're predicting—Jesus, it'll be a nightmare. The key is to not allow optional precinct-level absentee voting at the polling place."

"Long lines in the cities."

"Miles long," Shay said.

Both were silent for awhile, Shay pacing slowly and checking his silver wristwatch. As Matt checked to see if their conversation was being recorded, he kept his cell phone open near his ear in case one of the techs came in.

"We need election officials who look the other way," Carl said. "Otherwise it's too risky. And the mock elections they run on the systems before and after the election should reveal irregularities."

"Does it matter which kind of system is being used?"

"No. These guys"—Carl chuckled a bit, crossing his beefy arms— "they all want you to think they've got NSA-level security, but the truth is, manipulating the counting software would actually be easier than the machines themselves. It's like protecting the engine of a train and none of the other cars. And hell, in the smaller counties, the entire election is turned over to private companies with no checks or balances, so we just need to get into those companies."

Shay said, "Little bites. We can't get greedy. Adjust around the margins."

"Like you eat an apple," Carl said.

Again they were silent, and with a sharp twist of his head, Carl studied the hallway. Matt leaned back in his chair and spoke soft gibberish into his phone; seconds later, one of the technicians walked by, waved at Matt, and continued on down the hall.

If that had been Shay, or God forbid, Carl, they'd have immediately pounced on him. He scanned the recording equipment as Shay stressed the importance of a higher voter turnout. The knobs and screens and flashing little red lights looked like they belonged on the bridge of an Imperial Star Destroyer. He'd need to think of something else.

Shay was counting off on his fingers, recapping. "Secondly, we pick demographically similar counties. For the appearance of consistency."

"Just tell me where," Carl said.

Matt rose, snapped his cell phone shut, and crept out to the overhang. The storm had resolved to a light drizzle, and the sun was peeking through in the distance. One of the technicians, a lanky kid who was about as clean-cut as a marine, was taking a drag on a cigar. Matt lit up, asked about the cigar brand, and studied the kid's response. An expensive cigar, man. Top of the line.

Sliding a hundred-dollar-bill out of his wallet, Matt held it toward the kid. "Up for a little extra work?" The kid tried to play cool, but his eyes were wet like an old lady's on her birthday. "I know you guys are shipping all the video and audio to DC, and to Mr. Shay, but what's the chance you can get me just the audio tonight?"

"On a CD? Shit, that's easy."

Matt held the bill close to his face. "Quietly. Mr. Shay hates a suck-up, know what I mean?"

The kid giggled, snorted, and said he could slip Matt a copy by the time they were done with their meeting. Instead, Matt suggested, since they were so close to Columbus, maybe the kid would drive down to his hotel and drop it off. He offered to throw in another hundred, and the kid nearly swooned. After he'd called Broussard to get his hotel reservation, Matt handed the technician the hundred dollars, tossed his cigarette and lit another, and then gave the kid his final instructions: "Just the audio is fine, but I want all of it, including the half hour after the interviews stopped. And you say nothing. Got it?"

———⌣∿⌣———

Matt was hardly in his plush Regency room before the kid knocked on the door. Gratefully Matt included the courtesy bottle of Dom Perignon with the tech's second hundred.

It was there, standing by the door, that he noticed an odd briefcase in his luggage, piled up by some intern. Cracked tan leather, beaten. Shay's briefcase. The one no files went in or out of. The one that never left Stephen's hands. Well, apparently it had. Mixed up somehow. Matt looked at the briefcase, then at the CD just delivered to him, then the briefcase.

On the still slick balcony, he wrestled one of the room's chairs into a position where he could watch the sun setting over the Columbus skyline, and, after room service brought him a bottle of merlot, he ate the lamb shawarma plate he'd picked up from Aladdin's, swigged from the wine bottle, and listened through headphones to the rest of Shay and Carl's conversation.

"The counties must be large enough to have an impact," Shay said, "but not so large they'd require too many helping hands."

"One safe option is to piggyback off this gay marriage thing," Carl said. "What do you call it when people vote one way or another on a hot-button issue, but don't vote for president?"

"Fall-off," Shay said.

"Okay, so what if you programmed the results so that, say, 50 percent of these votes were automatically counted for one candidate or the other. That'd be impossible to trace. Difficult, at least."

Shay seemed to plop down on the table; *something* groaned with his weight. "We'll need a cover reason for exceptional voter participation. Maybe an aggressive direct voter contact campaign." He sighed heavily, no doubt missing his scotch. "But most importantly, with the checks-and-balances at the boards, we need help from Democrats. Not much, and it could be discreet."

"My specialty," Carl said cheerfully.

"I just don't know if we need this—"

"I know I'd rather *not*." Carl coughed, cleared his throat. "But at a minimum, we need to watch the other side. If we're capable, they're capable."

"Yeah but the do-gooders won't take that final step."

"Speaking of: are you gonna let Risen know about this?"

Matt sat up, a forkful of spiced lamb lingering in the air.

"Maybe," said Shay.

"He still worries me."

"You worry too much."

"Me?" They both laughed, and Shay said they ought to get to the rehash meeting. Carl added as they left the microphone's range, "Just remember, it only takes one person to fuck it up."

The recording trailed off into hiss.

Settling back into the chair, the late August sun burning through the haze left by the storm, Matt took a long drag from a cigarette. He had no intention of fucking it up, as Carl had so expressively put it. But you kept a bargaining chip in your back pocket. At all times.

He returned carefully to Shay's briefcase. Any moral resistance had been swept away by the conversation he'd just listened to and the fact that Carl had probably gone through his laundry and the laundry of every woman he'd ever slept with. Matt looked at the three wheels of digits. What would Shay use as a code? What was the only number he thought about? Two hundred seventy: the magic number in the electoral college. A moment later, the two flaps in the old-fashioned briefcase broke open. He again stared at the briefcase before slowly opening it.

He imagined first that he'd discover a file containing the details of the secret love lives of every key political player in DC, like the one J. Edgar Hoover kept. Or perhaps the background on some evil deed which would require yet another lie Matt would have to tell the entire world someday. Stacks of old-fashioned reel tapes, the kind that the Nixon CREEP committee kept? Or maybe a secret medical device for a hidden, tragic illness that would change how everyone thought of poor Stephen Shay.

He finally opened the lid and saw a brown paper bag. A gun? Matt had often imagined that Stephen would someday die at his own hand after some major political disgrace—an exceptionally pleasant thought at the moment. But reaching inside, he felt the slick gloss of magazine covers. Carefully he slid them out.

Monster Muscle. Kaged Muscle. Pump and Flex. Oiled-up bodybuilders on each cover—had to be at least ten magazines here—each of them grinning stoically, as if hiding their secrets. *Ironman.* Well that didn't describe Shay. What the hell would he do with these?

With a disturbed groan, Matt dropped the magazines onto the floor. The image in his head was persistent. And oily. He stuffed the magazines back into the bag, placed the bag as neatly as he had the patience for back into the briefcase, firmly closed the lid and fastened the snaps.

I'm starting to discover a whole new Stephen Shay, he thought.

He called Ellen, the travel coordinator who was staying down the hall, and a few minutes later, when he handed her the briefcase and explained who it belonged to, all the color drained from her face.

"Don't tell him it was mixed up with my luggage," Matt said, and helpfully shut the door on her.

Sometimes life handed you a little prize now and then, though it always came at a cost: in this case, the image of Shay greased up like a—no, don't think it. Sit on the bed and tuck this little trauma into your back pocket for a rainy day.

Some two hours later, he'd ignored Gail's phone calls and made a few of his own. Most of them business. After a brief jaunt to the state liquor store in the Short North, he returned to his room with a bottle of Blue Label and a couple packs of Marlboros, and he fidgeted in the darkness of his balcony with his cell phone, running up and down his contacts, passing Kris's name over and over. Shay called once to see if Matt wanted to meet him in the Regency's bar, where two and a half years ago, he'd returned after that wandering night out with Kris. No, he said to Shay, he was too tired. (And too freaked out. This he did not share with his mentor.)

The thought lingered: two and a half years of his life wrapped up in Kris, in a woman so different from him. Different orbits, different solar systems. It was the old cliché: she wanted to change him. Well, not quite. She'd just never expected him to change for the worse. But he had. Change happens, he'd heard somewhere, and sometimes it just felt like the world squeezed you between its massive paws, crushing you into the shape it wanted—demanded—and what were you supposed to do? Elude it? Fight it? He'd gotten, after many long years of struggling, to the place he wanted to be. (Kris glided through everything, it seemed. He'd heard Gail mutter as much when they were still dating.) And now, having arrived, maybe this was just the landscape, the reality, the way things were, not the dream of how they ought to be.

Matt's Journal, Day 180

Cherry blossoms without Kris. They look like dried and watered-down blood. I used to set aside at least one day for the blossoms, and I got Kris in on it, too—strange that she was so hesitant to appreciate their simple beauty, the subtle mosaic they formed.

This year I skipped it.

Like you, dear journal, old friend. I've neglected you, neglected everything. It's not too late? A summary? Driven to record our history, we write down the most meaningless details. Are we afraid of disappearing, afraid that we'll be forgotten?

Okay, here you go: post-Kris, the rest of 2003 I view as the wreckage left behind by a hurricane. I'd go through a month of heavy drinking, chain-smoking, then crawl back on the wagon for a couple weeks. Rinse, repeat. Got kicked out of three bars in DC and one in Maryland, which truly makes it an accomplishment on the federal level. Shay looked at me one day and said, "You drink too much, kid." Shay said that. So I've learned to pace myself, and have been happily oblivious ever since.

You want to know about my love life? Well, let's just take stock, shall we?

Shelly has seen Kris at the lower Starbucks. Says she's doing well. I don't go down there anymore. And there you go: my love life in a nutshell.

But of course what matters to you, my dear journal, is the work. The posterity of history! The inside story, wherein I reveal my true genius, my intellect, my savvy. It reminds me of a conversation I had with Shay back in 2000, after I'd gotten over the little game he and Webb had played with me about the press secretary job. Laughing, I said I'd always believed I was too smart to be manipulated that easily. "Are you kidding?" he said. "The smart ones are the easiest to manipulate." Then he waddled off without any explanation. Smart and ambitious, I think he ought to have said; ambition seems to be a stimulant, but it's really a sedative. You fall asleep and you wake up in a war and there's no way home. Congratulations!

But the work. Yes. Well, after the Massachusetts gay marriage ban was struck down, Shay's eyes glimmered, and we went to work ensuring that America saw all those video clips of gay couples tying the knot. Kensington kept yammering about wanting to give the federal Marriage Protection

Act his full backing, but Shay knew that wouldn't draw the right-wing Christians out in droves come this November. So he got the president to back off, much to the surprise of brilliant political analysts. Which left me spinning. I stammered that it was a states' rights issue. Sure. Good enough. Meanwhile, in Ohio, the RNC courted a Cincinnati group called Citizens for Real American Values whose name sounded innocuous enough, but whose official mission was "to save homosexuals trapped in their evil behaviors." As of this writing, the group has supplied nearly 90 percent of the $1 million raised to pass Issue 1. But, really, it's about states' rights. Honest.

I've heard nothing else about Shay's work in Ohio, really—nothing, I should say, about his more clandestine activities. He met with Kennetha Harris, the secretary of state there, a few times this winter; otherwise he's been skulking about the Midwest, dropping in on blue-collar bars, listening in, gathering, prying when necessary, but always retreating into the night. Not coincidentally, an urban legend has been circulating from St. Louis to Cleveland about a translucent blood-sucking vampiric blob. The authorities are looking into any connection, I'm sure, with the same eagerness with which they've come after me for the Redgrave leak. Which is to say, none at all. Even Judy Hill has held firm, despite threats of being jailed for not revealing her sources.

Redgrave is still alive, though. I have to wonder, if he was so guilty, why hasn't he been arrested?

And now we're hurtling toward the election. It is May 2004, and Raymond Kirk has had the Democratic nomination locked up for a month. Kirk is the kind of man I privately admire: an articulate and thoughtful veteran of Vietnam who never turns down new information when it becomes available; a man whose ethics are solid but whose political positions are allowed to shift with new wisdom. We, of course, are going to destroy him for that. Our numbers are down. The 2004 campaign already looks dirty, vicious, like a hooker you spot a hundred yards down the sidewalk and must nonetheless pass by.

Shay is still obsessed with Ohio, and the way he talks about my home state raises the hackles of my pride. He's like a lot of these consultant goons— they examine the state like proctologists, they don't learn about the people. It's no coincidence that Ohio birthed the Wright brothers and Tecumseh and Harding and Grant and John Glenn ... the list goes on. It's the fusion of the place. Am I proud? Damn right! We Ohioans are arrogant about our lack of arrogance. But we know, privately, how important we are. Let me put it this way: North Carolina contributed a pile of dirt and hot air; Ohio supplied the ingenuity and the courage. The Carolinians stood there gawking at the crazy Ohioans who were going to get themselves killed, and now they have 'First in Flight' on their license plates. I'll have to use that one day with the press. In Ohio, of course.

I guess that about covers it. Me? My mind frame? Let me tell you this: a few months ago, in the crisp, angry winter, when I thought a hearing over the Redgrave leak was inevitable, I began thinking about what else I could do. Maybe go back to Ohio, buy a little restaurant. Or a root beer stand, with a giant sudsy mug tipping back, and everyone would know me by name and wouldn't want anything from me other than a goddamn root beer float. But since then, I've come to my senses. I'm too stubborn to turn back—if turning back is even an option. There's no escaping who you are. Lately I've sensed that you can only hurtle toward the end of the track you've laid down for yourself. You go to sleep, you wake up, and you do your job. Your job is who you are. And it's only a problem when some reporter or senator quizzes you about what you did and when, and you have to think back; you simply can't gauge the time, you can't connect the dots. Don't they know it's been millions of years since Kensington took office? And they want me to make it coherent? Things happen. Seasons change. You go to sleep, and you wake up.

CHAPTER 9

Matt crossed the Rose Garden in the sweltering heat, picked up his pace along the west colonnade, nodded at the sentry inside, and wound through the hallways as he popped a few breath mints. In Webb's first-floor office, he found the vice president sitting awkwardly in his favorite chair, one arm high on the back and the other dangling low to scratch the thinly haired belly of his basset hound, Charlie Brown. Shay was lingering near the unlit fireplace, swirling a glass of scotch and holding it to the light entering from the west through a window. Gail sat near Webb's desk with her assistant, and Broussard and the president's secretary were chatting like lovebirds in a corner. Carefully he lowered himself onto the couch, crossed his legs, and tried to pinch away the hangover from dinner.

"Stephen, you're drinking too much," grumbled Webb.

"Mind your own business."

Jesus, it was like a family dinner in the Midwest: silence and malice. Without the food.

"Kirk has moved away from us on the war with Iraq," Shay said quietly, "and now he's in a tough spot. He has to oppose the war after supporting it. We need to go on the air now and define him as the flip-flopper. Hardly three weeks until their convention and they haven't been defining him. They're taking too long."

"Riding the numbers," Webb muttered.

Matt said, "Did you see the pictures of him dancing awkwardly at that fundraiser? Twisting back and forth like Chubby Checker."

Shay patted Matt on the back. "The visual. Perfect. Use it."

Webb nodded in approval. "What about the grassroots stuff?"

"The network is better than it's ever been." Shay cleared his throat. "We're able to put out anything we want immediately." He pointed a small finger at Gail. "The key to our operation is the individual influencers. It's right up your alley—the power of networking. Lately the message has been more complex than I'd like it to be."

"The gay marriage bans are working, though, aren't they?" said Matt.

"I think so, but that's just a segment. An important one, yes, but this flip-flopper ad is bolder, easier. No one likes inconsistency."

"Or thoughtfulness," Matt blurted. Shay and Webb glared at him. "I'm serious. Presidents are doers. Look at Reagan, for Christ's sake. I say we play up the ponderousness of his character."

"You won't beat his integrity," Webb said grimly.

"Don't be so sure," said Shay, and he looked at Matt. "I've got a job for you and Gail."

Matt nodded obliquely. No sense in pretending to be enthused when the rest of the room was so damn glum.

Webb's emotion seemed to shift, and with a profound pout he said, "The right track, wrong track numbers look hideous." He waved his bad arm toward a map pinned to a tripod. "In most of our target states, the mood is low, voters are still vulnerable. Even after we make the war on terrorism the focus, we start losing ground on the economy right away." Webb crossed his arms. "Just don't forget the other battleground states simply because you had a vision about Ohio."

One of Shay's caterpillar eyebrows slowly raised. "I've done some research in Ohio. I don't want to get into details, but Carl has identified some possible help on the other side."

"Other side—you mean Democrats?" Matt said. Finally this was coming into play. He wondered if Webb was read in on the vote manipulation idea, but judging by the anxiety in his eyes right now, that'd be a no.

"We can get a little help muddying the water," Shay was saying, "getting them to burn cash, confuse, misdirect. We have a Democrat operative that'll help us for a price. The Ohio Republican Party has used him before; he has enough influence to wreak havoc."

Webb stepped toward Shay and started to say something, but Shay held up his hands defensively. Take a picture, Matt thought.

"Every precaution has been taken," Shay said slowly. "Other than that, I don't want to say more."

Webb stood down. He'd begun pacing, though, and Charlie was following to see where his belly rubs would be coming from. "Let's get back to message. We want this campaign fought on security issues rather than domestic issues, so how do we keep them away from the economy?"

"The other side isn't exactly inspiring hope. Maybe we can turn the despair to our advantage, or at least blunt the damage. Maybe the subtle message is that, no matter what, things are going to suck for awhile."

"I can't say that on the air," Matt said.

Webb said, his voice a little more sprightly, "They know we'll do a better job keeping gas prices down and taxes low. So we offer a life preserver message. Hold on to us and the ocean won't swallow you up; let go of us and you'll drown."

Shay said, "Message phase one: he's a flip-flopper and we need a leader with a firm hand. Phase two: take away his military record advantage. Phase three: make sure they can't deliver a message of hope."

Webb sneered and smiled. "If there is no hope, then hope can't win."

———∿∿———

It wasn't until he, Shay, and Gail were holed up in a St. Louis bar a few days later that Matt understood what job Shay needed done. After a long campaign swing in Iowa and Missouri, the God's Will's entourage landed in a plush St Louis hotel that hosted a ten-thousand-dollars-a-couple fundraiser, but halfway through it, Shay dragged Gail and Matt to a bar he'd scouted outside the city. It was a typical blue-collar bar, with a neon Budweiser sign in the window and the smell of stale beer and cigarettes in the air. A sunken-cheeked man with deep-set eyes and yellow skin coughed a sound so scratchy it made Matt's throat sore. "Why are we here?" Gail said. "Does the campaign need us to catch TB?"

"Just a little ambience," Shay said, with a crooked grin.

Gail smirked. "Ambience? This looks like the bar scene in *Star Wars*." She pointed to three guys whose butts practically swallowed their bar stools. "Hell, that looks like a Jabba the Hutt family reunion."

Having been drinking since four that afternoon, Matt felt it his responsibility to inform Gail that she was a heartless bitch with a weight hang-up.

"Sorry," she said, "I know you like the big girls."

"You still gagging yourself in the toilet?" Matt sneered.

Shay shut them both up and explained once again what an asshole Webb was for believing that you couldn't react to your opponent's message. "Bullshit. His message and our message are two separate things that make one thing. Like hydrogen and oxygen make water. They'll try to use Kirk's war record, so it'll be a cowboy-versus-soldier comparison," Shay said. "America loves cowboys, just ask John Wayne. Maybe they don't speak the King's English, but they're straight shooters. Honest and charming."

Matt nodded. "And decisive. Charge in where others fear to tread. But that could be seen as reckless."

"Could be?" Shay said with a wormy grin. "Our cowboy is vulnerable to that, so let's steer them into an integrity war. Because it never works. All politicians are crooks. It's a dead argument."

Shay took a swallow of the Jack Daniels he'd ordered. Slumming it, Matt thought.

Shay continued, "The soldier is America's favorite hero: courageous, loyal, fearless, the best in the world. And unlike the cowboy, the soldier isn't reckless. He's highly trained. In a direct image comparison, the soldier wins." He scanned the room as he talked and pointed a stubby finger toward a young guy near the dartboard, wearing his camos. He'd probably just come back from, or was going to, Iraq. "We have to weaken that image. We laid the groundwork with the first round of ads, showing his indecisiveness."

Matt recalled the perplexed look on Kirk's face and the series of indecisive statements, culminating in "I didn't decide that way until I, err, ah, re-decided it."

"We have to finish him off with a direct strike on his war record," said Shay. His eyes tightened. "We need veterans to speak up against him, against his record. A separate committee to provide distance, of course. Gail, that's your job."

She seemed to jolt awake. "Got it. No tracks in the snow."

"Matt, you work with me on the ad copy and production. I want it low-key. When Gail's got them in place, make sure they say what we fucking want them to say."

As usually happened, Matt slowly gauged the foresight of Shay's plan; Kirk and his people would definitely go after Kensington's piss-poor experience in the National Guard, and this was nothing less than a pre-emptive strike.

"It'll overshadow Kensington's military record, or lack thereof," Matt said, smiling. Times like these, you almost played a different version of yourself. Momma told you to never lie, but your momma was never good at cutthroat anyway, was she? "You want these ads out before they start their convention, right?"

Shay's beady eyes popped. "Well before. Let's ruin their fucking picnic."

⸝⸜⸝

Two weeks before the Democratic convention, the ads started airing nationwide with heavy coverage in the Midwest. A woman whose husband had been a POW clutched a silk hankie—that and her dress just screamed "rich," but it'd take a week for anyone to notice and by then the ad would be off the air—and wept as she described the senator's hateful testimony after returning from Vietnam. "I'll never forget what Raymond Kirk did to my husband," she cried, as if Kirk had bound, gagged, and led her husband to Ho Chi Minh himself.

In the game of chicken they were playing, the timing seemed a brilliant stroke. The bloggers and even a few networks picked up on the story of the ads—brilliant when an advertisement became legit news, and got shown for free—and it became one of the top hundred searches on Google.

But Kirk, in a dour navy blue suit, had to ruin things on the Thursday night before the Democratic convention by introducing his vice-presidential pick: Noah Young. The one-term senator from Illinois, handsome, young, fit; Young was a perfect foil to Kirk's hangdog expressions and stiff gesticulations. The nation exploded with love for the Democrats and the first African American nominee for vice president on a major party ticket. And they'd just become a little more major.

Tuesday night of the convention, as thousands of signs jumped in a Minneapolis convention center, Webb hit the mute button and chuckled to himself. "The isolationists are gonna love this."

Matt leaned against the wall of the president's second-floor office, which was the real presidential office, the one where Kensington did most of his work. At that moment, the president was staring thoughtfully at the television, a little boy adamantly watching after his parents had told him to go to bed. Shay was two steps from drunk, Gail was on her phone. Same old, same old.

"This could be a problem," said Shay, ignoring Webb's comment.

"Stevie boy," said Kensington, "you're giving me an ulcer."

It looked like, Matt thought. Over the past few years, the presidency had streaked Kensington's hair gray and scalloped his cheeks and forehead with sizable wrinkles.

Shay tilted his head; it looked like a bus wobbling on two wheels, about to turn over. "We can't be sure how to take it. Polling and focus groups tend to be unreliable with the race issue. For his experience, he has a strong record."

"For his experience," Webb mumbled.

"Well, look at my experience, Dixie." The president eyed the pantomime on the television. Noah Young's wife was taking the stage. "It's a proud moment, you guys. Never woulda thought it."

"I don't believe his race is going to be a major issue," said Shay.

"And that's the way I want it: non-factor." The president spoke as firmly as Matt had ever heard him. "Don't get me wrong; I don't want to see Kirk in my chair, you know? But I'll be damned if we go down that route." He looked at Webb keenly, a glare Matt wished he used more often. "They can call me a half-wit and a cheater, but I do not want to be called a racist."

Webb shifted. Sometimes, when under pressure, he looked as if he was trying to find someone who could give him permission to go to the toilet.

"Mr. President, I agree with you, but—"

"Webb," Kensington barked. "It's not for discussion."

"Will's right," said Shay. "It's not for discussion because Young's not important. Webb, you'll treat your debate with him that way. Just another day at the office. Mr. President, you tell the world how proud you are." Shay turned to Matt and said in a lower voice, "And you hit the experience issue hard. And quietly. Otherwise, step around questions about Young like they're dog shit.

"Let's not overreact," Shay continued. "This is what conventions do: make it look like a race. Hell, Mondale tied Reagan, and Dukakis went way up. It happens every time and everyone acts like it's the first time."

The network went to commercial, and Webb turned up the volume when a chubby veteran in a glossy gray business suit started in on how Raymond Kirk *blah blah blah.* These guys didn't even look like soldiers, they looked like investment bankers, and now that the Dems had won a round with the selection of Noah Young, it would be imperative to up the ante. To play hardball. Fill in the cliché: Shay would use it. Imperative because, for the first time, it looked like Kensington could lose.

CHAPTER 10

A week later, nearing the Republican convention in New York City, Gail's group had mobilized again—their veterans held press conferences, they protested at Kirk's rallies, and the TV ads dipped into the netherworld of attack politics. The ads openly questioned Kirk's service record, showed an altered picture of Kirk at an antiwar protest, bombarded the Internet with closely edited clips of Kirk's testimony to Congress to make it sound as though he was charging every single goddamn Vietnam veteran with a host of atrocities.

Predictably, Kirk hit back, but to Shay's surprise, the ads were direct, almost austere. With the gravity of his years, Kirk looked directly into the camera and said, "It's not about the wars we've fought in. It's not about the past. It's about the future, about who will keep us from recklessly charging into wars that will tie us down for generations. We must be strong, but we must also be wise." And then, as carefully as they'd laced the Axis of Evil countries through the State of the Union address in 2002, Kirk listed the places where no one wanted to fight: North Korea, Syria, and Iran.

The lift from the convention was sizable for the Dems, and roaming Madison Square Garden with cameras in his face, Matt sensed a defeatism spreading through the faithful. Half the time he felt like he was tending to the wounded, convincing them that there was plenty of campaign left. Wednesday he watched from the sidelines as Ohio Secretary of State Kennetha Harris gave a live press conference explaining why, a few days ago, she'd demanded that registration forms in Ohio be on eighty-pound paper, even though it'd been revealed that even the forms in her office were on forty-pound. Boards of elections had already thrown out thousands of forms.

Keep on keeping them from voting, Kennetha, he could hear Shay say, and he wondered what she was getting out of the deal.

When her press conference was done, he wandered over, pulled her aside, and explained why she had bombed. "You don't have to actually answer the questions, you know," he said as if talking to a fifth-grader. "You say what you want to say. Otherwise, you're killing us."

"They're killing me. It's a new thing every day."

"No, it's not. That's the thing: it is *not* a new thing every day. It's the same thing, the same message, every fucking day."

He nearly patted her ass and sent her back out into the game.

The Republican Convention brought out something wonderful in him, no matter how poorly things were shaping up, no matter how blasé he felt about smearing the queers and the veterans. Interview after interview, mornings were a whirlwind of staff holding out his coffee and pumping him up as he rushed from one network to the next, grabbing producers and being the center of attention, Broussard at his side constantly, like Jacko's bodyguard. On one occasion, he'd actually had a doctor ask for his autograph, and as he signed it, he leaned over to Broussard and whispered, "We are a celebrity-sick culture, aren't we?" Broussard rolled his eyes. Like Shay and his scotch, Matt got drunk on the bright lights—and everyone knew it.

Thursday afternoon, having finished an interview in the CBS loge studio overlooking the floor, he wound his way toward the stage, past women in colorful Styrofoam hats covered with flowers and plastic elephants and young people in T-shirts with slogans like "America First" and "Kirk's a Communist." Where was that last one coming from? He edged near the podium, waiting for Broussard, and scanned the crowd. You could never get tired of the red, white, and blue, the gaudy beads and sunglasses, all that kitsch underneath the classic post signs for each state and territory, some of them affixed with bumper stickers for local candidates. Free exposure. He remembered watching the 1972 Democratic convention as a child and learning that America still had territories. As he looked out at the audience, he straightened his cuffs and tightened his tie, hoping that he could easily be spotted.

His phone rang, and a sheet of ice-water poured through him. "Kris?"

"About a hundred feet at your ten o'clock, Risen."

He spotted her on a platform behind the Texas delegation, in her work attire: white T-shirt, jeans, an albatross of cameras around her neck.

"Getting back to your roots?" he said.

"I guess," she shouted. "Sorry, I can hardly hear you."

"I'm glad you called."

"I'm glad you answered. I saw you pause."

Broussard was approaching, struggling to fend off an overzealous woman whose T-shirt claimed she was part of God's Will's army of believers. He turned away from his assistant, ducking toward the back of the stage.

"Why are you calling me?" he said. "I mean, not that I—have you …"

"Don't get worked up. I just … wondered about you."

"Me, too."

She laughed. "Well you should be. Wondering."

"Meet me for a drink tonight."

"I don't know."

"I've got a scoop for you, how about that?"

Several people in the audience had spotted him and were aiming cameras. Again, he ducked through a crowd, too late to avoid Broussard's clutch, though.

"Where are you hanging out?" she shouted.

He gave her the info as Broussard stared him down. Why, oh why this week? If he was more paranoid—and he was working on that—he'd guess that she was part of some vast left-wing conspiracy.

"Hey Kris, you know the only good thing about mistakes—they help you sort out the forgiving folks from the judgmental."

"We'll see about that."

———⌒⋀⌒———

It had taken him awhile to realize that they were in New York again and that it had been little more than a year since he'd gotten drunk and she'd walked out on him.

She brushed her curly brown hair over her shoulder and said, "Blitzed. You were wasted, Matt."

"Key choice of words there," he said with a soggy voice.

She didn't bite; in fact, throughout their conversation over some mediocre and half-warm Thai dishes, she kept a chilly distance, an almost curious tone in her voice, the way you would approach a first date. Slowly he'd drawn out the details of her life since last summer, connecting them to the barest of morsels Shelly had shared with him: Kris had worked the rest of the summer, then taken the year off; she'd flown to Europe, backpacked, and finally visited Italy. "Even Florence," she said with a grin, "and I managed to get out." She'd read, she'd sewn, she'd gotten back into yoga, and she'd even tried dating when she came back to the States. No one he knew, she said—that terrible phrase, meant to please, full of vagueness and an invitation to the imagination.

"You must be busy," he said.

"Since the primaries."

"I mean, dating."

She smirked and took a deep breath. "Not so much."

They avoided alcohol that night, sticking to green tea and then, after wandering a few blocks, a shot of thick Turkish coffee. As they walked, he noticed that she strayed near him now and then. Which was more heartbreaking? That she wanted to, or that she couldn't bring herself to?

His phone rang for the umpteenth time, and they both stared at it. "You're in deep shit," said Kris.

"You seem to have that effect on me."

"I'll just ruin your career."

"I may not have one in three months."

There was the walk to her hotel. The shy dance at the revolving door.

The friendly kiss on the cheek.

The lingering.

"Hit the road, Risen," she said, her heavy eyelids blinking furiously, some thought held back, some wish. Reluctantly he let go of her hand, drifted back to the sidewalk, and, in the gentle warmth of the night, said to himself that it could be a beginning. And that it was louder and brighter than any convention.

Cory snapped his fingers. "I said, tell me the fucking truth: did you or didn't you leak Redgrave's name?"

Matt leaned forward in his seat outside the lower Starbucks, pulling his eyes away from the statuesque woman who'd been approaching up the sidewalk. Glancing back at Cory, he winced at the rage flushing Cory's boyish face.

"No," he said absently. "I think it was Gail."

"You *think*."

He was tempted to tell Cory everything. Had been since Cory had called, demanding to meet. They'd been steadily drifting apart for a year, and there was nothing to blame it on—not the election, not even his drinking—nothing other than some lingering animus between them, the kind brothers carried for years.

"I think she's spreading my name for revenge. To take me out."

"Why would she do that?"

"We don't see eye-to-eye. I threaten her relationship with Kensington."

"Couldn't you talk to him, then?"

Matt shook his head. Poor Cory, still the naive dilettante. "It's not like that."

"Goddamn it, Matt, you've got to expose these people! Now!" His cousin's voice shook with a needle of fear. Just like Cory to be pissed and worried about him at the same time.

Calmly he tried to explain that Webb and Shay were calling the shots, and that, yes, they'd done some distasteful things, but it was in the name of national security. Hadn't Iraq simmered down after the Surge? Hadn't they been safe for the past three years? "Sometimes you do some dirty shit for the greater good," he said. Cory let him babble on, and he spoke with the easy tone of a person who privately believed that the worst was behind him; the Redgrave leak, the gay marriage amendments, the attack ads: it was all in the past or already in play, out of his hands. He'd never go back to it. Not after the election. Not if Kris would take *him* back. Briefly, even, he'd considered gracefully resigning after the election, if they won, and looking for a different line of work.

Cory firmly shook his head. "Dirty shit? Our ancestors expected us to do a lot better. To evolve. Go read the inscription at the Jefferson monument. With greater knowledge and understanding we're supposed to do better than our 'barbarous ancestors.'"

"He meant the British."

"No, Matt, he meant himself. And his contemporaries."

Suddenly Cory's eyes caught something over Matt's shoulder. A man had stepped out of the alleyway next to the coffee shop. He was pale under a greasy head of shoe-polish-black hair, and in the thick August heat, he was wearing a heavy brown business suit. His eyes darting, he said in a hush, "Good evening, Cory."

Cory had gone stiff and white. "Uh, George. This is my cousin."

Matt stretched out a hand. The man took it quickly and released it just the same. His skin was clammy, wet.

"George, what's it been? Years?" Cory forced an awkward smile. "How are you doing?"

Morosely he said, "I've been better. It seems I've lost my cat."

Once again, Cory's genuine goodness shone through. All you had to do was look at how he acted so concerned over the whack-job's cat.

"I'm sorry to hear that. Uh, have you looked for him?"

"Everywhere. But you know tomcats. He could be in Russia as far as I know." The pale man studied a young man making coffee on the street, one of the shop's summertime shticks. "Thing is, I didn't even know he was gone. For the longest time."

"I know how much your cat means to you. Have you put up reward signs?"

"Plenty."

"Well, give me a call, George. You have my number?"

"Soon as I can," the man said. Without glancing at Matt, he spun and walked away. Matt studied him awhile, gauging his limp, then with a crooked eye looked back at Cory.

"A guy I used to work with," his cousin said.

"What the hell, did he follow you here?"

"Yeah, strange guy. Real paranoid. He was always talking about GM stealing his patents. He, uh, spent ten years perfecting a corn stalk with a minimum of two ears of corn." Cory was still watching over Matt's shoulder. "I don't know, maybe he lives around here."

They sat silently for a few minutes, Cory lost in some trance while Matt observed the traffic up and down the Old Town streets. It'd been a good place to live for awhile, but maybe he needed to pack up shop and head somewhere else. Maybe Kris's cabin to write his memoirs. Slip away without much fuss. That'd show her what was important to him.

Idly he said, "I've been thinking about quitting."

Cory looked at him in horror. "You can't. You have to figure this thing out, Matt. You have to make it public."

Matt chuckled, gathered his laptop and suggested they meet again next week, before his schedule started flying him all over the country day-in and day-out. "We've only got a little time," he said with a mischievous grin.

"You're right," said Cory. "Look, I'm going to be really busy. Just promise me you won't give up on this, okay?"

"Sure thing," Matt said.

CHAPTER 11

A pair of glossy black eyes, wide as an owl's, reflected the image of a taxi speeding along the curving Tuscan road. On a hillside covered in blue irises, a man of considerable height lowered his binoculars and, from where he stood in the gloom of dusk, watched as the taxi came to a halt at the *ristorante* down the hill. The parking lot was empty, and this seemed to surprise the pale man as he stepped out of the cab; his head turned and turned, and for a moment it seemed as though he'd duck back into the cab. But he paid the fare, and Yuri watched as he headed into the restaurant.

With a groan, Yuri climbed the brief distance to the top of the hillside where his rental waited. He packed away the binoculars, and removed a second gun from the glove compartment. His cell phone rang; the owner of the *ristorante*, paid handsomely, pressed three even tones and hung up. Ball was inside, waiting at a table, and the owner and his staff would now be making their way toward the cellar.

Yuri pulled thin leather gloves over his quaking hands. They shook all the time now.

———⌁———

A year ago, nearly to the day, he'd been shot by Korovyov twice. As he'd dragged himself to his car, clutching the files on the Americans to his wet, bloody chest, the silliest tune haunted him—the lilting Gypsy song the professor, Ryukhin, had played for him. Those first pounding notes on the piano. The women's swaying voices, reminding him—no matter how much he wished they didn't—of Zaryana's sweet, maternal fretting. In the cramped coupe, speeding along, he imagined she sat

225

next to him. "Not too fast," she'd said, her grayish-blue eyes watery, a little bloodshot, "or there'll be no point to even making a hospital."

It was eight miles down the M-10 to a surgeon in Khimki, and he was admitted as Mr. Likhodeyev, the unfortunate victim of a mugging. How very white burned the hot lamps as the fiddle played.

When he'd woken, he was alone. As it had been for many years. His shoulder was wrapped and taped—little more than a flesh wound—but, through the bluish blur of his oxygen mask, he saw that his stomach was bandaged like the mummy of an Egyptian king. His feet kicked like a little boy's. In the movies, a man such as himself would have ripped it all away and staggered from the bed, but in truth he was so weighed down, so weak, that he could hardly breathe without the mask. Still, when the weasel-like doctor entered, Yuri muttered that he must get out, that he must be on his way. Impossible, the doctor said. It would take weeks. And besides, more tests needed to be done. They had found a tumor in a portion of his intestines that hadn't been blown away. "Thank God for your mugging, eh?" the doctor said cheerfully.

"Zaryana," he whispered.

By the time he'd left the hospital in Khimki three weeks later, he'd been diagnosed with colon cancer. A doctor also told him—with a straight face, mind you—that the car he'd parked outside the hospital had, in fact, been destroyed in a warehouse fire which claimed the lives of two American tourists and their Russian tour guide. His apartment had been scoured to the bone, and of course the Orbweaver program was gone, along with all of the files he'd brought with him to the hospital. But not all of his files were lost. He'd stashed various disks and notes in a chaotic pattern all over Moscow, and within a few days, he'd collected them and found a new apartment under a new name, chosen in a moment of inspiration: Mikhail Nikolaevich Abaddona. The first two names were a tribute to his dead colleagues, and as if called by him, they began to appear in his new apartment, nodding with approval, as did some darker force beyond the pale to whom Yuri had also paid tribute.

The chill of a Moscow autumn had fully descended, and walking shakily with a cane into Alexander Garden, Yuri considered the options the doctors had explained. The children gathered, but with only the pittance he'd thought to stash into a secret account, he had no *karofka* for them. Many months later, he would be ashamed to admit that he'd considered closing up shop, as he'd muttered that hot night to the American. His body was betraying him, all six-foot-five of it, every muscle, sinew, sense, even his brain, which lately seemed cloudy and given to moments of pinching hesitation. And visions. He'd never been one to consider the spirit, even after Nikolai and Mikhail had been killed in Florence. He'd seen many agents die. Many friends. But after Zaryana had died from the radiation poisoning from Chernobyl, he had to consider the problem of coincidence, the issue of fate, and the heartsick notions he felt of wanting to see her again. And now ghosts trailed him, said hello from beside fountains, waved to him from passing trains.

Still, there came no epiphany. One day, he'd been sitting on a bench in front of the Manege, and he seemed to remember what he had left to do. That was all. He had the doctors begin an aggressive treatment so that he might get back to his task, and they radiated his body—Zaryana held him, saying, "Now you know." From his frailty and anxiety arose a determination to see his final mission through to its completion. With only strands left of his silvery hair, he washed dishes in a filthy diner and took on a few odd jobs—a small-time hit here and there; he bought a laptop, had it fit with new security measures, and even tried to program a low-grade version of the Orbweaver software. Through the winter and into the spring, he took the pills he was prescribed, forced his hulking mass up and down stairwells, slipped into underground shooting ranges and boxing rings, and waited. One had to one's name only dignity and honor and perseverance, so what did it matter the length of the campaign?

———〰———

Yuri zipped his light tan jacket up over his shirt and the vest it hid. With a clearing of his breath, he began down the hill toward the ancient *ristorante*. The ivy-covered archway and giant stones of the patio had been set more than five hundred years ago and walked across by Machiavelli himself, no doubt, on his way home to his family's nearby vineyard. As Yuri neared the gravel parking lot, the pale man emerged from the rear kitchen door. Too slow, Yuri thought. These damn legs, this muddled brain.

He ducked behind an elm, waited a moment, and then paced in a crouch toward the American. Inside, they had probably not bothered to take his order; the total desertion of the restaurant was a clear giveaway. Stupid, stupid. Ball was probably thinking the same thing; he'd come alone, responding to Yuri's promise of answers concerning 'The Cat' Kaplan and Mendelsohn. He stood now in a grove of olive trees, holding his cell phone out and punching in some numbers, his back turned.

Yuri undid the safety of his .357. "We're getting old, aren't we?" he said.

Ball froze. "Y-yes," he whispered.

"Let's take a walk."

They proceeded into the rows of ancient grapevines where the dusk had fallen thickly. A few more steps in, Yuri told Ball to turn around, and he studied the pale face of the man who'd killed Mikhail. Like the other two Americans, like himself, George Ball had aged considerably, his skin a little looser, his eyes dimmer. It was tempting to sympathize with him.

Yuri produced a slip of paper, and when Ball took it, he reached into his coat pocket and held forth a tape recorder. "Read the message, Mr. Ball."

"I can't see, it's too dark."

A pitiful stall tactic. "Read the fucking message."

Slowly Ball began to read—his mind scrambling, no doubt, for any option, for any exit—and Yuri had pressed down the record button before he thought of something.

"Address him by name, Mr. Ball. And make sure you read evenly."

The American inhaled and began again.

"Cory, it's … your friend. Come to Florence. Alone. I'll leave an opera ticket for Thursday night for you at the desk of the Hotel del Rossi. Urgent, life or death."

Yuri ordered him to place the note on the ground, and the man tensed.

"What do you want to know?" Ball said.

"I know everything I need to know. Put the note on the ground."

"I can tell you things—"

Yuri squeezed the trigger, and the .357 kicked with a shock that sent a jolt up his arm and into his chest. Ball fell to the mossy earth, and for a second, Yuri thought he might join him there.

Wiping off as much blood as he could onto the stiff leaves, Yuri swept the American clean and rushed through the grove and up the long side of the hill toward his car, where he listened to Ball's message. It would do. The leak of Redgrave's name had caused considerable panic, he'd learned, but this Cory Risen was, by all accounts, a man whose loyalty was a fault; intel had pegged him as inviolate, a man who couldn't be turned but who followed his team members too closely, worried too much about them and not enough about himself. He would come to Florence and die.

At the car, Yuri's chest seized and the American's wallet flapped to the grass. His fat lips trembled; even the tear-shaped scar under his eye seemed to burn. He scrambled for the pills in his coat, popped the cap, poured a few down his throat, and swallowed. Night was on his shoulders, and he gasped like a man who'd just escaped with his life. And then he realized that he'd forgotten. Forgotten to ask Ball about the briefcase. This damn memory. Everything in its twilight. The ghost of Mikhail leaned on the hood of the car, his arms folded, a knowing grin bunching his fat cheeks and his beard, and he gazed at Yuri and nodded.

CHAPTER 12

Working himself into a lather, Matt watched the live feed of the World News on a monitor in CBS's Washington bureau. Republican protestors had struck another Kirk-Young rally, nearly all of them white and pushing sixty years old. That'll change our image, Matt thought as he watched one hill jack scream "Fucking socialist!" the expletive bleeped out, of course. "Commie traitor, go back to 'Nam!" shouted another, who stood next to a man parading around in a sandwich board of Young caricatured as a monkey, his teeth enormous, under the incredibly derogatory slogan, "It's black or white." Kirk they simply showed being hanged with the word in bold: *Traitor*!

"Clean campaign you're running," the makeup woman said as she looked him over.

"Those aren't my people," he said.

"They're all your people."

Seated, he held a copy of what CBS was calling a smoking gun: a letter supposedly written by the commanding officer of God's Will, implying that he'd received preferential treatment in the National Guard and gotten himself withdrawn, penalty-free, after only nine months of service. It was bullshit. It *looked* like bullshit to him—you used to be able to smoke in military bases, and yet the original was hardly yellowed—and Shay said he knew the guy on the other side responsible for the forgery. The media had been kicking themselves over missing this back in 2000, and CBS had slithered like muskrats down a riverbank slide to break the story. Sloppy, biased bullshit. He'd told every other network, and now it was time to drop CBS's anchor.

"Reaction from around the 'net over this item, sourced to CBS News just days ago," the anchorman intoned. You had to give him credit; no matter what he said, it sounded like the word of God. "And now, joining us from Washington with the administration's reaction, press secretary Matthew Risen. Matt?"

"Good to see you," he said to the screen.

"You've been on the record already saying this information is inaccurate, why don't you fill me in?"

Laughing condescendingly, Matt asked where he should begin. "The inconsistencies? The timing of the attack? Or that your staff picked the news up from a left-wing conspiracy fanatic's blog?"

"Libby Walter's the man you're referring to. He was a journalist first—"

"The worst kind. Every article on his site is an attack against the president and national security."

The last bit he threw in, of course; it didn't need to be true.

"So you're saying President Kensington did *not* use his family's connections to get that deferment?"

"I'm saying, that you guys have done a terrible job of reporting the facts. This is sloppy, irresponsible journalism." Heat was rising from his gut, even his groin—that nipple-tingling sensation—and though he calmed and deepened his breath, he otherwise let the anger flow. It felt damn good. No word from Kris for weeks, no word from Cory. Nothing was improving. "In fact, I'd say that this rests in your hands, you and the Democrats behind this mess." He allowed his hand to lift just a fraction, to give the impression of pointing his finger at the anchor without really doing so. "When you think about it, it's defamation."

Blushed crimson, the anchor stammered that the document had been reviewed by experts.

"What experts? *You?* You guys aren't saying, and why is that?"

"Matt, we only have a moment left. Could you describe in detail why you're convinced this isn't authentic?"

"That's your job. You and your buddies."

"But I'm asking—"

"Prove to me it *is* authentic, and then we'll talk. Until then, this is nothing more than a slanderous attack on the sitting president of the United States."

In the tin can of his earbud, Matt's words were overrun by the producer, and the anchor, still burning, gave a curt thanks. Matt barely managed to respond in kind. He flipped the earpiece out and tore off the lapel mike, handing it to a trembling intern.

"Another helpful interview with the Kensington administration," chirped the bureau's in-house producer, a slender woman who looked like she belonged at the opening of some art gallery in New York.

"Look, if you want another war, Bernice, I can get you that."

He rolled his eyes and stalked toward the waiting Broussard.

———⟨⟨⟩———

The next afternoon, after an exhaustive forty-eight hours of getting beat to death, the letter was declared a fake. Aim under the heart, he'd learned, and that's what he'd been doing. He'd reduced a few men to blathering and the edge of tears.

"Fucking brilliant," Shay crowed, toasting him at the Round Robin. "Though I worried you'd have a heart attack."

Matt shrugged and tossed back his licorice-tasting shot, savoring the burn as it slid down his throat. Frankly, my dear, he didn't give a damn about the truth of the National Guard letter. He just didn't want to get trampled by the press corps he'd managed to sedate the past few years.

"We're lucky," Shay said. "That letter really bailed us out. Ended the issue altogether."

"You mean the Dems bailed us out. It was sloppy shit."

"Sure."

Something struck him. They *had* been bailed out by the letter, pretty conveniently, and the Democrats had been all but silent, really; it was the media outlets doing all the barking, first in accusation, then self-defense, and now self-recrimination.

Matt threw his cigarettes on the bar. "Was it Carl? One of Gail's crew?"

"I told you, a guy in the Kirk cam—"

"You didn't trust me?"

Shay studied their reflections in the mirror behind the bar. "We just thought it'd be more natural if you didn't know."

Matt ordered a double.

"Come on, kid. We played a little cloak-and-dagger. Now they're skittish. Anything new comes up, they'll hesitate to run it. It's worth the gamble."

He described how Carl had worked on the letter himself, using an early 1970s-style font, but one that hadn't been created until much later. How he'd made sure to just nearly botch the signature. How he'd handed it off to Gail, who'd given it to someone she knew, who'd passed it to Libby Walter.

"The media should have figured us out," said Shay. "For the font to be off by just a little, that's the work of people who *wanted* the fraudulence to be discovered. The Dems would've been more careful, they knew there'd be experts involved—"

"Were you going to tell me?" said Matt.

Shay hemmed and hawed, as Uncle Jess would say, and it was clear that, no, he hadn't planned on it. Maybe the fix was in. Maybe Matt wouldn't get the chance to quit after the election—and with no Kris and a pissed-off cousin, who would he have left? Larry Bird? The impulse of hope was to lean forward, and so he'd naturally applied that energy to what he knew best: the election, spin, dirt. The pretty boy. The face. As he'd wavered and navigated, did a little hemming and hawing of his own, at least he could console himself that no one had gotten hurt. That his fuck-ups were his own and that he alone would pay the price. But even that rationale vanished: three days after the CBS interview, Raymond Kirk was dead by an assassin's bullet.

Air Force One climbed into the blue, cloudless autumn sky and leveled off. Once he'd finished a call with the Ohio press secretary about the rally in Cincinnati, Matt made his own climb to the second floor, which housed the airplane's kitchen and, hopefully, a grilled tuna sandwich prepared by the chefs from the navy. He gave absent nods to the Secret Service men and the occasional army support staffer, but when he reached the kitchen, the equivalent of a four-star restaurant, he batted his baby blues at the female chef. The food was the only thing about Air Force One he looked forward to anymore.

Waiting for his grilled tuna, he peeked around the corner at the briefing room next door. On the other side of the kitchen was an operating room staffed with two doctors and one surgeon. The second floor also contained a critical communications situation room, and from there he saw a young, crew-cut army corporal bolt toward the stairwell.

A few minutes later, he was stealing bites of the sandwich and gaggling with a group of reporters, all of them handpicked by him to ride Air Force One, and not the trailer plane, which nobody ever recognized, and which no one gave much of a shit about. As they talked about the lingering issues in Iraq, he unrolled what he called his "pep rally" speech, adopting his Nixon voice as he said, "Our opponents are an ideologically-driven and divided collection of cutthroat warlords who are primarily concerned with destroying each other."

"So you're confident the war in Iraq will end soon," a reporter said.

"Oh, I misunderstood," he said, grinning, trying not to seem weary of this act. "I was talking about the Democrats."

They were all laughing except for a serious young woman near the back of the gaggle. She reminded him, with her athletic frame and fierce eyes, of Kris. "Off the record, Matt," she said, and he tried to remember who she was and how she'd gotten on the damn plane, "do you think Ohio will be as important this year, and how do you approach the state?"

"Ah, my neck of the woods," he said, trying to light a charming fire in his eyes. "You know, to understand Ohio ... um, Amy?"

"Rebecca." She stared at him dourly.

"The diversity and the balance of power existed long before Europeans arrived. There were a multitude of major and minor native tribes in Ohio. The land, the rivers, the lake created a perfect habitat for diversity. Rebecca, to understand Ohio and the curse of balance, you just have to think back to the Seneca chief, Ogista." He paused to quickly flush down the last of the tuna with some water; he loved telling this story, and had bored Kris with it many times. "The Seneca and the Wyandot had been at war for generations, but in 1755 they joined forces to fight the British General Braddock. They kicked his ass, and they stopped on their way back home, intending to split up the next day. A joyous celebration broke out among members of the two tribes, but at some point over the course of the evening—you know, after some drinking, some carrying on—a fight broke out, and a member of one tribe killed a member of the other tribe."

After checking to see if he still had them, he went on. "War was about to break out when the Seneca chief, Ogista, proposed a slightly less bloody solution. He suggested that twenty members of the Seneca tribe battle twenty members of the Wyandot tribe. To the death. The last one standing would be declared the victor and the dispute would be resolved in favor of that tribe. I know it might sound outrageous, but sacrificing thirty-nine lives was less deadly than war would've been. The idea was accepted and the battle proceeded.

"And it was ferocious. Forty experienced warriors, trapped in a small area, hacking and stabbing each other until there was one survivor: Gahnele, Ogista's son. As the son knelt before his father, the chief raised his tomahawk and buried it deeply in his son's skull. I imagine him looking over the dead body of his son and saying, 'Your body belongs in this honored ground with the other thirty-nine brave souls.' He looked at the shocked members of both tribes and said, 'I have sacrificed my son for the good of our nation. So that we may live equally. Let the tomahawk never be raised between our tribes again.' And it wasn't, though Ogista lived out his days in constant sorrow. That spot is on the border of Stark county, the most balanced county in Ohio."

He waited a minute, like a college professor, gauging their reaction.

"Once the Europeans finally tipped the scales, they ended up doing the same thing, creating these pockets of communities, which is why we call Ohio a 'city-state.' Six unique tribes. Some say five, but I say six, Rebecca, because the north-central area is unique, and that strip from Dayton to Toledo is where all the good farmland is—"

A rush of army guards and Secret Service men passed by, interrupting his lecture. He was about to continue when Shay appeared in the hallway, whistled, and crooked his finger at Matt. "Quiz on Monday," Matt said, and he ventured a wink at Ms. Rebecca.

Shay ran his tongue under his lip impatiently. "Kirk's dead," he said, as if he'd been inconvenienced.

The news sucked the wind out of the plane like nothing Matt had seen. Even as Shay was telling him, cell phones started ringing up front. Television reports were tuned in. An immediate silence ensued, and as he followed Shay toward the situation room on the second level, Webb's voice boomed down the stairwell, "Jesus Christ!"

"What do we know?" Kensington said somberly, his hands folded as if in prayer.

Gail filed in, Broussard behind her, then the president's secretary and the head of the Secret Service POTUS contingency, Kate Schuto.

Video uplink connected them to Portsmouth, New Hampshire, where they'd made a campaign stop just a day ago, one of those common election campaign occurrences that now took on a more ominous character. Shay kept barking at the Secret Service agent there, who was trying to get word from another source, but one thing was clear: Kirk had been declared dead on the scene.

Across the country, ordinary people were asking why. But in the room, with its granite-like black table reflecting the agent's sweaty face, the concern was what it would mean. Already someone had muttered, "Backlash."

"Who the fuck did this?" Webb yelled at the agent.

"Please let it be a black guy," Shay said, and Kensington barked at him. But around the table, the programming of years of campaign experience and training kicked in; Broussard sighed that now they'd be running against an inexperienced African American, and Gail, typically, was on her phone with the ground team in Ohio trying to line up a local preacher to speak at the rally.

Moments later, Shay got an answer he wasn't looking for: the assassin was a white male, a former army corporal named Jerry McKee, who'd shot Kirk twice in the head and then turned the gun on himself, shouting, "Death to traitors in the name of a safe America!" before he pulled the trigger.

"Fucking insane," Matt whispered.

McKee's army record came up on the screen—he was a young man with a crisp flattop haircut who'd served for three years, one of them in Iraq, before being discharged for mental instability.

"Great, a white lunatic. That's all we need," said Shay, his eyes frozen on the screen. Then appeared a terrifying close-up of McKee, alive, in a mug shot from only a few months ago. In that picture, he was scraggly, his face patched by red blotches, his eyes heavy-lidded. Shay jumped back. "Burn that picture," he screamed. "No one can see that fucking picture!"

But there was no way to, of course. And there were too many pictures. By the time they'd cancelled the appearance in Cincinnati and headed toward DC, pictures of McKee carrying neon-colored, hateful signs at Kirk's New England rallies were going viral and being splashed on the networks' live coverage. With each new one, Shay pounded his fist against the thick leather seats.

———〰———

That night was a silent one. There was little information beyond what they already knew, and the question of security still hadn't been answered; it was ass-covering time, and the truth of how a man smuggled a .357 Magnum into an indoor rally wouldn't be answered for weeks, at the earliest. Stepping carefully around the obvious political questions, Matt did a round on the networks, expressing the sympathy of the administration and a vow to suspend the campaign. But he knew that overnight the news cycle would rejuvenate itself like some horror movie villain, and he'd have to spin the political impact of Kirk's murder. After his final interview, halfway between the press room and the president's office on the second floor, the illness of it all hit him, and he rushed to the bathroom, where, instead of the anxiety-driven vomit he'd experienced before, his bowels swelled and expressed their contents in an ugly stream.

As Matt neared the second-floor office, he passed a television monitor, and noticed that the twinkling-eyed commentator's eyes were dry. The spark of excitement over the election was gone, replaced by painful memories of a dead president, senator, and civil rights leader from years ago.

Shay was pacing the room with surprisingly long, loping strides. The small room was packed. Even the first lady was there, and naturally Webb had sought the comfort of his basset hound.

"Ohio, as I've said for three years, is the tipping point," said Shay.

He looked at Kensington, who stared blankly in return.

"We have to discuss this," Shay said.

"Yeah, looks like your Ohio prediction is coming true," the president said. "'Course a *premolition* is only valuable if you do something about it."

"Premo*ni*tion, dear," the first lady said quietly.

"Oh, yeah. Thanks honey." He laughed a little; on any other night, he'd have made his common joke about her being his personal English tutor.

Shay was unfazed. "Our ground operation in Ohio is nothing short of exceptional. We have established a multi-level marketing program with over a hundred thousand active volunteers. Those are realistic numbers, mind you. And we have the active support of statewide Republicans who, unlike in some places, know what they're doing—"

"This'll keep 'til the morning," growled Webb. "I still haven't called Kirk's wife."

"Wait—"

"Steve, let's give it a rest," said Kensington. "It's late, we're all tired. Let me just say one thing, okay? Now you're all really gonna be tempted to use the race thing. I'm telling you right now: don't." His exhausted face, scored by wrinkles, turned sour, and the look he threw at Stephen was even a little threatening. "No matter how tight things get. That's the last thing we need right now. Okay?" After a murmur of agreement, he nodded and said goodnight, his wife following.

Shay sulked in the corner, and Matt thought back to the Real Veterans Against Kirk campaign, all the mudslinging they'd done; sometimes, when you knew you'd been wrong, that's when you resisted the most. Was it possible Shay felt guilt? Finally?

The meeting broke up, and an hour or so later, Matt wandered through the deserted halls of the first floor. There didn't seem much point in rushing home. Shelly had called, asking if she should stay later, and what did he know that she didn't, but he'd heard nothing from Kris, nothing from Cory. Of course, no one realistically was worried about the president's well-being. Or his staff's. It was so goddamn clear that all of the ire, vengeance, and fear they'd stirred up in the extremist right—the isolationists Shay was obsessed with, the knee-jerk patriots with a dark gleam in their eyes—was responsible for the assassination;

the idea of an immediate threat to Kensington seemed like a joke, or a poor attempt at covering ass.

He passed close to Webb's lit office and, peeking in, saw that the vice president was just hanging up the phone with a faraway look in his eyes.

"You all right?" said Matt.

Webb nodded, that cranky visage of his nearly broken. "I can't tell you how badly I wanted to win this thing, but frankly, I'm not so sure we will. Or that we deserve to." He reached down and scratched the bristly hair of Charlie Brown, and the dog let out a pleased grumble. "Let me ask you something. Sit down. You want something? Scotch?"

"No, thanks."

Webb eyed him through those wide glasses.

"Did we do this?"

Matt looked away. In the three and a half years he'd been in the White House, not taking responsibility was almost as common as lunch. And it wasn't all scandal. Most of it wasn't, in fact. Things happened. Someone decided. Internally, you knew the players, you sometimes understood who made what call. But even within the confines of the White House, the language floating around so often kept floating. Still, he couldn't help but walk back through his misdemeanors, his crimes: exaggerating the evidence in Iraq, persuading the people based on lies and the seduction of his words; bullying the media into submission; outing Redgrave; staying silent about the gay marriage amendment's real purpose, and Shay's interest in manipulating the vote; sparking the outrage against Kirk with a few bitter and eager-to-please veterans and some carefully edited tape. Who had done all those things? Somebody. Sometime, somewhere. Things just happened.

"Yes," he said. "We did this."

Webb nodded weightily. "We demonized him," he said. "By my definition of a conspiracy, we conspired to kill him with words. We chummed the waters and this lunatic smelled the blood and struck." Matt cleared his throat but Webb raised a palm. "I'm just as responsible, Matt. I went on the same shows you did. What did you have us saying after the 2001 attacks? We only have to be wrong once?" Webb shook his head. "And now we have been. A lone lunatic. One guy. And along the way, how many people who might have stopped it—all those protestors at that rally in Portsmouth—I mean, they recognized this guy, he was a fixture—how many of them didn't do the right thing because they thought Kirk was a traitor? Not even 'thought.' Just … caught up in the emotion. Drunk on an idea that was, at best, an extreme exaggeration. And now a family is missing their father, Jeannie's missing her husband, and a soldier—a patriot—is dead."

Before he could think, Matt said, "We should have called him that when he was alive."

He looked up, his eyes wide and fearful. But Webb was nodding.

"I fucking hate elections," said the vice president. "Fucking blood sport. We should stick to hunting quail or pheasants."

"Shay has a blood lust."

"And it was unnecessary!" Webb pushed back from his desk a bit. "God bless him, but we were going to walk all over Kirk. And now we've jeopardized our cause—or worse, perverted it."

"What do you think about the race issue?"

"Doesn't matter at all," Webb said with the old declarative tone back in his voice. "But look, this is what I wanted to tell you: if we lose, you and I are headed for history's dung hill. You need a contingency plan."

"We're expendable."

"Shay has you and God's Will has me." He looked deep into the corners of the room and sneered. "Do you remember our talk on the boat a few years ago, Matt?"

"I'll never forget it, sir."

"Well, I had that talk with you for two reasons. I could see you were faltering, okay? But also, you and I may be very different stylistically, but we share something, and that's a belief in what we're doing. At least you used to. Look, I didn't invite you in here to challenge your loyalty or lecture you. Hell, I'm fighting some doubts for the first time in many years, and I don't give a shit who knows it."

Webb glanced down at his phone as if he was tempted to call someone and confess it. Then with a wry smile, he looked up. "Don't look so surprised, Matt. In this business, every day is a new day. But you keep working toward the same goal. You have to have a solid center, something you believe in. And people might hate me, they might say I sound like the Penguin"—his grin deepened—"but goddamn it, they better know that I believe in our course of action."

He frowned, agitated, as if he couldn't come up with the right words.

"This is why I hate elections," he continued. "It's like this: I see a boat in dock, ready to sail. And I know those people are headed into some rough waters. All I want to do is get on the boat, so I can steer it. Hell, obviously, I don't even have to be captain. But I can tell the captain where to navigate. But that gangplank. Everyone wants on, everyone wants to be the captain. And meanwhile, the boat's getting ready to shove off." Webb tented his fingers, his thumbs touching his lips a moment. "So you do what you have to. You push, you shove—you throw a guy overboard. And we say, 'Well, that's reality.' But it's a miserable goddamn reality."

Matt's Journal, Day 39

Each day I tell the world what a great tragedy this is and how we feel for the senator's family. Each day I lie. Each day I walk a delicate line between lauding Kirk, the man, and carefully belittling Kirk the politician's ideas. As if the two can be separated. Maybe that's it. I'm two different men, and having split myself into thin facsimiles, I've forgotten which is which, which one is true, and so I feel no shame in doing it to someone else. In Iraq, people die every day, civilians and soldiers, and we kill to protect a regime run by a guy who thinks he's a Mesopotamian Michael Corleone. Shay's a wreck, obsessed with the sympathy backlash and an invigorated, angry Democratic grassroots campaign, and, though we've stopped polling and we've grounded the ads, he's got independent groups working in the shadows, and the news, he says, isn't good. Sometimes it seems like he's forgotten Kirk ever existed.

The rest of us can't. Pundits and bloggers and voters and rock stars and Hollywood stars and even McCowan—long-jettisoned from our inner circle, increasingly vocal this past week—have been attacking the campaign and me personally for distorting Kirk's record and encouraging the lunatic fringe. The doctor who asked me for an autograph at the convention sent it back.

But we've received aid from a surprising ally, the new Democratic nominee; Noah Young has asked for restraint and unity despite all the blame. In the remarks he delivered at Kirk's funeral, he said, "A great statesman has died on our soil. Let not his death be in vain, let not his work and words go unheeded." The kind of oratory, I have to admit, that our guy has never been able to pull off.

Noah Young's speech reminded me of the one I was giving just before I heard the news from Shay, that Ogista story I like to tell. I've always practiced rhetoric by writing speeches for historical figures, trying to capture their voices, and I've been thinking about what Ogista might have said to the two tribes after he sacrificed his son:

The brothers of war are lies, fear, and vengeance, but the father of war is ignorance. War ends only when the pain is known and unbearable, so unbearable that a man can't go on. So it is today that all of you see my pain and know that if we don't stop, my pain will become yours. If I listened to the echoes in my hollow chest, I would ask my most loyal brave to take this tomahawk and crush my skull. But I will stay so that those who stand in the sun shall see my dark shadow and remember this day forever. So that you shall never be ignorant. So the sight of me will cause you to think about what war means.

Let the balance of the bodies of twenty Seneca and twenty Wyandot speak to all future generations, and may this balance stand forevermore on this land so tribes know that war always demands a high cost, and it is better to find peaceful and just measures to settle our differences.

War is only the last resort. Those that cry out for it must carry the heavy weight of truth that war is needed on their backs up a steep mountain. So heavy the weight that their footsteps cannot slide across the snow, but must trudge deep into the soil and crush the rocks under their feet. And if they can climb the great mountain, then it is time for war. Then and only then. If a chief is unwilling to sacrifice his own son, his own light, if he thinks that only others will pay, then the cost of war is not met, and he is a fool.

It takes little to become a chief or to start a war; it takes great sacrifice to stop one.

I won't be sharing that with Shay. Or anyone else. I can't help but wonder: if Kirk was the sacrificial son, who was Ogista? What hand guided the tomahawk? Or was it just the insanity of hate, of which Kirk is another victim in a long line of victims? Will we remain ignorant? Who will be next?

We had long discussions about the kind of picture we wanted from the funeral. The president was instructed to never smile, though it seemed only polite to smile at the fond remembrances told by friends and family. And so he was instructed, by Shay, to smile with his eyes. How he approached the widow and the children was rehearsed in the Oval Office, and his salute to the coffin was well-received. A man who dodged Vietnam and is called a patriot saluted the coffin of a man who chose to serve and was called a traitor.

Mom, Dad, I can't keep doing this, and I can't stop.

CHAPTER 13

Leaning against the rail of the veranda, studying the Tuscan valley below with its neat rows of grapevines and olive trees, it was hard not to dwell on Tess. The times they'd sipped espresso in the morning and wine in the afternoon; their making love at all hours. That first day, she'd met him at the replica statue of David, in Florence, just to talk.

"So you know it's against company policy, right?" she'd said, her eyes shining like rough-hewn diamonds.

How he'd stammered. "Asking a girl out g-gets me flustered," he'd said.

Tess had twirled a strand of her long, curly blonde hair. "Well it'd be a second date wouldn't it? I mean, the park, the statue, the view, a prearranged meeting: we're *on* a date, Cory," she'd said, laughing so beautifully, touching his shaking hands.

Now, from the overlook of the Hotel del Rossi, halfway between Siena and Florence, Cory wished he had one of those expensive Nat Shermans Matt used to smoke. Despite the beauty, despite the sun reflecting off the Roman marble ruins in blinding white shears, he felt heavy with the weight of returning to the scene of a crime, to the lush valley and Renaissance city where he'd been reborn, all right, reborn into anger and bitter, heartsick loneliness.

His cell phone chimed its alarm, and he straightened the cuffs of his tuxedo. Dressed for the opera. Crazy fucking George, always with his 007 moves. Grabbing his valise from his room, he jostled past a few tourists and hopped into the Porsche he'd rented just as his phone chimed again—a text from George. *Change of plans—D'addacio's café, Siena square.* Sighing, he shut down the growling engine, stalked back up to his room, changed into a sweater and blue jeans, the Glock 17

9mm fitting more comfortably against the back of his hip than it had beneath the tux jacket. Even so, it'd been years since he'd even handled a gun, and God knew that wasn't exactly in the training manual for a CIA number-cruncher.

The drive south to Siena on SR2 covered a good twenty-five kilometers, allowing him to work himself into a great amount of anxiety; that might have been his specialty, really, and the reason Redgrave had first approached him about working undercover. And it was precisely what Matt never understood, or never was capable of: looking forward to all the possibilities. He couldn't be sure that George's "problem" was the result of Matt's leak, but, well, he should never have had to consider it in the first place. He'd only talked with George once, the day after he'd come to the lower Starbucks; George was convinced there was a counterspy in their circle; Kaplan and Mendelsohn were dead, their deaths covered up rather messily, and now George figured someone was coming after him. They'd all worked for Wisconsin Foods. They'd all worked for Redgrave.

Sighing in the wind, pushing the machine to its height of speed, he thought he could smell the cherry fragrance of Tess's shampoo, a scent that tortured him in the Washington springtime. He'd known her so well—and yet not at all. They'd slept together, talked about their work in the CIA—but he'd thought she was just a stats geek like him, a geography buff whose degree had led her to one of the few government agencies interested in such things. That changed the day he saw her in the brassy lobby of the Hotel Bernini Palace with George, crossing the carpet and marble floor, heading briskly toward an elevator. He'd only seen George skulking about their office; he'd never talked to him. Less concerned that she was having an affair than that she was in trouble, Cory had followed them toward the elevator, then ducked into the stairwell and jogged up the steps, listening for the elevator doors over the clacking of his shoes on the tile. Out of breath on the fourth floor, he heard the clumsy shutting of the elevator, waited a moment, then peeked into the hallway. Tess and George disappeared around a corner—she'd been reaching behind her back—the glint of a silver handgun—and then shots, too many to count, and glass breaking.

He'd run to the corner of the hallway, terrified. Just as he'd worked up the nerve to peek, George stumbled toward him, his white shirt bloodied, and fell. Beyond the corner, a man was groaning in Russian—heavy footsteps approached on the carpet—and he grabbed George's gun and ducked low into the rest of the hallway in time to see Tess, pinned and trapped in the alcove of a service elevator, fall backward in a cloud of blood. Screaming, he lunged but was stopped by an explosion bellowing from down the hall, behind the three men. One of them was down and on fire. The others, crouching, turned toward him. He squeezed the trigger. Nothing. They were shouting in Russian. How the hell did you work this thing? he'd thought frantically, and, finally, pressing a small button, nearly shot off his foot. A bullet whizzed off the wall above him. His eyes halfway shut, he aimed down the hall and fired off as many shots as he could.

They were down. Everyone was down for Christ's sake. He scrambled to Tess, patting out a whisper of fire on her sleeve; her face was bloodied, her eyes frantic, wet, and dim. In the periphery of his vision, one of the men—hulking, brutish, his overcoat stained black and bloody—reached forward for a gun, and Cory tensed, clutching Tess, thinking it would be better to die here, right now, with her in his arms.

But then Redgrave's voice rang around the corner. Offering that briefcase. Saving his life.

That's what pissed him off so much about the leak. Those secrets were nothing special, really, nothing the Russians weren't on to. Langley had pardoned him, unofficially, considering he'd saved Cory's life, and probably George's, but they couldn't very well overlook that with the press breathing down their necks. So now Oliver was a goddamn target.

He pulled the Porsche to a stop, parking it just outside of Siena as all visitors were required. Unlike most Italian cities of any size, Siena had been saved from any bombing by either side during World War II, and nearly every street in the small city was no wider than an alley and lined with quaint homes, markets and restaurants, all of it pristine, untouched.

He made his way to the bottom of the famous square well-known for its reckless horse races, and climbed the slight incline to the coffeehouse. A mix of tourists passed, chattering in four different languages. Tess would have understood them all.

Half an hour passed. From time to time, he imagined the chilly gaze of someone behind him, and he would carefully look over his shoulder. A tiny old man, rotund, was playing chess with his granddaughter. Two sleek women were arguing in Italian. He checked his phone for messages, and with each passing minute, felt more uneasy. Maybe George had been intercepted. Maybe George was not George at all.

Dropping some coins onto his table, he slowly headed back to his car. He wasn't a fighter. He'd just done the job asked of him, stumbled, literally, into all of this. But if they wanted to fucking kill him, they'd have to come and get him.

And so they had. Pacing the cobbled street, he sensed a shadow behind him. He stopped at a shop window and saw in the dark reflection an enormous man with thinning silvery hair on the opposite side of the street. Watching himself being watched. From his pocket he raised a gun—

Cory broke into a sprint. As the glass shattered behind him, he banked into the first alley, then left onto the next street, which was lined with apartments. In the window of one, an old woman was slicing bread for a crippled old man, fresh fruit and cheese on their table, and he imagined their terror as he came flying through their door. No one else should get hurt today. He only needed to make it to his car, which sat at the crest of a gentle hill. The high ground.

But he'd never get the car started in time, and crouching next to a gas tank didn't seem like a wise idea. Near the edge of the town, he spotted a massive brick church, and he waited in the shade of its cornerstone. The Porsche was maybe twenty yards away. From the darkness of an alley, the other man appeared; he was indeed enormous, white-haired, thick-waisted, walking with a slight limp. Older than Cory would've guessed. Old scores. It was true. This was about Florence in 1987. Redgrave. Matt.

Aiming carefully, he just barely squeezed the trigger—like George had taught him, only after the nightmare—too late! always too late to change!—and as the Russian's left shoulder jumped back against a stone wall, Cory bolted for the car.

In the spinning of the tires, a nearly silent whistle shattered the rearview mirror.

—⁓—

There was no use in going back to the del Rossi. Forty minutes later he was in Florence, heading to a hotel he knew painfully well.

The next morning, he carefully watched the parking lot from the tiny balcony of his room, and he prowled the hallways and the lobby, imagining glances, stares—all of them as real as they needed to be, and a few of them from Tess. He saw her in a massive mirror in the Bernini lobby, as if she'd been trapped there all these years. Saw her at the elevator. In a hallway, reaching to her back for her gun.

The news about yesterday's shootout was vague, speculated to be connected to organized crime, which itself became an excuse for a story on some local leader's failure to crack down, etc.—politics was the same anywhere you went. As he watched the tiny television in the lounge, his cell beeped. Another message from George: *Ambush?*

He stared heavily at the phone.

Yes, he responded, and George—or his ghost—responded that they should meet at the Uffizi side of the Ponte Vecchio at midnight.

George couldn't spell for shit. When they'd worked together back in Washington, Cory had retyped all of his reports. The man had a doctorate, and he could barely spell Italy. But now "Ponte Vecchio" and "Uffizi" were spelled perfectly, as every text message had been, Cory realized.

So. George was dead.

In his room, he stared at the black finish of the Glock where it lay on the bed. God, he missed Tess. Missed her cherry blossom smell, her encyclopedic knowledge. Fifteen years hadn't blunted it at all. He'd thought it would. Thought he would move on, like everyone said, and that he could even let himself be in love with Carrie O'Malley. But now it was too late. If he stayed here, the Russian would find him. If he was able to get a flight back to the United States, the man would find him there. He pictured the creased face of his pursuer, the shock of cottony white hair; he was definitely the hulking man who'd reached for his gun that day before Redgrave offered the briefcase. He may have been the one who shot Tess. Lips trembling, tears trickling into his open, dry mouth, Cory snarled to himself, "End this." There were only two options. And Tess would never forgive him if he took the easier path.

Everything was the same at the beginning; people drifting by him at a public location, but this time Matt knew he was at the Washington Monument, sitting on a bench, his hands dripping in blood. As always, a police officer walked up to him. But this time he was next to General McCowan, who was also drenched in blood, a shower of it streaming down his face, his mouth sealed with military ribbons stitched across both lips. "Taps" played in the distance and then, as he saw the slumped body of the general, the blood on his own hands hardened into metal, like armor, and—

Matt woke in terror. Larry Bird stood over him, his tail twitching, and then rubbed himself under Matt's neck.

"Damn, buddy," said Matt. "Don't know what I'd do without you." He rubbed the cat's fat belly and reached for his phone. A message had come in from Cory hours ago marked urgent. It read: *Matt, need to talk to you ASAP.*

It was 3:30 AM, and he hadn't heard from Cory for weeks, and though it seemed likely he'd get another earful about the Redgrave leak, Matt felt a pang of fear. Cory was not impulsive. The last time he'd called this late was when he'd blown a tire outside of Baltimore.

Matt tried Cory's cell and got no answer; on a lark he tried the office, and got voicemail there, too. Cory's office, with its arch windows, had a perfect view of the Washington Monument; he'd cut across the Mall many times to meet Cory for lunch. Matt hung up, thinking he'd try later, dozed off a bit, woke with a start near five o'clock and tried calling again. Then he sent a message to Cory's phone: *Trying to reach you, call back.*

Around 7:30, he got Cory's secretary, who said Cory had left her a note sometime over the weekend explaining that he'd be out of town for a few days.

"Does he do that often?"

"Once, maybe," she said. "But ... well, I shouldn't say this, but I know how close you two are."

"What is it?"

"Nothing I can put my finger on, but he was definitely upset about something on Friday."

"Tell him to call me when you hear from him next."

On the Uffizi side of the Ponte Vecchio, a unique, three-story medieval bridge that was the site of an eclectic market, Yuri lingered near a high-end jewelry shop. Seven hundred years ago, the bridge had housed produce markets; now it was home to expensive niche stores and cafés, an outright monument to time and beauty; even as the Nazis were destroying everything in their path as they exited Italy in World War II, they couldn't bring themselves to demolish the bridge.

To his surprise, Cory Risen was standing openly under the middle arch, next to a covered-up kiosk, leaning against the stone wall and staring at the dark Arno flowing underneath. Something in the man's courage appealed to him; Mendelsohn and Kaplan had run; George Ball had offered to give up secrets in exchange for his life. But Risen had grazed him in the shoulder from twenty meters. His footsteps echoing against the stone mortar of the nearly deserted bridge, Yuri approached the American, keeping his Luger at his side. An idling moped quietly hummed down the street, but Yuri saw no one.

"Mr. Risen," he said softly.

The smallish man's shoulders quaked—he was laughing. "I don't even know your name."

"Yuri Nesterenko."

"FSB?"

"Retired KGB." He edged his gun away from his coat. To not trust his hands anymore, to leave the killing to this filthy instrument—it was painful, degrading. "You know that George Ball is dead."

Risen nodded.

"Walking around here," he said, "it's like being back in the Renaissance. It's like time stopped. Or that we never moved forward."

Yuri grunted, considering the point. "A friend of mine, a few years ago— his name was Kostya—he said things had changed, that time had slipped away. But men like you and me, we still fight the old wars."

"I'm not like you," Risen snapped. His voice riddled with tears, he said with a hiss, "I was a fucking researcher. I didn't even know Tess was covert until you killed her."

"She would have killed me."

"I know."

"I am here to kill you."

The American sighed. "I know."

Risen whirled, his gun hand leveling toward Yuri—but the younger man was slow, and Yuri, despite his pain and recently bandaged shoulder and treatments and age, caught the muzzle of the gun, angling it away. But then his hand all but exploded in a flash and crack of lightning—the pain shot up his arm—and he howled.

The American bolted, and Yuri shot wildly at his disappearing shadow. Blood seeped from the stub of his left thumb, a coldness spreading in waves. Stabbing like a heart attack. Stifling his hand against his coat, he willed himself on. In the darkness lit a faint red taillight, followed by the adolescent roar of the moped, and it retreated across the bridge, past the Torre dei Mannelli. Yuri bent down for Risen's Glock and ran toward the dark tower, stopping at the first unlocked car he found.

The cool wind drying his damp hair—he was sweating profusely now, fighting off shock—Yuri caught a glimpse of the moped on the Lungarno Serristori and jammed his foot against the accelerator. The Arno was nothing but a black wind. The wheel slick with his blood, he tried in vain to tear off a shred of his cuff. A lonely bus emerged from a cross-street. A taxi dragged along in its lane.

"So this is how it ends," said Nikolai's ghost from the passenger seat.

"Shut up."

Risen cut right, ascending a hill, and the hijacked car screeched in its turning, nearly sideswiping a lamppost. The darkness hung like a veil through which lights red and yellow burst—Risen cut left, still climbing, then right into an alley, narrow. Oncoming headlights illuminated the windshield, blinding him momentarily, and when he opened his eyes—had he blacked out?—he saw a gated driveway right in front of him. Swerving, he clipped a low stone wall, scraping the car's hull against it. The red light, a dot now, glowed up the hill.

By the time Yuri had caught up again, they'd leveled onto a plateau. Screeching around the curve, Risen's moped wobbled, drifted left of center, and in the lights of an oncoming van banked even harder to the left, scattering across the sidewalk of a plaza lit by floodlights and streetlamps. Risen leapt before the moped crashed into a tiny pond. Yuri screeched to a halt in the middle of the street and backed up in time to see Risen emerge from a shadow of a bush and hobble off into the park behind the plaza.

Slowly Yuri entered the indigo shade of the park, picking his way between bronze statues and hedges and trees. In the distance the lights of Florence flickered. This was Piazzale Michelangelo, high on a promontory—

With a groan, ill and defeated, Risen surged from behind a tree into Yuri. They both stumbled, the American landing an ineffectual punch. With a heaving, ancient grunt of his own, Yuri swung Risen into the base of the Statue of David replica.

Risen was immobile, clutching his chest just below the heart, his breath heaving and jagged, his lips curled, as if he'd already been shot.

Yuri removed his left glove, wincing as it stuck to the stump that had been his thumb. Pressing the glove between his wrist and his chest, he tossed the Glock at Risen's feet, and then withdrew his Luger.

Breathlessly Yuri said, "You loved her?"

"Always."

"Then you will see her again."

Raising his gun, he took careful aim and a long breath, and pulled the trigger. Blood and brain matter splattered across the lower legs of the Statue of David.

Still fearing a heart attack—weak from the chemotherapy drugs, his every muscle wailing—Yuri allowed himself a moment to steal Risen's wallet and cell phone. Patting him down, Yuri found in his coat pocket a picture of the woman with curly blonde hair: Tess and Risen locked in an embrace. The kind of photo one has taken on the street, on a whim, carefree. Gently he placed it back into the man's coat.

He staggered away, a see-sawing police siren echoing along the hillside. He would need to descend by foot, find a way back toward his own car near Ponte Vecchio. Just keep on, he thought. Keep moving. His head was light, weightless, and he looked at his thumb to stay sober and awake. This one had done what none of them had: twice. He'd nearly killed Yuri in this city fifteen years ago, and he might have finished the job tonight. As he walked, he pawed awkwardly through Risen's wallet and then checked the cell phone. Earlier in the day, he'd sent messages to a Matt Risen. The cousin who worked for the American president. That kind of connection wasn't a coincidence. Five messages had come in from the cousin, one of them just twenty minutes ago. He'd have to be taken care of. He and Redgrave. And they couldn't be drawn to Italy. Or Russia. Yuri would have to find his way into their country. As he winced over his missing thumb, having staunched it finally with a strip of his shirt, he decided to make a final journey home. One last trip to Alexander Gardens. There would be no return from America.

PART FOUR: UNINTENDED CONSEQUENCES

CHAPTER 1

As his phone rang and rang, Matt first reached for the nightstand and then stumbled out of bed, searching the room through sleep-deprived eyes for his damn phone until he staggered over his pants and nearly fell.

He dug out the phone, flipped it open, and heard only sobbing. "Who's this?" he muttered.

"Jesse." His uncle continued to mumble and sob, his voice a slick mess. "Something happened ... to Cory ... I don't know ... they say Florence. Cory, he's dead."

Matt sunk to the bed. A chill gripped him. He asked Jess if he was sure, how it'd happened, and his uncle could hardly answer him. Paula tried to take the phone, Jess fought her—"He's my boy!" shouted his uncle—and Matt looked away through his bedroom window at the dark, swept street. Horror of the past, horror at what couldn't be undone.

"Jess, I'm on my way," he said hazily. "Stay on the phone with me."

———〰〰〰———

When he saw, on the approach to Port Columbus, the frost on the ground shining in the breaking morning sun, he burst into tears. Too cold for late October, too much like winter, too late, too late. Life without Cory: the thought made him numb. He could feel the eyes of the handful of people on the plane looking at him—they knew him, didn't they? Knew what he'd done. He let the stinging tears dry on his face.

By the time he got to Jesse's home, the morning had cemented itself, the sky a dreary gray, the patchwork orange and brown leaves of the abundant trees lining the streets blowing listlessly away. Jess and Paula sat on the couch, both still in their nightclothes; once he'd sat with them, cried with them, asked the same questions—Florence? Italy?—Matt pulled himself up and fixed them coffee and toast.

While they ate, he paced on the back porch and told Broussard to get him a line with the State Department. "Skip that, get me the president. I want some fucking answers."

By 11 AM, the State Department had called. Cory's body would be in Ohio by the next day. Finally Matt's clout was worth a damn.

Jesse sagged as he hung up the rotary phone. His face fallen, wrinkles now entrenched that had been slight, even graceful, a few years ago. "They say he fell off a curb in Florence, in front of a truck. At three in the morning." His eyes shook, glassy. "Matt, they said he was drunk."

"But he didn't drink."

Jess stared at him.

"Jess, I'd have known. We were out all the time."

"The boy had his secrets."

"Not from me."

His uncle glanced away—in fury, in grief. Impossible to tell. Men like Jess held their emotions tight, even in the privacy of their homes. But it wasn't hard to know that he'd become accustomed to sameness. The same furniture, good for bouncing boys rooting for the Buckeyes. The same rotary phone, for collect calls to DC, at his good son's request. The stubborn persistence could only come from a man who'd seen too much change, who'd lost his wife, his brother, and his sister-in-law. What had he said years ago around Thanksgiving? Everything changes, the question is: into what? Never for the better, he might have said then, and would damn sure say now.

And you, Matt, what have you changed into?

～ᴧ～

Near the end of the day came a call. "Sorry to have to tell you," said the secretary of agriculture, "but Cory made some serious mistakes. I sent him there myself. Wish it hadn't turned out this way, Matt."

"What kind of mistakes? And why Florence?"

"Can't say, Matt. Sorry."

"What the fuck is this, classified?"

"Matt, let me call you back."

He never did, only a deputy or some shit. Sitting at the kitchen counter, caked in a filmy sweat, Matt stared at his phone. Something was not right. Not at all. The same dread that had filled him once the Redgrave story broke was now like a scent in the air, stale and numinous.

Shay picked up, drunk. "I've already been checking," said Shay. "I don't have much."

"How did you know?"

"Word gets around. We're looking out for you here, kid."

Matt sighed and shifted his weight. "I appreciate it, but I need a better explanation than the one they're giving me."

"There were witnesses, people from the Department of Agriculture who were with Cory and say he was intoxicated—"

"Bullshit."

"There were witnesses, Matt; that's all I can tell you."

"Who? Give me some fucking names."

"Just tend to your family, all right?" He heard Shay take a long swallow of his scotch. "I'll keep digging around."

Matt snapped his phone shut as Jess set down a cup of coffee.

Night. Sitting in silence in the old living room, while Paula was making the last of the arrangements with the church. Calling old friends, Carrie O'Malley—that had been Matt's job.

Silence and stillness. Uncountable cup of acidic coffee.

"I think, Uncle Jess, that Cory had given up on me."

"What the hell are you talking about?" Jess said sternly, a sign that the real Uncle Jess could fight his way back.

"My job and, well … he and I just disagreed strongly on some stuff," Matt said with a shrug.

"Cory never gave up on anything. Especially you."

Deep night, in the old bed, in the old room where they'd listed the names of girls they liked and their best features. Carrie O'Malley always came out on top for Cory, even then. Matt, he could never choose.

You think something is happening. Your mind replays scene after scene. A basketball. *Camelot.* Proud, brotherly smile. A girl named Tess.

You dream you are on fire in the ninth circle of Hell.

———∧∧———

Harsh, bleak light of morning, the plane has arrived, the funeral home calls: the body's been cremated.

"Who allowed that?" Jess shouts into the phone. "That's not what he wanted." He listens a moment. "In *Italy?*"

Uncle Jess in the red Naugahyde chair. "Matt, *do* something."

You call the White House. Shay.

A circle is being completed. The architecture revealed.

———∧∧———

The reverend had known Cory well. Once he had taken them both to a Reds game, late in a terrible season. The reverend and Matt were ready to leave long before the end of the sixth, but Cory insisted they stay until the end. The Reds were down by quite a bit and out came the boo-birds.

Cory glared at the Judas fans. Moments later he stood and cheered as loud as he could, whooping and hollering, "Let's go Reds," as the team ran out of the dugout to start the top of the ninth.

"You've got to stand up for your team no matter what," he said with a big grin.

People all around rolled their eyes. Except for one guy, who said encouragingly, "You cheer for all of us, kid."

"Don't worry, I will."

Over the white altar and the urn, the reverend said, "That's the kind of man Cory was."

Matt edged forward in his pew and bent his head. Rain beat against the stained glass of the sanctuary, and the church interior smelled of old carpet and older Bibles. Cory would have hated it.

Carrie O'Malley rose in her black dress and approached the pulpit. A few times she opened her mouth, her chest rising, until she could finally whisper the first words of "Danny Boy." Cory's favorite. They'd not a drop of Irish blood in them, but, given the community, it was easy to feel Irish in spirit. Her voice shimmered, gaining strength with each line, until the voice Cory had fallen in love with was sending him on his way.

The service ended, Jesse took the urn in hand, and the impressively large crowd began to disperse. A large constituency from the Department of Agriculture had made the trip to Ohio, despite Cory's supposed "serious mistakes," and none who spoke with Matt seemed the least bit ashamed of their dead friend. Even Warren, that childhood nemesis, teared up as he shook Matt's hand.

As Matt walked past Warren, he spotted a familiar head of peppered hair and stern, well-read eyes: Professor Redgrave.

Had they been friends? How? Cory would have said something. Unless he had. In the only way he could.

Matt clutched a pew, queasy. The long-distance calls, the weeks-long trips. A woman named Tess whom he'd met … in Florence.

Oh, God.

Matt caught the professor in the parking lot, caught him by the elbow and looked into the eyes of the man he'd ruined, eyes that returned his gaze with a fierce agony.

"Please," Matt stuttered.

Redgrave stiffened. "I can only tell you this: somebody in the White House has blood on their hands."

～ᴧᴧ～

From the vantage point of his car on the slope above the church, Yuri squinted through the binoculars. Ah, yes. Closely involved, Redgrave and this Matthew Risen. Though they parted abruptly, the two men were too well-connected, too entwined in the same disgusting system, not to be allies. Or perhaps had been forced into an alliance.

Yuri lowered the binoculars, then snapped them back, his attention caught by a man loitering near the church's billboard: a protective agent observing Redgrave. Another stood on the sidewalk along the post office next door. Obviously, the American president feared some scandal. What an enormous waste of manpower; even Kensington would realize eventually that, with his whole crew gone, Redgrave would talk sooner or later. He was dangerous. Yuri wouldn't be surprised if Redgrave caught a heart attack pretty soon.

Perhaps Yuri would, too. His heart beat irregularly, and his thumb pulsed in the cold winds. The bags under his eyes had turned purple. He'd barely made it to Toronto, barely crossed the lake to Pelee Island and then into Ohio. Mikhail and Nikolai spoke frequently to him with a nervous kind of chattering.

He pulled away slowly as Redgrave got into a forest-green Volvo. Taking down the old man was going to be tougher than killing Risen, who had no one protecting him. But he'd wait until Risen returned to DC, scour the hotshot cousin's apartment, and sweep away the trail of evidence. And then Risen would die. Then Redgrave. And then he.

⌒〜⋀〜⌒

Shay picked up and a bottle clanked against wood: no doubt his trusty bottle of McCutcheon on the nightstand, thought Matt. The receiver dropped once with a sharp sound painful as a bite, and finally, Shay pulled himself together enough to say hello.

"Little drunk, Stephen?"

"Matt. Yeah, sure, a little bit. How you doing, kid?"

He pictured the bloated, pasty white body rolling in its own filthy sheets, the conspiratorial eyes blinking in the lamplight. "Pretty fucking good," said Matt, "for a guy who killed his own cousin." He ought to have recorded the moment of silence that followed. A historical moment from a guy who seemed to have every answer rehearsed, who had every possibility forecast, who never doubted his ability to weasel the hell out of any jam.

"Professor Redgrave was at the funeral." Matt sighed, his sour, alcoholic breath drifting sharply into his nostrils. He let out a wheezing little laugh. "And the circumstances of Cory's death … this 'accident.' I can't believe I didn't realize a long time ago that Cory was CIA."

"You're jumping to conclusions, Matt. I'll get to the bottom of this."

"That's what you said a few days ago."

"Matt, you know these things take time."

"We killed my cousin! We killed my cousin and that is the bottom-fucking-line!"

Matt slammed the phone down.

Shay stared at the handset, confused by being hung up on. The shock and reverberation—it got him up and pacing, pacing through his expressionless hallways and into the clean, blank whiteness of his kitchen. A wild card less than two weeks before the election. No fucking way. The election was the key to securing a Republican grip and finally engendering war with Iran and a confrontation with North Korea—and it could all turn to tatters thanks to some pissant press secretary? Not a chance. Not a fucking chance.

He dialed Carl. "You were right about Risen," he said, the sleep still heavy in his voice. "Do you hear me? We need to deal with him. Did you know his cousin was an agent?"

"Bullshit. Cory Risen was a fucking clerk."

"Yeah, *was*. But whatever he was, he knew Redgrave."

"I'll find out."

"Don't bother. We shouldn't know, and we don't want anyone to know we know. I'll try and talk some sense into Risen, but be ready for anything."

"With pleasure," Carl said.

Chapter 2

It hadn't taken them long to spin his absence from the campaign. A week was all that was needed to turn a man from the reliable, good-natured face of the White House into—what was Broussard saying now?—a "man under great stress" suffering from "exhaustion," a pejorative unless you were applying it to an athlete. For anyone else, it meant a mental breakdown. He'd done it to others, and now his deputy was sticking it to him, saying that Matt "just needed some time to grieve."

Broussard, in a neatly-fitted suit, didn't look so hot himself; that short pubic hair of his was glistening under the hot lights, and he was straining so hard to smile that he looked childish, out of his depth. "Hang in there, Broussard," Matt said to the bar TV before he scanned the doorway again.

Outside the Round Robin Bar, a couple, young lobbyists, hurried by in the cold snap. A waiter was collecting the limp blue umbrellas from the patio tables outside—there'd been a warm day or two, and everyone had flocked to sit outside the Willard and have their pictures taken. The lobbyists, the tourists: they had no idea they were being used by those in power, and that beyond their uses, they meant nothing to a man like Shay.

He heard Broussard field another question about him. The bartender was trying not to stare.

"The debate tomorrow tonight in Cleveland won't be affected at all by Mr. Risen's absence," said Broussard with a poor attempt at a chuckle. "To be honest, I think the pace would be too much for him right now."

The props were being arranged, the stagehands scrambling scenery and lighting—yes, the stage was being set. Soon, to the whole world, he would be crazy.

The Round Robin's door opened and a man with the bookish appearance of an accountant entered. Not your typical Hollywood-brand spy. Thin gray hair covered the head of a thoroughly average-looking fellow. Maybe that was the real type the CIA looked for: the kind that could blend in. Which Matt had never attempted to do.

The agent ordered a coffee from the bartender and gestured with his finger toward a table in the right corner of the room, near the kitchen doors. It'd taken Matt eight calls to Redgrave to finally get a meeting with this guy, who subtly sized up the room before he sat down. Sitting close to him, Matt noticed a slight bent to his left eye, what in Ohio they affectionately called a walleye.

"I don't want to read about this in the paper," the man said with a glare.

"Look, I don't blame you for hating me, and believe me, you don't hate me as much as I hate myself. But I'm putting information together that can help Cory's father understand all this."

The agent, with a shrug, matter-of-factly said, "Cory used his Department of Agriculture job as cover. He had worked with Russian agencies to help provide food in Russia. And Afghanistan."

"Propaganda?"

"It's all propaganda. You should understand that." The man sipped from his coffee, his left eye listing toward the bar. "A KGB network of assassins had targeted Afghan rebels, including Hassan bin Chalabi."

Matt's eye's tightened. "Back when Hassan was a friend of Western democracy."

"Proving once again the stupidity of believing the cliché that the enemy of my enemy is my friend." He took a sip of coffee and cleared his throat. "We found out about this. Or rather, Redgrave discovered it during their cover work in Russia. Cory, Tess, George Ball, and Redgrave worked as a team."

Tess. The beauty from Florence. Matt lowered his eyes to the table and asked what had happened to her, but the man continued:

"Cory and Redgrave were strictly contract employees: information, pencil-pushers. Nerds. But Tess and Ball were covert agents. She was cool as a cucumber and Ball was an old-time CIA agent out of the E. Howard Hunt School. 'Crazy' was his cover. He was certifiable, but he could take on a new personality in a snap. He was an assassin. He looked after Cory, supervised him—and kept him out of the dirty stuff.

"On one occasion, however, Cory got caught in a crossfire and, to protect Tess and George, he shot two KGB agents."

"Cory?"

"Yes." The man's sterling eyes gazed back at his naiveté.

"And this happened in Florence."

"Yes."

Nausea dissolved through his stomach. "And Tess was killed that day, wasn't she?"

"Yes." The man's left drifted toward his nose as he, too, lowered his face to the table. "She told a hell of a joke. And could break your neck in six different ways."

They were quiet a moment with their private memories; it made sense, didn't it: Cory the idealist, the romantic, eager to help, dragged into a war above his pay grade and doing the right thing anyway.

"Unfortunately, a third KGB agent lived. And this is where your little bullshit treason charge comes into play: Redgrave exchanged a briefcase of documents—bottom-shelf info—for your cousin's life. But this Russian, he swore a vendetta. We call him The Butcher. All he needed was Redgrave's name."

Matt looked away, his eyes wet. "Then he just tracked him down."

"That's all I can say. It's more than I should say, especially to someone who's going crazy." He sneered at Matt. "Look, Oliver hasn't pieced all of this together, but I figure I have—you did what you were told, didn't you?"

"Just following orders," Matt said limply.

"We all do it. And we get our hands bloody for it." He leaned back and eyed the Round Robin's windows. "They'll throw you under the bus. And they won't protect you when Nesterenko comes to finish the job."

"Me?"

"Just a gut feeling. If we're right about this guy, he's an old-school commie, and your cousin was his enemy, and you work for the government: ergo you're the enemy. He'll come for you, then finish it with Redgrave."

Matt thanked the agent. "I know this violates every rule in your book."

The agent said bitterly, "I'm not here for you to get closure. I just want that bastard in the White House to know what he did."

The anger of the agent reminded Matt of the last time he saw Cory—those emotionless shark eyes, the only sign that Cory was hurting. All that he'd lost, all that he'd risked, gone in a single firefight—and then Matt had pissed it all away without even knowing. That final angry stare, cold, betrayed: like a curse.

"You know Carl Zalotnik?" said the man before he took a final chug from his coffee.

The name electrified him. Shay's goon.

"He's been lingering around in the promenade there." The man nodded through the Round Robin windows. "What say we leave through the proverbial back door, eh?"

On his signal, the man rose and Matt followed him through the kitchen, past steaming industrial pots and vats of grease, and out into the chill of the shade under the Willard along F Street. Despite his nerdish appearance, the man moved like a mink.

"A word of advice, Risen. Walk, don't run. If you're planning something, keep in mind that your life means nothing to these guys: Nesterenko or your own people."

"Shay," Matt whispered, a bit out of breath.

"Well, he has it comin'. I'd like to pull the trigger myself."

"He's in Cleveland, prepping for the debate."

The man looked at Matt dispassionately as he raised his collar to his cheeks. "Just remember *Hamlet*. You go on a revenge trip, and everyone usually ends up dead."

CHAPTER 3

Gail Turner scanned the small auditorium, her cat eyes prowling for anything out of the ordinary. Filling in for Matt was a piece of cake, really. Easier than she'd thought. The reporters didn't take to her, but fuck them anyway; she said what needed to be said, and that was it. Poor Matt. Always so stressed over insignificant things.

They'd chosen an intimate space on the Case Western campus. The stage was a circle, the two podiums angled just slightly toward each other, the twenty rows of seating in a fanning arc, each row a few seats wider than the one in front of it. If the arc had been completed, she thought, it'd look like Amsterdam's downtown. A small table sat in front of the stage for the PBS moderator, whom Gail had reminded politely to maintain fairness and decorum. Or else.

The Kensington campaign had loved the standing podiums when they'd anticipated debating Kirk. The president, while not tall, towered over the five-foot-seven Kirk, who exaggerated his diminutive stature with permanently hunched shoulders. Noah Young, however, stood at a fit six-foot-five. Coolly Gail had offered to allow a change in the staging, but the Young camp had politely declined.

Despite that minor defeat, as she stalked toward the holding room, Gail considered again how easy Risen had it. Everyone looked to you, everyone bowed. (Especially Broussard, who'd been ripped apart following his shaky press conference.) And filling in like this would endear her even more to the president. Quick work, and she'd be making the next jump after the election. One step at a time, she thought, like a stalking cat: one paw in front of the next in tiny, nearly unnoticeable steps, until she was in position to pounce.

Gail strode through the backstage spin room, home of the huddled masses: campaign workers and big contributors along with celebrities of all stripes, leaders of special interest groups, and local Cleveland leaders, prepared to declare their candidate the victor before the debate even started. They searched for any media-credentialed target in their path. Spin like a roulette wheel. Matt would have stopped to chat, she knew, but she passed through with hardly a nod to anyone. Let them chase her.

In the holding room, the president was surprisingly confident. Before he'd left for Ohio, Shay had shaken his head with disgust that the president didn't have sense enough to be afraid. The campaign was in free fall, he kept moaning; Young had awoken a sleeping giant with his demeanor and statesmanship, and now young people were drawn to his campaign like never before. But with a week to go, the president still maintained a five- to nine-point lead.

"Young needs something dramatic tonight," Shay growled to the president. "Don't give it to him."

"Gotcha. Get through tonight and we're home free. So I guess it's all on me." He snickered. "And that's the way it should be." He looked at the vice president and said, "Dixie, you've had too much on your back. It's about time I pick up some of the load."

Bless his heart, thought Gail, but the president, as Broussard and another handler guided him down the hall, well, he looked a bit like a Kentucky Derby horse being walked out of the stables.

"*Some* of the load?" Webb sneered.

Shay glanced into a monitor and yelled for someone to get the debate folks to lower the lighting a shade.

Gail walked Shay and Webb into a private viewing room. There they'd stay wired to the private focus groups across the country. She wondered if NORAD was as complicated. Webb reeked of Old Spice, Shay of stale scotch. She looked at the red-eyed Shay. "Are you living on liquor?"

"I barely woke up this morning."

"Where were you?"

He blinked. "Ah … Tulsa, Oklahoma."

"Probably fit right in." She sighed and cocked her weight over her hips. "You work too hard, Stephen."

"You don't have a fucking clue what you're doing," he muttered.

The moderator with his well-groomed beard, seemingly handmade suit, and sparkling manicure presented grandeur, but he spoke in a low and monotone voice that gave a polished dignity to the forum.

The opening statements were a contrast in styles and nothing of any surprise. For a moment, Young seemed nervous, but he'd made the jolting move from running mate to American focal point with surprising ease. He congratulated the president for the great success in warding off the terrorist threats, and thanked the now famous sniper who, with a single shot, had saved potentially thousands. But he quickly pointed out that with proper focus from federal authorities and—he looked at the president—"with the attention to detail by the White House that placed our defenses in position, our government saved our country from a horrific nightmare."

The compliment, along with a visual of the perplexed president, spoke volumes.

Shay looked at Webb and Gail. "He knew Kensington would give him that look," he grunted. "And that the camera would focus on it. Fucking brilliant. That's a man who understands the power of the visual."

The president stuck to the script and said nothing. Not even those who wrote his comments would remember anything the president said, and that would be a good thing.

But Young said a lot, even though he could have taken the easy way out and laid low on ideas. He steered the evening in a surprising direction: "Tonight, I will talk about a number of ideas I'm endorsing, not just as a matter of policy, but ideas which we as a nation should consider in a positive dialogue. And if elected I will pursue them. A trademark of my administration will be that I will not fear failing." He reminded his audience that after announcing a program, Franklin Roosevelt was asked, "What if this fails?" And Roosevelt had laughed and said, "Well, we'll try something else." Young straightened himself a bit and stole a glance at the president as he said, "But the fear of 'gotcha' politics has created a void of new and perhaps bold ideas. Not being able to discuss such ideas is a trap, and my administration will not just avoid that trap, but disarm it. Some will take their shots at us, and some ideas won't work out, but we will never fear a dialogue about substantial ideas, no matter how much we differ."

From the first question—about health care—it was clear that Young was too eager to actually put forth those grand ideas of his. He rambled on about "global economic realties" and "health care relief measures" though he was smart enough to describe in plain language the considerable tax relief he'd bestow on every American.

To each of these suggestions, Kensington tried a witty comeback. He couldn't resist, and each time his mouth opened, Gail could feel Webb and Shay tense beside her. Fifteen minutes in, and the president sounded like the incumbent president, and Young sounded like some idealist.

It got better—from Gail's perspective—when Young dove into the murky, jargon-laden pool of economics, claiming that the global economy dictated that the United States move the burden of taxation and health care away from taxing the employer-employee relationship, and therefore production, and shift to taxing consumption. "We must reinvigorate American production," Young said emphatically. "It will never reach the levels of yesteryear, but it can improve and provide opportunities for families." She watched Kensington jot down a note, probably to point out Young's pessimism that we could never reach the successes of the past. "This shift will level the playing field with our global competitors. Any item, whether it is a bike, or a broom, or a computer chip, or a car, carries the burden of health care and taxation if it is made in America. Japan, Germany, and many industrialized nations have turned to the value added tax for this purpose. As an example: an American-made car has several thousand dollars built into its cost to cover taxes and health care; a Japanese or German car has none. The person in Japan or Germany who buys the car pays the tax. With a 10 percent to 14 percent VAT, we should be able to eliminate the under-$50,000 dollar-tax bracket, and pay each American a $200 voucher to cover food and basics, no matter their income. This will also simplify taxation and recoup a great deal of unreported income, benefiting honest taxpayers."

"You said a mouthful," Kensington sneered to begin his response.

And it got even better with a suggestion by Young that America could massively expand rail service and high speed rail without spending a great deal of new money. "With one minor sacrifice," he said, then paused before adding, "If we combine many of the resources we spend on transporting mail and move them to a passenger rail service, trains can move people and mail from city to city and double their productivity."

"Is he talking about trains?" Webb crowed.

With a sanctified, raised palm, Gail said, "Here's to four more years!"

Onstage, the president smiled. "Now let me get this straight. You want to change snail mail to glacier mail?"

Young smiled graciously. "No, Mr. President, I want to melt the glacier that has frozen Washington into a mountain of inaction and I want to provoke thought."

"Well thinking is a good thing—I think, too—but I think we ought to think through what we, uh, you know, *think* about."

"Jesus, man, just run out the clock," Webb grumbled.

Gail turned to see Shay staring at his BlackBerry, his brows bulging, the caterpillar eyebrows practically sweating.

"What is it?"

"I have to go."

She and Webb echoed one another: what?

But Shay had snatched his suit coat from the back of a chair and was struggling to fit it around his stubby arms. "We've already won, anyway," he said. "So long as Kensington doesn't say something horrific. Just do what you do, Gail, and try to show a little personality now and then."

Slowly, the clock did run down, and Gail sprang out of the holding room with no need of direction, though she and Webb had spent the final minutes going over the obvious talking points.

The spin room was truly spinning. Opinions flew in the glare of television lamps. Young's camp stuck with a "for once we had a debate about ideas" script, but like their candidate, they made only confusing explanations of the ideas themselves. Gail ripped them apart. "Specifics," she snapped. "Where are the specifics? Anybody with half an education can throw out some ideas, but it takes experience to know and communicate those specifics." She remembered something Matt had told her: the media hate not knowing what's about to happen; it makes them look like idiots. And so she pounded away at the "improvisation" of the Young campaign.

"Like jazz?" one black reporter asked.

"Sure, like jazz," she said, then practically slapped her own hand against her mouth. "It has its place," she stammered, "improvisation does, but not here in a presidential debate."

Damn it. Where had Shay gotten to?

———∿∿———

A long walk off a short pier. Why not? Matt tottered a bit at the far corner of the East Ninth Street Pier, the Lake Erie water turbulent and black until it sloshed in the moonlight and was lit a sea green. A name floated back to him—from a history class?—literature?—yes, Woolf. Virginia Woolf. Rocks in the pockets. He'd explained Cory's real occupation to Jesse, explained how he'd inadvertently exposed him, and then Matt had gotten drunk again at the Oakland Grille—what was left? Oh, yes. Shay. Webb. Kensington, that dumb motherfucker. If it ended like *Hamlet*, so be it.

Lights encroached on the long promenade of the pier. Though a police officer had walked by, studying him, no one had tried to remove him, so at first he didn't pay any mind to the steady approach of the two front beams. Someone shouted his name and he turned. The Rock and Roll Hall of Fame rose like some angular, Egyptian monolith, a heavenly palace of the dead, and in the light it cast across the pier, a short man in a black woolen coat walked toward him slowly between the opposing rows of trees. Unearthly floodlights cast wild shadows on the nearly bald man who had once been his teacher.

"Hey there, Matt," Shay said cheerily. A little anxious, too. "Going for a swim?"

"It'd be your lucky day."

Shay's limo had parked in the roundabout. All the cars that would park on the pier for a trip on the Goodtime II were gone this late in the season, and so they were alone in the eerie light of the Museum and Browns Stadium to the west just beyond the dead hulk of a floating steamship museum. Shay rubbed his hands together and kept his distance.

"I almost chose Terminal Tower, but I figured you'd try to throw me off," Matt said with a bitter laugh. "I'm a decent swimmer."

"Where the hell you been, Matt?"

"Columbus first, lovely motel. Then Marion, to tell my uncle why his son was killed. What about you?"

Straining to sound chipper, Shay said he'd been watching Kensington try to give away the election. Matt looked out across the vague motions of the massive lake in front of him.

"So what's it going to be, Matt?"

"A scotch neat," he said with a weird chuckle.

Shay approached carefully and said, "When was the last time you shaved? Hell, bathed?"

"Don't know."

Shay, with a thick dose of sympathy, said, "I know what you're thinking. But believe me, Redgrave needed exposing. History will prove us right."

Matt's cackling laughter rang across the water.

"Find out anything more about Cory?" he said with something like a giggle.

"Same. I'm telling you, the police reports are accurate."

Matt stared intently at his former mentor. "Here to carry Webb's water, huh? Like you always do."

Shay's eyes lit up like struck matches. "If that's what you think, you're a fucking moron. I am not here for the president, or the vice president; I am here for you. I know you're thinking some strange stuff, but trust me, Matt, you have no way to hurt us. You know we can take care of our problems." Shay turned to the water beating against the pier. "In fact, you wouldn't be that big of a problem; you'd be a goddamn opportunity. As the president would've said before he turned into God's Will, we'll ruin you so bad, you couldn't sell pussy on a troop ship."

"He still says that. He's a fraud."

Shay snorted. "Like me, I suppose?"

He turned and glared at Shay. "No. That's the problem." He raised his hand, as if raising a drink. "And here's to problems."

Shay went for his coat pocket, and instinctively Matt grabbed the little man by his woolen lapels; the look of fear in Shay's eyes was startling, like some newly discovered land.

"Just my BlackBerry," Shay stuttered.

Matt let go with a shove. Down the pier, Shay's driver had stepped out of the limo. Hell, it might have been Carl down there.

"Taking a call?"

Shay shook his head and held the phone up to Matt. "Your message. *Concede.* Really? Are you that fucking naive, Matt, after four years of this? No one concedes, no one confesses." He shook his fat head, his turkey neck wobbling. "Do you remember what you told me and Webb back in 2000, when you thought you had to fight for the job with Gail? Those words of hers? 'In politics you're rewarded for success, not loyalty.' Do you want to know why that's true, Matt?" His voice had risen to a thin shriek, his face blotchy and red. "Because, Matt, the betrayal of loyalty is an easy fix; success is not. You, my smug little friend, are an easy fix."

"We'll see what the press has to say about that."

"The press? They lost their balls after Iran-Contra and don't even know where to fucking look."

They lapsed into another silence. The odd laughter that kept bubbling up from Matt's lungs wouldn't stop, and he leaned against a mooring post for ships that no longer docked here. Shay was right, of course: it wouldn't take much to silence Matt. He needed more proof, and needed to get it before someone like Carl silenced him for good.

"Look, let's not end this in an ugly fashion," said Shay. "Take a vacation. The campaign can justify it. Wherever you want. Hell, take a month with your girlfriend up there in, what is it, Shenandoah? You've earned it. Just get things under control, then come back when the election's over and cruise for as long as it takes."

"I'm out of bullshit, Stephen."

"Hey, I've got enough for both of us." Standing next to Matt, leaning on a different mooring, he shrugged with a self-deprecating laugh. Or one designed to be so. "Don't go off half-cocked. Why spoil things for yourself?"

After a long silence, Matt said, "Do you understand that the person I cared about most, for all of my life, is dead? And we caused it, Stephen."

"It's just not true," Shay said. "Like I said, I have a mountain of bullshit, I could make something up, but I'm not bullshitting you because I want the truth about Cory just as much as you."

"That's good bullshit."

Matt turned and headed back down the pier.

"Hey! Hey!" Shay's shoes clacked on the brickwork. "You do this, and you'll end up just one more dead bug on the windshield as we power on. And for what? This delusion?"

Matt spun, his fists clenching. "Delusion? You told me to spread that story!"

"Matt, I did no such thing."

"You fucking stood in my office and told me that Redgrave was CIA!"

Shay swiveled his head, his eyes wide and innocent.

"Prove it," he said.

With a groan Matt pushed into Shay, his forearm digging into Stephen's throat. He pinned him against a thin tree, which shook the few remaining leaves to the bricks around them.

"Go ahead, Matt," Shay said breathlessly, his weak and purple lips twisted in an ancient-seeming grin. "Get it all out. See how it feels."

"You're a fucking monster!"

Some force pinched his shoulder and threw him back. He landed on the brick and concrete with a snap, and his arm went numb. Above him towered Shay's driver—not Carl, but some other faceless shadow-man, a hulking brute who was now dusting off Shay's lapel.

Shay leaned over him a little. "Maybe I am, Matt. And maybe you're trying to do the right thing. I could give a fuck. I told you: how it gets done is for the sewers. *What* gets done, that's important. That's history."

His elbow slowly beginning to howl, Matt tried to pitch himself forward, but his back tightened and with a gasp he fell back. Shay and his driver walked off through the opposing trees, their shoes crushing the leaves underneath, and Matt gazed at the salt-light of the Hall of Fame museum and its windows into the land of the dead.

CHAPTER 4

For the next several days Young continued to throw out ideas, and, while most were beaten down, the steady flow had the talking heads debating either the merits or flaws of Young's strategy and ideas. But for the first time in anyone's memory, it was a campaign of ideas.

Gail could see that Shay was torn about attacking Young, but the campaign decided to run out the clock with a prevent defense, every football fan's least favorite strategy.

—⁓⁓—

"What the hell happened to you?" Kris said at the door of her Old Town apartment.

It was the first time Matt realized what his appearance must be like, hair messed and matted, his eyes red, skin gray, and face unshaven.

"Kris, you were right. Cory was right. I don't understand why it took me so long," he said.

"I'm so sorry about Cory …"

With a wrenching sob, like the slap of waves against a break wall, it all came pouring out of him: what Kris already knew—his role in the leak; Shay; Webb—and what she didn't know—Cory's job and why he'd died in Florence. How he'd met Shay in Cleveland, how he'd made it back to DC and nearly gone straight from the airport to the *Washington Post* before he remembered what a young Cory used to say: "Right time, right place." And so he'd had the cabbie turn around, and he'd hidden in his apartment, thinking, sobering up—

"Slow down," she said. "Let's get you some food."

"Why are you home?"

"You caught me between flights," she said from the kitchen. "I'm supposed to be in Iowa tomorrow."

"I want to expose Shay and Webb before the election," he said.

She poked her head around the corner, a can opener in hand.

"What did you say?"

"I realized I needed a better plan than just bursting through the front door of a newspaper and spilling my guts," he said, sipping at the soup she'd microwaved.

"So you burst through my door."

"I'm a hell of a guy, I know." He wiped his mouth and looked at her sternly. "I'm in a war with the greatest manipulator in the world. He's got unlimited resources, and I don't. So I have to think like him, anticipate his next move. As soon as he realizes I'm not backing down— after that beating I took at the pier—well, he's going to up the ante." His eyes softened. "He might come after you, or Shelly."

"I will kill anyone who touches that girl," she said, her voice shaking.

"Not before I do," he said with a little smile.

"Matt, these people … it's not that different from what I saw in Bosnia. It's the depth of the human heart: pride. Righteousness. They think they can do whatever it takes."

"If I call Shay and suggest a meeting, he'll figure I'm trying to trap him. But I don't know if I have time for anything else."

"You need to spin him."

Matt perked up. Had he heard a car door slam? They could be watching … listening. Carl could knock on the door any minute. He held a finger up to Kris and reached for the notepad where she'd scribbled down a grocery list, flipped a new page, and wrote, *Don't talk.*

Her eyebrows crinkled.

Hastily he wrote, *Meet at Chadwick's 1–4 tomorrow—through window with wine rack. You film it. Have Shelly come over to feed LB at noon.*

He then carefully slid the pen onto a second page and wrote a grocery list to serve as a decoy. If Shay's cronies were watching, they'd do anything to get the note. He tore off both slips, simultaneously folding them together carefully. Sliding over to Kris, he feathered her hair and said, "I love you," kissed her—she murmured in shock—and he slid the instructions into her hip pocket, keeping the grocery list in his hand.

Pulling away, he barely saw her hand before it slapped him.

"You fresh!" she said, trying not to laugh.

"I'm insane, remember?"

"Your lackey Broussard never fails to mention it."

"He's just doing his job." Matt sighed. "That's all we ever do, isn't it? And it gets us into this." He looked at her, and now the urge to kiss her was not for the sake of deception or an observant camera. "You let me in. You didn't even yell at me. Why?"

She pursed her lips, shook her head. "I don't know." Taking his scraped-up hand, she traced the lines of his bones. "I always thought you'd come around. That you were more than you allowed yourself to be."

"It's hard knowing."

She kissed him now, brushing back his greasy hair, and when she pulled away, she suggested with a gleam in her eye that he could use a shower.

"One more thing," he said. "Tomorrow around seven, I need three or four reporters—whoever you can gather—to meet me at the Round Robin Bar. Tell them I want to address all these insinuations that I'm losing it."

"Done. Shower."

"Maybe I should just go."

She yanked him off the sofa and pushed him toward the stairs. In the bathroom, she ran the water while he stripped, protesting the entire time, until the noise of the shower head suddenly made sense.

"That's the loudest shower in DC," he said.

"Took you long enough to figure that out," she said, unbuttoning her blouse.

Under the water, they held each other. Not needing to whisper, Matt thought out loud, figuring that Shay would mumble and maybe even cover his mouth at Chadwick's, rendering his audio recording useless. "Play to his pride," Kris said as he soaped her back gently. "Get him worked up. There's a reason he doesn't go in front of the cameras, right?" He nodded, grinned. Such a devious woman. With her video, and maybe some photographs, the images could back up the words. They'd make a hell of a team.

He left a few hours later, and, stepping out into the cold air, he felt a new pressure on his shoulders, a new kind of goal. His entire career in DC, he'd only done what somebody else told him to do; now the impetus was his. His alone.

As he walked toward the subway, a woman staggered in front of him, apparently intoxicated. She bumped into him, apologizing with remarkably slurred words—"Been looking for my dog," she mumbled— and he felt her hand slide into his pocket and pull out the grocery list. He smiled and wished her good luck.

—∿—

The next day, at twelve o'clock sharp, Shelly arrived at the door, throwing herself into his arms. "Kris didn't say anything other than to come here at noon," she said, and he slid her a long note. As she read, he watched her eyes flicker; she was a bright kid, and she deserved so much more than her parents were providing her. If this all worked out, he'd have to do something about that.

"Don't worry," he said, "Larry Bird's a tough old coot."

"Who's worried? I'm not worried."

"If there's any trouble—*any*—don't mess around."

By one o'clock he was headed into Chadwick's, immediately taking a spot at the bar in front of the window with the wine rack.

He asked the bartender, "Could you open the blind so I can get a little sunlight?"

"We got a row of windows up front with a couple of tables open. Why not there? Plenty of sun."

"Don't want to be too public."

"So you come to a public bar? Besides, we never open these."

Matt handed him a twenty. "Maybe you could just humor me?"

The confused bartender reached up and pulled the blind. Matt studied the window and hoped Kris had found a place to shoot. The recorder he'd affixed to his chest with electrical tape was a poor imitation of something he'd seen in a movie, but if he was careful, fairly still, and thought to hold it a bit by crossing his arms, it should do the job. On the television behind the bar, MSNBC reported on a Young rally in New Mexico, their anchor letting slip her disappointment over the recent tracking reports: Kensington had regained the momentum for the first time since the assassination of Kirk.

The hours dragged on. Maybe Shay wasn't having him followed after all? Then he recalled the way he and Webb had gleefully made him sweat over the press secretary job. Just another manipulation. Maybe he'd heard them last night—at least until they'd gone into the shower—and knew Matt was planning something for tonight. Even still. No way he could resist, not after the obscenity-laced phone message Matt had left in the morning.

Sure enough, Shay stormed in at a quarter to four. Matt fumbled to press the record button through his shirt before Shay thumped down onto the barstool next to Matt, not making eye contact until he'd ordered his drink. His gaze was long and steady, almost amused, but clearly searching for a read of Matt's intentions. It was like being scanned by an alien.

Once the scotch had arrived, he took a sip and kept the glass held to his lips. He whispered, "First I'll kill that bitch Johansen, and after that the kid, then you, no matter what it costs. I'm thinking it'll be an angry CIA agent, popping a traitor in retaliation for his underhanded release of a CIA agent's identity. We'll be sympathetic, of course—poor Matt, he went crazy under the stress—but we'll be dutifully appalled by your actions."

Well that hadn't taken long.

"You'd think a CIA agent would be angry with *you*, Stephen."

"Let him. I had nothing to do with it."

"That's not what's in my notes."

"Notes," Shay snickered. "Notes disappear."

Matt watched Shay in the mirror behind the bar; his big head filled half of the frame. "I know one thing; my message will get through to someone."

"We might have to drag our feet after the election, but it won't *cost* us the election. That's in the bag."

"I'll disgrace you at the very least."

"Me?" Shay let loose a full belly laugh. "You little bastard, I don't feel disgrace. I don't even know what the hell that is."

"Which explains those men's magazines. *Kaged Muscle* ring a bell? You know, the body builders all oiled up. That'll be in the story. Just for fun."

Shay stared past the wine rack as the setting sun beat down on the bottles. His face was as flushed as a chardonnay. He glared at Matt.

"Oh, that's a hateful look," Matt said. "See the same in my eyes? Huh?"

Shay drained his tumbler of scotch and pushed himself off the stool. He collected his coat around his narrow shoulders while he gazed at Matt. "One last lesson, Matt. The great lie is that in this country, every voice counts. That we're a true democracy." Shay's voice was smooth, steely. "We're not. You ought to know that. It's what you're trying to do now. Lift your voice to the top, right?" His eyes narrowed behind his watery eyeglasses, those barest of outlines around his twinkling, devious pupils. "You, my washed-up little protégé, are nothing but an attention whore trying to make himself out to be a hero. Your cousin was just a piece in the puzzle, and you're nothing but the dirt on his grave."

Shay stalked out. Matt's hands shook, and it required all of his energy not to go out and pound that balloon head into the cement until it popped.

He waited a while and then walked into the bathroom. From his cell, he texted Kris to meet him at his apartment. With Shay alerted and with Carl on the loose, he and Kris needed to move fast. He ripped the tape recorder from his chest and rewound it, listening to Shay talk about killing; it was the smallness of the man's voice that made the words so terrifying. Shay was precise. Surgery, he'd said once. A scalpel, correctly inserted.

Matt hurriedly walked home, listening for footsteps or car doors. As he rushed toward the steps of his brownstone, he turned in time to see a man's sleeve and a hand holding a black baton—then blackness, a swirl of texture and sound. His legs scraped against the concrete of his steps. Framed in an intense halo by the lowering autumn sun, a shadow of a man propped him against his own door.

"Last warning."

Tires screeched and his eyelids fought open. Down on the sidewalk Kris's head jerked back from a blow. The man's arm was slung through her camera strap. She was calling him. Matt got to his knees as his stomach tried to empty itself. Fight, damn it, a voice in his head screamed. Cory's voice? He saw Kris land a knee into the man's thigh—he was wide as a wall, bald, and rather stubby—and he howled, snapping the camera strap. It clattered to the ground.

The door swung open behind Matt, and all he saw was two legs rush past, screaming. Not until she bolted down the steps did Matt see in Shelly's raised hands a baseball bat and a golf club. Kris had grabbed the man by the ear, and it squirted blood—from a distance, like a pen's purple ink had exploded—and Shelly swung the bat level and sure into the man's torso.

"Bitch," the man grunted.

Matt pulled himself up by the handrail of his steps and planted one foot, then the next, trying to descend. The man pushed Shelly away from him and took off down the street, hobbling though he ran.

Kris and Shelly, out of breath, stared at Matt. Another wave of nausea passed through him, and he vomited over the rail.

"Matt, come on. Keep looking at me."

"Is he gonna be okay?"

His head felt weighted by bricks, his neck too thin and rubbery. Each time he opened his eyes, the scene was different: Kris in his face, a bruise swelling her cheek; ascending the stairs again, Shelly crying; the echo of voices in his apartment.

"Your camera," he muttered.

"I've got it. Your tape recorder?"

He patted down his pants pockets. It was gone.

"You trust me?" Kris said frantically. She kissed him once. "Do you?"

He nodded.

CHAPTER 5

That night, Yuri parked on the Old Town street, having passed by his target a few times. Two lights on downstairs, one upstairs. He lit a cigarette and watched the brownstone for awhile. He'd been trailing Redgrave the past few days, to be certain his protection detail was consistent—it was—and had found Risen only yesterday. Then he'd promptly lost him. How quickly everyone in this city, in this entire country, moved. He'd forgotten. And where, of course, were they going? Had they any idea? Of course not. Flailing about, here to there, with no sense of direction, without morals or integrity, believing in their country only when it suited their immediate needs.

But he'd found Risen's apartment now, at least. He reached for the Luger, screwed on the silencer, and opened the car door. His bandaged thumb throbbed, and he popped an aspirin before he crossed the street. Late in the hour, it was deserted, and he peered at the address before he took one of the steps. In the streetlight's glow, a watery pile of vomit had pooled in the scrubbed grass. So Risen was a drunk. All the easier.

He peered through the window by the door, noting that some music was playing. Classical. Bach's cello suites, if he wasn't mistaken.

Creeping to the backside of the apartment, he disappeared into shadow. Each adjacent apartment was dark, and he worked in the velvety darkness toward the rear door. Pinching a small flashlight with his teeth, he manipulated the lock until it clicked, and he slowly swung the door open into a laundry room. A cat's food dish sat near the washer.

The music was louder now. Coming from the kitchen. Allowing his breathing to relax, Yuri poked the Luger's nose into the kitchen. Nothing. A small stereo played the cello suites, the cat gut texture of the cellist's instrument somehow unleashing such beautiful rising and falling patterns of repetition. Like life. They killed your friends, you killed their friends. Over and over. There was no progress any more, not in these times.

From the center of the living room, he peeked up the stairwell. Then the den, where, on a coffee table in front of a gas fireplace, lay a few bloody gauze pads. He crouched a moment: stray bloody smears of fingers, too. Someone better not have done his job for him.

As he neared the stairwell again, the only light upstairs shut off. He smiled to himself. His rubber soles elicited hardly a squeak from the stairs, and he paused to let his eyes adjust to the dimness. A bit of moonlight cast a pale block of light on the wall. Below, the cellist gained in his frenzy, the notes spiraling up, up, up.

Yuri whirled into a bedroom—the spare, and hardly furnished— and kicked through a sleeping bag that had been laid out on the floor. A few teenager's magazines, a tube of lipstick. A pillow that smelled of lilacs. A security light with a timer, still warm. The bathroom, too, was empty, but clearly the province of a single man like Matthew Risen. Five different colognes, various hair creams. A real pretty boy, from the looks of him on the television.

The only room left upstairs was the master bedroom. Its door was only slightly ajar, and he aimed the Luger through the opening, then nudged the door aside with his foot. Two lumps under the sheets. A pitiful attempt at the illusion of two sleeping bodies. One by one he edged open the walk-in closet doors—again, nothing. His nostrils flared as he exhaled deeply. Crouching near the bed, disgusted that he'd lost Risen again, Yuri wondered if his prey been tipped off. Or if he'd run because he'd already been attacked.

He'd just emerged from the back door when he heard a pair of footsteps coming along the sidewalk beside the apartment. With no time to even lock the door, he hopped from the stairs into the grass and aimed at the corner of the brownstone. The first appeared in the darkness as little more than a shadow. His breath caught. The second followed closely.

"Carl says this back door's real loose," said the second.

Yuri holstered his Luger as they went up the steps. Maybe they were here to guard Risen, maybe to kill him. Either way, it didn't matter. He needed to be silent here and to trust his hands one last time.

The woman agent fidgeted with the doorknob. "What the?"

Her partner did not respond. And before she could even turn around, her neck, too, was in Yuri's hands.

No blood. Good. He could leave no trace, otherwise Risen might return only to run again, or the police would get involved. His severed thumb throbbing, Yuri stood over the two bodies: each wore a black leather jacket, they carried no identification, and each was packing a revolver. He sneered at the thought that he may have saved Risen's life. For the moment.

CHAPTER 6

Matt stood with one foot on a half-buried rock and gazed across Kris's Shenandoah property, the rolling valley stretching out in the same waves the early settlers must have fallen in love with: the promise of expansion, freedom, seemingly unlimited resources. From the top of the hill, it always looked that way. What could be used, what could be consumed, and what would be lost in the process?

He stretched his sore neck to the left. Everything, he thought. Everything could be lost.

Kris lay nestled in her favorite armchair, and down the verdant hill, Shelly was leading Larry Bird around by an improvised leash of twine, though, given his corpulence, old Bird wasn't running anywhere. Matt lay next to Kris and pulled her jacket across her chest; though the morning sun was unrelenting, the chill was, too.

"How's the pain?" he said, gingerly lifting her bandaged left hand, which their assailant had apparently pinned to the side of a parked car; he'd missed it during his fading in and out.

"Fine," she said, "though I'm glad I got the pictures before we got jumped."

"They won't prove much without the recording."

She rubbed his arm, reaching over the exposed root of the cradle and kissing him.

"You couldn't have known Shay would act so quickly."

"I bet those reporters were pissed," Matt said with a chuckle, and he winced. The painkillers they'd gotten prescribed by the emergency room doctors in Woodbridge weren't quite doing the trick.

"Ah, they owed me," said Kris. "They'll owe you, too, once they find out what's going on."

Shelly held Larry Bird up to the sun like some odd sacrifice, and the cat's meow echoed thinly up the hill.

"Shay knows about this place. We can't stay here long."

"You need to rest."

"The election's in five days, Kris. I can sleep after that."

"Or when you're dead." She tightened her grip around his arm. "I'm not fond of you dying, you know," said Kris. "In case you were wondering if I thought that hero shit was hot or something."

"You went along with it."

"I didn't really think they'd try to kill you. Or me, or Shelly."

By noon they'd taken a nap and cooked a lunch with the stores Kris kept in her cabin. She'd called in to the news organizations that were expecting shots from her, saying she'd come down with the flu; remember this, Matt thought; remember how much she's sacrificed just in the past few days.

They were chatting on the stonework porch of the cabin when his phone rang. He looked at it suspiciously and then answered. "Yes," he said.

"Risen …coworker of Cory's …" The deep, manipulated voice broke up with interference—it was amazing he'd gotten reception, even this high on the hill—but he could make out a few words, "package you need … Cory's … tomorrow at eleven."

"Tell you what," said Matt. "Why don't you go fuck—"

"Did you know Cory … Shay talked?" said the voice. "Figure … could use."

"What do you want?"

"Justice. Meet me … Ag Department lot, wide open … parking lot facing Cory's window. Can't risk … my office. Eleven o'cl—"

With a click, the voice disappeared. The birds were the only sound for awhile.

"It's a trap," Kris said once he'd explained.

"I know that parking lot. It's the Department of Agriculture. Right there on the Mall, a Friday afternoon. Terrible place for a trap."

Kris studied him over the rim of a steaming coffee mug. With Larry Bird asleep in her lap, Shelly stared absently at the cat's bushy fur; she'd gone through violent swings of emotion, crying out in her sleep, crying when her parents hadn't even noticed that she didn't come home last night, and yet forcing herself to cheerfully crack jokes about going out for the softball team now that she knew how to swing a bat.

"We'll go with you," she said.

"No, you won't," Matt said. "You and Kris need to go somewhere. A motel, deep in Virginia. Ohio, maybe. God, I've got to get Jesse and Paula out of their house."

"And what, you go strutting back into Washington all by yourself?" Kris said.

"Someone needs to look after Shelly."

"Someone needs to look after *you*," said Shelly.

He blew a gust of air through his tense lips. The plan he'd woken to this morning—the remnant of a dream, perhaps, or that constant nightmare—seemed to make even more sense now that this stranger had called. He still had a few friends left.

"Do you trust me?" he said, smiling gently at Kris.

"It's them I don't trust."

He looked at Shelly, then at Kris. Words that only a few months ago would have tumbled out—perhaps sincerely, perhaps not—now clogged in his throat. "You two ... you're all I have. You're precious to me. I think I have a way you can help from here, but you have to listen to me, please. We have to be out of here as soon as possible."

The two women, who would've gone to war for him, relaxed a little once he explained his plan. He called a car rental company in Luray and then dialed his uncle's house. Jesse answered breathlessly, and for a moment, Matt feared the worst. After some explanation, Jesse, too, calmed down, and Matt gave him a phone number to call, a direct line to a senator; he should tell the man everything, including what had happened to Cory, and then ask him to do a favor for Matt. "And then Jess, I need you to get the hell out of Marion."

CHAPTER 7

The next morning, Matt stopped at a country diner and devoured a large plate of ham, eggs, greasy home fries, and maybe a gallon of coffee, careful in his corner booth to keep an eye on the parking lot. Like the friend of Redgrave's had instructed, he'd sat as close to the kitchen as possible. With stationary he'd picked up at a convenience store in Luray, he hastily wrote duplicates of the same confession, folded and stuffed them into envelopes, checking his watch, eyeing his cell phone in anticipation of Kris's eight o'clock check-in. *We're fine, and it's on,* her message said. *Jess and Paula in Fred.*

A few hours later, he pushed into DC and heard on the news that Senator Joseph Rose had called a noon press conference at the steps of the Capitol building. The talking heads barely gave it their attention, focused as they were on the race and the reported seven-point gap that'd opened up for Kensington. Matt gritted his teeth, rushing across the Beltway, his eyes glancing between his rearview and the clock on the rental's dash. He parked at the Jefferson Memorial, and with some time to spare, he walked up the steps of the monument and watched swarms of people of all ages and from several states and a few different countries. He read the inscription that Cory had told him to read, which was engraved on the southeast panel:

> "I am not an advocate for frequent changes in laws and constitutions. But the laws and institutions must go hand in hand with the progress of the human mind. As that becomes more developed, more enlightened, as new discoveries are made, new truths discovered, and manners and opinions change, with the change of circumstances, institutions must advance also to keep pace with the times. We might as well require a man to wear still

the coat which fitted him when a boy as civilized society to remain ever under the regimen of their barbarous ancestors."

And what had Matt done but help squeeze the country into the small coat of intolerance?

On a lengthy circuit, in full public view among the tourists—Carl would have to kill him for everyone to see, if that's what was going to happen—he crossed the tidal basin, winding his way to the Mall and the base of the Washington Monument. Throughout he had the nerve-fluttering sensation of being watched but saw no one trailing him, no one on his tail, no suspicious eyes staring back at him and quickly looking away. He checked his watch: quarter to eleven. He gazed up the spine of the Washington Monument. Why had they always built them so tall, so high that no man could reach without losing sight of where he stood?

～৵~

It was by luck that Yuri had found Risen again. Early in the dawn, a car had stopped near Risen's apartment, and a tall, bald man in a tight, black leather jacket had gotten out, cased the brownstone and, pausing only a moment to look up and down the street, hopped back into his car. A gut instinct led Yuri to follow the car, and he'd stayed on the man all morning, watching him talk every five minutes, it seemed, on his cell phone, and then snap it shut and light a cigar. Thirty years in the business and you developed a feeling for these things: the man was CIA, and given all the news there'd been about Risen's "exhaustion," and the two operatives Yuri had killed last night, it was clear that Risen was being hunted. And then the image clicked: the bald man was the Wrestler, whose image Yuri had come across before the Redgrave leak. So Risen was being hunted by his own government. For a moment, he'd considered his options: what Risen had to say clearly would embarrass the United States, and in the old days, he would've actually protected Risen long enough for the scandal to emerge. Weaken the enemy state: a prime directive. Oh, Kostya, those old urges faded with reluctance, didn't they?

By the time he parked behind the man's car near some garish museum, Yuri had come to his senses. Risen had to die, and any delay would only make it more difficult to execute his revenge. And Redgrave would become such a problem, the U.S. government would definitely find a way to get rid of him, probably by "natural causes," eventually doing Yuri's work for him. Besides, if he went after Redgrave now, he'd be killed in the attempt with so many guarding the supposed traitor. And so he trailed the bald man, whose nose was as sharp and pointed as a shrike's beak, down to the grim, dirty tidal basin, and then back along a trail toward the Mall, until he found himself staring at the Washington Monument and, at its base, on a bench—Matt Risen.

Near eleven o'clock, Risen got up from the bench and passed a theater. The man Yuri had been following slid carefully through the crowds. Yuri tightened his black woolen overcoat and did the same.

———◊◊◊———

As he slipped the last of the prepared statements into a mailbox on Jefferson Drive, Matt felt the vibration of his phone. Shay. Maybe they were tracking him, getting a fix on his location via the cell phone; hell, maybe they would do something stupid. Becoming a martyr was a small price to pay for his sins.

"Hey there, Stevie!" he practically yelled into the phone.

"Matt. I've got Gail here; she says Senator Rose's office is planning some stunt. I don't suppose you're headed to the Capitol, are you?"

"I'm sure you know the answer to that."

"You'll never make it up the steps, you dumb bastard."

"Then shoot me in front of the whole world."

He imagined Shay's stunned, pasty face; in Shay's world, no one was ever willing to die for his beliefs.

"I will!" Shay burst. "Goddamn it I will! And it doesn't take this administration to get what we need. I don't care who's in power; if it's us, we'll grab it, and if it's Young, we'll tighten the vise grips and make sure he knows he'll never get a second term unless he goes along with us. So if you think you're going to fuck up this election for us—"

"Stephen, I'm disappointed that you don't get it. I'm not working an election, for once." Matt shouldered the phone as he crossed Fourteenth Street, eyeing a bearish man on the opposite side of Jefferson with a shock of silvery hair. "It's about the truth, Steve. You don't speak for this nation. You only speak for a few people. And the rest of them are catching on. You remember how Hitler rose to power by burning down the German parliament building and blaming it on the communists?"

"The Reichstag … yeah, it worked for him. He got elected and he got his war with the Soviets."

"But how easy is it to get the Germans to go to war today? You've inadvertently raised the bar for war. And it's only getting harder. Too many people sitting around coffee houses talking. The old style isn't going to work anymore."

"It's timeless, you dumbfuck."

Matt paused and stepped across Jefferson Drive toward the parking lot by the Ag Department.

"We've outgrown the coat, Stephen."

"Outgrown the *what*? Listen, asshole—"

"You're breaking up, Stephen."

"They'll just think you're crazy—"

Matt snapped shut the phone. He cut through the browned hedges and scanned the stocky gray brick of the Ag Department for Cory's window as he walked. Many times, he'd hiked from the White House over this way, always checking that second window from the left for a glimpse of Cory at his desk. Today the shade was drawn. The window was one of only two that overlooked this particular lot, which was always empty, like it was now.

What seemed at first a supernatural chill, he soon realized, was the sudden shade caused by a few overbearing trees. Even leafless, their clustered branches blocked out the sun. And the view from the street. In fact, the entire parking lot was cut off, surrounded by a tall line of hedges, some shaped into cones, others as long and thick as walls. Even the driveway to the parking lot was hidden by a massive elm. His stomach seized. With the noisy traffic passing by and the seclusion of the shaded lot, no one would know he'd died here.

Carl stepped out from the tree line along the north edge of the building, a revolver in hand. It caught just a glint of sunlight.

"Hey there, Matt," he said, his voice low and cheery. The scant wind buffeted his black leather jacket. "Helluva way to go, huh?"

All the blood drained from his head. That voice on the other end, when he was back in Shenandoah. The Jersey accent.

"It was you," Matt said.

Carl twisted his lips and cheeks into a sneer and raised the gun.

A shot snapped—or was it two?—and the stone of the building splintered with a crack. Matt's eyes tightened and he spun, tripping to the macadam. The shot—from his right, or his left? There: a huge man in a black overcoat, his left thumb bandaged, pushing through the hedge with a gun raised. The man from the sidewalk. Matt scrambled back but otherwise was immobilized by the sights before him.

Carl had fallen to one knee, snarling, pressing his left hand to his bloody right shoulder. He leveled his gun at the newcomer, and with an echoing report, both toppled—Carl with a grunt, and the massive stranger with a primitive howl.

Cautiously Matt picked himself up from the macadam, patting himself down for blood, then sprinted to the fallen man in the black overcoat. His silver revolver, equipped with a silencer, had fallen a few feet away, and though he wondered if this man wasn't some secret ally, a friend of Rose's perhaps, he kicked the weapon a few feet farther. Bent over, Matt studied the heavy creases in the old man's forehead, the purpled bags under his eyes, the oddly-shaped scar under his right eye, and he pushed back on the thin white shock of hair as he looked into dimming eyes. He looked as old as Uncle Jess. Almost as old as Webb.

"I ... I should've killed you first," the man stammered in a thick Russian accent.

With another howl the man struggled forward, and Matt recoiled.

"Useless," said Yuri Nesterenko, sitting upright dumbly. He might have been weeping, his breathing now swift puffs, and he fell back with a thud. "Sunk," he whispered. "Sunk in madness."

Matt ought to have been enraged. Ought to have finished the bastard off. But instead he could only see Cory—up there, at his window, waving him on.

———⁓ᴧᴧ⁓———

Staggering the last hundred yards, Matt saw that using Senator Rose's prestige had worked: spread out in front of the Capitol was a fleet of television cameras, light reflectors, and a turbulent sea of reporters held back behind a red rope line. He approached the crowd from the side, heading for the point of the V formed by the ropes. In front of him, the reporters buzzed, some shouting questions before he'd even reached the podium. One of the Senator's aides extended a hand, admiration in her worried eyes. He straightened his tie and then his steel blue suit as he gazed at what would be his background: the stretch of green lawn, the stub of the Ulysses S. Grant Memorial, the glittering reflective pool, and, in the far distance, like a white needle pointing to the sky, the Washington Monument. His breath stuttered along for a moment as he surveyed the mass of reporters, many of them tipped off by Kris. He'd shaven, he hadn't had a drop to drink since leaving Marion, and still, he knew, they'd bought so far into the White House's portrayal of him that he must have looked now like an escaped inmate.

"I'll keep my comments today brief," he said, to test his voice and steady his nerves. He inhaled deeply and thought of Cory in the window of his office. "I'm here today to confess … to moral treason. I am responsible for the leak of CIA operative Oliver Redgrave's identity to the press. I was not alone; my accomplices were Stephen Shay, Gail Turner, and others." A ripple of chatter spread back through the crowd. "While what we did may not fit the legal definition of treason, it certainly fits the moral definition. I will testify to Congress, or to any investigator, if asked.

"My testimony will include firsthand knowledge of an interest by many leaders in this country to expand the war in the Middle East. There is no specific timeline for expanding the war except to see it done in either the second term of this administration or in the near future."

They were clamoring now, below him; in the old days—funny to call them that—he would've been grinning, soaking up their attention, looking for the next opportunity to lay down a one-liner. Studying them now, studying their worried and confused faces, he felt a rush of relief, a lightness of truth.

"Too often in our history, provocation has enabled those with visions of empire to justify their expansion. Surely there have been times when a call to arms has been justified, but, often, many have seen through these motives and challenged our country's march to war. And for that they've been called un-American and weak. But it has become clear to me why Teddy Roosevelt said there is no greater act of patriotism than to speak out against a war.

"I don't hold myself to be one of these courageous Americans. If I were, I would have stood here a long time ago. As a member of the Kensington administration, I can tell you that we celebrated the fact that 77 percent of Americans thought that Iraq was behind the 2001 attacks, that we'd tricked that many people … an even higher number than we'd hoped. This administration and perhaps the next one are waiting for Iran or its supporters to make a mistake. No matter who is elected, those who seek to build an empire will not rest. It shouldn't be forgotten that President McKinley and President Kennedy were pressured and compromised into supporting wars not of their choosing. It can happen again."

In the back of his mind, he heard a difference in his voice; now that the truth was pouring out—the messy, confusing truth—his voice nonetheless escaped more freely from his gut, his chest, his mouth. To his ear, the pitch of his voice had lowered from that sarcastic, tense yapping of four years ago.

"Because of my actions—actions sanctioned by the names I've mentioned—people close to me have died. My grief … is endless. And if you doubt my sanity, just look back to the small parking lot on the Washington Monument side of the Department of Agriculture building, between Jefferson and Independence, and you'll find two dead bodies there. Both were there to kill me before I spoke to you today."

A few reporters bolted from the crowd.

"I'll take only two or three questions. The rest will be answered over the coming weeks; however, let me restate especially for any camera that missed it"—he paused and looked across the Capitol lawn, the weeping statue in Peace Circle shining, though dirty from the soot of traffic—"I will plead guilty to treason if charged."

There was a long silence as stunned reporters who'd never experienced a moment like this tried to process the information. The pause, however, was brief. The mass erupted in unison, while still more broke away frantically for the building down the Mall and the promised scene at the parking lot.

⁓⋏⋏⁓

Shay studied the television monitor in his office. That opening panoramic sure wasn't the typical "steps of the Capitol" shot, but damn Matt had given them something good to use: the great, subtle loneliness of the monument; the solitude of the lone truth-teller, facing the massive Capitol. "Yeah, kid," he muttered toward the television, "that's a hell of a visual."

Matt's Journal, Day 3

And then I left the Capitol, hailed a cab at Garfield Circle, and was gone. Don't know if I'll ever go back, unless they subpoena me, which seems less and less likely. I'd been on the phone with Kris and my uncle and few well-wishers, including Senator Rose, when I heard a report on the cab's radio. We were just getting into Old Town. No bodies, they said. No bodies where Matt Risen said—nay, promised—there would be bodies. The first reporters on the scene found two workers with industrial street painters covering the lot, they said, in "fresh yellow parking stripes." One of the workers said he'd seen me lurking around about an hour beforehand. Nobody had called the police. Nobody found any shell casings or blood. "Seemingly discredited," was the kindest way they put it.

Probably shouldn't have expected anything less. Shay is thorough. Or maybe it was Webb. He's been quiet during all of this, and when he's quiet, that means he's watching. Maybe I was lucky to get out of there before the clean-up crew arrived.

That was yesterday. Today I'm at Aunt Marie's farm in Fredericktown, and the smells of manure and pumpkins and hot apple cider off her stove are godsends. I've done what I can. Is it enough? Will it ever be enough? Don't know. I'm watching Kris show Shelly how to carve a pumpkin while she's telling some story to Jess, and Paula is shooing Larry Bird off the picnic table where she's braiding cornhusks with Marie; for me, right now, that's enough.

Tomorrow is Halloween. Old ghosts in the fields, one of them going long, taunting me to throw him the ball. Old men around the country will go begging in their masks. Whichever they need to wear.

How long will the world suffer the deadly arrogance of leaders who think they can know the unknowable and who assume they can anticipate the outcomes of every action, no matter how small? When the infinite number of factors are considered, the weaknesses of individuals and their often incomprehensible reactions to circumstance guarantee that the only certainty is the unintended consequence. Perhaps it is as minute as a grain of sand blown into the eye of a horse by an exploding rocket on the plains of Afghanistan, his rider—a future leader, a Gandhi of his people—thrown off and killed against some rock. The chain of events never breaks. We can only imagine so much.

CHAPTER 8

Cleveland, Ohio. 6:00 AM

Esther Johnson went to her closet and, with a weathered but soft black hand, pulled down her best hat, a gray cloche with a scarlet silk flower and a thin veil that draped partially over her face. She was locking her door from the outside when a taxicab pulled up and dropped off the young woman who lived two doors down from her. Esther watched the woman stumble up the steps. Her shirttail was hanging half in and half out of her short skirt. Convinced that she was a prostitute, Esther made a note to say a special prayer for her tonight.

When Esther turned the corner at the elementary school, she couldn't believe what she saw: the line must have been a hundred people deep, all of them eager and nervous like they were waiting to cross the river Jordan. She took her place in line. Inches later, the line had only grown. Several people glanced at their watches. "I've gotta be at work in half an hour," the Latino woman in front of her said. In time, the woman walked out of the line and left, allowing Esther to inch closer to the voting machines. There were only two. For the entire district? It must have been some mistake; there'd been four for the primary. And the poll workers seemed so confused, they didn't know which way was up. An older man, stocky and clean-shaven, said from in front of her, "Tell you what: they know most people down here are Democrats. They're just trying to drive people away."

"Have a little faith in people," said Esther, but the middle-aged lady behind her pointed to the cars pulling out of the lot as the children's buses were pulling in.

"Looks like they got what they wanted," she said.

When she finally entered the booth, sometime near eight-thirty, Esther stared at the two names for president. On the one side, there were all the reasons she had always been a Democrat. And that crazy war. It sure looked like Kensington stole the last election, and he'd been a horrible president. But the nation was losing its moral center. Abortion and drugs all over. And she'd barely gotten a chance to know Noah Young; she liked his look, his eloquence, and he'd make a lot of people proud … if he wasn't just another DC hotshot. She skipped to the top and cast all of her local election votes. Nearly all her choices were Democrats. Lingering over the gay marriage ban, she sighed and closed her eyes. No wonder the line had been taking so long; a body couldn't halfway think in these booths, and these decisions … Lord. Talk about weighty. She thought about that poor girl stumbling home in the wee hours of the morning. Used to be that love felt right and good. Like an old Smokey Robinson song. That wasn't the Democrats' fault, but neither did they take much of a stand against sin. And it didn't matter much that Young was black; he was young, naive, and she worried for him like he was some grandson about to get himself in trouble on the street. Holding the cross she always wore around her neck, spinning it with her finger and thumb, she voted for the ban, then reached out somewhat impulsively, hesitated, and voted Kensington.

As she left the school, a young woman full of silliness bounced up to her with a clipboard in hand. Beside her stood Esther's friend Wynn, a Democratic activist. "Who'd you vote for, ma'am?" said the girl.

Esther glanced at Wynn and smiled. "Young," she said. "Voted Young."

She walked away shaking her head. She'd been a Republican for only two minutes and already she was a liar.

Van Wert, Ohio. 8:15 am

After moving through a short line in the middle-school gym with only a five minute wait, Lynn Curtain pulled shut the heavy cloth of her voting booth and slammed shut the door on gay marriage. Swore she could feel the Lord guiding her fingers toward that touch screen. Love the sinner but hate the sin, and the only way to show that was to keep the law—God's inspired law for this land—intact. Then she stared at the choices for president and searched her mind for a decision. After a long wait, she realized she couldn't vote for any of them after all the strange and hateful stuff she'd heard in her church. Young was a socialist, they said, but Kensington seemed to want to get them involved in any war possible. No, she was satisfied with the one vote she cast. She walked out, spotting some campaign literature on the ground, littering the area, and so she picked it up and threw it in the trash can. Then she headed back to her fort of a home and prayed.

Newark, Ohio. 5:45 PM

A videocamera filmed outside a barbershop, capturing the front of an old last-of-its-kind building in a town surrounded by big-box stores and strip malls. It could have been anywhere in America, but the two-foot, glass-encased cylinder with spinning red and blue candy-cane stripes, and the large "Tucker's Barbershop" sign over the recessed entryway said, "small business, in middle America." Just the visual they needed.

"All right, walk inside, Gary," said a producer from the van outside. "Keep it slow."

Inside, two of the three barber's chairs were empty. An array of magazines, some of them yellow-edged and tattered, was scattered on both bay window sills. Red vinyl-covered chairs with black plastic armrests lined the wall. A dust–covered poster on a dust-covered wall offered customers their options via sketches of hairstyles from the 1960s. The producer trailing the cameraman held the microphone end of the headset close to his mouth and muttered, "Jesus, it smells like scorched coffee in here."

"Let's get this going," said the producer in the van.

Jim Tucker snapped his gum with the crack of a gunshot as the producer inside asked how business had been. "Sucks," Jim said. "Half of the million-plus strip malls around here all got a haircut franchise.

The producer pinned a microphone to the barber. He said, "Jim, count to ten for me so we can get a sound check." Jim dutifully counted.

"Okay, we're live in ten seconds. Just look at that camera as you reply, just a few inches above the lens."

The reporter they'd brought along—improbably named Trent Law—didn't beat around the bush. "How did you vote?"

"I thought about it. It was tough, you know. But, uh, Kensington."

"What made it tough?"

"That Risen stuff didn't set well, and I almost went with it, but Shorty over there,"—he pointed to a barber's chair occupied by a small man in a tan hunting jacket, his hunting license as visible as his Kensington's army of truth button—"well, he keeps up on this stuff better than me, so he convinced me the guy was nuts. If I was wrong you'll have to blame him." Jim smiled at his friend who now owed him for making him famous. "Besides, the other guy seemed too weak to protect our country in a time of war. And I didn't hear much about how he'd help us around here."

Back in the studio, hundreds of miles away, the election night host looked at his panel of experts. "Does the fact that a guy so likely to go with Kensington—and indeed, he ultimately did—but still, that he had last second doubts, does that give anyone pause? Should we maybe rethink the Risen impact?"

"For a nanosecond," said one of the commentators. "But no, no October Surprise here."

They all laughed.

Columbus, Ohio. 6:30 PM

Marge Scarborough stood with several volunteers next to the mayor of Columbus, passing out coffee to the more than two hundred mostly African-Americans standing in line to vote. A few walked away, shaking their heads. "I gotta get to work," a man muttered, "my shift starts at seven."

Tall and lean, the mayor was patting people on the back, encouraging them to stay in line and stick it out. One lady told the mayor that if she didn't leave the line in five minutes, she would be fired. He flashed a genuine smile and pulled out his cell phone. "How about letting me call your boss and see if he'll let you come in a little late?" A TV camera filming the long lines spotted the mayor and suddenly the lady, the mayor, and his phone call were on television. The boss couldn't say no and, to boot, his dry cleaning business had received a free commercial. "Thank you," the woman whispered.

Seeing one trembling old lady about to fall, the mayor asked Marge to help him find a chair. She ducked into the school, following him into an empty hallway where she spotted the teachers' lounge. As he helped her lift a high-backed, overstuffed chair, the mayor said, "You voted already, right?" Oh yes, she replied. Out in Hilliard, early in the morning. Hardly a wait there. The mayor nodded, and she noted the look of disappointment in his eye, which she suspected had something to do with the secretary of state.

"The war really turned me around," she blurted as they neared the outside door. "Then the assassination, how crazy things were getting—even that guy's speech at the Capitol—just made me realize even more how lucky I've had it out there in Hilliard."

They set the chair down for the old lady. A man behind her said he'd move it along as they progressed up the line.

"Well you look like you've been working for a long while," the mayor said to her. The strangeness that she, Marge Scarborough, nobody famous, was talking to the first African American mayor of Columbus still hadn't entirely worn off.

"I owe it to the world," she said. "I voted for Kensington four years ago."

"You've more than made up for it," the mayor said.

Two hours later, Marge felt her eyes well up when she saw the old lady exiting the high school gymnasium with her chin a little higher than it'd been when she'd come in. She passed a frustrated young man who looked like he was about to dash. The old woman patted his forearm and said, "They ain't never gonna make a line long enough to keep me from votin'."

"Yes ma'am, I hear you," he said, planting his sneakers on the concrete.

Dayton, Ohio. 9:00 PM

The camera started filming the front and then the inside of the normally quiet tavern. A soft glow of orange lights framed the window behind the bar, silhouetting bottles stacked neatly, awaiting consumption.

Forest Morgan: the name led to a very apt nickname: Tree. He was tall, with broad, powerful shoulders and a round bald head, medium-sized ears, and large earlobes his wife referred to as his acorns. His bass voice resonated in a tone so low, it was said to shake the bottles behind the bar.

"Horrible lights," the forty-something cameraman said to the producer.

"Make do!" The kid couldn't have been older than twenty-two. What a punk.

The smell of smoke from years of tar-filled breath permeated the bar, leaving deep stains in every nook, particularly the tiles in the ceiling that, once white, were now the color of strong tea.

Tree studied the nervous cameraman taking orders from the punk producer who was, in turn, getting yelled at by some fancy-pants host back in New York City. Proof that shit rolled downhill.

Couldn't have been more than twenty people in the place, and a fight broke out. Well, a shouting match. The world watched as a drunken man in a Reds hat and a man in a UAW windbreaker jawed at each other about conspiracies and socialism.

Tree Morgan smiled sheepishly at the interviewer. "They're both buddies of mine. That ain't normal for around here, just so you know."

When asked how he voted, he said firmly, "Young."

The UAW man held up a fist and grinned at the Reds fan. "I won *that* goddamn fight, asshole." As the network scrambled to censor the union guy, the man in the Reds cap lowered his head and disappeared out of the frame.

"And why Young?"

"Just some doubts there at the end. About Kensington and his mob." He glanced toward the beaming man in the UAW coat.

———～₩～———

In the crowded hotel suite, Shay paced frantically, weighted by questions and a good half-gallon of scotch. He caught his own reflection in the mirror and studied himself for a brief moment, as long as he ever dared: eyes that darted back and forth and a perpetually pale face—whiter than usual, paler than it had been here in Denver four years ago—which only revealed more obviously scores of bluish veins. In fact, there wasn't a drop of blood in the face of anyone in the room; close friends, staffers, and family members of the president were pallid. The only facial color was to be found in an Asian Indian college friend of the president's and the always rosy complexion of the first lady. Otherwise, Zombieville. And they didn't even know how frightened they *should* be. North Carolina was slipping away, Ohio was a toss-up, and they had an ugly fight developing in a state no one had expected to be thinking about.

Kensington whined, "Damn it, look at that map! Nothin' but a red sea—hell, I'm carrying 80 percent of the country—but we're locked in a dead heat? Stephen, you know anything about North Carolina?"

Shay just shook his head. "It doesn't look good."

He turned back to his phone and the source from the middle of country. The middle of the goddamn country: God's country. Twisting his thick, hedge-like eyebrows between his fingers, he listened to the bad news and wondered from what hellhole Matt Risen was watching tonight.

———∿∿———

Matt pushed the final mile up the slope of the hill they'd affectionately named Johansen Mountain, the burning only pushing him harder. In the cabin ahead, the lights glowed humbly except for the occasional flicker of the television. On that thrilling night four years ago, he'd have never imagined struggling through a five-mile run in the Shenandoah Valley, to say nothing of his fervent hope that Kensington would be defeated. No tingle in the nipples tonight.

He opened the door to see Shelly banging on the television. "Come on, you son of a bitch!"

"Language!" he and Kris shouted at the same time.

Kris grinned and tossed him a bottled water from the second-hand coffee table. He chugged the icy water and asked what was happening.

"Chaos," Kris said.

Shelly had lifted Larry Bird onto the console, and his weight seemed to steady the antennae. "Stay," she said, before joining them on the couch and observing loudly that Matt stank.

The thrilled analyst with the twinkling eyes and crooked smile, who, four years earlier, had scribbled electoral college notes on a dry-erase board, was tapping a transparent screen, combining various states into blue and red ranks, playing out scenarios like a general before D-Day.

"I liked the dry-erase-and-wet towel approach better," Matt said.

"You old fogy," Kris said, lacing her fingers through his. "No way the networks pass up that high-tech visual."

"It's all about the visual," Shelly muttered, in a trance.

The cost of the screen could have paid for an in-depth investigation of the Redgrave affair, but getting the channel surfers to pause was more important than a journalistic breakthrough, he supposed. The possibility of a thorough investigation seemed unlikely, even if Young won; Matt's confession had gotten swallowed up by the election itself, and a new administration would only succeed in embarrassing the Republicans—Young seemed too willing to take the high road for that.

The analyst's eyes lit up and bulged a little as he described each scenario. The results were coming in faster than four years ago, but not as coherently. Many states long considered solid looked shaky; others that had been shaky looked solid. And then Ohio came up on the board.

"Come on, Buckeyes," Shelly said through gritted teeth.

The announcer drowned them, his face going to static as Larry Bird yawned and readjusted his weight. "Folks, this is going to be as close in the electoral college as four years ago. We're still waiting to make a prediction about Ohio, but keep in mind: four years ago, Ohio was the turning point." He inhaled sharply and continued in that late-inning, punctuated style of his, "But it is possible, at this point, that we could be headed to electoral college deadlock. If Ohio goes for Kensington, he will have reached the 269 votes that will guarantee at *least* a tie. With the Republican party in control of the House of Representatives, that may be enough. Remember that Congress confirms the election results. This was a factor in Al Thornton's decision to concede four years ago.

It would be a moot point if Kensington also carries any one of half a dozen states."

Shelly glared at Matt. "Why'd you have to do such a good job in Ohio, jerk?"

As Kris snickered, Matt thought of his many trips into Ohio with Shay, their clandestine meetings with Carl, and how Shay always kept him away from Kennetha Harris.

"Hey, some things you just can't go back and fix."

"Yes, it's official!" shouted the analyst. "President William Kensington has won Ohio, which gives him 269 electoral votes."

Shelly groaned and dug herself into the pillows at the end of the couch. As he rubbed her shoulder, he tightened his grip on Kris's hand; in the maelstrom of the past two weeks, he'd nearly forgotten how much campaigning he'd done, and how closely he'd be tied forever to a Kensington victory.

—\\\\—

"—gives him 269 electoral votes. Senator Young has remained at the same level for a little over an hour, and he trails in each state that remains," the analyst said. Shay watched the idiots around him raising their glasses; you give a fool ten dollars and he thinks it's a hundred. "So to achieve a tie, Young must win everything that remains—and he trails in all of them. One bright note: African American turnout is extremely high in places like North Carolina."

Bright note, my ass, Shay thought. They should have doubled-down on those urban centers in the South. Goddamn.

He kept one ear on the line with his source in the plains.

Gail Turner was on with her contacts at both CNN and Fox, a cell phone pressed to each ear and one on the mahogany table next to her. "The stuff we've been hearing all day about the exit polls is being confirmed by the early results. Which is shitty news, Stephen."

Boy, she was really catching on. With Matt you at least didn't have to endure the constant and obvious evaluations.

As Gail was about to address the room, Webb announced, "With the exit polls and the results we have, our team is calling every single state remaining for Young, including—oh Christ—Colorado."

Kensington glared in steely anger at the television. Slowly the rage dissipated, but that was only the surface of things, the image the president wanted to project. Shay knew better. The president would remember this defeat for a long time to come.

Gail said, "That's what I have from CNN, ABC, and Fox. All remaining go to Young."

"A goddamn tie!" Webb barked.

"Well it's 269 to 269," said Kensington, tilting his head thoughtfully. "So we go to the House and win the sucker. But doggone it, I wanted to win this one with an *un-irrefutable* mandate."

Everyone stared at him for a moment in silence, the only tittering far to the back of the room, near a baby grand.

Gail Turner said, "Good thing the current Congress selects, because we're losing seats like we're giving them away."

"Congress is turning?" the president said. The childish hurt in his voice was unmistakable.

"Fuck you very much Matt Risen!" one staffer said.

Webb pointed a finger at the staffer. "Now hear me clearly: we know some of this lies at the feet of Risen, but no one—and I mean *no one*—gives him the blame, or what some will see as the credit. We tell the media that our internal polling showed we had a problem for some time."

"It *is* the current Congress that decides, right?" the president said to his wife.

"Yes, Will," said Webb, and his hunched shoulders maneuvered his arms and hands to grip his younger boss's shoulders in a fatherly and somewhat terrifying manner. "So we'll hold on. It'll be bumpy, bumpy as hell, but we'll hold on."

Shay had just turned from this tender idiocy when Kensington said his name. "You've been silent, buddy. Unusually, shockingly silent. What's goin' on?"

Shay just looked grimly at the room and went back to his phone call.

Webb said with a snarl, "Stephen just has to face the fact that he blew it."

Oh, that was the final fucking straw. He whirled and lunged, his stubby arms just reaching Webb's before the Secret Service got between them. He writhed in one agent's grip while the other released Webb.

Kensington smiled. "Wouldn't be election night if we all didn't get to see Stevie being held back by an agent," he said with a chuckle. "Put a cell phone on the floor in front of him, let's see that Irish jig of his."

Glaring at Webb and then at Gail, Shay said, "This is a hell of a lot worse than what you all think!"

"They let Thornton get back in the ring?" said the president.

Webb chortled. "Just Stephen being an asshole."

"You simple bastard," said Shay. "You held me back. All of you wanted to pussyfoot with this guy because of the assassination and his race. And now we have goddamn lost the entire thing."

"He's got the insanity virus from Matt Risen," said Webb.

"Did we call another state incorrectly?" Gail said, her voice weak for the first time Shay could recall.

"Shit!" an aide cried. "Listen to this!" He cranked the volume on the widescreen plasma.

"That's right ladies and gentlemen, it gets stranger by the moment," the twinkling-eyed announcer was saying. "Nebraska, as we said earlier, is the home of the split electoral college, just as it is in Maine. Each congressional district is assigned one electoral vote. And fittingly, for this bizarre and possibly historic night, the Lincoln area congressional district is being carried by Senator Young."

Webb said, "We checked this! We checked the exits! It was safe!"

The president flapped his tie up and down. "But we won, Dixie. We got the 269!"

"Get the state director of Nebraska on the phone, Gail," Webb said. "I want to know what the hell is going on there."

Shay covered the mouthpiece of his phone. "I'm talking to him now; I've been talking to him all night while you were celebrating." He uncovered the phone and felt heat tearing through him. "Just know that you're through, asshole. You get handed one of the easiest jobs in America and you fucking blow it. I will personally make sure you never even work a goddamn school levy!"

The president stood and ran his tongue under his lips as Shay tossed the phone toward the piano and collapsed into an armchair.

"You let me down, buddy," said Kensington. He towered over Shay, his eyes strangely cool.

Shay kept the president's gaze but cocked his head so the rest of the room would hear. "It seems our opponent ran a campaign in Nebraska that no one knew about. Under the guise of impacting Iowa and Missouri, Noah Young's campaign bought extensively on Nebraska television. And then, our dumbfuck state director ignored all the signs that Young's people were running some kind of stealth ID program in the district. Polling callers pretending to be national network pollsters interviewed tens of thousands of people in that congressional district. Our guy got suspicious but just put his head in the sand. They were turning out the positive voters all day." He swiveled his pounding, throbbing head and leveled a glare at Webb like it was the last of his life. "And Dixon over here didn't think we needed an influencer campaign," Shay said, vulgarly spitting out the vice president's name. "Well, we didn't have one in those parts."

"It was just goddamn Nebraska!" Webb squealed.

Gail said, "Can't we just have Congress throw out the results or refuse to give up the office somehow?" The pace and volume of her voice slowed until it was like she hadn't spoken at all.

The commentator, grinning crookedly, said, "In case you missed it, we have a stunning development—"

Webb grabbed the remote and changed the channel. "You can tell how glad he is that we lost by that fucking twinkle in his eyes."

If you had stood at the foot of Johansen Mountain, you would have heard the shouting. Might have even heard the earth shake a little bit and seen in the small windows of the stone cabin on the hill's plateau a trio of bouncing silhouettes. In that cabin, for the moment, the losses were eased and the mistakes were forgiven. And if you'd kept your eyes trained on that hilltop, you'd have seen, a few minutes later, a shirtless man fling open the door, whoop at the sky, and commence a victory lap around the modest cabin until two women—one practically a sister, the other practically a savior—tackled him to the ground in a mess of laughter and shouting and the meows of an overweight cat.

CHAPTER 9

Webb slumped past his secretary's nearly empty desk and into his office. A shadow created by the harsh glare of the sunlight stood behind his desk. He strained a moment. "Grover! Who let you in here?"

Grover Alexander turned in the sun's white aura. "We've got some business."

"Answer my question: who the fuck let you in here? This office might be mine for only a few more weeks, but I don't get unannounced visits!"

Alexander smiled, put his hand on Webb's shoulder, and, with the other hand, motioned toward the chair. "Don't waste time, Dixon. You've done enough of that. What transpires over the next few years may depend entirely on this conversation. Believe me, it's in your best interest."

"Did I miss the strategy meeting?"

"Don't be conspiratorial. You know that's not how things work."

No, Webb thought. It was like he'd described to Matt that night years ago on the yacht—in the aftermath of an event, like a lost election, all the players knew their parts. Nothing need be said.

"Okay, just get on with it."

"We've lost several years and, frankly, my investors aren't happy. They have a plan to keep things headed in the right direction in the Middle East, and it involves Shay." Webb chuckled. This ought to be good. "Immediately after Noah Young takes office, Shay will head to Pakistan to advise our allies in Pakistan and throughout the Middle East on how to broaden their support in their own countries. But sometime early in the next year, Al Jazeera will report that an American government agent known to have strong CIA connections is advising the Pakistani government. A day or two later, documents will be discovered that suggest Shay is quarterbacking an all-out extermination effort against terrorist sympathizers, extremist governments, including assassinations—"

"That's supposed to stabilize the Middle East?"

"In the long run."

"And get Shay killed."

Alexander shrugged.

Webb shook his head. "That's not what Shay does!"

"You know that, and I know that, but every enemy and paranoid, conspiratorial nut, and every terrorist enabler who hates us will be sure that Shay is there to help our Pakistani allies seize absolute control of Pakistan, thereby strengthening America's hand in other Arab states. The fear level in Pakistan goes up, their government destabilizes, which leads to a shift in power, which leads to Iran doing something stupid … and on down the chain of dominoes."

Alexander smiled confidently. "And with that, the new president will be culpable because there will be memos that suggest that he was aware of and endorsed the Shay effort. So, like Kennedy and the Bay of Pigs, he'll have some serious culpability. But now it'll be a Bay of Pigs with a twenty-four-hour news cycle and nonstop analysis. And it was the Bay of Pigs that forced Kennedy's hand in Vietnam. He couldn't look soft with the communists again. And if he falters—Young, that is—then we get back control of the White House in four years. The question of who can handle terrorism will be case-closed. And we'll never lose that recognition for the rest of our lives."

Webb thought of Kennedy, a man he begrudgingly admired, and drew a circle on his desk with a forefinger. "That Bay of Pigs conspiracy story is bullshit, Grover, but then again, you're full of bullshit. And here's another thing: the fact that Pakistan has the bomb doesn't concern you, or your investors?"

"They're your investors, too, Dixon." Alexander glared under those white caterpillar eyebrows of his. "And Pakistan having the bomb is a goddamn plus. Makes them more frightening to everyone."

"I'm one of them. The basis of mutually assured destruction is that both sides want to live. But if one side is in a hurry to get to heaven, that's a very high risk."

"It has to be."

Maybe it was the Cold War terminology, but Webb thought briefly of the shootout between Shay's CIA lackey and the insane Russian near the Ag Department. Two old soldiers fighting an old war, it seemed. He imagined the great irony, that their bodies had mingled in an incinerator somewhere, and that over a million years their ashes would fuse together.

"Grover, it's time for us to wake up: we can't anticipate everything. The infinite, possible factors guarantee that something unexpected will happen and we'll only end up empowering people bent on destroying Israel and the United States, not to mention the rest of Western Europe. Unintended consequences: what you're suggesting may cost lives in Amsterdam, Paris, London, Brussels Berlin, or in Omaha."

"Omaha can burn in hell." Determination strained Alexander's face. "It only took the Democrats eight years to destroy what Reagan built, and they never had the kind of momentum they have now. All you've worked for is at stake."

"And so I do everything your way?"

"All you have to do is send Shay to Pakistan. Then you work with the necessary agencies to develop the paperwork that will be turned over to the new administration. Just create the impression of a thorough briefing. What could be worse for Noah Young than to appear to be working with Shay or Dixon Webb? People hate you, and that'll trap our young president into making mistakes."

Webb looked up at Alexander. "You know I don't want it to end here, but I just don't feel it anymore. Too much uncertainty. We were so certain, and look how that panned out. I can't believe I'm saying this, but I hope Shay doesn't take your offer, the poor bastard. I'm not doing it."

"Dixon, I—*we*—aren't asking." Alexander turned back to the window.

"Is that a threat?" Fucking sycophant! Errand boy! The red rose in Webb's face. "You can't."

"It'll be surprisingly easy, Webb. We'll just say you're as mad as Risen, depressed about the election. And we'll bring you back into the Redgrave thing."

Standing in front of a portrait of the slyly smiling Ronald Reagan, the red in Webb's face drained to a cold, sickly white. That son of a bitch. Never should have gotten behind him, never should have gotten out in front of him. All that old money, he didn't know the value of hard work, or loyalty—and he wouldn't hesitate to bury ol' Webb under a rock somewhere.

"That's why he wanted to do the Redgrave thing. Shit, I knew he was good but … No, I have another choice."

"Which is?"

Webb shoved his index finger in Alexander's face. "I can help you and your fucking hide-behind-the-curtains, chicken-shit boss find your path to hell."

Alexander grunted. Nodded with some pity. "Goodbye, Dixon. It won't be long till I piss on your grave."

"Not if I get to you first."

"Don't get too worked up. Your heart problems and all."

Webb followed him to the door, the words and the anger tying his tongue until he managed with one final spit to shout, "Hey errand boy, fuck you very much."

───∿───

Upstairs in his box-strewn office, Shay sat at his desk and fed documents into a shredder. The cold seeped in through the poorly insulated window despite the bright sun, and he thought meanly of driving himself home—himself!—in all the fucking snow that'd fallen in the morning. Hearing the faint sound of someone breathing, he looked up over his shoulder to see Grover Alexander standing in the doorway in a shiny gray suit, studying him with something like sympathy.

"Fuck off, Grover."

"Stephen, our fighting needs to be over with. It comes with the turf, and it can be a good thing—friction sharpens the sword. There were times I hated you. Hell, most of the time. But there wasn't a moment I didn't respect you."

"What do you want?"

"I want to talk about what you do next." Alexander lifted a stack of folders off of a chair, piled them on the carpet, and sat down, brushing back his bushy white hair like he was Paul Newman or something. "Now look," said Alexander, "there may be a hearing about the Redgrave thing, but Risen has too little credibility to generate much controversy. The pressure will be on the Democrats to move past it. So I can't believe anybody's going to prison. Thank God Carl and that other guy took each other out."

"Don't talk about Carl."

Alexander grinned. "Okay, okay. Hard feelings there. But, thing is, you and I, Shay, well, we both let our country down. We fucked up. I'm doing my part, and so should you." Alexander reached across the desk and began to fidget with a paper clip. "Our allies want you in the Middle East."

Shay squinted at him and repressed a giggle. "Doing what?"

"Pakistan. We need you to go there and help the government reach out to their people. Expand their support, you know, just like you were running a campaign. And this is a very big deal, Stephen; if I were you, I'd ask for a million bucks."

This time he couldn't repress the laugh. "Okay, now you want to tell me what the real assignment is?"

"You know everything I know."

"You don't know half of what I know," Shay said. "One million for two months work? What am I, a major league baseball player? Come on. You know and I know that Pakistan doesn't need an American political consultant."

"No, they need the best political consultant in the world."

Shay raised his small hand. "Flattery from your mouth is like gems from a sewer."

Alexander jerked as if he'd been shocked by the paper clip; he leaned forward and maybe stopped himself from doing something brash. Took him a full thirty seconds to regain his composure.

"So, I go to Pakistan and advise the government," said Shay, "and then who is it that reports my presence? *The London Times*? *Washington Post*? Oh, no ... Al Jazeera?"

Alexander's eyes darted back and forth across the cluttered desk.

Shay nodded and smiled slyly. "And so, once it's known throughout the Middle East that an 'American Empire builder' is advising the Pakistani government, the Pakistani government falls, the fundamentalists take over, and they start doing stupid shit, which paints Young into the corner." Even he had to admire the grandeur of it all.

"You've thought it through."

"Have you? Young could take a hard line, unite the world, kick some fundamentalist ass, finally capture bin Chalabi, and get reelected. We'd make him more popular than ever."

Alexander tilted his head in agreement. "And we'd get what we want, a stronger presence in the Middle East. Parties don't matter."

Shay picked up a polling book and dropped it in a box. "Option two: he starts thinking about the Nobel Peace Prize."

Alexander chuckled. "That sure worked for Carter. See what I mean? Win-win."

Shay leaned back and stared out at the blanket of snow on the South Lawn and the covered swimming pool. It wasn't like he had a number of options left. Lose in this town and you were branded for at least a few years. Even him. Besides, it'd only be a couple of months, and then he could afford to buy his own goddamn driver.

"I need an answer, Stephen."

"You know, Moliere once said of writing that it was a lot like prostitution: first, you do it for love, then for a few friends, and finally for money. For me to play the schmuck, tell 'em it'll cost five million."

———⁓⌣———

In the hallway by the empty Oval Office, Alexander opened his phone, texted Gail, and then dialed a number. Looking behind him, he said softly to the voice that answered, "Shay's in."

"Good. He ain't ever coming back from Pakistan."

Alexander nervously studied the hallway and pressed the button for the elevator. "We just need to take care of Webb. He's resisting."

"Dixie's a tough nut to crack."

"Don't worry about it; Gail can get the memos taken care of, and then your plan is underway, Mr. President."

EPILOGUE

Kris lugged a suitcase down the steps of his townhouse with a bump and a clack. "In a hurry or something?" Matt said, sidling up to her.

"Just want to be ready." With a sureness of purpose, she kissed him as she dragged his hands across her shoulders. "And make sure I've got the rest of my day cleared," she added. "For you."

"What am I going to do for two weeks?"

"Probably look for a job, huh?"

They ate breakfast to the sounds of Beethoven's cello suites, and he dropped a few bits of egg down to Larry Bird. By noon, they'd settled onto the Naugahyde couch he'd ordered to replace the old leather one that reeked of Gail, and they turned on the lead-up to the Inauguration ceremony. It was an astounding sight: thousands upon thousands of people filled the Mall, more than he'd seen at any election night victory rally, even Young's back in November.

Kris sipped from her coffee. "Where do you think Shay is right now?"

"Judy Hill told me last night, on the phone: Pakistan."

"What?"

Matt laughed. Imagining Stephen sweating his ass off in some Humvee without air conditioning was like a gift from the Big Man Upstairs. "And Gail, get this, took a job with one of the Kensington family companies."

"So she can stick close to God's Will."

"Nah."

Kris stared at him incredulously. "They're totally screwing, Matt. You didn't know that?"

"Bullshi—"

She pressed a finger to his lips, her radiant blue eyes sparkling, searching him. "In your own backyard. I'm ashamed. By a degree of separation, you've slept with the president. Not many men can say that."

"I'd say we screwed each other pretty directly."

"Careful. It's the visual, Matt, it's all the visual."

Their frivolous mood simmered as the ceremony began. On the steps just above where Matt had made his impassioned confession, a plea for sanity and justice, the nation's first black president put his hand on the Bible. Rubbing each other's hands as they watched, Kris and Matt listened to the words being spoken with the weight of stone, the burden of time and trouble, and the hopes of the thousands on the Mall and the millions watching. Dignity, thought Matt. We've regained our dignity.

"Never seen anything like it," Kris murmured. "Everything's changed."

"Not everything," said Matt. "Not the way laws are made, not the way the powerful maneuver. There's just a new player. If the coalition stumbles, or breaks apart, or gets caught up in finger-pointing, the hawks—the empire-builders—will be waiting."

"But Young's got the grassroots organizations," she said. "Local groups, young people who aren't afraid to stiffen their spines—"

"And they'll have to. Every day. There'll be bad days, disappointments and disagreements, but the tens of thousands who work out of beliefs and convictions, and not the few who seek the bright lights, money and excitement, can never forget what they're up against." He kissed her forehead as the new president waved to the cheering crowd. "The campaign never stops."